'Joe Ide is the best ne   ime. And Isaiah

... returned or renewed
'This is one of the most remarkable debuts below.
written with exceptional panache and a fine ear for dialogue, it intr...
the world to an LA private detective who might just become the Holmes of
the 21st century'   *Daily Mail*

'Fantastic detective debut about LA and rap moguls'
                                                      India Knight, *Sunday Times* Magazine

Praise for *Righteous*

'He is the first new crime writer I have read in ages who truly feels like an
heir to Elmore Leonard'   *Daily Telegraph*

'Joe Ide [is] the best thing to happen to mystery writing in a very long time'
                                                                                                    New York Times

'Witty and confident, with a bustling plot, this is a worthy follow-up to
Ide's excellent debut'   *Guardian*

'Ide writes with confidence and a sharp wit'   *Sunday Times*

Praise for *Wrecked*

'Joe Ide's IQ novels are an electrifying combination of Holmesian mystery
and SoCal grit'   *Time*

'Blazing . . . Ide is still the hottest of recently-emerged crime writers. He has
populated Southern California with wildly entertaining characters, from
those hinted at offstage to the motormouths whose priceless talk fills his
pages'   Janet Maslin, *New York Times*

'With writing so sharp you may cut your fingers on the pages, Joe Ide's latest IQ novel, *Wrecked*, is outrageous and laugh-out-loud funny, a page-turner with devastating observations'

Attica Locke, Edgar Award-winning author of *Bluebird, Bluebird*

Praise for *Hi Five*

'Savor the freshness, vividness and ingenuity of the author's prose . . . Hit men, henchmen, bagmen – they all wander in and out of a highly diverting book that crackles with life and vividness' *New York Times*

'Engrossing . . . The author is skilled at developing the humanity of every character, regardless of their perspective. It's a hallmark of Ide's evolving style that allows *Hi Five* to stand on its own for first-time readers, even as the series deepens longtime fans' engagement . . . *Hi Five* succeeds on so many fronts as it sets IQ and the series' characters on an uncertain path down darker roads' *Los Angeles Times*

'Stellar . . . Readers will root for Ide's distinctive lead every step of the way. This innovative series continues to show promise for a long, high-quality run' *Publishers Weekly* (starred)

Joe Ide grew up in South Central Los Angeles. His favourite books were the Conan Doyle Sherlock Holmes stories. The idea that a person could face the world and vanquish his enemies with just his intelligence fascinated him. Joe went on to earn a graduate degree and had several careers before writing *IQ*, his debut novel, inspired by his early experiences and love of Sherlock. Joe lives in Santa Monica, California.

www.joeide.com

Also by Joe Ide
IQ
Righteous
Wrecked

HI FIVE

Joe Ide

W&N

WEIDENFELD & NICOLSON

First published in Great Britain in 2020 by Weidenfeld & Nicolson
This paperback edition published in 2020 by Weidenfeld & Nicolson
an imprint of the Orion Publishing Group Ltd
Carmelite House, 50 Victoria Embankment
London EC4Y 0DZ

An Hachette UK Company

1 3 5 7 9 10 8 6 4 2

A CIP catalogue record for this book is
available from the British Library.

ISBN (Mass Market Paperback) 978 1 4746 0895 4
ISBN (eBook) 978 1 4746 0721 6

Printed and bound in Great Britain by Clays Ltd, Elcograf S.p.A.

MIX
Paper from
responsible sources
FSC® C104740

www.orionbooks.co.uk
www.weidenfeldandnicolson.co.uk

To Esther Newberg and
Zoe Sandler

They found a failed screenwriter and
sent him on his way.

Love takes off masks that we fear we cannot live without and know we cannot live within

— James Baldwin

HI FIVE

PROLOGUE

Isaiah Quintabe's East Long Beach neighborhood hadn't changed much over the years. It was the hood when he was growing up and it was the hood now. Gangs, street crime, poverty, drugs, and violence were constants, facts of life. Isaiah didn't know the statistics but from his perspective, things were getting worse. Not a surprising viewpoint when your job was fighting human suffering and indifference.

As the area's only unlicensed PI and unofficial ombudsman, there wasn't much he hadn't seen. Murders, robberies, burglaries, scams, bullying, kidnappings, addiction, rape, child abuse, loan sharking, questionable suicides; runaway children, husbands and wives. There were cases of great consequence and those of very little, but all were crucial to the victims, whatever the size of the injustice.

Someone had stolen Mrs. Marquez's Pomeranian, Pepito, and was holding it for ransom. The kidnapper left a note on her porch. There was a phone number and a demand for five hundred dollars *or your dog will be drownded in the ocen.* She called the number while Isaiah listened in.

"Yeah?" the man said. "Who's this?"

Isaiah immediately recognized the voice. It was Freemont Reese, a young hooligan who was so stupid and cowardly even the gangs rejected him.

"This is Mrs. Marquez," she said. "You stole my dog?"

"I sho' did," Freemont said. "Did you read the part about the money?"

"How do I know you have him?" Mrs. Marquez said, Isaiah nodding his approval.

"Because it's sitting right next to me watchin' TV. You want me to put him on the phone?"

"I mean, what's the dog's name?"

"His name? I don't know. He hasn't told me yet."

"It's on his tag. You know, the one hanging on his collar?"

Freemont told her to meet him at McClarin Park and sit on the bench nearest the south entrance. "You better have the money," he said. "Or you can go get yourself a cat right now."

Mrs. Marquez went to the park and sat on the designated bench. She had twelve dollars in her purse. Isaiah stayed well back and watched. He spotted Freemont near the restrooms, peeking around a corner. He didn't have the dog. Isaiah circled and got behind him.

"How are you, Freemont?" Isaiah said.

Freemont jumped. "Hey, man. Don't be sneakin' up on me like that! I might have shot your ass."

"With what?" Isaiah said. "The gun you have in your sock? Where's the dog?"

"What dog?" Freemont said, just realizing it was Isaiah.

"The one that belongs to the collar you have in your hand."

"This? I found it."

"Where's the dog?"

"I don't have to tell you nothin', Isaiah, and you can't make me."

"No, I can't, but I know who can."

"Oh, yeah?" Freemont sneered. "And who is that?"

"Your mother," Isaiah said.

Freemont's face crumpled in on itself like a wadded-up napkin. "Hey, man," he said, putting his palms out, his voice rising an octave. "She ain't got nothin' to do with this." Freemont lived with his mother, Oleta, a bony, fearsome woman with no sense of humor and nails jutting out of her eyes.

4

"Do you remember that time I helped her out?" Isaiah said. "Her boss at the shoe store wouldn't pay her overtime and I made him give it up? She was grateful. Really grateful."

Freemont shook his head and looked to the heavens. Maybe someone up there would have his back.

"Bring me the dog," Isaiah said. "And if there's a scratch on him, I'll lock you in a room with Mrs. Marquez and a baseball bat."

Mrs. Marquez was thrilled to get Pepito back, and she brought Isaiah a soul-warming pot of *calabacitas con puerco*, a hearty stew of vegetables, spices and pork cooked in butter. Isaiah wished she had more dogs that were stolen.

He was happy to have helped her like he was happy to help anybody, but lately he'd been wondering if he had a higher calling. The traditional notions of success bored him. He had a nice place to live, food on the table, and a fast car to drive. Getting a nicer place, more food on the table and a faster car didn't interest him at all. A lot of people seemed to enjoy power. Controlling the lives of others, telling them what to do, determining their fates—the idea made him cringe. He could barely control his own life, let alone determine his fate. Isaiah in charge of Isaiah was plenty. Maybe he should just shut up and get on with it.

He had a girlfriend now, Stella McDaniels. They'd been seeing each other for three months. She was a violinist, first chair, in the Long Beach Symphony Orchestra. He'd met her on a case. On her way to rehearsal she'd stopped at Beaumont's store to get a bottle of water. She was late and didn't lock the car. When she returned, her violin was gone. A Giovanni & Giuseppe Dollenz violin made in Italy circa 1855. When she was in high school, her parents had used their life savings and cashed in their IRA to buy it for her. The instrument was insured for fifty thousand dollars, but over the years it had increased in value and the payout wouldn't cover the cost of anything comparable. The symphony season was starting and she was frantic. She got a rental but it was like wearing someone else's shoes, the same thing but unfamiliar, and when you're playing music at her level, feel was everything.

*   *   *

Stella had come up the hard way, like Isaiah, like everyone in the neighborhood. Her family lived on the border between Long Beach and Compton, the hood if there ever was one. Isaiah asked her when she knew she was going to be a musician. "I've always known," she said. "There was never a day I *didn't* know."

Her parents were working people and couldn't afford music school or even music lessons. She used a relative's battered, tinny-sounding instrument and practiced relentlessly. A friend of her mother's owned a laundromat. At age nine, Stella was sorting lights and darks, stuffing wet clothes into the dryers and folding sheets by herself. She used the money to pay for music lessons, but she could only afford three. The teacher recognized almost immediately that Stella was exceptionally talented and lowered her rates to next to nothing. In high school, Stella worked two jobs after school and in the summer. She got a better teacher, played in junior orchestras and earned a music scholarship to the California School of the Arts. She entered competitions but was disappointed. There were other exceptionally talented violinists who were better than her. She would never command an audience of her own.

After graduation, she gave violin lessons to children, taught music at a small college, substituted in local orchestras, played in Vegas for Michael Bublé and finally, finally, got a spot in the Long Beach Symphony. It took her seven years to work herself up to first chair. A prestigious position. She was the principal soloist as well as leader of the section. The other musicians would take her directions on inflection, dynamics, bowing and numerous other things. Her first solo would be her proudest moment and the proudest moment for her family.

Where to start? Isaiah thought. East Long Beach had a legion of car thieves, but the violin had been stolen right outside of Beaumont's and she'd been inside the store for only a minute, two at the most. Someone was Johnny-on-the-spot. A local walking by or someone on his way into the store. Beaumont's was in gang territory. Locos Sureños 13.

Isaiah went to see the gang's entrepreneurial leader, Manzo. They weren't friends but they respected each other and sometimes traded favors.

They met at Café Michoacán, Manzo's new coffee place. Manzo was thirty-five or so, dressed in nice chinos and a black shirt, inked-up, bulked-up arms coming out of the sleeves. He was the only gang leader Isaiah had ever heard of who invested the gang's money. Manzo had told Isaiah he was going to open a Starbucks for Mexicans and here it was. Clean, modern, comfortable seating, display cases for Mexican pastries and beautifully embroidered story cloths on the walls. Mexican jazz was playing. Isaiah thought he recognized Juan José Calatayud but he could have been wrong. The place was nearly full. A mix of young and old staff. Not a Corona poster or a sombrero in sight. It could have been an actual Starbucks save for the solidly Latino faces.

"Cool place," Isaiah said. "Congratulations."

"Yeah, it came out better than I thought," Manzo said, sipping his latte. "Another year, we'll be profitable. I'm thinking about a franchise." Manzo funded his enterprises with drug money so he had no loans to carry. "You think it'll go?"

"I don't see why not," Isaiah replied.

Manzo's stated mission was to get his gang off the street but so far, he hadn't succeeded. The members who signed on for the investments didn't quit banging or dealing. The dividend checks were another income stream that paid for the same shit gangstas always dropped their money on: weed, guns, electronics and cars.

Isaiah told Manzo about Stella.

"A violin can be worth that much?" Manzo said.

"I guess so. I don't know much about it."

"Who's Stella?"

Isaiah shrugged. "Client."

Manzo smiled. "Is she paying you?"

Isaiah smiled back. "Do I ask you about your personal life?"

"I'll talk to the fellas about your violin," Manzo said as he got up. "Coffee's on the house."

Manzo put the word out to the homies who put the word out on the street. The khan of the Locos wanted the violin and if you happened to have it in your possession, your best option was to return it or suffer a life-threatening injury. Two days later, it came back. There were a couple of new scratches on the fretting board and a dent on the scroll, but they were cosmetic.

"Alfredo had it," Manzo said. "He gave it to his eight-year-old daughter as a birthday present."

"Thanks," Isaiah said. "I owe you one."

"I know."

It cost Isaiah a favor but it was worth the effort. Stella was nice to look at and a good listener, sifting through your words like she was panning for gold. She talked about music with intensity and passion, and Isaiah wished he still felt like that about his work. Stella was a few years older and had been through the relationship wars. She said she was done with being cool, buying cool things, hanging in cool places and, most of all, cool men.

"I'm not cool?" he said.

She smiled. "No, you're not. And that's what's cool about you."

Isaiah was driving over to Stella's place thinking about how he envied her and wished he'd taken a path like hers instead of his own. To be brilliant at something the world recognized. He wondered what that could be. His brother, Marcus, had told him many times, he could be anything, do anything he wanted, and nothing could stop him but himself. Was that true? Could he really be anything he wanted? Maybe so, if he knew what that was.

He was nearing Stella's place when he saw Grace. He did a double take and nearly rear-ended the car in front of him. He couldn't believe it. Was it actually her? He hadn't seen her in two years, since she'd left for New Mexico and taken his heart with her. She was going in the other direction, driving the same '09 white GTI. The New Mexico sun had burnished her skin, the pale green eyes hidden behind mirrored sunglasses, her hair tucked messily under a baseball cap. Isaiah had given her his dog, Ruffin, for protection, and there he was, head out the window, tongue flapping, happy as could be. *Isaiah who?* In an instant, Grace was past him. He tried to make a U-turn but was boxed in by the traffic. He yanked the car over into a red zone, got out and clambered onto the roof. He stood on his tiptoes and craned his neck, but the GTI was gone.

He was confounded. Why had she come back? How long had she been here? His heart was thudding like he was mid-marathon and losing. Was she back for good? The car still had its California plates. Why hadn't she called him? Had she forgotten him? Or maybe she'd just arrived. Yeah, that made sense. She'd made the long drive and wanted to get herself together before they met.

Except her car was clean. No road dust, no bugs on the windshield, so she'd been here long enough to get her car washed, and he didn't remember her ever wearing sunglasses or a cap even on sunny days. Maybe that was something she picked up in New Mexico. Sure, that was it. It was hot out there—but it was hot here too. Maybe she was hiding from someone and in disguise. Maybe she was hiding from him. He felt hollow and a little sick. The torch he'd been carrying all these months had smoldered but never gone out. He could feel it crackling into flames again. What to do? Track her down? It was tempting, but wait, he told himself. Calm down. She has her reasons. Be patient. She'll call. She had to, didn't she?

CHAPTER ONE
Come to Justice

Beaumont's corner store, Six to Ten Thirty, had been a fixture in the neighborhood for more than thirty years. Like people his age tend to do, Beaumont wondered what his life had been about, stuck here in this cramped, un-air-conditioned space with the Red Vines, the packages of Kotex, the cans of frijoles, the racks of chips and coolers full of Budweiser, the hard liquor behind the counter. There was a time when he thought about moving on, doing something else, going someplace where he could be outdoors and breathe some clean air. But after his wife, Camille, died, he didn't see the point. Why bother being anywhere in particular if the love of your life wasn't there with you? Beaumont had two grown children. Merrill was a traffic engineer in San Diego. His daughter, Katrice, was locked up in Vacaville for carjacking. These days, one out of two wasn't bad.

Beaumont heard rowdy voices coming up the street. He sighed, dreading their arrival. It was never a group of police officers or a troop of Boy Scouts or some other kind of law-abiding folks, and sure enough, four hooligans from a Cambodian gang came in with their white T-shirts, gold chains and tattoos. Maybe one of these days somebody would break the mold, wear a bowler hat or some penny loafers. The chubby one was the shot maker or shot supervisor or shot daddy or whatever they called the ringleader these days. In Beaumont's eyes, the kid didn't look any different from the others, but that's what they used to say about black folks so he crossed that off his observation list. He wondered if there was a nationality left that didn't have gangsters. Even white people who'd never been closer to the hood than one of Biggie's CD covers walked around talking like they'd been born in East Long Beach with a Glock 17 in their nappies.

The Cambodians dispersed into the store. There were fish-eye mirrors everywhere but these guys were past shoplifting. They had money. They still made Beaumont nervous but he wasn't afraid of them. He'd been in Vietnam and had seen action that would have these punks crying for their mamas.

They came back with a pile of junk food and dumped it on the counter.

"How you doin', Chief?" Chubby said. He was the leader for no apparent reason Beaumont could see.

"I'm doing just fine," Beaumont said.

"I been meaning to ask you. What do you do with yourself all day besides sit back there and jerk off?"

"And I've been meaning to ask you," Beaumont retorted, "what do you do all day besides lie around being an asshole?"

Chubby slow-blinked twice. "You know, one of these days your store might burn down."

"And one of these days your mama's house might catch on fire. I know where she lives, son."

Chubby tightened up and let one shoulder sag like he was going to throw a punch. Beaumont put his hand under the counter. He hadn't fired the .45 Colt Commander since Phnom Penh but the gesture made Chubby hesitate. The moment teetered on the edge of violence.

One of the other guys said, "Hey, fuck this guy, Lok. We got shit to do."

Chubby had his eyes locked on Beaumont's. "I'll be back, Chief."

"And I'll be right here," Beaumont replied.

Beaumont thought he might clean the gun, see if it still fired when he heard a big engine revving and the Cambodians shouting *get down!* The salvo of bullets came through the window like copper hornets, spider-webbing the glass, exploding the tiny boxes of Tide, cans of chili and SpaghettiOs, the coolers shattering, the whole candy section blasted apart, a confetti of paper towels and toilet paper fluttering in the air.

Beaumont couldn't get down fast enough. He'd barely bent his knees when he was hit in the shoulder. "Oh God, I'm shot!" he shouted. Then the second and third bullets struck him in the chest. He twisted around, grabbing at the shelves and sliding to the floor, dragging bottles of Smirnoff and Early Times down on top of him, a fleeting, silver moment of consciousness streaking past as he closed his eyes and the world was gone forever.

Isaiah was on a case and didn't hear about the shooting until the next day. Dodson came over to tell him.

"Beaumont?" Isaiah said. "They shot *Beaumont*?" Dodson looked the same, maybe a little heavier, but the same. Homeboy uniform, short, cocky, swagger in his chromosomes.

"I talked to his son," Dodson said. "He said Beaumont's hurt bad, doctors don't know if he's gonna make it. You want to go to the hospital?"

"No, the store first."

Isaiah and Dodson hadn't worked together since the 14K Triad case. The partnership had gone bust, but since then they'd fallen into an easy comradery that Isaiah cherished. It was the most solid, reassuring thing he'd had in his life since Marcus was killed. As long as he and Dodson didn't spend too much time together, the relationship worked fine.

"I'm telling you, this gun shit is getting out of hand," Dodson said. "I was over at Raphael's crib buyin' some weed? Three of them East Side Longos was there and check dis. They all had brand-new Berettas, that compact model? Julio said the whole damn gang has them. They bought them like team jerseys."

"How's Micah?" Isaiah said.

"He's doing aight," Dodson said. "Big-head boy thinks he can walk, stumbling around with his feet all wide apart, little hands up in the air, and making goo-goo noises that Cherise says are words. That's a fortunate lil' muthafucka, growing up proper-like. Got love all around him, don't have to worry about nothin'." Dodson's face didn't match the words. He seemed far away and brooding. Strange for him.

"You okay?" Isaiah said.

"Yeah, I'm cool. I think I'm coming down with a cold." Isaiah didn't believe him. Dodson's gears were grinding on something too private to talk about.

Isaiah had heard about him only sporadically. After the Walczak case, Grace's mother had given Dodson a not-so-small fortune. That was a while ago and he hadn't mentioned it since. A couple of times, Isaiah saw him driving a tow truck. Dodson had seen him but pretended he didn't. Isaiah wondered what that was all about and whether his friend was hustling again.

The police had come and gone. Beaumont's store was boarded up, yellow tape hanging loosely across the open door. Isaiah and Dodson had known Beaumont since they were kids. The crotchety old man was one of the good, hardworking people who made up most of the neighborhood. He'd never hurt anybody or caused any trouble. He ran his store, loved his family, smoked a cigar in the park on warm evenings and went fishing with TK and Harry Haldeman. Now he was dead for no reason at all. Isaiah hated the term "random violence," as if it were an anomaly, worrisome only if you were unlucky, and not a plague on the community that infected everyone with the belief that killings were an ordinary part of life.

"This is bullshit," Dodson said, shaking his head in disgust. "Mutha-fuckas ain't got nothin' better to do than kill people minding they own business?"

Isaiah said, "Do you know what happened?"

"Drive-by. Around one in the afternoon," Dodson said. "No witnesses." The bullet holes in the store's façade were large, wood splintered around them. "Big-ass bullets," Dodson noted.

"Could have been nine-millimeter but I'm thinking .45s," Isaiah said. Dodson looked at the splotches of dried blood on the sidewalk where a gangsta had been hit.

"I hope he died," Dodson said. "Lok's people were the ones that got shot at. Cops haven't identified the shooters. They were on the news asking for help, which means they don't know shit." Isaiah shook his head. One third of the murder cases in the US go unsolved and he was fiercely determined Beaumont's wouldn't be one of them. He put his hands in his front pockets and looked off a moment. "Let's talk to Mo."

Across the street from Beaumont's was a vacant storefront that used to sell vacuum cleaners. A wino named Mo camped out in the vestibule for part of the day. He used to hang with another wino named Dancy but Dancy died of liver cancer. Nobody knew he had it until the coroner found a tumor as big as a fist. None of the other winos could remember saying Mo's name without saying *and Dancy.* Mo still said it, though his friend had died months ago.

Mo was sitting on a greasy sleeping bag with his back against the door, eating noodles from a Styrofoam cup. His shopping cart full of overstuffed garbage bags was parked beside him. He'd probably tried to flee when the shooting happened but it was a drive-by, over in seconds.

Isaiah and Dodson approached him.

"Hey, Mo," Isaiah said.

"How you doin', Isaiah. Is that you, Dodson?"

"Yeah, it's me."

"Bad day," Mo said, shaking his head. There was lint in his gray hair, hands as dirty as the sidewalk, his layers of clothes stuck together with grime. "Beaumont was a good man. I cried like a baby when I heard he was dead. Seems to be goin' around. Wasn't no cause for that. No cause at all."

"You saw the whole thing, didn't you?" Isaiah said, going right at him.

Mo choked on some noodles and wiped his mouth on a sleeve infested with every germ in the world. "No, I didn't. I didn't see nothin'. Wasn't even here."

"*Mo*—" Isaiah said, a warning in his voice.

Mo slurped down the last of the noodles. "I see no evil, hear no evil. That's the only way to get along out here."

14

"You saw everything, start to finish."

"Imm-possible," Mo said with a sharp nod. "I wasn't even here."

"Stop lying, Mo. In the morning you hang out around the Coffee Cup because Verna passes out leftovers, and then around lunchtime you come over here because Beaumont gave you a free beer if you swept the sidewalk and kept the trash area clean. You were here, Mo."

"How you know all that?" Mo said. "You been followin' me?" Isaiah glared. Mo cringed. "Okay, okay. Y'all don't need to be like that. Ain't much to tell no ways. Some thugs went into the store, came out again, and then this pickup goes by, somebody on the passenger side started shooting. Br-d-d-d-d-d-d-it! Just like that."

"Was it loud?" Isaiah asked. "You've heard gunshots before."

"Shits yeah it was loud. Almost broke my hearin' system."

"What kind of truck was it?" Dodson said.

"You mean the brand? I don't know. Ain't had a car since I drove through a fence and landed in some lady's fish pond. Big fish in there, orange and white. When the lady stopped screaming at me, she said some of 'em was a hundred years old. You believe that?"

"Color?" Isaiah said.

"Like I said, orange and white."

"I mean the truck."

"Black."

"Did you see the driver?"

"He went by real fast," Mo said. "But it was a white boy, had a cap on backwards, you know how they do."

"You sure it was a white boy?" Dodson said.

Mo nodded adamantly. "Positivity," he said.

"Anything else stand out to you?" Isaiah asked. "Anything at all?"

"No, I don't think so. You believe that lady's fish was a hundred years old?"

Intensive Care was a familiar scene to Dodson. He'd been here many times in his gangsta days, the room dim, his homeboy diminished and frail no matter what his size, the badass bled out of him, lying there in a mess of tubes, white tape and catheters, family members crying and solemn, like the boy's life meant something, the slow beeps and barely oscillating lines warning you the end was near. Save for the medical equipment, Beaumont might have been lying in state.

Beaumont's son, Merrill, was there. The old folks described him as *a nice young man;* a ranking just below TV star in the hood. Merrill was standing next to the bed. Dodson and Isaiah shook Merrill's hand. The only things Dodson could think of to say were clichés. Probably the same with Isaiah.

"He respected you, Isaiah," Merrill said. His eyes were bloodshot and brimmed with tears.

"And I respected him too," Isaiah said.

"I appreciate you coming, Dodson," Merrill said. His tone suggesting Dodson's presence was as unexpected as it was unnecessary.

"I'm sorry for your loss, Merrill," he said. "Beaumont was a good man."

Glints of anger sparked off Merrill's eyes and he turned away. Dodson knew why. He was one of the kids that stole from Beaumont's store and told him he charged so much he must be a Jew and painted graffiti and pictures of big dicks on the walls and said shitty things about Camille when she was bald and stripped down to the bone with cancer.

Merrill said, "Dad is gone and he won't recover. I'm waiting for his sister to arrive before I pull the—" He wiped the tears off his face with his shirtsleeve. "Before I end it." He took his father's hand.

Dodson, Merrill and Isaiah had known each other since middle school. Merrill and Isaiah were good students and hung out with other good students. Dodson was on the other side of the playground, smoking weed with the fellas and trying to convince girls to meet him in the bathroom.

Dodson lived across the street from Merrill. They'd watched each other grow up with the wary, amused contempt of rival religious groups. Dodson and his crew taunted Merrill at every opportunity; about his pastel polo shirts and his fucked-up haircut and his lame-ass backpack.

They would have beat him up for sport if Beaumont hadn't known all their parents.

Dodson's father threw him out of the house when he was seventeen. Nobody would take him in and he was living in Lateesha's car with the Saran Wrap windows and cat hair fossilized in the seats. It was a school morning. He woke up with crust in his eyes, Buckwheat hair and the taste of weed and cheap wine in his mouth. He was standing at the curb, brushing his teeth and rinsing his mouth out with a warm Dr Pepper. He was just realizing how stupid that was when Beaumont drove by. Merrill was in the passenger seat. They made eye contact, a moment so humiliating Dodson wanted to shoot him.

Dodson and Isaiah left the hospital room, Isaiah with that look on his face, the one that said he was pissed off and wasn't going to let this go. Dodson was angry too, but for some reason, he couldn't get his mind off Merrill, standing at his father's bedside holding his hand.

Dodson had to babysit Micah, so he drove Isaiah home. He stayed distant and tight. Not like him. He was usually talkative to the point where you wanted to put your hand over his mouth. A tension crept into the car, the imminent kind, where something important was going to be said and it was only a question of when. But nothing happened.

"Thanks for the ride," Isaiah said as he got out of the car.

"Yeah, I'll see you later," Dodson said.

Strange, Isaiah thought, that Dodson had come over in the first place. He could have told him about Beaumont over the phone. There was something weighty on his friend's mind. He'll talk when he's ready, Isaiah decided, knowing that was true about himself.

He ate a bowl of oatmeal standing at the kitchen counter and thought about Grace. Where she was, what she was doing and who she was with. Why hadn't she called? He imagined a dozen scenarios. She had a deadly disease, she was disfigured, she was homeless, she lost his phone number, address and email all at the same time. Or maybe she had amnesia or had become a heroin addict, joined a cult or was married with a couple of kids. He was driving himself crazy so he went to Ari's gym to work out.

Ari taught Krav Maga, a mixed martial art developed by the Israeli military. Isaiah had been attacked and beaten numerous times over his career. Belatedly, he'd realized he should take self-defense more seriously.

Ari was the same as he'd always been. Built like a concrete pillar, silver hair in a flattop, fists big as sledgehammers.

"Let's go, Isaiah," Ari said. "Show me what you've learned."

They sparred, Ari saying, "Too slow, Isaiah. Isaiah, keep your balance. You are leaving yourself open, see?" as he slammed him to the mat.

"Don't you think you could be a little encouraging?" Isaiah said.

"Maybe later," Ari said, pulling him to his feet. He put his hands on Isaiah's shoulders and looked like a father sending a son off to war. Ari knew what wars were like and for him, they were never over. "Remember, Isaiah," he said. "Fight to win, and it doesn't matter how. Don't stop, don't give up. Whatever you do, keep fighting."

Isaiah was far more skilled than he'd been only a few months ago. He'd been jogging and lifting weights at home, getting his body fat down to nine percent, pro-athlete range. His muscles were cut, steely six-pack, his arms corded with veins. He was pleased when he looked in the mirror but embarrassed too, vanity being new to him. He wished Grace could see him.

Ari had told Isaiah his kicking was weak and he lacked leg strength. Isaiah worked on it hard, leg squats and kicking the shit out of the heavy bag.

"Kick *through* the bag," Ari said. "Like you're trying to kill someone on the other side."

After his workout, Isaiah went home, showered and changed. He thought about Beaumont. The shooting was obviously gang related, but Isaiah didn't know any white gangs in the area.

He made some calls to a few contacts who'd spent time in one prison or another. He found out there's a skinhead gang in Signal Hill called the Starks—a German word for powerful and strong. In the joint, the Starks hung around with the Aryan Brotherhood and the Nazi Lowriders.

Isaiah didn't know anybody from those organizations, but he did have an acquaintance named Kevin Boyd. Kev didn't belong to any of the gangs. He was more of a closet racist who hated niggers and Jews in the privacy of his own home.

They'd met about a year ago. Kev was drunk and his car had broken down not far from Beaumont's. Some local thugs were beating him for trespassing. Isaiah happened by and told them to stop. It was a sign of respect that they backed off. Kev promptly pronounced Isaiah as one of the "good ones," right up there with Michael Jordan and Derek Jeter. Presently Kev was serving seven to ten in CCI for armed robbery.

Getting permission to visit someone in prison was a lengthy process. You had to fill out a Department of Corrections questionnaire, available only if the prisoner sent it to you. There's also a background check and a bunch of other hoops to climb through. Isaiah called Carter Samuels, a police officer and former client, who got a message to Kev to call Isaiah, which Kev agreed to do for a fifty-dollar contribution to his commissary account.

"The Starks call themselves white nationalists but it's bullshit," Kev said. "They're not real believers."

If you call yourself a white nationalist, Isaiah thought, you are a white nationalist. "Who's their leader?" he asked.

"A guy named Sidero Bernal. Weird name for a white guy, huh? He tells everybody it's Latin but who knows? He's a vicious little prick. Even the Mexicans and the nig—blacks—leave him alone. He's done some crazy shit."

"Like?"

"Like he stole some gasoline from the motor pool and set a guy on fire. He made a shiv out of a toothbrush and a shaver blade and cut a guy's Achilles' heel. He locked this one poor asshole in a dryer and watched him go around and around until he blacked out. That kind of crazy shit. It's the joint so nobody saw anything."

"Is he in there now?" Isaiah asked.

"I'm not sure. The Starks have a house they call the Den. It's in Signal Hill."

"Give me the directions," Isaiah said, and wrote them down. "One last thing. Don't tell anybody I asked about them."

"I won't," Kev said.

"I mean it. I know people in there," Isaiah said. "You rat me out and you'll be wearing an apron and calling somebody hubby."

"I get it, okay? When do I get my fifty bucks?"

Signal Hill was east of Long Beach, nothing separating the two hoods but lines on a map. Isaiah took Willow toward the airport and stopped by the Sunshine Cemetery to visit Marcus's grave. He regretted it. Looking at the headstone brought back terrible memories. Marcus, with his beautiful smile and sterling goodness murdered in the street. His killer, Seb Habimana, was dead but it was no consolation. Isaiah cried for a while and left.

He was feeling faint. He hadn't eaten anything since the previous night. Beaumont's death and Grace's sudden appearance had squelched his appetite. He stopped at a park and forced down an energy bar. Kev's directions weren't very specific, but eventually Isaiah found the dirt road that led to the Den. It was an odd area next to the freeway. Drive down the road and whoever was at the other end would see you coming.

Isaiah drove past the road. Immediately adjacent was a grove of trees and past that was a vast parking lot, both surrounded by tall, chain-link fences. Isaiah parked on the street, walked by the empty kiosk and crossed the lot. It seemed to be a storage depot for the city—office trailers, rows of earth movers, cranes and other heavy machinery. A few men in orange hard hats were driving forklifts, taking rolls of rebar and bags of cement into a warehouse. Isaiah made a mental note like he did whenever he was in new surroundings.

He walked through the grove of trees. Grove was something of an overstatement. There were desiccated eucalyptus, exhausted palms and stunted pines. The ground was covered with pine needles and litter, one of those nasty places where you might step on a hypodermic needle or a used condom.

It was a long walk. Isaiah was sweating by the time he reached the opposite tree line. Just across a dirt road was the so-called Den. It was an old, two-story thing with boards missing from the front steps and scabs of paint flaking off the gray wood. Everything in and around the place looked broken.

Mo said the car involved in the drive-by was a black pickup. There were cars around but no black pickup. It was probably hidden somewhere until the heat wore off. A group of Starks had gathered on the front porch, in their teens or twenties, passing around a joint and drinking cans of Coors. Their uniform was the same as every other gang in the country: oversize shorts or jeans, gold chains, tats, shirts and caps with slogans on them. NO JEW WILL REPLACE ME. MAKE AMERICA GREAT AGAIN. WHITE SUPREMACY IS REAL.

White supremacy, Isaiah thought. What a joke. In what fields of endeavor did these assholes imagine they were superior? Art? Science? Ending world hunger? These people hadn't shown their superiority in anything besides burning crosses, wearing pointy hats and inventing new kinds of swastikas. And why were they always complaining about losing jobs to minorities? What jobs and minorities were they talking about? Did they mean they applied for work harvesting crops but were turned down in favor of an undocumented immigrant? Or that they wanted to build airplanes but Boeing overlooked them and hired engineers from India and Korea? Or they had an opportunity to be a bank president but the board of directors chose a fellow Jew? Their problems weren't because of the niggers, faggots and wetbacks. Their lives were of their own making; they had no one to blame but themselves.

Isaiah used his binoculars and tried to pick out the leader. Could be the guy sitting on the top step. Scrawny, shaved head, mandatory tats and a terrible case of acne. There was something hyena-like about him. The malicious grin, maybe, or the dull, merciless eyes. Next to him was a big guy. Really big. He was shirtless, inked up, bulbous belly, his skin pink from the sun that glinted off his bald head. He looked lethargic but dangerous, like you were in a canoe and a half-submerged hippo was staring directly at you.

The others were seated around them like acolytes. They were the two leaders or maybe leader and second lieutenant. The others listened when the hyena talked and laughed when he laughed. A red-haired woman sat beside him, bored, like I've heard this shit a hundred times before. Hyena said something sharply and one of the guys got up immediately and went into the house. That's him, Isaiah thought, Sidero Bernal. And Kev was right. He didn't look like his name. A white guy like any other.

Did he shoot Beaumont, or was it one of the others? It didn't really matter. Isaiah thought about revenge but he knew better now. Revenge, served cold, hot or any other way was a form of self-mutilation that scarred you as much as your victimizer. But these murdering sons of bitches would come to justice. Of that, he was sure.

CHAPTER TWO

Are You Okay, Weiner?

Isaiah took a shower to wash off the smell of racism. He'd just finished dressing when the doorbell rang. Out of habit, he took the collapsible baton off the coffee table and put it in his back pocket. He looked through the peephole and opened the door. On the other side of the security screen stood a man in his forties or early fifties. He wore an electric blue suit, crisp white shirt, gold tie, gold tie clip, gold cufflinks, and fat gold Rolex. A-type, Isaiah thought, struggled early, has money now, and feels the need to show it off.

"Can I help you?" Isaiah said.

"Are you Isaiah?" the man asked in a tone that sounded like *are you the garbage man?*

"Yes. Who are you?"

"Dwight. I work for Angus Byrne."

"That's too bad."

Dwight smirked. "Sure, anything you say."

Dwight had a puffed-up build, a square head, his salt-and-pepper hair shiny and combed back. He reminded Isaiah of John Gotti—cunning eyes and a smug, cruel face. He was restless and fidgeting, seemingly embarrassed; a flunky who was too old to be doing a flunky's job.

"Say what you want or I'm closing the door," Isaiah said. Dwight turned his head and nodded at the Maybach idling at the curb, a stretch

23

Mercedes, snow white, gleaming like a block of sculpted ice. "Angus wants to talk to you. Five minutes."

"Why?" Isaiah said. "Did he lose a shipment of machine guns? A box of hand grenades go missing?"

Dwight sighed impatiently. "It's five fucking minutes, okay? Don't give me a hard time."

"Sorry, I'm busy," Isaiah said. "I've gotta go do something important like wash the dishes or sweep the floor."

Dwight puffed himself up even more and growled through the screen like a mafioso. "You're making a big fucking mistake."

"I make them all the time," Isaiah said as he closed the door.

He ate some soup standing at the counter. He'd been tempted to accept Dwight's offer; a chance to get a read on a bad guy was always a good thing, but Isaiah loathed Angus Byrne. He was one of the biggest arms dealers on the West Coast, another prince of darkness living the life of royalty. His weapons had robbed parents of their children and turned children into orphans. They had gunned down husbands and wives and grandparents, teachers and nurses and laborers in the field, and Isaiah wouldn't abet Angus in the smallest way. The old man had probably sold the gun that killed Beaumont.

Isaiah knew what Angus wanted. He had a case, he needed help. Why else would he be reaching out? Isaiah would never work for that asshole. The man was pestilence, a virus, a stinking glob of human offal. Making the smallest effort on his behalf would be like burying yourself under an outhouse. You'd never get the filth off.

Later that afternoon, Isaiah was holding a bag of groceries, trying to put in the key and thinking about Grace when three men rushed him from behind. By the time he heard them and dropped the groceries, they were at his back. He whirled around and caught the first attacker with an elbow and heard the guy's nose snap. It was Sidero, the dull hyena eyes going wide and bright. He howled, spun away, blood spurting on the lawn. The second man was Dwight, grinning and eager, his gold tie undone. Isaiah ducked under his lunge and punched him in the crotch. Dwight screamed and doubled over, clutching his balls like they were trying to escape. The third attacker was hippo man from the Den. He bear-hugged Isaiah from behind. Isaiah pushed up on his arms and ducked, slipping out of the embrace, but Dwight was on his feet now. He came at him with his teeth bared, snarling, hitting Isaiah with a flurry of angry punches to the midsection, enjoying himself. He only stopped because the others told him to. They dragged Isaiah into a van gasping for breath. Sometimes a six-pack helps.

They drove to Newport Beach, an upscale area south of Long Beach. Dwight was driving, shooting glares in the rearview mirror, Isaiah bookended between the others. If he wasn't so winded he'd have taken them on. Sidero had his head back, holding a T-shirt against his bloody nose.

"If it was just you and me?" he said nasally. "I would hab killed you."

"If it was just you and me," Isaiah replied, "I'd have broken more than your nose."

Hippo man was taking up most of the seat. The sleeves of his T-shirt were cut off by necessity and apparently he'd run out of deodorant.

"Could we open a window?" Isaiah said.

"Christ, you stink, Hugo," Dwight said. "Don't you take a shower?"

"Eben I cad smell it," Sidero said through his T-shirt.

"Shut up, Sidero," Hugo said. Then he leaned forward and tapped Dwight on the head with a sausage-like finger.

"Listen, asshole, you don't say shit to me, okay?" Hugo said. "Or I'll fuck you up bad. Stop the car and I'll do it right now." Dwight smoothed his hair, looked in the mirror and sighed like he was bored.

"Sure, Hugo," he said. "Anything you say."

Angus's house was a monument to sterility. A stack of cement blocks, painted white with smoked windows and bands of oak across the front for that homey feel, the cheapest possible way for a developer to build a luxury house. Fuck aesthetics. Fuck architecture. Houses sold by the foot.

Isaiah was ushered into the study, nearly cringing when he saw Angus. He'd always been repulsed by the man's impossible ugliness. Angus was at his desk, talking on the phone. He was wearing a suit that was too young for him and reeked of cologne that smelled like limes. When he saw Isaiah, he dropped the phone.

"You nimrods," he said. "You were just supposed to bring him here, not beat him up. Can't you do anything right?" He glared at Sidero still holding the bloody T-shirt to his nose. "What happened to you? Weren't there three of you?"

"Des," Sidero said, "but—"

"And you get *your* face busted up? How does that happen? Did you have your hands in your pockets? I wouldn't be surprised if you hit yourself in the face, you goddamn moron! Stop bleeding on my fucking carpet and get the hell out of my sight!" Sidero hurried out of the room.

Angus was a stooped, skeletal old man, Ebenezer Scrooge with thinning hair dyed too brown and an antique scowl. His face was inexplicably lumpy, like someone had pressed his knuckles into a hunk of cookie dough. Add big startled eyes, a mustache and ears like sideways satellite dishes and you had an aging Mr. Potato Head after a car accident.

"Why are you standing there, Dwight?" Angus said. "Get the man some water and an aspirin. Dwight took a second too long to respond to Angus, testing his patience. He left the room tugging at his sore balls.

A brown dachshund slept next to the unlit fireplace. Angus looked at the dog with concern, as if he hoped it hadn't been disturbed. "You okay, Weiner?"

"This is kidnapping," Isaiah said, "and if you think I won't press charges, you're dumber than the people who work for you."

"I know you're angry. I'm angry too," Angus said. "I'm surrounded by idiots. Give them a screwdriver and they'll stab themselves in the forehead. Do you want a drink?"

"No, I don't want anything except to get the hell out of here," Isaiah said. "Say what you're going to say or I'm out."

"I want you to work for me," Angus said.

"No chance. I'd rather work for a serial killer," Isaiah replied. "At least they murder people one at a time."

"You haven't heard what I want you to do."

"Like I said, no chance."

Dwight returned with an ice pack, Tylenol and a bottle of water. "Here," he said, and Isaiah waved him off.

"My daughter's in serious trouble," Angus said.

"I don't care," Isaiah said.

"Could you just listen for a minute? This is important."

"I guess you didn't hear me. *I don't care.*"

"You handle this for me and I'll pay you fifty grand."

"Fifty grand won't buy you breakfast," Isaiah said.

"Taking the high road, are we?" the old man said. "I realize we don't walk on the same side of the street, but you can't take it out on my kid."

"Oh, yes, I can," Isaiah retorted. "You're a plague on the world, Angus, and I want nothing to do with you, your kid, your problems, your dog or anything else." Isaiah moved toward the door. Hugo was standing in front of him, his arms folded across his chest. "I'm going home," Isaiah continued, "and you need to get out of my way."

Angus wasn't used to being challenged. The lumpy face had flattened, the big ears turning red. He took a moment, nodding, thinking, and then he said casually, "I have a question for you," and Isaiah knew from his tone that something bad was coming.

"I was wondering," Angus went on, "can you play the violin with a broken hand?" Something cold and sharp pierced Isaiah's gut. Dwight smiled. "I'm not a medical man," Angus continued, "but I think it would be impossible. Even after they put it back together. You'd lose flexibility." Dwight cracked his knuckles.

Isaiah restrained himself. Outrage would have no effect on Angus. Pleading or arguing would only make him more confident of his position. There was no doubt he'd carry out the threat. He'd have Dwight and the Starks slam Stella's long, graceful fingers in a car door until they splintered.

Angus was known for his vindictiveness. Jose Modesto cheated him on a deal and left town. Three and a half years later, Jose came back and his wife found him upside down in a barrel of tar with his feet tied together. A rival named Teddy Walsh went missing. The next time anybody saw him, he was lying under an industrial steamroller like a poster of himself. There was no way Isaiah could protect Stella 24/7 and if he told her about the threat what would he say? That he'd brought his virulent world into hers? That she'd have to be on guard all the time, even when she was home rehearsing Vivaldi? That wherever she went she'd always be in danger of losing her ability to play music? Isaiah remained blank but he knew his eyes revealed his fury.

Angus smiled like a skull in the catacombs. "Like I said, I want you to work for me. My daughter, Christiana, makes custom suits, has a shop here in Newport Beach. A man named Tyler Barnes was shot and killed right in front of her and the cops think she did it. It's ridiculous bordering on idiocy. The girl is spoiled and capricious, but she wouldn't kill anybody."

"Who is Tyler Barnes?" Isaiah asked.

"He worked for me," Angus said.

Isaiah snorted a laugh. "A guy who worked for you got shot in your daughter's shop?"

"It's not funny. It's my flesh and blood we're talking about."

"What did Tyler do for you?" Isaiah said, still amused.

"Finance and logistics," Angus said. "He handled the money and got things organized. He was honest, smart—and classy. None of that flashy stuff. He could have been from another time, another era. He had manners. He lived in one of those historic homes and drank vintage wine. He was also the best employee I've ever had." He shot a snide glance at Dwight. "This asshole has been with me for fucking decades and hasn't come close." Dwight's jaw tightened and stared off at his anger. If he didn't want to kill Angus, Isaiah would be very surprised.

"Tyler was a homo," Hugo said.

"No, he wasn't, Hugo," Angus said. "Maybe you should suck some dick yourself. It might make you smarter."

"Suspects?" Isaiah said.

"Ponlok. Know him?" Angus said.

"Sure, I know him. He's a thug like you."

"He's trying to run me out of town and I'm doing the same. We're at war. That's why I have all these dimwit monkeys hanging around my house. Lok couldn't get to me so he went after Tyler." Isaiah had doubts about that. Angus went on. "I still can't believe they got him. He was a former Marine, always armed, and on the lookout for an attack."

"Was Tyler from LA?" Isaiah asked.

"From Oregon, somewhere on the coast," Angus said. "Why do you ask?"

"I was wondering if Tyler and Lok had some prior beef," Isaiah said.

"None that I know of."

"So what do you want me to do?" Isaiah asked.

"What do you *think* I want you to do?" Angus snarled. "Get my daughter free and clear."

"If your daughter didn't do it, then she *is* free and clear. I don't see the problem." Angus hesitated. Isaiah said, "You think she might have done it, don't you?"

Angus was glaring now, his ears bright red, his breathing faster. "No, I don't, goddammit! That's not possible!"

"Okay, let's say it is Lok's crew," Isaiah said. "I'm supposed to find out which one of them pulled the trigger and convince the cops he's guilty? That's impossible and you know it. It's stupid and a waste of time. If your daughter did it, that's not my fault or yours."

Angus's gaunt body seemed to swell, his breathing pumping noxious fumes into his system, the cartoon face contorting into a freak-show exhibit, grotesque and terrifying, a Stephen King clown come to life. A small, white scar on his temple glowed brighter. "My daughter is precious to me," he hissed, spit bubbling between his teeth. "Christiana is the only person in the world I care about and you will get this done no matter what it takes, *do you understand?*" He was shaking, palsied with fury. "Fuck this up and I swear to God, I'll cripple your girlfriend and break you in half!"

They looked at each other, death rays coming from Angus's eyes. Isaiah didn't react, his usual response to threats, his gaze steady and unrevealing, his face blank as unbuttered toast. Angus's rage dissipated into what appeared to be sadness or despair. He turned away and looked out of the window. "Hugo?" he said. "Tell Sidero to drive him to Christiana's place. She's expecting him."

Seething, Isaiah went outside. Sidero was leaning against his black pickup truck, the hyena wearing a backward baseball cap and a swollen nose. It was slightly off center, wads of Kleenex stuffed in his nostrils.

"Get in," Sidero said.

"You shot Beaumont," Isaiah said, stepping closer.

"Who's Beaumont?"

"Remember that drive-by? The Cambodians you shot at? You hit the man who owned the store. He's in the hospital. He's dying."

Sidero grinned and stuck his neck out so their faces were nearly touching. "The fuck do I care? Now get in the goddamn car."

Isaiah whipped an elbow across his nose. Sidero screamed and fell back into the truck and slid to the ground. He had his knees up and was rocking back and forth, his hands cupped around his face, blood spilling between his fingers. He tried to get up but Isaiah put his foot on his chest and pushed him down again. Sidero took his hands off his face and looked up, snarling. "I'm gonna put you in the ground, motherfucker!"

"No, you're not," Isaiah said. "You're too stupid to put me anywhere." He walked off and heard the punk shouting.

"A bullet in the head, nigger. Wait for it!"

Isaiah went home, put on some music and tried to calm himself. He doubted Lok was Tyler's killer. Ponlok called shots for the Cambodian street gang, TEC. If they wanted to kill Tyler, they wouldn't shoot him in somebody's shop. They'd spray him with bullets from a moving car or send a newbie to do a walk-up and blast him from three feet away. Isaiah resisted the urge to call Angus and tell him to fuck himself. He thought of Stella looking at her crippled hands, her crippled life. *Go to work, Isaiah. Shut up and go to work.*

CHAPTER THREE

Alters

Angus's daughter, Christiana, lived in Newport Beach, not far from her father's place. The drive there from Long Beach was depressing, the transition from want to bountiful, from struggle to ease, from peril to relative safety. Isaiah wondered what algorithm of race, history, economics, politics and law had led to a divide so deep and insoluble. Experts had explanations, but it was like describing the universe. Whatever your vantage point, there was so much more to wrap your head around.

Christiana's condo was in a posh building, marbled and mirrored, all potted palms and glittering chandeliers. A woman opened the door.

"Hello, Isaiah. I'm Gia, Christiana's mother." She was in her sixties, short silver hair, genteel in her mannerisms, primly dressed in a sweater set and pearls. Isaiah was incredulous. This woman married that evil old man? "I'm assuming you spoke to Angus," she said.

"Yes, I have," Isaiah said.

"I apologize if he was—well, his usual self. We've been divorced for nineteen years," she was quick to say. "All we have in common is Christiana." She led him into the living room. Isaiah stopped and stared. "I know," Gia said, embarrassed.

The décor, if you could call it that, was chaotic. An Edwardian armchair, a poster of the Clash, a Turkish throw rug, a Chinese throw rug, a convincing reproduction of a Tiffany lamp, a convincing reproduction of Monet's water lilies, an antique pine dining table, a porcelain bird clock and myriad other things that had no connection to one another. It was like a 7-Eleven and the prop room on a movie set had collided in the living room. Clothes were hung on the backs of chairs and piled on the furniture. Beer cans, fast-food debris, golf clubs, gambling chips, crumbs, a broken tennis racquet, pizza boxes, miscellaneous stains, and a bunch of other random stuff were scattered across the marble floor.

"I'm sorry for the mess," Gia said. She looked helpless, like a child lost in TK's wrecking yard. "It's hard to keep up with things," she said.

Why not get a housekeeper? Isaiah thought. Why not get ten? Angus could pay for them out of his penny jar. "May I get you something to drink?" she said.

"No, thank you," he said.

"Please, sit anywhere." There was irony in her voice. Isaiah found a spot on the black leather sofa, between the HOME IS LOVE pillow, a giant stuffed panda, a stack of tabloid magazines and a scuffed leather jacket.

"Is Christiana around?" Isaiah said.

"Yes, of course. I'll get her."

She left. There had to be other people living here, Isaiah thought. scanning the room again. Rabid teenagers or schizoid decorators. Strewn on the coffee table were an empty bottle of Grey Goose, a tumbler imprinted with bright pink lipstick, assorted beer cans, a charred bong, a half-eaten container of sushi, a lacy pink thong, an open bag of peanuts and a paperback romance novel with a viking on the cover.

Piled in a corner were shoes. Lots of them. Pumps, stilettos, oxfords, cap toes, basketball high tops, patent leather thigh-highs, ballet slippers, motorcycle boots and who knew what else. Usually Isaiah could get an idea of what someone was like based on their belongings, but this made no sense at all.

Christiana came in. She'd inherited her mother's looks—slim and pretty and she moved with an elegance Isaiah associated with swans. Her clothes were another matter, like she'd stolen them from a hooker.

Short-short skirt, tank top that said LET'S PLAY, spiky heels with straps around the ankles. She smelled like booze and cigarettes.

"Hello, Isaiah," she said in a soft voice. "Thank you for coming."

She looked for a place to sit down, glancing wearily at her mother. Hard to believe she was responsible for this chaos. Her nails were bitten to the quick, he noticed. You'd think she'd be biting them now, though she didn't seem nervous, more weary, more sad. She had peculiar scars, a thin line of raised skin around both wrists. Somebody had tied her up and not with rope. Christiana moved the stuffed panda off the sofa and sat down. Her mother pushed the laundry aside and took the Edwardian chair.

"These aren't my clothes," Christiana said. She looked at her mother. "I think Marlene lost again. There wasn't any money in my wallet." She gently rubbed her hands together while she spoke. There was a spot of blue paint between her thumb and forefinger. Odd. Isaiah wondered why they weren't her clothes or who Marlene was and why she was stealing.

"Your father said you witnessed a murder," Isaiah said.

"Well, I—" Christiana hesitated, seemingly embarrassed.

"It's simpler if I do this part," Gia said. "I'm sure you understand." Isaiah didn't, but let it go. "It happened at Christiana's shop," Gia continued. "She makes custom suits." She smiled, trying to brighten the moment. "Christiana has a wonderful reputation and her reviews are always five-star. Most of her customers are regulars." She tensed, getting to the hard part. "Last Friday night, Tyler Barnes was shot—killed—right in the showroom. Christiana and Tyler were the only ones there." Isaiah didn't understand why Christiana couldn't tell him that herself.

"Did you see the killer, Christiana?" he asked.

Gia interjected. "No. She wasn't aware there was a shooting."

"You didn't hear the shot?"

"No, she didn't," Gia said.

"Tell me what happened," Isaiah said. Gia started to speak but he raised a hand.

Christiana looked down at her lap. "Tyler and I were in front of the mirrors for a final fitting." Her brow furrowed, she pinched her lips together, straining, like she was kicking herself for not remembering. Gia was gripping her knees, restraining herself from speaking.

Christiana sagged, exasperated, like the whole exercise was pointless. "I don't know what happened after that."

Isaiah was puzzled. More harshly than he intended he said, "You don't know? It happened in your shop while you were there." Gia tried to say something but Isaiah raised his hand again. How could Christiana not know? he thought. Was she an alcoholic? Did she have blackouts? Transient amnesia? Christiana hunched her shoulders like she was cold. Then she bowed her head, closed her eyes and went perfectly still.

"Christiana," Isaiah said. "Are you all right?" She didn't move. He waited for her to speak and realized something strange. *All the shoes were the same size.* Christiana lifted her head and looked at him sharply, sneering.

"That stupid bitch doesn't know anything," she said. "You might as well talk to a donkey." The change in her voice was startling—loud, abrasive and nasal like she had a cold. Her posture was different too, slouched and fuck-you indifferent. She put her hands behind her head, stretched her legs out in front of her and crossed her ankles. "You're not going to find out anything. Not from that idiot."

"What idiot?" Isaiah said. "Who are you talking about?"

"Are you an idiot too?" she said. "You act like one."

"I'm not sure what's happening," Isaiah said. He looked at Gia. She was mortified, her hand over her mouth.

"I'm so sorry," she said. "I thought Angus told you."

"Told me what?"

"Christiana has multiple personalities."

Isaiah was stunned into silence. Christiana was grinning, enjoying his confusion. She laughed like a squawking blue jay.

"Woo-hoo!" she said. "This is fucking great! Look at him! He's fucking lost!" She picked up the beer can. It was empty. She frowned and tossed it aside.

Isaiah tried to stay calm and recalibrate, see if this was real. "You're not Christiana?"

"You gotta be joking."

"Then who are you?"

"Jasper. Jasper Hicks," she said as if Isaiah should already know.

"Jasper is from Arizona," Gia said. "He's eighteen years old. He dropped out of high school and—"

"I can talk for myself, okay?" he snapped. "Why the fuck are you still here, anyway? Why don't you go home?"

"Were you there that night, Jasper?" Isaiah said. Jasper was so different from Christiana, Isaiah started thinking of him as an eighteen-year-old dropout from Arizona. Jasper yawned.

"Yeah, I was there," he said. There was something oddly theatrical about him, like he was trying to be an asshole, like an actor who hadn't mastered the part. Christiana had seemed quite authentic. "Too bad," Jasper went on. "That idiot comes in to get a suit and ends up dead."

"I'd like you to answer a couple of questions."

"Why should I?" Jasper was grinning again. "Gimme one good reason." He grabbed the bag of peanuts and began tossing them in his mouth.

"I'll give you a reason," Isaiah said, tired of this bullshit. "If Christiana goes to prison, so do you." Something got stuck between Jasper's teeth. He hooked a finger into his mouth and tried to dig it out. "You were telling me about that night," Isaiah said.

"Gimme a second, will you?" Jasper said. He took his finger out of his mouth and frowned, his eyes crinkling into a wince. He looked like he was getting carsick. "I need a beer," he said. He bowed his head, took a deep breath, and when he lifted it again, Christiana the swan was back. It was uncanny, like shape-shifting or a special effect. She pressed the back of her hand against her forehead.

"I'm getting a migraine." Her voice was soft and fluid again.

"All right, dear," Gia said gently. "Take your pills and lie down. I'll be in in a minute." Christiana left. Isaiah didn't know what to think.

Should he believe this? It bordered on the ridiculous, but as far as he knew the phenomenon was real.

"She actually has multiple personalities?" he asked.

"Yes," Gia said. "She was six or seven years old when the first one appeared. As she got older, more came and went."

"How many of them are there now?"

"Including Christiana? Five."

"Five," Isaiah said flatly.

"Christiana, Jasper, Marlene, Pearl and Bertrand," Gia said. "It's not an unusual number. There have been some cases where the alters are in double figures. *Alter* is what we call an individual personality."

"Jasper didn't like Christiana," Isaiah said. "How is that possible? They're the same person."

"They are but they aren't," Gia explained. "To them, they're entirely different people. Different lifestyles, memories, experiences."

"Is Christiana aware that Jasper doesn't like her? I mean, do the alters communicate?"

"Some do, some don't," Gia said. "Think of the condition as a house. Each alter has their own room. Some doors are open and others are closed. With Christiana and Jasper, it's open but not very often. One alter might hate another and be friends with someone else. They might be jealous or protective or completely indifferent. One may not know another even exists."

"What happened to Christiana when Jasper took over?"

"It's as if she were unconscious," Gia explained. "She'll have no memory of what happened after the switch out. If Jasper or any of the others got into a traffic accident, Christiana could wake up in the hospital with no idea how she got there." Isaiah had another question but was dreading the answer.

"Did any one of the alters witness the whole thing?" he said. "The shooting from beginning to end?"

"I can't say for sure," Gia said, "but probably no."

"So each alter only saw part of it?"

"Yes," Gia said. "If they saw anything at all."

*   *   *

Christiana lay on the bed, the migraine throbbing. She didn't mind. The voices of others were jabbering at her, asking questions, scolding and making fun of her. Sometimes she could turn down the volume, sometimes not. Everything in her life was sometimes. She was supposed to be on top of things, in charge, but that was far from true. From her perspective she had all the responsibility but none of the control. She felt both angry and defeated. She should have tried harder to keep Jasper from switching out. If only she knew what the jerk had said. Did he give something away? She groaned, less for the migraine and more for her predicament. If Isaiah succeeded one way, they were home free. If he succeeded another way, they were doomed.

CHAPTER FOUR
Stopping Power

Isaiah left Christiana's and went home. He was stunned by what he'd seen. Anxious too because he knew so little about her condition. Isaiah wasn't a speed reader but he was close. His facility for understanding and remembering was exceptional, even as a schoolkid. His teachers remarked on it all the time. He also had the ability to hone in and conceptualize the central ideas, foregoing the details until they were needed.

He read articles online and downloaded several books. Multiple personality disorder has its beginnings in childhood. If a child is severely abused for a sustained period of time, the physical and psychological damage can last a lifetime. In rare cases, the abuse is so unbearable the child's psyche fractures into different personalities. As Isaiah understood it, the fracturing was a way to break up the memories so no one personality had to endure the horror of remembering the whole experience. These personalities, or "alters" as Gia called them, can be completely different, as different as Christiana and Jasper: age, ethnicity, sexual orientation, personality, mannerisms, even eyeglass prescriptions, can vary wildly. Christiana was apparently the "host" alter who functioned day to day, the alters changing or "switching out" depending on circumstances.

The dry, technical language didn't describe the overwhelming awe and fear you felt watching someone transform into an entirely different person or your revulsion imagining what had happened to that helpless child. The monstrous images made Isaiah hate Angus all the more.

Mental illness was a grim reality these days. Isaiah had dealt with its ugly guises since he began his career. Lester Collins stabbed a hallucination that turned out to be his girlfriend. Missy Laws drowned her baby girl in the toilet because she thought it was trying to poison her milk. Jake Lamont jumped in front of an Amtrak train because he thought he was Iron Man.

Multiple personalities was way beyond Isaiah's experience. The case had only started and he was already feeling overwhelmed. Angus wanted to get this resolved before Christiana was arrested. He knew though, that if Christiana went to trial, her attorneys would likely claim not guilty by reason of insanity. At best, a long, bumpy, uphill road. For the most part jurors didn't look favorably on the insanity defense, thinking it might be a scam, easily faked. Everyone all had relatives who were nuts but didn't commit crimes.

The defense was not helped by cases of actual fakers. Vincent "The Oddfather" Gigante, head of the Genovese crime family, was often seen shuffling around Greenwich Village in his pajamas and slippers, talking to parking meters, muttering incoherently and drooling on himself. He was a former boxer and a lot of people thought he'd taken a few too many straight lefts to the head. He was declared unfit for trial and it kept him out of a courtroom for a decade. But another jury didn't buy it and Gigante was busted for racketeering. Later, he admitted it had all been a ruse.

Sometimes the insanity defense worked. John Hinckley Jr., who'd nearly killed President Reagan, was declared legally insane. So was Andrea Yates, who'd drowned her five children in a bathtub. Steven Steinberg's lawyers argued Steinberg had been sleepwalking or in a "dissociative state" when he stabbed his wife twenty-six times. It worked for him, but for the vast majority of cases it wasn't a good strategy. Only one out of four people using the insanity defense was able to convince a jury.

Isaiah had seen a couple of his cases go to trial. He had watched defense attorneys and prosecutors alike trying to explain the legal standards for the insanity defense. They were difficult to understand and even more so to apply. *Was Mr. Smith's behavior the result of a mental disease?* That is, was it involuntary, something he couldn't control, like coughing when you have a cold? How were you supposed to know if Mr. Smith's neurochemicals had shorted out when he hit his grandma with a hatchet? *Did Mr. Smith know right from wrong at the time he committed the crime?* What does that mean? That before he hit Grandma with a hatchet, Mr. Smith said to himself, "I know this is wrong but I'm going to do it anyway"? Sorting through the arguments was confusing and often heated for twelve strangers, each with a different understanding of what it all meant.

The next morning, Isaiah, Christiana, and Gia met at Christiana's shop. The showroom was pretty and charming. Soft lighting, diaphanous curtains, hardwood floors, antique furniture. The window in the door had been reglazed; there was new glass and the doorframe had fresh paint on it.

"Nice place," Isaiah said.

"Yes," Gia replied. "Christiana has good taste."

Christiana stiffened. Apparently, her mother's assessment wasn't appreciated. She was dressed in what Isaiah assumed were clothes of her own choosing. Stylish but subdued.

"Tell me about Tyler," Isaiah said. Christiana shrugged.

"He was a good customer," she said simply.

"Did he have an appointment?" Isaiah asked.

"Yes. We were doing the final fitting on a new suit," Christiana said. She smiled sadly, and tears welled up in her eyes. "It was linen. Very beautiful." Isaiah wondered what was so meaningful about linen.

"How was he?" Isaiah said. "What kind of mood was he in?"

Gia tried to give Christiana a tissue but she brushed it away. "He was…upset," she said. "Not himself. He was usually very low-key— no, that's not right. Easy. Comfortable. He was always that way."

"What was he upset about?"

"He wouldn't say…but it was something about…" She hesitated again, reeling in the memory. "Someone had disappointed him," she said. "He had to tell Angus something and he didn't want to do it. He said it would be really bad."

"That night," Isaiah said. "Start from the beginning."

"Pearl was doing the final measurement," Christiana said.

"How did you know?" Isaiah said. "Weren't you switched out?"

"Yes, but sometimes, if she lets me, I can see what she's doing."

"Why would Pearl do the final measurement? Isn't that important?"

"Christiana and Pearl are very close," Gia added helpfully. She was going to say more but Christiana silenced her with a glare.

"And then?" Isaiah said.

"I needed my scissors," Christiana said, "and Pearl went to get them for me."

"I'd like to meet her," Isaiah said.

"I don't know if she'll want to," Christiana said too quickly. "She's very shy but I'll ask." Christiana went still, blinked a few times. "She doesn't want to come out," she said. She shrugged, as if there was nothing she could do. "I doubt if she'll have anything to say," she added.

"Wait a second," Isaiah said, turning to Gia. "You just said Christiana and Pearl were very close." Gia froze. Christiana was tight-jawed, caught in a lie. Isaiah passed over it. "She has to know how important this is," he said. "Please, ask her again. Tell her there's a possibility that she could go to prison, and I'd give you the same warning."

Christiana took a deep, reluctant breath and bowed her head. Pearl appeared. Isaiah would have sworn under oath that she was smaller and younger than Christiana. She was looking at the floor, her head pulled into her neck, shoulders hunched, hands clenched in her lap. That feeling of theatricality was there again. A peasant girl questioned by the gestapo.

"Hello, Pearl, I'm Isaiah."

"Yes, I know," she said. She bit her nails.

"Do you know why I'm here?" Isaiah said.

"Yes. You want to know about…that night."

41

"What do you know about Tyler?"

Pearl hesitated. She looked furtive, as if someone might be eavesdropping. "Christiana can't hear me now," she said. "You promise you won't tell her?"

"I promise."

"Tyler wasn't a good person," she said.

"Why?"

She thought a moment and shook her head. "He just wasn't." She looked resolute so Isaiah moved on.

"Can you tell me what happened?"

"I was measuring Tyler for the suit and Christiana asked me to get some scissors," she said.

"Show me what you did."

Pearl led Isaiah to a doorway with a curtain drawn across it. Her walk was different from Christiana's. More tentative, like she wasn't sure she should be going where she was going. Isaiah and Gia followed her through the curtain. It was new, the fabric stiff. A throw rug bridged the two rooms. The design didn't fit with everything else, white angular shapes over a forest-black background. It was chosen in a hurry, Isaiah thought. To cover the bloodstains, difficult to get out of hardwood. The shooting happened here, he realized, between the two rooms.

They entered a large workroom. There was a cutting table, a computer nook, a door to a bathroom, an alcove kitchen, numerous shelves with rolls and rolls of fabric and a single sewing machine. There was no way for a lone woman to pay the rent in this neighborhood with suits that took weeks to make. Isaiah suspected Gia did much of the labor and Angus was supporting the shop. Guilt will make you indulgent. Pearl looked like she was standing on a frozen lake and the ice was moving.

"I came through the curtain," Pearl said. "And then Tyler came up behind me and put his arms around me." She squirmed, embarrassed. "He kissed my neck and then he picked me up and whirled me around and that's when"—she started to cry—"he was shot. He kind of grunted, and then he fell down and pushed me through the curtain back into the showroom." She shook her head vehemently. "That's all I saw."

"Did you get a look at the killer?" Isaiah said.

"For a moment, before Tyler turned me around," she said. "It was just a blur."

"Where was the killer? Can you show me?"

Pearl pointed to a spot on the floor. "About here. I don't remember anything after that."

"Why did Tyler kiss you?" Isaiah asked. "Were you in a relationship?" Pearl shook her head. Isaiah thought about pressing it but moved on. "Do you know who came after you?" he asked. She shook her head. "Do you know if any of the others saw anything?" She was fearful now, as if Isaiah was extracting a terrible secret.

"I don't *know*!" she said. "I have to go now or I'll get in trouble." And she was gone. Christiana returned.

Isaiah suppressed his impatience. "So Pearl went into the cutting room," he said. "Then Tyler was shot and she switched out. When you came back, where were you?"

"It was very confusing," Christiana said. "I was kneeling beside Tyler...he'd been shot in the back of the head." She started to cry and put her hand over her mouth. "There was blood everywhere." She turned away. "It was so awful...so horrible." She wept. Gia offered her a tissue and Christiana pushed it away, preferring the back of her hand, smearing her mascara. Another oddity but Isaiah let that go too.

Isaiah went to the spot Pearl had indicated and tried to imagine what happened from the killer's point of view. The guy came in the rear entrance and saw no one at first. Then he started toward the curtain and Pearl came through it, followed by Tyler. Tyler grabbed her, whirled her around exposing his back, and the killer shot him in the head. Tyler fell to the floor, pushing Pearl through the curtain and back into the showroom. That's why the curtain was replaced. It was splattered with blood or full of bullet holes or both. If Tyler was moving, it was possible the killer had missed a shot or two.

Isaiah went back into the showroom, Gia trailing. He examined the freshly painted front doorframe. He put his finger on a nearly undetectable hole that was spackled and painted over. It was small, a .22.

Gia was looking over his shoulder.

"How did you know it was there?" she said.

"When did you get here that night?" he asked.

"About fifteen minutes after Christiana called me. When I arrived, she was sitting next to Tyler's body, holding him, crying and saying things I didn't understand. It was so awful. I didn't know what to do."

"When did you call the police?" he said.

"I don't know," she said. "Ten minutes later? I can't remember." Isaiah sighed.

"Did I do something wrong?" she asked.

"No. But the police would think it was suspicious that Christiana didn't call them immediately. What did she tell them?"

"Nothing coherent. She was hysterical. The alters were coming and going at random. It was a mess."

"Did you tell the police about Christiana's condition?"

"Yes," she said, "but they were very skeptical. I don't think they believed me."

"Do you remember if the police were focused on anything?"

"They asked a lot of questions," Gia said, "but they wanted to know about the front door. Christiana always keeps it locked at night, but it was open. She said she hadn't used it but she was on video. She came out the front door and ran down the block out of camera range. There was blood on her clothes. After a minute, she came back."

"And she has no recollection of that?"

"No."

"Any other video?"

"Everyone who came into the shop went out again," Gia said. "After hours, there was only Tyler and Christiana. No one else." There was a time gap, Isaiah thought, between the killer shooting Tyler and Christiana going out the front door and another gap between her return and kneeling on the floor beside him. He wondered which alters filled those gaps and what they saw.

The killing looked like a professional job. The spot Pearl indicated on the floor was about twenty-five feet from the curtain. If the killer could hit Tyler in the back of the head from that distance, especially when he was moving, the killer was a very good shot. He'd only missed once. Hit men in the movies used 9mms and .45s but the pros used .22s. They're lighter and quieter, especially with a silencer. And the bullet bounces around in your skull, shredding your brain. It made it harder to match the bullet with a gun.

Most people bought larger-caliber weapons for self-protection because they thought they needed *stopping power*, which made no sense to Isaiah. With a nine or a .45, you stood a far greater chance of shooting through a wall and killing your neighbor. If you're an intruder, you are, by definition, clandestine. Whether you're there to grab an iPad or a serial killer about to hack a family into chunks with a meat cleaver, you're nervous and twitchy. The foremost thing in your mind? *Don't get caught.* A gun going off—*any* gun, will send you sprinting the hell out of there, and no one, no matter how vicious and determined, will hang around for a shootout.

Isaiah wondered: If the killer wasn't on video, how did he get in? Isaiah went out the rear entrance. The building was twelve stories tall. All the rear doors to the shops faced the parking lot. There was no camera over Christiana's door because of the awning. It was dark blue, with CHRISTIANA'S CUSTOM SUITS in fancy script. Two cameras were attached to the building, each with a different view of the lot. The building was hemmed in on both sides by other buildings and there were cameras in the passageways too.

Isaiah got the key from Gia and went up on the roof. He stood at the parapet directly over Christiana's awning. The only way to get down was by rope or something similar. Each story was approximately ten feet, times twelve equaled one-hundred twenty feet or forty yards. You'd have to be incredibly strong to descend that far on a rope. Getting back up again would be virtually impossible. Rappelling maybe? Unlikely. In the movies, hit men were cool, smart, athletic and highly trained. They lived in luxury apartments, drove Maseratis and wore designer clothes. They were experts at mountain climbing, skydiving, waterskiing, piloting helicopters and wielding samurai swords.

In reality, they were near-psychotic, none-too-bright wretches; lonely and pathetic, too inward to have normal relationships. As far as skills were concerned, pulling a trigger and staying on two feet were all you needed to know.

If the killer was lowered on a rope, it was raised by someone else. Two people, then. A team. Isaiah walked straight back from the parapet to an HVAC unit. There was a ring of bare metal on a painted stanchion. It could have been made by a rope sliding back and forth. So. The roof guy looped the rope around the stanchion and let it out little by little. But once the shooter reached the awning, he'd have to grab on to a support bar and swing under it. An athlete, then. A small one. To help the shooter get back up, the roof guy would have to pull the rope up a little at a time while the shooter climbed. He was strong. Another athlete.

The whole thing made no sense. Why did the killers choose to kill Tyler in the shop? Especially with Christiana there as a potential witness? Maybe, as Angus had said, it was because Tyler was an ex-marine and hard to target, or maybe there was a reason. Maybe Tyler was *supposed* to be killed in the shop.

It was discouraging. Isaiah wasn't the police and he didn't have a lab for testing DNA and microfibers, or a database to search for similar MOs. His resources consisted of himself and sometimes, like now, that wasn't enough. He thought about Gia and Christiana. Why were they waffling around? Why all the furtiveness? Why did Christiana reprimand Gia with those looks and brush off her attempts at kindness? What bothered Isaiah most was that Christiana had lied about her ability to beckon Pearl. Under the circumstances, Christiana should have been forthright. Her reluctance didn't make sense. Unless she was hiding something.

CHAPTER FIVE

Potato Gun?

Angus was in his favorite booth at Geller's Deli. He was hungry and impatient. He wondered how Isaiah had gotten on with Christiana and what new kind of bullshit would happen next. Hugo was near the front of the restaurant, covering the front door. Dwight was across the aisle, wearing another ridiculous suit. It was green and shimmered gold when the sun hit it at an angle. It reminded Angus of a chameleon except the lizard was probably smarter. As usual, the moron was antsy. He was reading the paper—why, Angus had no idea. Who gives a shit about the news? Dwight put down the paper, crossed his arms across his chest and sighed for the hundredth time. He picked up the paper, read something and put it down again. He ran his hands through his shiny hair while his foot tapped aimlessly on the floor. The guy was always on simmer, Angus thought. Useful at times but mostly it was annoying.

"Hey," Angus said. "Could you cut it out?"

"Cut what out?" Dwight said.

"Everything," Angus replied. "Just sit there. You're fidgeting like a four-year-old."

Sidero was sitting at Angus's table looking sheepish and stepped on, his nose mottled green and black.

"Where's my fucking sandwich?" Angus said.

"How would I know?" Sidero said.

"Well, find out, goddammit."

Angus grew up in Welch, a bleak coal town in McDowell County, West Virginia. The town slogan was "The heart of the nation's coal bin." Angus's father was a miner, coughing and exhausted every moment of his life. His mother was busy having eight children and drinking to forget her responsibilities. She whipped whatever child wasn't doing a chore. The kids at school were unmercifully cruel about Angus's looks, calling him ugly and shitface and the Creature from the Black Lagoon. They bullied him, beat him up, pushed him into ditches full of filthy water and mashed coal dust into his face. They chased him home. A date with a girl was as unlikely as wealth.

Angus went to work in the mines when he was fifteen, the HR guy mistaking ugliness for age. Angus knew it was a shit job but once you're down there it was a hundred times dirtier, more dangerous, back-breaking and soul crushing than anyone could imagine. "Mine shaft" was a fancy way of saying a hole in the ground, a hole darker than the coal itself, built room and pillar, wooden supports, no roof bolting, the air stifling and poisonous, no safety equipment but a stupid helmet with a flashlight on it.

Kids these days didn't know shit about hard work and neither did their parents. You had no idea what hard work meant until you were hacking away at a wall of coal with a goddamn pick and then shoveling blank chunks into an endless succession of carts or using an air drill, big as a 50mm machine gun, burrowing holes in the walls that held the mine together—*all fucking day long*. If you want to grow up to be a tough motherfucker, work in a coal mine. If you want to grow up to be angry and fearless, work in a coal mine.

Angus left the mines when he was twenty-one. His ugliness was like a criminal record. His job interviews averaged three minutes long. He could tell right away how his appearance affected the interviewer, even if the guy was a chinless warehouse supervisor with a lazy eye and boils on his forehead. Angus had hated his looks when he was a kid but he hated them more now, where the consequences were food and rent and dignity. And loneliness. People were afraid of you, as if ugliness was a parasite that bored into your skin and laid eggs in your bloodstream.

Angus learned to love guns in the National Guard, where he was assigned to the Detroit Naval Armory. His unit watched over row upon row of cases, shelves, lockers and wall racks of M14s, M16s, M40s, Winchester 1200s, Colt Commanders, M40 sniper rifles and a variety of machine guns as well as land mines, grenades, mortars and rocket launchers. Angus didn't get to fire the weapons but he appreciated their engineering and artfulness. How they slid, snapped, clicked and cocked. How the parts moved with oily smoothness and how satisfying it was to snap a clip into a sidearm or work the bolt action on a sniper rifle or rack the slide on a riot gun. *Clack-clack!*

But what made Angus smile when he arrived for work each morning was how the guns held unimaginable power. The power he saw in the movies and on TV; how guns controlled, persuaded, coerced, terrified, overwhelmed and saved the day. And the very best thing about them? The thing that gave you goose bumps and filled the empty chamber in your psyche? *You didn't have to be powerful to use them.* You could be a skinny, awkward, hideously ugly, prematurely balding goober like him and still make the baddest motherfucker in the UFC say "excuse me, sir" and get the fuck out of your way.

Some years later, when Angus was well into the business, he walked into the Crazy Horse on his regular night, wearing an Armani suit, a gold Rolex speckled with diamonds and a pink-diamond pinkie ring as big as your knuckle. Most of the strippers approached him only as a last resort, but not Gia, the new girl. The first thing she said was "Wow, what a cutie!" and they both laughed. They went in the Champagne Room and she said, "I'm gonna make you cum in your pants." She nearly succeeded too. He kept her there until closing time paying for lap dances ten at a time with hundred-dollar bills. They talked while she straddled him and ground her sex into his.

"I bet you do something illegal for a living," she said.

"Then you'd win the bet," he replied.

She mashed her tits into his face. "I love dangerous men." He had to pull back so he could catch a breath. "I bet you have a nickname," she said.

"Top Gun," Angus said.

"Oh, baby." She laughed. "We're going to get along just fine."

Angus estimated he'd spent five grand on lap dances before she agreed to see him outside the club and another five before she'd fuck him. She'd look at him while they did it, talking dirty in a steady stream. *Come on you ugly motherfucker give it to me give it to me harder, harder you fucking monster, stick it in so deep I can feel it in my toes.* His ugliness didn't matter because it was acknowledged. You're ugly and I'm a whore. Why should that stop us from having fun? If you have money, you're Val Kilmer, Steven Seagal, or anybody you wanted to be. Maybe you don't have a star on the Walk of Fame but you could buy the fucking sidewalk all the way to the ocean. They had Christiana but he didn't want to think about that.

Isaiah entered the deli through the back. Angus had a napkin tucked into his collar and was demolishing an enormous sandwich, his lips shining with grease. He was talking to Sidero with his mouth full.

"Two entire crates of PX4s and you don't know what happened to them?" Angus said.

"I told you already," Sidero said, tired of hearing this. "I never got them. I waited at the warehouse for three hours. I called Dwight. He didn't know anything so I called Tyler. He said there was a problem."

"Did you ask him what the problem was?" Angus asked impatiently.

"No."

"Well why the hell not?"

"Because he was busy and didn't have time to explain," Sidero replied. "And by the time I called him back he was, you know—dead." Dwight coughed to stifle a laugh and then laughed outright.

"Get out of here, you fucking idiot!" Angus shouted at Sidero. He threw his napkin at him, adding, "Go sit in the goddamn car." Sidero shrugged, smiling as he passed Isaiah without a word. Dwight had a toothpick in his mouth, swiveling it around and smirking, one foot tapping on the floor. He gave Isaiah a look. *You'll get yours, asshole.* Isaiah had the feeling Dwight was capable of anything. Hugo was at a table near the front. Plates were scattered around him, littered with bones, bread crusts, empty bowls, congealed gravy and miscellaneous scraps. It looked like the other cavemen had just left.

"You want something?" Angus said as Isaiah sat down. "Food's good here. I come here two, three times a week. No place like it in my fruity neighborhood. Try the Reuben. It'll give you a coronary but it's worth it."

"Why didn't you tell me about Christiana?" Isaiah said.

"I thought you should find out for yourself," Angus said. "What did you think?"

"What do I *think?*" Isaiah said, "I think it's impossible! Five alters? *Five?* I'll have to interview all of them and *if* they show up and *if* they saw something and *if* they tell the truth, it may or may not add up to something. Did you know there's nothing on the video except Christiana and Tyler?"

"Yeah, it's a problem." Angus took a bite so big, he looked like a boa constrictor swallowing a pig. "I'm still surprised the killer got him. Tyler knew his shit."

"There were two hitters," Isaiah said. "They worked as a team. Have you ever heard of something like that?" Angus stopped chewing and thought a moment.

"No. Never."

"They were professionals," Isaiah said, "and that lets off Lok. He would have sent his own people and they'd have shot Tyler in a drive-by or a walk-up."

"Yeah, I suppose you're right." Angus was focused on the sandwich again, chewing and chomping and grinding and gulping. It looked like a lot of work. Sauerkraut and cheese oozed from between his yellow teeth. "But that's not my problem."

"It *is* your problem," Isaiah retorted. "How am I supposed to find two professional killers who aren't on video, left no evidence and may or may not have been seen by five different personalities? It's not possible, Angus, and you know it."

"Did you tell him about the deadline?" Dwight said.

"I'm getting to it," Angus snapped. "If you'd shut up and let me."

"What deadline?" Isaiah said.

Angus found another napkin and wiped the grease off his mustache. He said, "If the police arrest Christiana, it means they've made the case. She'll be in the system, locked up. She won't last a week, and for murder she may not get bail. You have until then."

"Until—but they could arrest her tomorrow," Isaiah said. "They could arrest her *now.*"

"That's my point," Angus said. "Get your ass moving, Isaiah. You know I don't bluff." He threw the napkin down on his plate. "Let's go."

They went out the back door, Hugo and Dwight leading the way. Hugo hesitated at the door, looking around for possible attackers. If there were any, Isaiah thought, they wouldn't be where you could see them.

"Even if I find the hitters, what then?" Isaiah said. "I'm supposed to convince the police when there's nothing to convince them with? This is a dead end, Angus. Whatever happens happens."

Angus turned to face him. Tufts of white hair were sticking out of his nose; the mustard and corned-beef smell was sickening. "I'll tell you what's *not* going to happen," Angus said. "My daughter is *not* going to prison." His voice was gravelly, the big startled eyes narrowing into cut marks. You could see the fury rising in him, this stooped old man who could sell death as easily as an ice cream cone. "Do you understand?" he said. *"Do you understand?"* There were flecks of spit at the corners of his mouth, his chest expanding with every breath. *"DO YOU?"*

Isaiah held his gaze and said nothing. Angus whirled around, got in the car and slammed the door. Hugo got in. "Get to it, asshole," Dwight said. He cracked his knuckles. "Or you're fucked." He spat out his toothpick and got in the car.

"Drive, Sidero," Angus snapped. "What are you waiting for? Your nose to heal?"

Isaiah watched the Maybach sail away, a white cruise ship on an ocean of gray asphalt. He wondered if Angus was, on some level, happy with his life. If the intrigue and violence were downsides or perks. What did Angus enjoy? The power, no doubt. But that was transactional. He obviously loved his daughter, but who loved him back? The dog. It was always the dog.

Isaiah was getting in his car when a black Navigator with spinning chrome rims went speeding past. Isaiah recognized the car. Guda was driving and Guda was one of Lok's gang. Isaiah called Angus.

"A black Navigator's coming up behind you, Ponlok's crew," Isaiah said. He heard gunshots and the call went dead. He heard more gunshots. Very close. He got in the Audi and raced out of the lot.

The Maybach had crashed through a chain-link fence. The front two wheels hung over a wide cement culvert. Hugo was shooting from behind the car, Dwight hunched down, a gun on the ground beside him. He was cursing and patting his pockets—out of ammo. Sidero was in the driver's seat, lying sideways, trapped by his seat belt. Bullets were smashing through the windshield, showering him with broken glass. "Help! Help me!" he screamed. "Get me out of here!"

Guda and another guy named Tag were shooting at them from behind a parked truck. They had extra ammo, timing the clip changes so the salvo was nearly continuous. Angus was in the culvert itself. He stumbled toward a big drainpipe and disappeared inside. If Guda and Tag got around Hugo, Angus would be trapped in there.

Isaiah drove past, made a turn and parked in an alley. He went to the trunk and opened a plastic box labeled WEAPONS. He hated firearms but there were times when he needed to defend himself. The pepperball gun was out of ammo but he did have a gun. A potato gun. A pistol, to be exact. He'd made it himself from PVC pipe, some couplers, epoxy, a ball valve and a CO_2 cartridge. It looked like an oversize Luger put together by a drunk plumber. Potatoes rot, so the ammunition was made by putting a dollop of epoxy in the same piping as the barrel and letting it harden. The resulting ammo was like oversize rabbit pellets as big around as a nickel. The gun was surprisingly powerful against soda cans and vegetables. Isaiah had never fired the one-shot contraption at a person.

There was a manhole in the middle of the alley. Isaiah used a crowbar from the trunk and pried it open. Then he climbed down the ladder into the drainpipe, two inches of mossy, smelly water trickling through it. Isaiah could almost stand upright. He had used the manhole as an escape hatch before, but he'd come in through the drainpipe end. He jogged into the dark, keeping his head low. Angus was coming toward him, the sunlight behind him.

"Who's that?" Angus said, terrified.

"Isaiah."

"What? What are you doing here?"

"Saving your shitty life," Isaiah said. He saw Guda's silhouette at the entrance to the drainpipe. "Lie down," Isaiah said.

"Lie down in this muck?" Angus said.

Isaiah couldn't waste time arguing so he judo-tripped Angus into the slimy green water.

"Fuck, it's filthy!" Angus said.

"Get as low as you can," Isaiah said. "Do it if you want to stay alive." Isaiah leaned against the wall and conformed his back to the curve of the pipe.

"What's that you've got?" Angus said.

"A potato gun."

"*Potato* gun?"

"Shut up, will you?"

Isaiah and Angus were just out of the sunlight's reach. Guda would have to be pretty close to see them. His silhouette was getting larger but it was large already. Guda was huge. Six feet, two forty if he was naked and hadn't eaten breakfast. He'd spent years in the yard at Corcoran lifting weights and doing one-handed push-ups with his feet up on a wall. You wondered how he got through a door or put on his pants.

"Angus?" Guda called out. "I'm coming for you, asshole." He was closer still. You could make out the gun in his hand. The maximum range for the potato pistol was about forty feet, but the impact would be greater the closer he was. Isaiah wondered if rabbit pellets made out of epoxy would have any effect on a walking condominium.

Guda saw the shaft of light coming down from the manhole. "Shit," he said, probably thinking Angus had already escaped. Guda jogged forward, water splashing on the sides of the culvert. He was fifty feet away...forty...thirty...twenty...He saw them. He raised his gun and Isaiah shot him in the face.

"Fucker!" Guda shouted. The pellet was far from lethal but it hurt like a son of a bitch. Guda turned away, his gun falling in the water. Isaiah charged. He kicked the big man in the back of the knee and he fell to his knees. He was trying to get up and turn around. Isaiah threw a punch, a glancing blow. Guda caught his wrist, his grip like a car crusher. He whipped Isaiah around in front of him and slung him into the wall.

Guda got up. He was more monstrous in the dark than he was in the daylight. Isaiah went into a defensive crouch, one hand held open at his left cheek, the other in front of his face. Guda came at him, slogging through the water with his hands out in front of him, ready to grab. Isaiah stepped between them and threw a punch but Guda leaned away. Then he hit Isaiah so hard all the air left his lungs in one heaving wheeze. Isaiah fell backward into the water and in an instant Guda was on top of him, his huge hands around Isaiah's neck, shoving his head underwater. He writhed and choked on the filthy water.

Guda's weight was unyielding. He hauled Isaiah up for one sputtering breath and plunged him back under the water. *I'm going to drown. I'm going to die!* Again, Guda hauled him up, screamed something in his face, and then stopped and stared in disbelief.

"Isaiah?" Guda said. "IQ?" Isaiah was too waterlogged to answer. Guda grinned and laughed. "You helped out my sister, Emmy! Remember you kept her outta jail? She was looking at five to ten, she got kids and everything!" He lifted Isaiah out of the water and beamed. "Come on, get up. Shit, Isaiah. You my boy!"

*   *   *

Angus called. The first words out of his mouth were "This doesn't change the deal."

"I didn't think it did," Isaiah said.

"Tell me something," Angus said. "Why did you do it? If I was dead you'd be free and clear."

"You wouldn't get it."

"Yes, I would."

"No, you wouldn't. It would require some understanding of human decency."

"I owe you," Angus said grudgingly. "But it doesn't change the deal."

Hugo had done well, Angus thought. The big oaf had balls and a good thing too. Dwight was a vicious son of a bitch, but stupid as a goldfish. And fucking Sidero. *Help me! Somebody help me!* The pussy. For all his Nazi bullshit he was a goddamn coward. One fat, tough motherfucker like Hugo was worth a hundred cunts like him. Every day Angus thought about kicking Sidero out into the cold, cruel world but he'd made a promise, goddammit. One of the few he'd kept.

The attack had shaken him. That gook bastard Ponlok had nearly gotten him. The Mexican and black gangs were bad enough, but since when did the Asians get into the mix? In Angus's day, Asians were the "good" minority, the kids who sat at the front of the class, raised their hands all the time, dressed like Beaver Cleaver and made robots for the science fair right after cello practice. Except for Jackie Chan and that chick on *Hawaii Five-0,* Asians were boring.

Angus had seen UC Irvine students riding to school on their bicycles. Was there some kind of law that made them wear ugly glasses and a backpack? And those haircuts. There must be a barber somewhere who specialized in the gulag look.

That Isaiah saved Angus's life was confusing. Why would he do something like that? The human decency thing was a bunch of hooey; no one's that goody-goody—well, except for Virginia. If Angus had been in Isaiah's position, he would have driven away, thanking his unbelievably good luck. All the shit Angus had seen in his life, he thought there was nothing left to surprise him. Isaiah did. Was he really going to return the favor? Not unless it cost him nothing. Not unless it played to his advantage.

Isaiah's clothes were drenched with sewer water and he tossed them in the trash. He threw up twice. He took a shower, dressed and put on some music to settle himself down. The case. There wasn't much he hadn't seen before but he'd never heard of a team of hit men. A second person was another variable, somebody else to control and communicate with; somebody else to make a mistake or rat you out. Isaiah wondered if he was interpreting the clues correctly. Was it really a two-man job?

Most of the employment opportunities for contract killers were in the drug world. Take out a rival, a rat, a thief, or someone who cheated you on a deal. There were the gangs, of course, but they used people from their membership lists. The problem: how to identify the killers. If they were professionals, they were also professional at laying low.

Isaiah could find out himself but asking Dodson was quicker. He was a former drug dealer and had better connections. Isaiah was hesitant. Did he really want to hook up with his belligerent semi ex-partner, who always needed affirmation and tried to prove they were equals? It was Isaiah's one conceit: *No one* was better at what he did, even though what he did didn't have a name. PI didn't quite capture it. It was for Stella, so he made the call. "I need your help," he said.

"Say the word," Dodson said. He was a little too eager, not like him at all. Even if he was eager, he'd usually put up some kind of resistance or make it about something else.

"I need to find two hitters," Isaiah said. "They work together. A team." He told Dodson about Angus, Christiana, Sidero and the Starks. He told him about the circumstances of Tyler's murder and his theory about the MO.

"Damn, man," Dodson said, "I never heard of shit like that."

"I need to know who these people are," Isaiah said. "Can you reach out for me?"

"Yeah, I can do that," Dodson said. "But let's say I hook up with somebody that knows 'em. They're not gonna tell me how to find them."

Dodson was right. Isaiah thought a moment. He was never going to locate the hitters himself. Which meant the hitters had to come to him. "Ask your contact to send a message," Isaiah said.

"To the killers?" Dodson said. "What message is that?"

"Tell them IQ is coming for them."

CHAPTER SIX
No Loose Ends

Another fucked-up day on the 710 at rush hour. Sal was late and there was a stain on the new suit. It was a smudge, kind of oily, maybe from that In-N-Out double-meat cheeseburger or maybe the fucked-up car. What difference did it make? Annie would be pissed if the stain was from their new Rolls-Royce. The suit was uncomfortable, the cheap fabric smelled like chemicals, as if their house three blocks from Long Beach Gas and Oil didn't stink already. The suit was for a job interview. Work had petered out and there was nothing left to do but go legit. Of course the fake social security number had gummed up the computer. It was embarrassing, getting out of there before somebody called the authorities.

Sal dreaded going home. As soon as Annie saw the stain, the shit would start. She'd bought the suit so the stain would somehow be an insult, and then she'd pout and sigh, bang pots and pans around, or sit on the sofa with her arms crossed and stare at the TV like her eyeballs were frozen. The passive-aggressive stuff was infuriating. And the *nagging*. It was like living with your mother, mother-in-law and the high school vice principal all at the same time.

The beige stucco house was small, with a chain-link fence and a blotchy lawn. Inside there were flowered drapes, thin beige carpet, and a lot of maple furniture bought at thrift stores. Bric-a-brac with no sentimental value and photos of families that weren't theirs lined the shelves. Annie was in the kitchen, sulking while she stirred creamed corn, which she knew Sal hated.

"Hi," Sal said. She sat down at the breakfast table to hide the stain and took the scrunchie out of her hair. The pencil skirt and the jacket felt like a wet suit. Annie said you had to wear heels with the outfit or it would look weird.

"Why are you so late?" Annie said.

"Because rush hour is rush hour," Sal said. "You've seen it, haven't you?" She took off the fucking heels and rubbed her feet.

"Oh, that's nice," Annie said. "Why don't you shave your armpits while you're at it."

Sal tipped her head back and looked at the ceiling. "Oh my God, will you give it a rest?"

"Dinner will be ready in a minute," Annie said. "Don't you want to wash up?"

Dinner was agonizing, Annie sighing and picking at her food like she was looking for something in particular. Sal pushed the creamed corn to one side and ate little bites of the fucking meat loaf.

"Don't you like it?" Annie said. Meat loaf was one of the three things she knew how to make.

"It's great," Sal said. "It tastes better the fourth time in two weeks."

"Well, don't eat it, then." Annie stood up, snatched Sal's plate away and dumped it in the sink. "I try real hard, you know." Sal didn't apologize and didn't care. Enough of this bullshit; she was done with it.

"You're really a pig, you know that?" Annie said as she banged the dishes around.

"And you're really a bitch," Sal replied. "And could you please take that fucking apron off?"

"No, I won't. You're not the one who does the laundry."

Sal pushed away from the table and stood. "Okay, I've fucking had it. You've got to stop bullshitting yourself, Annie. We are not going to have kids and you'll never be a mom. You're a goddamn killer, just like me. Snap out of it, will you? You're being ridiculous."

Annie wasn't indignant anymore. She was angry in the way only Annie could be, her voice like an axe hitting an anvil, eyes fierce and blazing, balled-up fists, her steely arms tight as piano wire. She took a step back and rested her hand on the countertop. There was a gun in the drawer beneath it. Sal pretended not to notice.

"Take it back," Annie said.

"Take it back?" Sal huffed.

"What are we, eleven years old?"

"I'm warning you, Sal," Annie said. "Take it back."

"Or what?"

They locked eyes a moment.

"Or we're through," Annie said.

Neither of them cried. Sal didn't want to stay in the house. She was in the bedroom, packing and wondering where she'd go, when she heard Annie's phone ring. Moments later, she came in.

"That was Terry C, the guy in Dallas?" Annie said.

"Yeah, what about him?" Sal said.

"He said Angus hired an investigator to find us. His name is Isaiah something. They call him IQ. He's after us."

"Where is he?"

"Here. In Long Beach."

They looked at each other. They had a rule. Always work out of state. They had another rule too.

"No loose ends," Annie said.

"I'll pack the gear. Leave in half an hour?"

Isaiah was at the condo again. He'd made an appointment with Marlene and she was already an hour late. He was restless and anxious and worried about Stella. Christiana could be arrested at any time. The mess in the living room was depressing. It was too much of a mess, an excessive mess, like the alters were purposely trying to fuck up the place. Gia was haggard, scurrying around, putting trash in a garbage bag. She stopped and wiped her brow. "Would you like some coffee?" she asked.

They sat at the breakfast table amid the stacks of crusty dishes, spilled cereal, greasy pans piled on the stove, the room smelling of burnt toast and coffee.

"I try," Gia said, "but I can't keep up. Christiana refuses to get a housekeeper." Isaiah sipped his coffee and set his mug down between splotches of dried egg yolk.

"What do you do at the shop?" he asked.

"Christiana selects materials and does most of the sewing," Gia said. "The rest is up to me. I create the pattern, order the fabrics, keep the books. Pearl does all the little things."

"I wondered about that," Isaiah said. "Why does Pearl take the measurements? Isn't that important?"

"Yes, but Christiana doesn't like to be touched," Gia said. She sipped the coffee, her eyes studiously avoiding him. She was tense, he thought. She wants to say something but doesn't have a way to get into it. What would she want to talk about? Probably Angus, he decided. She'd been quick to say they'd been divorced for a long time. Maybe she wanted to explain.

Isaiah said, "Tell me about you and Angus." Gia instantly brightened. "I was young, stupid and a stripper," she said with a small laugh. She seemed relieved to have said it. "How's that for a combination? Angus was a regular at the club. He wasn't what you'd call attractive but he threw money around like it was nothing. Very appealing to a hardscrabble kid from East Side Chicago. Disappointed?"

"No. We all have a past," Isaiah said.

"We were quite a pair, I can tell you," Gia said, shaking her head. "We did crazy things. Parties, drugs, all that nonsense. I was a real rock-and-roller. I loved to dance." She made another small laugh. "It's amazing, isn't it? How you can be so different from your past? For a while, I worked with Angus. Criminals love hot chicks. They liked dealing with me. Angus was so belligerent and hateful—and jealous. My God. If anyone looked at me the wrong way, he'd have his goons beat the guy to a pulp."

"Do you still see each other?" Isaiah said.

"Yes, fairly frequently, actually," she said. "Angus fires his bookkeepers when he thinks they're too nosy. I don't ask questions and I know all his secret codes."

"What happened when Christiana was born?" he asked.

"Angus was worse. She was a usurper, competition for my attention. He hated her. He...did things to her."

"Did you know about it?" Isaiah asked.

Gia's whole body sagged, inhabited by a pain so awful she'd become a slave to the alters, forever paying down a debt she could never pay off.

"I didn't want to know," she said, "and I was in a drug haze most of the time. Or I was out partying. Or asleep. Or screwing some stranger."

"What did it?" Isaiah said. "Why did you leave?"

"It was Christmas, of all things." Gia tore a paper towel off the roll and dabbed sweat off her face. "Christiana didn't get the present she wanted and was whining about it. Angus got upset but it was way over the top. He started yelling at her, calling her an ingrate and a bitch and...other things. He threw a marble ashtray at her. I got in the way and it hit me right here." She put her finger above her right eye. "I had to get stitches. And it didn't end there. Angus knocked a couple of my teeth out, broke a rib, and that was it. I took Christiana and left." She breathed a deep sigh. "I should have done it before. Long before."

Isaiah agreed but didn't say it. "And then what?"

"It was hard. By that time, the alters were in charge." Gia shrugged and sighed. "Angus got married again," she said. "A Filipino woman named Virginia. I heard they were in love and Angus was very happy. They had a baby but Virginia died in childbirth. The grandmother took the poor thing. For a long time, Angus didn't give it a name." Isaiah glanced at his watch.

"Why are the alters so unresponsive?" he asked. "Don't they realize they're in serious jeopardy?"

"They might only be vaguely aware of what happened," Gia replied, "if they're aware at all. Or they might think it hasn't anything to do with them. It's somebody else's mess."

Isaiah hated downtime. "I want to look around," he said.

"Sure."

Gia led him through the hall toward the bedrooms. It was a huge place.

"In general," Isaiah said, "do the alters get along?"

"Some do, some don't. Christiana tells me they argue about everything. What to wear, what to eat, where to go. Everything."

"With all that going on in her head, how does she function?"

"The others are like background music or people talking in a bar," Gia said. "She can ignore them if she wants."

"Does one alter know what the others are doing?" Isaiah said.

"Sometimes, but I honestly couldn't tell you who sees what. Maybe one alter can see everything. I've heard of that happening."

Isaiah didn't know why he wanted to see the alters' rooms, but at this point in his career he didn't need a why. He had been in his acupuncturist's office, waiting for his appointment, and saw a pointillist painting on the cover of a magazine. People in a park in old-fashioned clothes, sitting, walking, lounging on the grass; men in top hats, women carrying parasols. When you looked closely, you could see the whole canvas was comprised of tiny dots. Isaiah's work was something like that. Putting dots on a blank canvas, seemingly unrelated, some in bunches, some disconnected, shapeless spaces in between. Keep adding dots, no matter where they landed, and eventually something took shape. Looking in the bedrooms was like adding dots.

"Christiana and Pearl's room is to the right," Gia said.

"They share a room?" He had to remind himself they were one person.

"The others have their own rooms. It's not necessary. It's silly, really. I've never heard of anyone doing this but Angus is indulgent. He wants Christiana to have everything. Even privacy from herself."

Pearl and Christiana's room was pretty and happy. "Fortunately they have the same tastes," Gia said. "If they didn't, the room would look like the living room." There were soft colors, prints of Monet's water lilies and Renoir's *Two Sisters,* diaphanous curtains like at Christiana's shop.

Two beds neatly made. A designer suitcase and a carry-on jammed tightly underneath the bed. Odd, Isaiah thought. Buildings like this had private storage. There was a closet with two sets of clothes and two different styles. Chic and shy. On Christiana's side, there were a couple of new sundresses with the tags still on them.

A pair of beautiful jade earrings were on the dresser. Isaiah wondered if they were real. He tossed one of them up in the air and caught it. Noticeably heavier than a pebble the same size. It felt cool, smooth and soap-like. Real jade. Real expensive. There were travel brochures on a small desk. Fiji. Christiana and Pearl had dreams of going away.

There were photographs on a side table. "Christiana insists on having them," Gina said. "They weren't exactly happy times." In one photo, Christiana was seven or so; Angus, beatific, cradling her. She was asleep or pretending to be. Her mouth was open a bit and most kids her age slept with their mouths closed. Her body wasn't slack enough for sleep. Why be awake in the arms of your victimizer?

Another of mother and daughter sitting at a vanity, their backs to the mirror. They were both wearing lavender dresses and forced smiles; Angus was probably the photographer. In the mirror, Isaiah could see a large framed photo of Chuck Berry in that famous pose—hunched down and aiming his guitar like a gun. Gia said she was a real rock-and-roller. A family photo, Christiana was nine or ten, expressionless, dressed like Shirley Temple in another lavender outfit, apparently Gia's favorite color. Ugliness had not come to Angus later in life. Even back then he was the Mr. Potato Head monster except with more hair. He looked proud, as if saying, *Aren't we one happy family?* Gia was young, hot, dressed expensively, a huge diamond engagement ring that glittered like the sun on a breezy sea. If nothing else, she'd enjoyed Angus's money. The photos were reminders, Isaiah thought, to Gia and Angus and what they'd done under the guise of doting parents.

There was a single photo on the nightstand. It was of a house, more like a cottage, with a porch and a brick chimney. It was rustic and charming and at the edge of the sea. A dark forest behind it. Isaiah thought it was strange, a photo singled out like that.

"Whose house?" Isaiah asked.

Gia shook her head. "Christiana never said."

Jasper's room. About what you'd expect from a dumb, unsupervised, eighteen-year-old asshole. Isaiah stopped and stared, Gia looking over his shoulder.

"Did I mention Angus was indulgent?" Gia said. "He even gave Jasper a job for a while, until Jasper kicked his dog. The ultimate sin. I'm going to go. Look around wherever you want."

The dense smell of things unwashed, unsanitary and unappetizing wafted into Isaiah's face. It was the smell of neglect, of not caring, of contempt for order. Piles of dirty laundry, stuff spilling out of drawers, food splatter on the walls, the floor strewn with trash, beer cans, empty bottles of Everclear, a pair of heavy black boots with zippers on the side and a studded monk strap. The left sole was nearly worn through. Posters were thumbtacked crookedly on the wall. The Ramones. Kiss. Dead Kennedys. The New York Dolls. Twisted Sister. The sheets on the bed were knotted with stains Isaiah didn't want to look at. A battered toolbox underneath it. A cheap scimitar, a crowbar and a Fender Stratocaster leaning against the dresser.

Bertrand's room was orderly and spartan. Dockers, polo shirts, and sturdy shoes precisely arranged in the closet. A poster of the Dallas Cowboys Cheerleaders. Books on self-defense. A small collection of baseball hats. A framed, stock photo of a man, woman and a boy, the kind that comes with a picture frame or a wallet. Made bed with military corners. No dust bunnies under the furniture. There was a cluster of dents in the drywall, broken through in a couple of places. Isaiah looked at them closely. Fist marks. He wondered if all the alters were like this. Off kilter. Odd. Familiar yet not quite credible.

Marlene's room was like a whorehouse after the DEA had come and gone. There were a variety of thongs, nighties, nipple-less bras, crotchless panties, and a dildo the size of a bluefin tuna. There were condom boxes torn open and a plastic bottle of lube called Unicorn Spit, donut flavored. The only neat thing in the room was a folded sheaf of freshly laundered T-shirts. The one on top showed part of the logo: UST. "Lust," Isaiah said aloud. Meeting Marlene should be an event.

Marlene's liaisons had left behind some items. A BMW key ring, a leather bra that was too big for Marlene, a charcoal-gray vest, expensive material, and a pair of Converse All-Stars, men's size ten and a half. That must have been funny, Isaiah thought, the guy humping away when Marlene turned into Pearl, who screamed, who turned into Jasper, who shouted, *What the fuck?* Isaiah would have left his shoes behind too.

The rooms felt staged. As if a director had told the prop master, *I want to see a party girl's room. Really wild, like a slut, you know? Okay, this guy's a real tight-ass. An accountant, maybe. Like completely boring.* Copied lives. Torn from magazines, seen on TV, read about in the tabloids.

Isaiah had read that each alter plays a role and that these roles helped the victim cope. Christiana's was to be pragmatic and rational. Pearl was submissive, a useful quality when dealing with an abuser. Alters didn't like intrusiveness and Jasper's role was probably to keep people away. Evidently, Marlene was overtly sexual, also useful given the situation. Bertrand's role remained to be seen.

A deep sadness descended on Isaiah. He wondered what form of wrath Angus had wreaked on his own daughter to create a human being this fucked up. What would be horrific enough to shatter a child's selfhood into so many jagged pieces? Cruelty to kids infuriated Isaiah. Working for a perpetrator was sickening. He felt sorry for Gia. All these years living with a real-life Hydra, never knowing whose face would appear, five personalities making demands that would never end. He admired her doleful acceptance. Her brave perseverance.

Later in the day, Dodson showed up at Isaiah's house unannounced.

"I put the word out about them two killers," he said. "Heard anything?"

"Not yet," Isaiah said.

"You don't look so good. The case got you down?"

"Some, yeah."

Weird, Isaiah thought. Not enough time had gone by for him to have heard anything and Dodson could have called. He couldn't worry about that now. He had to find Marlene—or Bertrand or Jasper. Any one of them would do.

Gia called. In a small, embarrassed voice, she said, "Marlene was here and then she left."

"Did she say where?" Isaiah said.

"No, and when I asked her she said, 'I'm going to have fun.'"

He thought a moment. "How did she say it?"

"How?" Gia said.

"Was she happy, like *Yay, I'm going to have fun?*"

"No," Gia said thoughtfully. "She was more...determined, like she was going to have fun, hell or high water."

"When she left there, what was she wearing?" he asked.

"Tight skirt, low-cut blouse, heels."

"Perfume?"

"Yes. Something horrible."

"Did someone pick her up?"

"I think so, yes," Gia said. "I heard a horn honk and then she ran out."

Isaiah was aware that Dodson was listening intently. He ended the call and turned away to concentrate. Okay, he thought. Tight skirt, heels, perfume, honking horn. She went on a date and was going to have fun, but not like *Oh, boy, I'm going to Disneyland!* fun. More like she was going someplace reliable, where she'd had fun before. Good thinking, Isaiah, that narrows it down to ten million places.

All right, back up. Start where you always do. What do you know about her? The first time he'd heard Marlene's name was when he met Christiana. She was embarrassed because she smelled of booze and was wearing Marlene's clothes, salacious like the ones Marlene was wearing tonight. Wherever Christiana had been, it had been Marlene's choice, not hers. He remembered Christiana talking, soft voice, graceful, hands fluid as she gestured. *Her hands.* There was something about her hands. What was it? Something didn't fit. Isaiah nodded to himself. There was blue paint between her forefinger and middle finger. Wait, *was* it paint?

No. It was on her left hand. The alters were right-handed. She also didn't smell of paint and who wore clothes like that to touch up the bathroom? Okay, so how else would you get blue coloring between your forefinger and middle finger? *What, Isaiah, you know this. What is it?* Shooting pool. You chalked the tip of the cue stick with blue chalk to give it a little more stick. When you stroked the cue, that's exactly the spot where the chalk would leave residue.

Hypothesis: Marlene had been shooting pool before she switched out with Christiana. It was likely a one-off. Being good at pool required discipline and patience, and judging from Marlene's room, those were not qualities she admired. There were no pool halls in Long Beach itself but quite a few in the surrounding area. Christiana smelled of booze though. That meant Marlene had been drinking, and no pool hall Isaiah knew of served hard liquor. Okay, so maybe she was shooting pool but not in a pool hall. There were bars that had pool tables but a place to have reliable fun? That seemed unlikely, and why would Marlene dress like that to shoot pool in a bar? It didn't fit—Marlene bent over a table in a tight skirt and heels drinking Grey Goose on the rocks while she lined up a shot on the nine ball? No, back up again. Let's suppose she was someplace where playing pool and drinking were secondary activities. Something you did while you were waiting to do what you came for.

Isaiah's avatar stood in the doorway of Marlene's room. There were loose poker chips on the floor, the heavy embossed kind used at casinos. When Christiana came in wearing Marlene's clothes, she'd said to Gia, "I think Marlene lost again." Had she lost money betting? Okay, maybe she went to a casino. Which one? Bicycle Shop, Hollywood Park, Pechanga, San Manuel, Morongo? There was a stack of clean T-shirts on the bed, the one on top said UST. This was like *Jeopardy!*, which Isaiah never watched because it was too easy. The T-shirt didn't say LUST. It said HUSTLER. There was a Hustler Casino on Redondo Beach Boulevard, where you could drink, shoot pool and gamble the night away.

"Gotta go," Isaiah said.

"You got something?" Dodson said.

"Maybe."

"Can I come with you?" Dodson said. There was an awkward moment. Dodson had revealed himself. He wanted to be included. Isaiah considered it but he had to get on with this.

"Not this time," he said.

* * *

Isaiah drove away from the house, wondering about Dodson. Why did he want to tag along? They'd dissolved their partnership by mutual consent. Had he changed his mind? Deal with this later, he thought. Then he downshifted, punched the accelerator and felt his head sink deeper into the headrest.

Dodson was embarrassed. He shouldn't have reached out to Isaiah so soon. He'd been too needy. Patience, he told himself, but he had none. He had to get going. He had to get off his ass. Desperation hung you out there, exposed and vulnerable. Shit, he hated that. And he'd been troubled by something else too. He wanted to go back to the hospital. He didn't know why. Beaumont wouldn't know he was there and he owed Merrill nothing. Or maybe he did. Like what? He wondered. He hadn't seen Merrill since they were kids. This kind of bullshit was agonizing. You didn't have answers so you couldn't make yourself feel better, especially when you didn't know what the questions were in the first fucking place. This wasn't like him, all this confusion, inner turmoil. "Get on with your gettin' on," he said aloud. "What the fuck is wrong with you?"

CHAPTER SEVEN
Deep-Fried Baseball Mitt

The Hustler Casino was just another casino. Bordello colors, brass railings and sparkly chandeliers, dozens of tables and hundreds of gamblers playing Hold 'Em, Omaha Hi/Lo, Pai Gow, No Bust Blackjack and three-card poker. It seemed like people should be smoking. Off in an alcove were pool tables. No one was playing. You came here to gamble, baby. If Marlene was here, she was playing cards.

Isaiah's clients had told him numerous times that his ability to pick a face out of a crowd bordered on supernatural. Instead, it was a product of rigorous training and retraining himself to observe and remember. At a glance, he took in your facial features, profile, eye and hair color, body type, posture, tattoos, shoes, clothing, hand gestures and how you walked. It took him nine seconds to locate Marlene.

Marlene was playing Hold 'Em at a no-limit table, no chips in front of her. She was fuming and had evidently lost everything. She got up to talk to the supervisor. Mischievous, overtly sexual, her hand on his chest, she asked him something. He shook his head. In the next instant, she was a snarling bobcat, cursing at him. She shoved past him and went to the bar.

A man was waiting for her. Big, brush cut, a no-neck behemoth wearing a red muscle shirt and gold chain. How's that for originality? Isaiah thought. Marlene complained to the guy, who nodded sympathetically while he stared at her tits. They ordered drinks, Marlene bitching, unceasingly. She went on so long the guy got tired of nodding and looked past her at the big-screen TV. When Marlene seemed to be winding down, Isaiah left. The couple would have to wait for the valet to bring their car around.

Twenty minutes later, they came out of the casino and Marlene was *still* bitching.

"Okay, okay, I get it," the guy groaned.

"No, I don't think you do," she said. "And by the way, I saw you with that girl, the one with her skirt slit up to her navel?"

"What about you and that dude in the suit?" he retorted. "Why didn't you just take your tits out and motorboat him?"

"He was nice and polite, okay?" she said. "Something you should learn about. Where's the fucking car?"

As good a time as any, Isaiah thought. He walked toward them. "Marlene? Hi. I'm Isaiah."

"Oh, Christ, not now, okay?" she groaned.

"It's important and you know why," Isaiah said.

She glared. "I said *not now*."

The guy stepped between them. He actually said, "You heard the lady. Now start walking, pal."

Isaiah avoided confrontation but this was urgent. "How about I buy you both a drink?"

"How about you go fuck yourself?" the guy replied.

Marlene put her hand on his bulging arm. "Yeah, tell him, Tony." His name was *Tony*? Of course it was.

"Look, it's really important," Isaiah said. "It'll only take a few minutes."

"Didn't I tell you to fuck off?" Tony said. He came toward him with his palms out, ready to give him the Big Shove, the bully's first move. Most people backed up, which put them at the point of greatest impact. Isaiah swung his left forearm around and knocked Tony's right arm inward, then stepped left out of the big man's grasp. Tony's momentum carried him forward. Isaiah stuck his foot out. Tony tripped, staggered forward, and sprawled on the pavement. He stayed there groaning a couple of moments and got up slowly, bleeding from his nose and mouth.

"Great. Nice going, Tony," Marlene said. "A guy half your size is kicking your ass." She wasn't going to cooperate now, Isaiah thought.

He went back to the Audi to wait it out. He'd tail them to wherever and try to get Marlene alone. The couple was heading toward Tony's car. She was yelling at him, telling him he was a pussy and why didn't he do something. Isaiah sighed and closed his eyes, put his head back. *God help me.* He heard Tony's car door open and close. They were leaving. Isaiah sat up, started the engine, used the paddle shifter, and put the car in drive. Sometimes he didn't have the energy to shift manually. He was about to engage the seat belt when Tony yanked the passenger door open. He was bleeding and raging, and frightening. He lunged over the console, grabbed Isaiah with one hand and hit him with the other. Isaiah put his arms up to protect himself. He wished he'd taken up Dodson's offer.

Marlene was pounding on the window, egging Tony on—and then *she shut Tony's door.* The two men were trapped in the front seats, a space no bigger than a bathtub. Isaiah was six foot, one sixty-five. Tony was taller, wider and sixty pounds heavier. The only way to maneuver was by squirming, and neither of them could get his legs out of the footwells, their knees stuck under the dashboard. Isaiah tried to get out of the car but Tony yanked him back.

"Get him, Tony! Get him!" Marlene shouted gleefully.

Tony pulled Isaiah's upper body across the console. Isaiah couldn't get loose and there was no room to throw a punch. They thrashed like two bears fighting in a closet, growling and grunting, greased in their own sweat, breathing in gulps, their body heat trapped inside, the windows dripping. Tony's blood was splattering on the seats, the dashboard, Isaiah.

Tony got his massive arm around Isaiah's neck and squeezed. Isaiah felt his head swell and his lungs clamp shut. He tried to pull the arm away but it wouldn't budge. He kicked and wriggled but it was no use. He'd pass out soon or suffocate and die. *Think, Isaiah, think.* The car was in drive and starting to roll. His foot couldn't reach the brake pedal. He had a flash memory of fighting Gahigi at Seb's house. He bit down on Tony's arm. Tony screamed but didn't let go, squeezing even tighter. *Think, Isaiah, think.* The car was picking up speed. Marlene was running alongside, shouting, "Stop the fucking car! You're gonna crash, you idiots!"

Isaiah let one hand go and the pressure around his neck doubled. He was breathing through a throat the size of a dime, his face expanding, his eyes about to spurt out of his head. He squiggled a hand underneath him and depressed the cigarette lighter. Endless moments passed while it heated up, the black tide of unconsciousness lapping at his brain.

At last, the lighter popped up. He plunged the glowing hot coil into Tony's arm. The big man screamed and let go. Gasping, Isaiah struggled to sit up but Tony didn't quit, his rage morphing into lunacy, his features masked with blood, a tooth missing from his raving, open maw and Isaiah realized, *Tony's on steroids!*

Tony grabbed him and tried to pull him over to the console again, screaming with uncontrollable rage. Isaiah held on to the steering wheel but Tony kept yanking like a pit bull clamped onto the seat of your pants. There's a four- to five-percent grade on parking lots so that rain doesn't pool and the car was in drive. It moved faster. And faster.

Tony finally looked around. "Hey," he said stupidly.

"Let...me...go!" Isaiah croaked.

Tony released Isaiah and tried to get out of the car, but the door locks had locked automatically. He pushed the wrong button and the window buzzed down. "How do you open this fucking thing?" he yelled. He rammed his shoulder against the door and when that didn't work he tried to climb out of the window. His bulk got stuck there. He panicked and started screaming, "Get me out of here! *Get me out!*"

Woozy from the lack of oxygen, Isaiah struggled back into the driver's seat a moment too late.

"Oh, shit!"

The Audi bumped over a parking block, the jolt nearly bucking Isaiah out of his seat, the car smashing through a thick hedge, branches scraping and snapping, Tony's upper half taking a beating while he screamed like a toddler. The car slowed as it came out of the hedge and then plunged down a steep dirt incline, bulldozing through ivy and azalea bushes, a chain-link fence coming next. It was no match for thirty-five hundred pounds of steel and aluminum. The car mowed down the fence and hit an even steeper concrete incline, the front end of the car crashing into a culvert, the shocks bottoming out, the momentum carrying it forward, nose down, sparks flying as the bumper scraped against ground, coming to a stop in a trickle of mossy water.

Quiet. Metal creaking, something hissing, the smell of gasoline. Isaiah groaned and moved a little to check for broken bones. He had to shoulder the door to get out.

Tony was still stuck in the window, cuts all over him, his muscle shirt torn, his gold chain ripped off, blood oozing from his nose. "Could you give me a hand?" he said.

"Fuck you," Isaiah said. He blinked twice and his stomach lurched. "My car." The bumper was on the ground, the grill smashed, the front tires were blown out, the headlights and windshield broken, mirrors dangling. Green antifreeze was leaking, oil dripping. Isaiah couldn't speak. Dazed and disbelieving, he walked around the car. "Could you *please* help me?" Tony said.

Isaiah put his head in his hands.

He found the '09 Audi S4 when he was a teenager, working at TK's wrecking yard. It had been totaled in an accident and he'd lovingly restored it. It took him years. It cost him money he couldn't afford. It was the only car he'd ever wanted. He couldn't look at it anymore and turned away. Marlene and a security guard were standing at the top of the dirt incline.

"You guys okay?" she said.

"You stupid bitch," Isaiah said.

"You guys stay put," the security guard called down. "An ambulance is coming."

The paramedics pried Tony from the window, checking him and Isaiah for injuries. Neither wanted to go to the hospital and had to sign release forms. The cops took statements.

"You know what's wrong with this world?" the cop said, looking at Tony. "Too many assholes."

The police left. Tony took off before Isaiah could kill him. A tow truck came and yanked the Audi out of the culvert. When Isaiah got back to the parking lot, Marlene was waiting for him. Oddly, she was calm and seemingly puzzled, like she couldn't imagine how something like this could have happened.

"Well, that was a disaster, wasn't it?" she said. "You never know what life is going to throw at you." Isaiah was too pissed off to speak. "I never liked Tony," Marlene went on. "He was such a show-off. And what a temper! He flies off the handle, just like that."

Wait a second, Isaiah thought. *You never know what life is going to throw at you? He flies off the handle, just like that?* Was this the same woman who cussed out the casino supervisor, trapped Isaiah and Tony in the car and urged Tony to bust Isaiah up?

"You're not Marlene, are you?" Isaiah said.

"Me? Oh, heavens no. Not for all the tea in China."

"Who are you?"

"Bertrand, of course," he said with a bright smile. "I'm hungry. How about we get something to eat?"

They took an Uber to Denny's. "I like Denny's," Bertrand said. "I come here all the time. Try the country-fried steak. It's really good."

It had taken Isaiah a few minutes to recalibrate. Marlene was Bertrand now. The raving bitch was suddenly cheery and mannerly and, well, nice. A grown-up Opie in a woman's slutty clothes.

Bertrand drank a glass of water in a long series of gulps. "Ahh! That really hits the spot. Sorry about the runaround. What a night, huh?" He shook his head with weary affection. "Marlene, Marlene, Marlene. That girl is—how should I say it? Loose. *Very* loose, if you catch my drift. She's constantly getting herself into scrapes. Tonight wasn't unusual. Not in the least. She is definitely cuckoo." Bertrand crossed his eyes and made circles with his forefinger. "And if you can believe it, she gets jealous! Some nerve, huh? I mean, *really* jealous. *Women.* You can't live with them and you can't live without them."

The waitress was standing there, looking at him. Her nametag said JANET. Bertrand held up his glass. "Hi, Janet. Could I get a refill, please? It's excellent water." She looked at him a moment and moved off. "I've heard a lot about you, Isaiah," Bertrand said.

"From who?" Isaiah said.

"Oh, I hear things in passing," Bertrand said. "Nobody really talks to me. Not very polite, given what I do for them."

"What do you do for them?"

"I am—what should I call myself?" Bertrand said. "It's hard to talk about these things without tooting my own horn." He looked off as if the right word were over there by the kitchen pass-through. "I am...the guardian, so to speak," he went on. "When one of them is in trouble, that's when I step in. Day or night, rain or shine." Isaiah wanted to laugh but didn't. Some guardian. He didn't show up until everything was over and it was time for a snack. The Cowardly Lion came to mind.

Janet brought another glass of water. "Thank you," Bertrand said heartily. "Much appreciated."

"What can I get you?" Janet said.

"Country-fried steak, of course. It's your best dish."

"Oh, yeah? I'll make a note of that."

"You wouldn't happen to have root beer, would you?"

"No, we don't," Janet said.

"Darn," Bertrand said. He was really disappointed. "I wish they'd put it on the menu."

"Yeah, me too," Janet said. She looked at Isaiah.

"Bacon, eggs and coffee, please," he said. She nodded and moved off. Isaiah said, "What can you tell me about that night?"

Bertrand sipped his water and smiled at the glass admiringly. "Really refreshing. Best water I've ever had."

"Bertrand?" Isaiah said.

"Yes?"

"What do you know about Tyler?"

Bertrand frowned. "Didn't like him, didn't like him at all. He was a meddler and a troublemaker."

"How so?"

"I'd rather not talk about it," Bertrand replied. Isaiah was about to push back but didn't.

"Did you see anything that night?"

Bertrand nodded emphatically. "I sure did."

Janet returned. "I forgot to ask you—how do you want your eggs?"

"Scrambled," Isaiah said. She left. "Go on, Bertrand. You were saying?"

Bertrand leaned forward. Isaiah did too. "You would not have believed it," Bertrand said, confidentially. "Never saw anything like it, and I've seen a thing or two, believe me." Suddenly his expression changed, his placid face contorting to disgust. "Oh, crap!"

"What's the matter?" Isaiah said.

"The music," he groaned. "Why do they have to play that junk?" The fifties classic "Maybellene" was playing. Bertrand waved at Janet. "Excuse me. Could you turn off the music?" She rolled her eyes and turned away. Bertrand huffed. "See if she gets a tip." He sat there fuming and muttering until the song ended. "Well," he breathed. "I'm glad that's over."

Isaiah wondered what that was all about but pressed on. "You were telling me what happened that night," he said.

Bertrand was about to speak when Janet brought their goddamn fucking food. He was delighted. He stuck his face over the plate and breathed deeply. "Ahh, nothing like it." He took a bite of what looked like deep-fried baseball mitt, a splotch of white gravy on it. "Oh, darn. It's cold." He waved his hand. "Oh, Janet—"

"Bertrand," Isaiah said. "No more Janet, no more water, no more eating. *Tell me what you saw that night."*

"All right already," Bertrand said, a little miffed. "It wasn't very pleasant, I can tell you. I was near the curtain, on the showroom side. I was flat on my back. Don't ask me why, and Tyler was lying in front of me and he was, well, dead. Completely dead! I had blood all over me, it was *really* unpleasant. I heard someone in the workroom. I couldn't see because of the curtain so I said, 'Hey, what's going on over there!' Like that, you know? Really forceful."

"And then?"

"And then I looked through the curtain and I saw someone running toward the back entrance."

"What did he look like?" Isaiah said, getting excited.

"It was a she," Bertrand said.

"A woman? Are you sure?"

"Of *course* I'm sure." Bertrand slipped in a quick bite of baseball mitt. "I'm not a stupid person, you know. I didn't see her very well. She was facing the other way. She was really small, almost like a kid, and she was wearing black, head to toe, like one of those—what do you call them? Ninnies?"

"You mean ninjas?"

"I suppose. I don't speak Chinese."

"And then what did you do?"

"I got up and went after her," Bertrand said. "And this is the crazy part. I come out of the rear door, I look up and the ninny woman was climbing up a rope! As you can imagine, I was very perturbed. Obviously, she had something to do with Tyler. I said, 'What do you think you're doing? Come down here right now!' She ignored me."

"Keep going," Isaiah said.

"Well, now it gets confusing. You see, when there's too much stress, the alters, including myself, get a little, what's the word? Jumbled. We get together—in Christiana's head, of course, and everybody starts talking and switching out really fast. Anyway, this was happening when I went back inside and I switched out. I don't know what happened after that."

"Anything else?" Isaiah asked hopefully.

"I'm afraid not," Bertrand said. "I'm going to finish my supper now. Jeez, I'm still thirsty." He raised his water glass. "Janet? Over here?" Isaiah closed his eyes and sucked in a deep breath. Here he was, beat to shit and his car was totaled and what had he learned? That the killer was a woman. Interesting but it made no material difference. Bertrand was still waving at Janet.

"Janet? Could I get some more water?" She gave him the finger. He reared his head back. *"Well!"*

Christiana switched out with Bertrand and caught a taxi home from Denny's. She went into her room, ripped off Marlene's clothes, and threw them in the hallway. "FUCK!" she screamed. She'd only heard parts of what that dolt had said. Maybe it helped, maybe it hurt, maybe it did both. Everything was out of control.

She retreated into the house, the one inside her head. It was a nice house. Very modern, everything clean and neat and bright. No loud colors, no clash of styles, nothing like the condo. She had no idea how it had come together. There was so much she didn't know the how and why of. Her life was part-time. In the office at nine, clock out at nine thirty. In the office at eleven fifteen, clock out at a quarter after one. What happened the rest of the time was either hearsay, piecemeal or a total mystery. If it wasn't for Gia she couldn't function at all. It was unbearable. Dependent on someone you wanted to hurt in the worst way possible. Another thing she couldn't deal with, another thing shunted off to the others.

She could hear them calling out and arguing and crying. They were no help. They only made things more confusing; a blaring cacophony while you were balanced with one foot on a pinhead. She was alone in spite of them. She was isolated in spite of them. She had no love because of them. She hated them as much as she hated herself. The situation was impossible, the definition of futility, a lingering death without actually dying.

She couldn't help Isaiah, she only knew what she'd told him. Did he suspect what she suspected? That one of the others had plotted to kill Tyler? They had a reason and a good one too. Marlene? Possible. Jasper? Possible. Pearl? No—well, maybe. The crime was so egregious she might have been forced over the edge. Bertrand? Another maybe, but not by himself. He took his protecting duties seriously and he might have seen this in the same light. Could they have hired the killers? At one time or another, they'd all had access to Angus's contacts. Some of them they'd met. Some of them were contract killers or knew them personally. It wouldn't have been hard to convince them that they were acting on Angus's behalf.

She was afraid when Isaiah talked to the others. What if one of them said something that exposed their guilt? Her only hope was that the case would lead Isaiah somewhere else. Another migraine was coming on, she could hear it rumbling like a faraway avalanche. It would be here soon, huge and enveloping. She welcomed it. The pain was real, it had substance and constancy; you knew what it was and what it was doing. It wasn't some unpredictable, shape-shifting, parceled-out headfuck that came at you in flashes so horrifying you had to flee yourself and black out and let somebody else take the hit. There wasn't room for all her hatred and so much of it was swallowed, choked down and hidden. Stay steady, she reminded herself. She had to think her way through this.

She took a shower and scrubbed off Marlene's perfume. She thought about suicide. She'd tried it before but as soon as the thought entered her head, there was a chorus of complaints, admonitions and pleas. Kill herself and she killed them all. One voice rose above the rest but she couldn't tell whose.

"Get us out of this, asshole. That's your fucking job."

She lay down on the bed as the migraine barged in, the pain punching holes through her skull, her eyeballs swelling, her mouth a rainless desert wash. Memories swirled and shrieked, the kind she couldn't stand. She felt the wire coat hanger cutting into her wrists and smelled her own feces, the drunken laughter like a death knell. She groaned and thrashed and then, gratefully, she blacked out.

CHAPTER EIGHT
Starsky and Hutch

Isaiah was pissed. Marlene and Jasper refused to be tied down. It was ridiculous and frustrating. He thought about Grace. She was here in Long Beach, probably within walking distance and she still hadn't called. He couldn't wait anymore. He had to *do* something. He remembered Grace's friend, Cherokee, the pale girl with collar tats, her hair shaved on one side of her head. An easy person to remember.

TK had sold him a five-year-old Kia on the cheap. He drove over to Ross Dress for Less and bought a hippie-looking handbag. He added to it a wallet, an old ring of keys, a couple of flyers, some makeup and some change. He went to the art store where he had first seen Cherokee talking with Grace. He knew what he was doing was stupid and underhanded, bordering on stalking, and he knew it was Grace's choice whether to see him again. Amazing, he thought, what you could block out of your mind when you really wanted to. He knew love was powerful, but what he hadn't understood was that it strung you out as well.

"How can I help you?" the guy at the counter said.

"I found this bag," Isaiah said. "It belongs to someone named Cherokee."

"Oh, sure, I know her. I can give it to her if you want."

Isaiah ate lunch across the street at Carl's Jr. He ate half the burger and stopped. Fast-food joints cooked the shit out of everything. He was feeling more and more ridiculous. He was about to leave when Cherokee showed up. She went into the store and two minutes later came out again, looking annoyed and talking on her cell. Isaiah followed her to a building on Kenmore, far enough away from his house that Grace wouldn't run into him.

The rush of adrenaline blew his self-discipline and common sense right out of his head. He *had* to know what she was up to. He snuck into the parking garage and found Grace's GTI. He used a slim jim and easily opened the nine-year-old car. The alarm went off but nobody paid attention to them anymore. In the backseat were a box of dog treats, two bottles of water, a roll of paper towels and a man's white shirt, size large. There was paint on it so maybe she wore it when she worked. Or maybe it belonged to her boyfriend, a world-famous artist from Barcelona.

A shopping bag held new tubes of paint, a bundle of brushes, sunscreen, nail files and other miscellanea. The receipt for the art supplies was from a local store. It was dated two weeks ago. He was as hurt as he was mystified. *Two weeks* and she hadn't called him. The glove box next. Her old address on the registration. A hairbrush, a tangle of USB cords and a broken pair of sunglasses, the same ones he'd seen her wearing. They were too big for her. Did she borrow them from Señor Barcelona?

Isaiah drove home, debating whether to call her. He decided it came down to his opening line. It had to be casual, breezy. *Hey, saw you the other day. Thought I'd give you a call.* No, that's stupid. Maybe get right to it. *Okay, so how come you haven't called me?* No, that's more stupid. *I'm hurt that you didn't call me.* No, extra stupid and now he was feeling bad for being a creep. *You broke into her car, Isaiah? You violated her privacy? What's wrong with you? Is this who you are? A guy who skulks around and rifles through a woman's things like a perv?*

He got resentful. He'd found her long-lost mother. He'd saved her life—well, she'd saved his too but that was beside the point. The point was, they'd been together, they'd been more than close—and that letter she'd sent. *Kind and wonderful Isaiah* my ass. She'd been here at least two weeks and not one word. "What a bitch," he said aloud, the sentiment lasting about five or six seconds because that's when he saw Grace sitting on his front stoop. He pulled into the driveway and got out of the car. He approached her slowly, like some rare bird that might flee at the slightest wrong move. As he drew closer, she stood up. My God, she's beautiful, he thought, and then she smiled and the criteria for beautiful took a leap into the clouds. "Hi," he said. He wondered how the moisture in his mouth could disappear so quickly. His tongue felt chapped.

"Hi," she said.

"Come on in," he said. She entered, Ruffin right behind her. Isaiah had been so overwhelmed he hadn't noticed the dog. It gave its former master a couple of disinterested sniffs and lay down on his spot next to the bookshelves.

"How are you?" she said. Her mouth was dry too.

"Fine. You?"

"I'm okay."

"Sit down. Want something to drink?"

"No, thanks," Grace said. She sat on the edge of the couch. He stood with his hands in his front pockets. "The thing with Cherokee's bag?" she said. "I knew it was you."

He shrugged, embarrassed. "I saw you before, so—"

"I wasn't avoiding you."

"You've been here for two weeks," he said. It just slipped out.

She frowned. "How do you know that?" Then she smiled and shook her head. "Never mind." She took in a yoga breath and let it out slow. "I've been working up the nerve to see you. I'm sorry, I shouldn't have been such a wimp."

"It's okay," he said, still thinking about Señor Barcelona. "I know you're busy."

"I didn't forget you. I thought about you all the time. Every day." The pale green eyes were as he remembered them. Wise and sorrowful and compelling. "Are you angry with me?" she asked.

84

"For what?" He shrugged. "You don't owe me anything."

"Yes, I do. I owe you for all kinds of things."

"Naah." He shrugged again and hoped he sounded breezy. "It's okay, really. I didn't have any expectations. I'm just glad to see you." Grace got up. He thought she was leaving but instead she came over, put her arms around him and kissed him.

They didn't talk even after they made love. They spooned and breathed and held on tighter, sunlight through the window a golden comforter. He could hear sparrows twittering, the occasional car going by, and Mrs. Marquez gossiping with the mailman. It made him feel good, the world out there while they were here; enclosed, safe.

Eventually they got up and took a shower together, smiling the whole time. They dressed. She sat on the bed, drying her hair with a towel and looking at her painting on the opposite wall.

"It doesn't scare me anymore. I don't dream about it."

"I'm glad."

They sat on the back stoop, drinking Heinekens, Ruffin sleeping in the shade of the lemon tree. It was easy and right and perfect, Isaiah's quiet excitement so profound he wanted to jump up and run around the yard.

"What brought you back?" he said.

"What brought me back?" She smiled and elbowed him. "*You*, of course. Are you seeing someone?" she asked.

He hesitated, fearful of fucking this up and afraid to tell the truth. "Yes, I am," he said.

"I've been away for two years," she said. "I didn't expect you to wait for me and I didn't mean to interrupt your life. You should keep seeing her."

"I don't want to see her," he said. "Not anymore."

"Is it serious?" she asked. He thought a moment.

"Not like you and me."

"Really, Isaiah. It's okay," she went on. "You shouldn't break up with her just because I randomly show up on your doorstep."

He shook his head. "So I keep going out with her while I want to be with you?" he said. "No, that isn't right for anybody. I have to break it off." But not now, he thought, not before Stella's big concert. Her first performance as a soloist. Her family's proudest moment.

Stella was a wonderful person who deserved only the best. She would be hurt and he felt lousy about it. He hoped she wasn't in love. Had he given her the idea that he was? He dreaded the thought. Stella was probably rehearsing now, completely wrapped up with the music she loved and the thrill of performing. The least he could do was not screw everything up.

Ruffin was lying on his back with his legs in the air, wriggling around, scratching himself on twigs and fallen leaves.

"I don't think Ruffin recognizes me," Isaiah said.

"Sure he does," Grace said. "If he didn't, he would have only sniffed you once."

He told her about the case. Angus and Christiana and the threat against Stella. He told her about Beaumont, and Sidero and the Starks and their clubhouse called the Den.

"That's unbelievable," she said. "Angus sounds insane. Where is this *Den*?"

"On the way to the airport. I stopped at the cemetery to visit Marcus's grave. I shouldn't have. Made me cry."

"That's okay. Nothing wrong with that."

He told her how he almost fainted and stopped in the park to eat an energy bar and how the Den was down a dirt road and hard to find. He said he should have taken the freeway because it would have been faster. He was surprised he went into such detail, but it made him feel better.

"Who do you think hired the killers?" she asked.

"I usually have a feeling about it, but I truly don't know."

"Can I help?"

"Absolutely not."

She sipped her beer. "I've changed a lot," she said, "but I'm not completely there yet. I'm still weird, you know? I get paranoid, and sometimes I'll shut you out or be pissed off for no reason, or I might disappear for a while but it's me, okay? My craziness, not yours. I don't want you to think I'm all sweetness and light."

"You mean like me?" he said, and they laughed. She said she had to go over to Cherokee's and clean up.

"Can you keep the dog?" she asked.

"Sure. At least that way I'll know you'll come back."

She kissed him and said, "I wouldn't worry about it."

Sal and Annie got a room at the Crest Motel on Long Beach Boulevard, the hovel being one short step above a prison cell. It smelled heavily of weed and perfume. Hookers used the rooms as their offices. The sheets may or may not have been changed.

Annie raised the corner of her lip. "Ugh," she said.

"Did you see the soda machine?" Sal said. "There's no soda in it and there's a fucking anchor chain holding it down."

Annie turned on the TV as soon as they closed the door. It was instinctive, a way to fill a room with something other than tension. She put a towel on the bed, lay back and watched *The Real Housewives of Atlanta* or Miami or Winnipeg or Jupiter. They were all the same. A bunch of spoiled, ridiculous women who didn't do anything but eat lunch, bitch at each other and overdress.

Sal checked the equipment. The ropes, pulleys, masks, black outfits and Annie's tightrope shoes, thin leather and flexible so you could curve your foot around the wire rope. And guns. Sal had taught Annie to shoot back in Loomis. Sal carried a Walther PPQ .22 with a Q El Camino suppressor, which made no more noise than a stapler. Annie insisted on a 9mm, saying her small size made her more vulnerable. There was no talking to her.

They met on set, a romantic comedy with a circus for a backdrop. Annie was a featured player with no lines. The director had chosen her on the spot. She was seventeen, photogenic, cute and very tiny, which was mandatory if you were a member of the world-famous Flying Morettis, a staple of the Ringling Brothers Circus for twenty-five years.

Sal was a stuntwoman, six years older than Annie. Sal rolled out of speeding cars, jumped off buildings, charged through breakaway doors, and had fistfights on top of trains with Matt Damon. She was fit, boyishly attractive, shoulders wide like a swimmer's, her hands calloused from lifting weights and doing power slams with an exercise rope. She'd marveled at Annie. A fairy princess in her pink tutu, chin up as she balanced herself on the high wire, fluid arms out wide, somehow teetering and graceful at the same time.

Annie had grown up in the circus. The Morettis lived in a trailer like all the other acts, a portable community that went from city to city, opening and closing like one of those birthday cards where a bunch of happy elves or singing squirrels popped up. There was no chance to make friends. You only went to a real school for part of the year and there was nobody to hang around with except the other circus people.

Annie liked performing but her parents were disciplinarians with a lot of rules, curfews and lectures. Annie ignored them and spent most of her time running around with Oscar and Manny. Oscar was part of a family of clowns and Manny's family had a dog act; the yipping Jack Russell terriers drove everybody crazy. The three misfits formed a mini-gang and called themselves the Big Top Boyz. They smoked dope, vandalized, stole whatever wasn't welded down and got into fights with the locals. It was fun until Oscar and Manny took turns raping Annie behind the hay bales, the horses lifting their hooves and stirring restlessly.

Ringling Bros. closed for good about a week after the movie ended. By then, Sal and Annie were together. The Morettis moved to Loomis, a rural town right outside Sacramento. Mr. Moretti had family there. A nice place if you liked peace, quiet and hanging out with farm animals. Sal loved Annie and followed her there. Sal's career was over anyway. An assistant director tried to play grab-ass and she put him in the hospital with a dislocated shoulder and two black eyes. She had a little savings and lived in a shabby guest room just down the road from the Morettis.

It was blissful being together all the time, but they had no money and no way of making any until they saw a rerun of *Bonnie and Clyde*.

Bank robbery was out but robbing people seemed like a good idea. Annie wore a halter top and short shorts and walked down Stone Road or Sierra College, waiting for some random asshole to pull over and say, "Need a ride?"

Annie would reply, "No, I need to get laid." Then she'd take the man to a predetermined spot. It was off the road, isolated, under a copse of trees. Smiling prettily, she would touch the guy's cock and say, "You're in for the time of your life." The man would be ecstatic. Whoever heard of an enthusiastic hooker? After he got his thing out of his pants, Sal would appear at the window with her Sig Sauer and a wide grin.

"Hi," she'd say. "What is that? A one-eyed hamster?"

Annie would take a picture of him. "What would your wife and kiddies think about this?" she'd say.

Then they'd rob him, make him strip, and take his car to a chop shop in Sacramento. They'd done this about a dozen times when a man who looked like the retiring head of the physics department changed the program. He and Annie were driving to the spot when he stopped the car and punched her. Then he dragged her out, punched her a few more times and started ripping her clothes off. Her screams brought Sal running and she shot him. The guy would have lived, but Oscar's and Manny's lurid grins were flashing in Annie's eyes and she finished the guy off with a rock, bashing his skull into bone fragments and brain matter until she exhausted herself. It took a lot of time to wipe everything down. Their DNA was probably all over the place but they weren't in the system and there was no way to trace them.

"He deserved it," Annie said as they hosed off the blood. Sal didn't answer. She knew about the rape but still couldn't believe so much rage was inside her tiny, perfect girlfriend. They moved to Sacramento. Their income situation was no different than before so they went back to their routine. They killed another man when he tried to take Sal's gun away, and it went off in his face. They never talked about the killings. It was like a family secret, buried but still moving around inside its coffin.

About a week after the second killing, Sal said, "I'm going to get a job." Sal got work in a Vietnamese restaurant. Her major duty was to take phone orders. People were complaining they couldn't understand Mr. Dao's thick accent. Sal also washed dishes and mopped floors. None of the other workers talked to her and she didn't try.

Annie waitressed in a bar. She had no experience and had to give the owner a blow job before he'd accept her application. He never knew how close he'd come to getting his entire crotch bitten off. Both Annie and Sal were depressed, gaining weight, fighting a lot, drinking a lot, and nearing despair.

Among Annie's regulars at the bar were two black guys. They were older, the kind who wore fedoras and patent leather shoes and kept their sunglasses on indoors. Their names were Sonny and Rolando. Annie thought they were pimps. She chatted them up with her blouse open, flashing her little titties, and they tipped her extravagantly.

The bar was separated into two rooms by a low partition, plastic ferns sticking out of it. One afternoon, Annie was cleaning a table behind the two men and overheard them talking. They wanted to kill somebody named Eric, discussing who could do the job and ruling out everybody they knew. In the middle of the conversation, Rolando turned around and said sharply, "You didn't hear this, girl. You understand?" Annie nodded.

She told Sal and the next day they approached the two men. Annie said, "That guy you were talking about? Eric? We'll take him out for you."

They laughed. "Oh, yeah?" Sonny said. "You big-time killas, are you?"

"We've killed two people," Annie said. "A third won't be a problem."

"What'd you kill 'em with?" Rolando said. "A hatpin? Your finger-nails?"

"We killed them with this," Sal said. She lifted her shirt and showed them the Sig.

"Whoa, whoa, girl," Sonny said, putting up his palms. "Don't be waving that around." The two men glanced at each other, starting to take this seriously.

"You ain't playin', are you?" Rolando said.

"No, we're not," Sal replied.

The men hesitated, no doubt wondering if they were being set up.

"This isn't a scam," Annie said. "Even if it was, two players like you would know in a heartbeat." They nodded—true dat. Annie had poked their egos. She was good at that.

"Anyway, what are your alternatives?" Sal said. "Some brainless street kid with a record who smokes dope before the job? That's what Eric will be expecting. But two cute white girls in dresses? Annie could still be in high school. He'll never see us coming."

They went outside and got in Rolando's giant SUV. The men made the women lift up their shirts and open their pants and checked them for wires.

"If we give you a down payment," Sonny said, "how do we know you won't run off with the money?"

"We won't," Sal said. "We want to work for you again."

Eric was a drug dealer. He was in his forties, a white guy with a comb-over and belly fat hanging over his belt. He listened to rap music and dressed like a teenager. Rolando said Eric was expecting a hit and traveled with two bodyguards who knew what they were doing. The women watched them, followed them, got a pattern down. There were very few openings. Eric was either in his car, a crowded club, partying with a bunch of women or safe in his apartment on the seventeenth floor of a high-rise.

Sal snuck a peek inside the building. A guard was at the kiosk 24/7. Guests had to sign in and there were cameras all over the place.

"It's impossible," Annie said.

"Maybe," Sal replied. They sat in the bar, talked and drew diagrams. They chose a Saturday night, when Eric was likely to be drunk or high. They parked across the street from the building at midnight. Eric usually didn't get home until one or two in the morning. They were both nervous, silent the whole way over.

"You okay?" Sal asked.

"Yeah," Annie said. "I'm good."

They were both skilled at makeup and wigs. They'd worked on themselves a long time, coming up with looks that were radically different from their own. On camera they would be unrecognizable. Sal could be conventionally attractive when she wanted to be. She wore a short skirt and heels, trudging through the lobby looking exhausted and lugging a heavy suitcase.

"How can I help you?" the guard said.

"I'm Eric's daughter. Eric Mehlman? Is he in?"

"I'm not allowed to tell you that, miss. Can't you call him?"

"I have, but he doesn't pick up." She hung her head. "We're not exactly getting along."

"Well, I'm sorry I can't help you," the guard said. "Those are the rules."

She made puppy eyes. "Can I wait in the lobby? Please?"

"Sure, that's fine."

Sal sat on a sofa and tried to look miserable. Twenty minutes went by. She could tell the guard was uncomfortable—this poor, bedraggled girl waiting and waiting, making him wonder if he was being a tight-ass. She went to the desk.

"I know this is asking a lot, but could I please use the bathroom?"

"Sorry, there isn't one in the lobby," the guard said.

"*Please?* There's nothing else around here. Don't make me go in the bushes." She looked like she was going to cry.

The guard sighed. "Okay, okay," he said. "Right around the corner there's an office. The bathroom's in the back. Don't be long. I could get into trouble."

"Oh, thank you, thank you!" She found the bathroom, locked the door and waited. Ten minutes later, the guard came and knocked on the door.

"Miss? Are you okay?"

"I'm sorry," Sal mewled. "I'm having...female problems."

"Oh, my God. You've got to be kidding."

While the guard was away from his desk, Annie ran across the lobby. She was wearing her hooker outfit; short shorts, a tank top and a girly pink backpack. She got on the elevator and rode up to the seventeenth floor. There were only four apartments. Eric's was 1702. She set her backpack down, sat next to it and waited.

*　　*　　*

The guard kicked Sal out and now she was waiting in the car. Just after one a.m., Eric arrived. He got out of the car, said something to his bodyguards and went inside. Thank God there wasn't a woman with him. Sal texted Annie. *He's here.*

Eric Melhman got off the elevator and found a girl sitting next to his door. She was cute, really cute. She looked exhausted and was wearing next to nothing. That backpack was bigger than she was.

"Hello," he said in his friendly voice. "Anything I can do for you?"

"Yeah," she said in a tiny voice. "I'm waiting for my father."

"Here?" He nearly laughed. "This is my apartment. I've lived here for six years. Sure it isn't one of the others?"

The girl looked panic-stricken. She stood up and took a slip of paper out of her cute little shorts. "No. I wrote it down. See?"

"Well, I'm sorry," Eric said, starting to feel sympathetic, "but you've got the wrong one. Can't you call him?"

"I did but he won't pick up. We're not getting along."

"Friends?"

"I just got here from Ohio. I don't know anybody." She started to cry.

I wouldn't mind a taste of that, Eric thought. He liked spinners. You could move them around, do things. Maybe she'd be grateful to someone who offered her a place to rest, good food and the best cocaine outside of Bogotá.

"Come on in. Take a load off and we'll figure out what to do."

"Thank you. That would be great."

Annie had never seen such a lavish apartment. It was something you'd see in *People* magazine or on *Entertainment Tonight.*

"Wow," she said.

"Yeah, it's nice," Eric agreed. "I decorated it myself."

"You did a good job."

Eric went into the kitchen, chose a bottle of wine from a rack. He used a fancy corkscrew and poured her a glass. "Here. Villa Domaine Vincent Grand Cru, eight hundred dollars a bottle. The best thing you've ever tasted. Swirl it around in your glass and smell it first."

Annie swirled, sniffed and sipped. It was the best thing she'd ever tasted. "Wow," she said again. She knew she should have shot him by now but it occurred to her that a drug dealer who lived in a place like this might have some quality coke lying around and maybe some cash as well.

"Are you hungry?" he said.

"Yeah, a little. I haven't eaten since I got off the plane."

"Then I will make you the best ham and cheese sandwich you've ever had in your life."

He stood at the cutting board and made a sandwich with meat rolled up in wax paper and thick cheese he sliced himself. He was humming, showing off, handling the knife with precision. Annie heard her phone ping. It was Sal, wondering why she wasn't back yet. Annie drew a gun out of the backpack.

"Drop the knife and get down on the floor."

"Hey, what's all this?" he said. He didn't drop the knife.

"I said, drop the knife and get down on the floor," she said.

He smiled and shook his head. "No, sorry, sweetheart, I don't take that shit from—"

She shot him in the foot, the bang muffled by the silencer. Eric howled and fell on the floor. She took his phone and his wallet. She found a Whole Foods shopping bag and dropped them inside.

"Hey, I'm bleeding to death!" Eric shouted.

"Where's your stash?" Annie said.

"What stash? I don't have any—" She shot three rounds close to his head, chipping the marble floor and splintering a cabinet. "Okay, all right! In the bedroom."

"Get up," Annie said. Groaning and dragging his leg, Eric found a safe in the closet. He blubbered while he worked the combination. "Hurry up," Annie said.

* * *

Sal was afraid. This was taking too long. *What are you doing, Annie?* Eric's bodyguards were still in the car, arguing about something. What were they waiting for? Her stomach wrenched. Maybe Eric was supposed to text them and tell them he was okay. "Oh, shit," Sal said. The bodyguards got out of the car. They ran inside and Sal ran after them. *What the fuck are you doing, Annie?*

There were bundles of cash and a baggie of coke inside the safe. Annie laughed and dumped it all into the shopping bag.

"That's everything," Eric croaked.

She shot him twice in the head. She walked into the living room, wiped down everything she'd touched. She started for the front door and stopped. She grinned and said, "Bling!" She went back into the bedroom.

The bodyguards ran across the lobby. The security guard got up from the desk and stood in their way. "Sorry, you can't go up there."

"Why?" one of them said. "You know who we are."

"It's regulations, fellas. You know that. I have to call him first."

The bodyguard shoved the guard so hard he hit the floor and somersaulted backward. Both men got on the elevator and as the doors were closing, Sal pushed her way in.

"Get out," a bodyguard said.

"Why? I live here," she protested.

He grabbed her and flung her out.

Annie was dropping Eric's Rolex collection into the bag when she heard pounding on the door. She went out into the living room. Men were shouting, the pounding continuous. The cops would be here soon. There was only one thing she could do: shoot the men through the door and run for it. She got into position, aimed about chest height and stopped.

The gun. A fucking .22 peashooter Rolando had given her. This was a lux building and the goddamn door was heavy and thick. Maybe she'd take the men out, maybe not, and they would no doubt return fire with 9mms or .45s. Annie was sweating and she never sweated, even when she was thirty feet off the ground, standing on Pietro's shoulder, posing like a maidenhead on a sailing ship. Her only option was to open the door fast and let 'er fucking rip. "Ready, Annie?" she said aloud. She wished she could talk to Sal, say goodbye, say she was sorry. She put her hand on the knob and tightened her grip on the gun.

Sal didn't want to be in the lobby when the cops arrived. She'd returned to the car and heard sirens. She couldn't wait around until she was spotted. "Goddamn you, Annie!" She banged her fists on the steering wheel. "Why didn't you stick to the fucking plan?" Terrified and angry, she drove to the end of the block, turned and drove alongside the building. She was wondering what the fuck she should do when she jammed on the brakes. She saw her tiny partner climbing down from balcony to balcony with a Whole Foods bag over her shoulder, a hundred feet between her and the concrete below. Annie looked calm, measured, her steely nerves shining like a sword. "Oh, Annie," Sal said, wiping tears from her face.

Rolando and Sonny were impressed, paid them the rest of the fee and added a tip. "You some bad little bitches," Rolando said. "You like them two female cops on TV. You remember that show?"

"*Starsky and Hutch*," Sonny said.

"Naw, that ain't it," Rolando said.

Word spread. Sal and Annie got work and a reputation for pulling off impossible jobs. In the movies, professional contractors are in demand and highly paid, one more figment of a screenwriter's imagination. Starsky and Hutch worked sporadically and made a sporadic living. It was not glamorous, fun or dignified. They traveled around and killed people.

*　　*　　*

The room at the Crest Motel smelled like mold and roach powder. Annie had a voracious appetite and ordered a pizza.

"What are we going to do?" she said.

"We can't set up at Isaiah's house," Sal answered.

"Why?"

"Because we'll be two white chicks in black clothes sitting in a car in the middle of the hood, that's why. We don't exactly blend in."

"Could we call a truce, please?" Annie said. "So what, then? He could be anywhere."

Sal thought a moment. "We need help."

"From who?"

"We have to call the client."

CHAPTER NINE
Whore of the Vampires

"When I was a kid, my auntie Georgina got sick," TK said. "She was old and deaf and had to be spoon-fed most of the time. So one day I goes over there to babysit. Nobody else was around 'cept my uncle, who was almost as messed up as Georgina. So I goes into the bedroom and she's a-settin' in her wheelchair and I see she's tilted to the right. Well, I don't want her to fall on the floor, so I went over and pushes her straight. Two minutes later, she's tilting to the left and I have to do it all over again. This went on the whole damn afternoon. Right, left, right, left, right, left. Well, I'm about to push her out of the chair myself but then my uncle comes in. He gets real close to her and says, 'How you doin', Georgina? This young man treatin' you all right?' And she said, 'Oh, he's treatin' me just fine, but he won't let me fart.'"

Grace laughed and laughed. "I love you, TK. I really do."

The moment she arrived, TK had held out his arms. "How you doin', baby?" he said. She rushed into the embrace, put her head on his chest and cried into his oily coveralls. "Oh, now, now. Stop all that nonsense. I ain't nobody to cry over."

He told his joke and they strolled around the wrecking yard, Ruffin back on his home ground, sniffing and peeing and sniffing and peeing and chasing ground squirrels. She remembered sleeping in the loft that

Isaiah had fixed up for her and running from Walczak's crew and hiding in the Passat and shooting at them with Mr. Brown.

"How's your life going?" TK asked.

"It was rough for a while but I'm better now," she said. "Mom is safe and the Walczak thing is behind me."

"Somethin' like that would've broke most people's back," TK said. "I don't know how you came out of it in one piece." Grace wondered that too. TK lit a Pall Mall, squinting as he exhaled. "How's Isaiah doing?" he asked.

"Great. Except for the case he's working on."

"Y'all are together now?"

"Yeah, we're together."

TK chuckled. "Two shy folks who don't like people and do most of their talkin' to that dog? That's a match made somewhere but it sho' wasn't heaven." They walked in silence a bit, her arm through his. Something was wrong, she thought. TK was brooding and tense, wanting to say something. She waited, letting him get there on his own. They were all the way back to the warehouse when he said, "Grace, I got something I want to talk about."

"Are you okay?" Grace said. "You're not sick, are you?"

"No, no, it's nothing like that." He lowered his voice. "It's about a woman. I, uh—I have feelins for her." TK's first wife had died, and his second wife left him. Grace thought he'd lost interest in women. He was elderly, white haired, made mostly of sinew and gristle, but damn appealing if you liked honesty, the inner strength of heavy machinery and jokes ranging from hilarious to god-awful. "Other folks might not understand it, but this woman is—" He stopped, unable to describe her.

"She must be something special," Grace said.

"She is that." TK smiled and shook his head like he was admiring a tornado or a tidal wave. "See, I don't go for no ordinary women. I ain't got nothin' against 'em but I need some *vitality,* somebody with some get-up-and-go. Somebody who makes me want to get up and go with her." Another surprise. Grace thought he'd want a woman as laid back as he was. TK sighed. "Problem is, the woman don't know I'm alive. I might as well be a lampshade or a tin can for all she cares."

"Have you introduced yourself?"

"I started going to church 'cause that's the only place I'd see her, but I ain't said nothing to her."

"Does she know your name?" Grace asked.

TK looked down at the ground. "No, I haven't talked to her yet," and Grace realized he was intimidated. "What's so hard about talking to her?" she continued. "You've done a million things that were scarier than that."

"I haven't courted a woman in fifteen years," he said. "I'm nervous as a goddamn teenager." He took off his STP cap and wiped his brow. "But I suppose the main reason is her. She's not friendly, for one thing. No, I'd say she's one step short of a snappin' turtle—and opinionated too, one of them people that's right all the time, which makes you wrong all the time, and if she's got a sense of humor, nobody knows about it."

Grace didn't think she sounded nice at all and wondered if TK had left out some things. "Well, maybe start by introducing yourself," she said. "You know, saying hi."

He shook his head woefully. "It's not that easy. I need your help, Grace."

She was getting a bad feeling about this. Like he was asking her to go swimming in quicksand. "I'm not sure I can," she said. "Like you said, I'm shy, I don't like people, and I'm most comfortable when with the dog."

"Yeah, I know. But I got nobody else to ask."

"Right."

"Look, all I want you to do is size her up," TK said. "Get a feel for her, see what you think. There's a church picnic at the park and I was hoping you'd go with me."

"Sure, if you want. What's the woman's name, by the way?"

"Gloria Simmons. She's Dodson's mother-in-law."

They heard tires crunching gravel and Mos Def's "Close Edge." She smiled. A bright red convertible drove into the yard, Deronda bobbing her head, waving her arm in the air like she just don't care and dancing in her seat.

"Whassup, baby sista!" she shouted. She got out of the car and they hugged. "Watch my nails. Them sparkly things cost money." Deronda was jangling with bling, hair up and elaborate, her smile as big as the grill on a Cadillac Eldorado.

She's so beautiful, Grace thought. "What are you doing here?" she said.

"TK gave me a call. Damn, I'm glad to see your pale ass. Whassup, TK? How you doin'?"

"I'm old and slow but I'm doin' all right."

"Have you seen Isaiah yet?" Deronda asked.

"Yeah," Grace said. "We're sort of together." She wondered why it was so hard to say.

"Dang, girl," Deronda said. "All the men who would rise up on you and *that's* who you pick? He's a good person and all that but as a boy-friend? You could hook up with a workaholic hedge fund manager and have more fun."

"Maybe," she said, "but he's the one."

"He's *the one?* Oh, my muthafuckin' God. You done lost your mind."

"That seems to be the consensus."

Deronda thought a moment. "What are y'all doin' tonight?"

"Me? Nothing really."

"Aight, then," Deronda said, delighted. "It's a girl's night out, baby sista!" She looked at Grace and paused, her smile fading.

"What's the matter?" Grace said.

"Girl, we need to do something about your appearance."

Deronda took Grace to get a manicure and pedicure. She'd never had either. It seemed more complicated than repairing the Hubble telescope. Cutting, filing, soaking, prepping the cuticles, first coat, second coat and other stuff she didn't bother watching. The same for her toes too. Who had time to do this? She wondered. Deronda had the manicurist apply what she called *design features,* which took even more time. When the job was finally done, Grace's nails were a quarter-inch long and looked like Jackson Pollock and Willem de Kooning had decorated ten little Christmas trees. She didn't understand how she was supposed to eat, drive, open a door. Live. She wondered if her toes were supposed to be visible from space.

"Don't you think this is a lot?" Grace said.

"No," Deronda replied. "I'd say that's just enough."

Grace had always resented how much crap women went through to look *presentable,* a word her father had used when she was a kid. But she dutifully explored Cherokee's closet and found a simple black cocktail dress that hadn't been worn since 1994. Grace examined herself in the mirror, turning this way and that. "That's not bad, don't you think?"

Deronda looked at her like she'd just arrived from Upper Rubber Boot in patched coveralls and a straw hat. "That's the saddest dress I've ever seen," she said. They took the dress over to Deronda's apartment. She raised the hemline three inches and borrowed some stilettos that made Grace wobble like a newborn giraffe. Then she slicked back Grace's hair with something that made it look wet, and did a gothy thing with her makeup. Stark black eyebrows and long fake eyelashes, black eye shadow and bright red lipstick.

"You white girls like this look," Deronda announced.

"We do?"

"Makes you look all dramatic."

"I'm not a dramatic person."

"I know," Deronda said. "But try."

Bling next. Big hoop earrings, a neck chain with a dollar-sign medallion, clinking hoop bracelets and a belt with a heart-shaped buckle as big as an actual heart. They stood in front of the mirror together.

Deronda smiled, pleased with her work. "What do you think?"

Grace stared at herself, incredulous. "I look like a vampire who decided to be a whore."

Grace had never been in a real nightclub before. "Jesus," she said. It was overwhelming, the swarm of dancing bodies, the ear-shattering music and the dense, booze-mixed-with-sweat-mixed-with-pheromones smell.

"Whoo-yeah, baby, we gonna party tonight!" Deronda said. "I got to find my people—oh wait, I don't believe it. There's Junior!"

"Junior?" Grace said.

"You don't remember him? You robbed his house."

"I didn't see what he looked like. I was in the dryer."

"Let's go say hello," Deronda said.

"Didn't you do something painful to his dick?" Grace asked.

"Balls, honey," Deronda replied. "I twisted 'em so hard they almost came off in my hand."

"Now there's a nice thought."

As they approached Junior, Deronda said, "Don't he look like a pug? Every time I see him, I want to open a box a Milk-Bones."

Junior was lounging on a flouncy pink sofa, his arm around a hoochie girl with thighs like sleeping walruses.

"Hello, Junior. Remember me?" Deronda said.

"Yes, I remember you," he said indignantly. "You impaired my sperm facilities for an entire generation. I believe you owe me your condolences."

"Do you really think talking like that makes you seem smart?"

"A good vocabulary signifies perceptivity," he said.

"Maybe," Deronda replied, "but you sound like a can of alphabet soup blew up in your head."

"Who're you supposed to be?" the hoochie girl said to Grace.

"A friend," Grace said.

"A friend of Deronda's? Shee-it, girl, you need to meet some new people."

"And you need to shut up before I tear the weave outta your head," Deronda said.

Junior flicked his hand. "Be gone, you felonious bitch, before I grab you by your giblets and ensconce your ass on outta here."

"Uh-huh. And I'll see you at the pound, you little dog-face monkey."

Deronda and Grace plunged back into the crowd, circling the dance floor. Deronda smiled, big and broad. "I got me a new man."

"Really?" Grace said. "That's great."

"He's a good one too. I thought they were extinct like dinosaurs or dodo birds."

As they approached a table, Grace said, "Is that him? He's gorgeous."

"Ain't he though," Deronda said. He stood up. "Grace, this my boyfriend, Robert," Deronda announced proudly. "Robert, this is Grace."

"I've heard a lot about you," Robert said. He had warm eyes and a charming smile. "Please sit down. May I get you something to drink?" Grace glanced at Deronda. *Oh, my God, is he for real?* Deronda's sister, Kalina, was there, along with her friend Nona, plus Nona's boyfriend, Jermaine, and another fine brother who called himself Whip. Everybody laughed and drank, shouting over the music, the back-and-forth nonsensical and fun.

As uncomfortable as she was in her Whore of the Vampires outfit, Grace was glad she came. It was great to see Deronda so happy. Cuddling with Robert, feeding him the cherry from her drink, whispering things that made him smile and shake his head. Whip, who looked really young, was all over her; flirting, teasing and joking, buying her drinks and stroking the back of her hand.

"She got a boyfriend, you know," Deronda said.

"It's okay," Grace said. "I'm kinda liking it."

Whip smiled condescendingly. "Can you dance?"

"Let's go find out," Grace said, taking off her shoes. She danced. No posing or moves, nothing planned or premeditated, nothing to please the crowd. Over the years, she'd developed her own boogie; a blend of the jazz lessons her mother made her take, Axl Rose's snake dance, the hula dancers she'd seen when her dad was based in Hawaii and the headbanging she'd picked up in her punk days. The sistas weren't appreciative but the bruthas were diggin' it. *Go on, baby, move that thang. Look at the bootie on the white girl! She must be high on somethin'. That bitch gonna have a heart attack.*

Grace heard none of it. She was gone from the world, dancing amid glittering bursts of color, coils of mist, shooting stars and a beckoning horizon, and as the room spun around and around her, she thought, *Oh, Isaiah. It's all because of you.*

Isaiah was waiting around for Gia to call him. She was trying to pin down Marlene and the pressure was getting to him. Christiana's imminent arrest, the futility of solving an unsolvable case, Stella in danger and not being with Grace. Here he'd waited all this time for her and—*no, don't go there, Isaiah. Keep your eye on the ball.*

Gia called, upset. "Something happened. The police called Christiana but Bertrand answered. They wanted him to come down to the police station. They said they had a few more questions. I told him to talk to the lawyers first but he went anyway. He said he wanted to clear the whole thing up."

"*Shhhhit!*" Isaiah said. He couldn't keep running around like this. Instead of trying to catch Marlene, he'd follow whichever alter appeared and stay on that one until he or she switched out with the two alters whom he hadn't interviewed. Marlene and Jasper.

Bertrand was in an interrogation room, waiting, strolling around the tiny space with his hands behind his back, looking at the walls like every one of them had a view. He tapped on the two-way window. "Excuse me. Hello?" He tapped again. "Could I get some peanuts or something? And a root beer. An ice-cold root beer would be great." No answer. "I know you're in there, you know. I watch *CSI* all the time."

The two detectives came in. Bertrand had forgotten their names but they were both round and bald. He thought of them as Humpty and Dumpty. They were looking at him funny.

"Is there something wrong?" he asked.

"You're dressed…different," Humpty said.

Bertrand looked down at his clothes. He was wearing what he always wore: Dockers, a short-sleeve checked shirt, a leather belt and sneakers he bought at the drugstore.

"Why don't you have a seat, Miss Byrne," Humpty said.

"It's mister."

"What?"

"It's Mister Byrne," Bertrand insisted.

The detectives glanced at each other. "Okay, *Mister* Byrne," Humpty said.

They sat across from each other. Dumpty leaned against the wall with his arms folded. They made Bertrand sign a paper waiving his right to an attorney.

"Okay," Humpty said. "We can start now."

"Did you hear me about the peanuts?" Bertrand said.

"We don't have any."

"Well, you don't have to be mad about it."

"I'm not mad," Humpty said.

"Yes, you are. I can see it in your face."

Humpty's voice rose. "I'm telling you, we don't—"

Dumpty cleared his throat and Humpty took a breath. "We just want to clear up a few things," he said. "Let's start at the beginning. Tell us what happened."

"Right," Bertrand said, happy to get going. "I was sitting on the floor next to Tyler's body and it was *very* unpleasant, I can tell you. Well, I got up, looked through the curtain and the first thing I saw was the ninny woman going toward the back entrance."

"'Ninny woman'?" Dumpty said.

"Wait a second," Humpty said. "That's not the beginning. The whole thing started with you and Tyler in the showroom, didn't it?"

"Not for me," Bertrand replied.

The detectives looked at each other. "What do you mean 'not for me'?" Humpty said.

"I *mean*," Bertrand said, speaking slowly as if that might help, "I didn't enter the picture until, like I said, I was sitting on the floor next to Tyler's body and I saw the ninny woman—"

"I don't think I'm following," Humpty said. "You had to be in the showroom first. You had to see Tyler alive before he was dead."

"Not necessarily," Bertrand said.

"Who's the ninny woman again?" Dumpty said.

"Okay, back up," Humpty said. "You told us before that you were measuring Tyler for a suit."

"No, I didn't," Bertrand said. "Christiana did."

Humpty squinted and shook his head. "But you're Christiana."

"You know who you should talk to?" Bertrand said. "Pearl. She was there before me."

"Wait," Dumpty said. "Who's Pearl?"

Bertrand shrugged. "I don't know. She's just . . . Pearl."

"We haven't heard the name before," Humpty said. "Here. Write down the names of all the people who were there besides Tyler."

"Sure," Bertrand said. For clarity's sake, he wrote the list in block letters.

CHRISTIANA
PEARL
ME
NINNY WOMAN
MARLENE AND JASPER BUT I'M NOT SURE

Bertrand slid the list to Humpty. "There you are," he said, like this was highly unnecessary.

Dumpty read over Humpty's shoulder. He squinted like the list was out of focus. Humpty took a big breath, like Bertrand did when he was in the bathtub, just before he dunked his head underwater.

"Okay, Miss—*Mister* Byrne," Humpty said. "I'm confused. When we interviewed you at the shop, you never mentioned all these people."

"You didn't interview me," Bertrand replied. "You interviewed Christiana." Humpty and Dumpty looked the way you look when somebody is speaking in a foreign language you've never heard. "I don't mean to be rude or anything," Bertrand said, "but have you ever done this before?"

"Yes, we have," Humpty said. He was frowning now. He had his big hands splayed on the table and was leaning forward. "Okay," he said, like he was the one who needed patience. "One more time from the top."

"Sure, Humpty," Bertrand said.

"Humpty?"

Bertrand felt sorry for him. A guy his age and couldn't do a simple interview. "You're kind of old to be a rookie, aren't you?" he said.

"I'm not a rookie," Humpty said.

"It's okay. Everybody's got to start somewhere."

"I'm *not* a—"

"Wait," Dumpty said, coming off the wall. *"Who the fuck is the ninny woman?"*

"Which one is in there now?" Dodson said.

"Bertrand," Isaiah said. "Or at least I think it's Bertrand."

"So the—what did you call them, alters? They could change back and forth like, whenever?"

"Yeah," Isaiah said, "whenever."

Isaiah was on his way to the police station when Dodson called. He said he had nothing to do and was wondering if he could help with the case. A startling admission. The Dodson Isaiah knew would never admit to needing something he couldn't get for himself. Something was up. Now they were sitting in the Kia across the street from the station. Isaiah caught Dodson up on the case.

"That is some crazy shit," Dodson said, shaking his head.

"Yeah," Isaiah sighed.

Bertrand came out of the station. "That's him," Isaiah said, noting the clothes. Bertrand looked furtive and annoyed, like he had to do something he didn't want other people to see. Hurriedly, he walked around the corner of the building and out of sight.

"No, wait, I don't think that's him anymore," Isaiah said. "His head is too erect, too much attitude, too much—"

"Booty," Dodson said.

"That's Marlene."

By the time they got to the corner of the building, she was nowhere to be seen. There was nothing around but office buildings and more office buildings. Nothing of obvious interest to Marlene. But there, between a building and a billboard, Isaiah saw a bronze sailor in a crow's nest, one hand shading his eyes, the other pointing at *land, ho!* The Windward Mall.

They hurried over. "What's Marlene like?" Dodson asked.

"Party girl. Promiscuous. Gambler. Trades on her looks."

There was nothing special about the mall. A rotunda, food court, shops on three floors. Lots of people carrying shopping bags, dragging their kids along, clusters of teenagers yakking, sullen men sitting on benches, sighing and glancing at their watches.

"Split up," Isaiah said, wanting to get rid of him. Dodson nodded and left.

Obviously, Marlene came here to shop. Isaiah went from Victoria's Secret to the Skin Spa to the Jewelry Mart. He was on his way over to a shoe store when Dodson called.

"I got her," he said.

Dodson was waiting outside Night Moves, a store that specialized in what Deronda called the *come on and get some* look. "Party girl like that," Dodson said. "She was embarrassed about them clothes she was wearing."

"Right," Isaiah said. He wished he knew more about women.

Marlene came out of the store and dropped Bertrand's clothes in a trash can. She saw Isaiah and groaned.

"Oh, for Christ's sake. What do you want?"

"I want to talk."

She stuck her head forward, opened her eyes wide and shook her head. "I'm telling you, *I don't know anything.*"

"Just a few minutes," Isaiah said. "It's for your own good." Apparently, that was the wrong thing to say.

"My own good?" she said, her tone hardening. "Oh, really?"

"You could end up in prison," Isaiah said, angry now. "Is that what you want?"

"I'll look after myself, Sherlock," she snapped. "In the meantime, leave me alone." Dodson was looking at her, knowingly and slightly amused.

"Who are you?" she said.

"I'm Juanell Dodson," he replied as if it was common knowledge. "What are you making such a fuss about? It's only a conversation. If you don't know anything, you don't know anything. Just talk to Isaiah for a quick minute and we'll be on our way." She sighed, only half convinced. "The Hyatt's across the street," Dodson went on. "A cocktail hits the spot in the middle of the day." He smiled his hustler's smile. "You must be thirsty, trying on all those clothes." There was a flash of recognition in Marlene's eyes.

"Lead the way," she said.

Dodson and Marlene crossed the street together, Isaiah trailing. He was sullen, thinking he could have convinced her himself if he'd had a little time. This was aggravating. They'd only been together for forty-five minutes and Dodson was competing with him already. Well, he could compete all he wanted but he was not, repeat, *not*, going to win the day.

Marlene sauntered, hips like a metronome. Men gawked and she glanced at them as if to say *you wish*. Dodson chatting her up—how hot she looked, how she should be in *Playboy*, how it should be against the law to walk like that. She laughed and took his arm.

They got a table in the bar. She slipped off her shoes, curled up in the chair like a seductive *S* and looked at them with Marilyn Monroe eyes. Corny, Isaiah thought. He almost expected her to sing, "Happy birthday, Mr. President." Dodson was smiling appreciatively.

"Stop it, girl, my zipper's about to bust." She laughed.

The server arrived. "Good afternoon," he said. "Welcome to the Hyatt. What can I get for you today?"

"May I order for you, Marlene?" Dodson said gallantly. "There's a drink here I think you'll enjoy."

"I wish you would."

"Two black martinis, please." The server looked at Isaiah.

"And for you, sir?"

"He won't have anything," Dodson said. "He's driving."

Marlene giggled. The server left. "What's a black martini?" she asked.

"Vanilla Absolut, touch of Kahlúa, a little whipped cream and a chocolate swizzle stick."

"Sounds yummy," she said.

"Could we talk about that night, please?" Isaiah said.

She waved her hand. "Oh, it's such a bore. Can't we talk about something else?"

"Marlene, you could go to prison," Isaiah intoned like a parent. "Do you understand what I'm saying? They can lock you up for years. *Years.*" She reacted as if she was hearing this for the first time. She looked at Dodson for confirmation.

"No joke, girl," he said. "Ain't no men in there, either, 'less you wanna be passed around by the guards. Tell him what he needs to know and we can enjoy our drinks in peace." She nodded as if that was sensible.

Isaiah restrained his irritation. "What did you think of Tyler?" he asked.

Marlene made a face, half angry, half disgusted. "He was such a pretentious asshole. He made a big deal out of wine and he drove one of those so-called vintage cars. Some kind of old Mercedes. It didn't even have airbags. And he lived in this old creepy house like it was supposed to be cool or something." She shifted around, exposing more thigh. "I mean I'm sorry he's dead and everything, but—" She shrugged.

"So you knew each other?" Isaiah asked.

She sneered, "Oh, he knew me, all right. He was like every other man I've met and, of course, he *adored* Christiana. Everybody *adores* Christiana. I hate that selfish bitch. All she thinks about is herself." That was surprising, Isaiah thought. The charge seemed to fit Marlene perfectly.

"What did you see that night?" Isaiah asked. She seemed to take the question seriously. Her brow was bunched up. She was nodding, staring past him, trying to remember. *Come on, Marlene. Give me something.*

"It's hazy, okay?" she said. "Sometimes something happens that's too freaky for us to handle so we kind of go berserk. We start switching out all over the place."

"Okay, but what did you, personally, see?" Isaiah said.

"Nothing really," she said.

"You don't remember *anything*?" he said, trying to keep the desperation out of his voice.

Marlene shook her head. "Just a bunch of flashes...but I did feel a temperature change and I was sweating."

"Where were you?" Isaiah said.

"Um, I was standing just inside the front door, looking at Tyler's body." She shrugged. "After that, just snippets. I can't really remember them."

"That's all?" he said.

"That's all."

The server brought their drinks. "Just in time," she said. She clinked glasses with Dodson. They sipped, suggestive smiles on their faces. "Mmm, this is good," she said. Dodson raised his eyebrows and smiled at Isaiah. *What's the matter, son? Your freakishly large brain couldn't work this out?*

Isaiah paid for the drinks and left. Grudgingly, he was grateful Dodson had extracted the info from Marlene, as little as it was. It chafed, like it always did, how Dodson could manipulate people so easily. It made you wonder if there was anything beneath his superficial appeal; whether he thought about anything other than being slick.

Okay, Marlene, Isaiah thought. She said she'd just come in the front door of the shop and felt the temperature change. Was she the alter that ran down the block and back? There was no way to know for sure. He felt another wave of futility. Even if he completed the timeline, so what? How would that prove Christiana's innocence? What exculpatory evidence could he give to the police? He dreaded and feared what came next. Jasper. If he didn't know anything that broke the case, the case was over.

CHAPTER TEN

You Can't Buy a Backbone at the Store

Dodson drove home from the Hyatt. He'd briefly considered having sex with Marlene. She was certainly willing, but it was wrong on so many levels he dismissed it. Still, he'd never turned down pussy before and it depressed him even more than he already was. The last couple of years had been hard on him.

Grace's mother had given him a hundred K for his help in the Walczak case, but Cherise had insisted on putting most of the money into Micah's college fund. Dodson argued he could invest the money and make a bigger contribution somewhere down the line. *Somewhere down the line* is not the phrase to use with a mother worried about her child's education. Very reluctantly, Cherise said his portion would be twenty thousand dollars and that was generous given what tuition costs these days.

"Besides, I know you, Juanell," she said. "You're not going to *invest* in anything." She said the word with the same inflection she used to say *a wasted life* or *down the toilet.* "I know what that means."

"Oh, you do?" Dodson retorted. "Tell me, then. What does it mean?"

"It means you'll partner up with one of your shady friends and put the money into something shady and even if you make money, you'll have to hide it from the IRS, but you won't care, you'll just have more money to invest into something else shady with your shady friends and end up in trouble with the law."

Dodson didn't say anything. He wondered if Cherise was psychic, a question he asked himself all too often. "I had no such intention," he said. "I nearly lost my life earning that money. I should get a bigger cut. It is *my* money."

"No one is saying you didn't earn it," Cherise said. "Nevertheless it's *our* money—don't shake your head like that. It's our money the same way my salary is *our* money, which you've been living off of for most of our marriage, and I'll also remind you Micah is *our* child. You're not some bystander. You're his father. You're responsible for his future, don't you get that by now?" Dodson hated it when she said things like that.

He used the twenty K to buy part interest in a tow truck from Freddie G, a former partner in the crack business. He didn't tell Cherise about Freddie; a man had to make some decisions for himself. Dodson's father had worked at a towing company after he got back from Iraq. He was an alcoholic and took his son along to do the heavy lifting. Dodson loved it. Shimmying under the car; setting the tow hooks, the wheel straps and the breakaway chains; his father operating the winch from inside the truck, proud when the boy was done. "Pretty fast," he'd say, looking at his watch. "You almost beat the record."

Dodson's new business went well for a couple of months. Until one day the police showed up, shut down the towing yard and confiscated the truck. Freddie G had been selling the cars Dodson towed in for cash. They were both arrested but fortunately, *very* fortunately, Freddie told the cops Dodson had nothing to do with that part of the business. Cherise never said anything but it made him feel worse.

Now he was adrift all over again. Since losing the money he hadn't found anything lucrative or prestigious enough to suit his family-size ego or idiosyncratic skill sets. He spent most of his time napping, eating, watching TV and sitting on the balcony looking down at the roof of his car. He'd gained weight and sometimes didn't bother changing out of his bathrobe, putting on regular clothes just before Cherise came home from work. If he felt energetic, he'd go to McLaren Park, smoke a J and bring a baggie of Doritos crumbs to feed the pigeons. He liked to watch them squabble and bump each other aside, hustling for a living like everybody else. Sometimes he'd listen to Mo and the other winos tell stories about fortunes lost, wicked women and how the government was spying on their cardboard houses and had satellites that only watched black people.

Cherise's mother, Gloria, felt bad for her daughter but she was delighted with Dodson's failure. It was clear proof of what she'd been trying to convince Cherise of for years. That Dodson was a bum and a loser, a mistake to be rectified. Gloria and Dodson took turns babysitting. It was shortly after the tow truck debacle when they inadvertently met in the living room.

"Oh, *it's you*," she said with utter contempt.

Dodson said, "Yes, it's me because I live here and this is my apartment, a fact you should have realized a long time ago. I guess it's difficult, given your age, deteriorating eyesight and the gradual loss of your mental capacities. Maybe you should be looking for an old folks' home. I'd be glad to help you."

"You don't contribute one penny to the rent," Gloria replied. "So it's not your apartment, it's Cherise's, who should have married Earl Cleveland and never let you in the door. Do you have a job yet?"

"I'm between projects," Dodson answered.

"You mean you're between stupid ideas," Gloria said. "It's a good thing too. One more of your ideas and everybody'd be in the poorhouse."

Dodson couldn't defend himself, a first for him. They needed some things for the baby. He'd go to Costco. That would be useful.

"Where're you going?" Gloria said as he put on his hoodie.

"Shopping."

"Why?" she said. "You can't buy a backbone at the store."

It was two weeks before Beaumont was shot in the drive-by. Dodson was sitting in the kitchen minding his own business and eating a bowl of Cocoa Puffs. Cherise came in. Even in the navy blue business suit, she couldn't hide how fine she was. Sometimes, like now, he couldn't believe they were actually married, that she'd chosen him from all the other men out there who would have mushed a dogsled across Siberia to get with her.

She sat down at the table across from him and stared with that *we need to talk, it's serious and it's not about me* look in her eyes. He ate another heaping spoonful of cereal. He knew from experience this would take a while.

She said, "We need to talk."

"Do we?" he said.

"Yes, we do. Look at me, Juanell. It's time to face the music."

"What music is that?"

"That you've become a lazy bum."

"I don't believe I've heard that song before. Who sings it?"

"I do," Cherise said, "and don't get smart with me and don't eat when I'm talking to you." He sighed and put down his spoon. She went on. "Financially we're getting by, but that doesn't mean you shouldn't be working. I am not your banker, I am your wife and I expect you to be upright and productive."

"That might be a little much right now," Dodson said. "How about I go for the upright part and leave the rest for later." Cherise was glaring at him and drumming her nails on the table. She used clear polish she applied herself and only added color during the holidays. When her guard was down and she wasn't upset about something, her voice reminded him of the jazz singer Shirley Horn—sultry and smooth, like good bourbon poured over warm molasses. Whispered in his ear, it made his heart do the mambo and increased his sperm count by fifty or sixty percent. Now she sounded like Patty LaBelle after she lost her makeup bag.

"Let me ask you something," Cherise said. "Do you want to live with a woman who ignores you, doesn't talk to you, and will only have sex with you on your birthday, assuming she hasn't thrown you out?"

Dodson thought the first two sounded all right. The third was alarming. "No," he said. "I think that would be very unpleasant."

"I expect you to have a job by the time I get home," she said.

"By the time you get home—*today?*"

"Yes, today."

"That ain't enough time to fill out an application," Dodson complained.

"It is if you get out of that damn bathrobe, brush your hair and walk fast," Cherise said. She got up and came around to his side of the table. He thought she was going to hit him but instead, she leaned over and gave him a lingering kiss, the one that said *you're my hero and if you get this right, the nagging will stop and I will bone you to sleep for the rest of your life*. As she went out of the door, she said, "Today, Juanell. No excuses."

After she left, he finished off the bowl of Cocoa Puffs. He would have had another but the box was empty. He went into the living room, sat on the sofa and turned on the TV. He thought better with some background noise. The voices made him feel he wasn't alone. Nine-to-five jobs were out, he decided. He imagined what his résumé would say. Dope salesman of the year 1996–97. Regional distributor of counterfeit Gucci bags. Assisted unlicensed private detective in saving his girlfriend from some crazy motherfuckers from Abu Ghraib. No legit business would hire him unless everybody else in the job market was struck down by the measles or got run over by a fleet of giant buses. The only possibilities left were criminal. He could join El Cuchillo's car-theft ring or sell fake lottery tickets for Alonzo or be security at one of Big Hanja's massage parlors. Probably not what Cherise had in mind.

There wasn't time to be fucking around but he went to the park and smoked a J. He only had one choice. One terrible, humiliating choice. He couldn't do it. But he had to do it. Couldn't do it. Had to do it. Couldn't. Had to. He picked up the phone and dialed. Then he disconnected. Dialed. Disconnected. Dialed. Disconnected. He thought of Cherise. "Fuck it," he said and made the call.

He was waiting in a booth at the Coffee Cup. He drank decaf so his anxiety and growing sense of shame wouldn't turn him into ashes. Ten minutes went by. Twenty minutes, each passing second a reminder he was being deliberately disrespected. At thirty-two minutes, he couldn't take it anymore. He got up just as all eyes went to the front door. A woman came in, dressed for a New Year's Eve party at Kanye's house, hair in elaborate curls, bling jingling.

She grinned when she saw him, sashaying over, doing a little dance move, her famous backside like two potbellied pigs fucking under leopard-skin tights. She set her Gucci bag on the table and sat down. Dodson gave it a quick once-over. The stitching was even and clean, the hardware solid metal, no chips or dark spots, GUCCI nicely engraved on the buckle. The logo pattern was the way it was supposed to be; one G facing forward, the other G facing backward. The letters were evenly spaced, the font was correct. It was the first authentic Gucci bag Dodson had ever seen.

"I'm sorry I'm late," Deronda said, not sorry at all. "Business, you know how it is. Busy, busy, busy. Making money is hard work, ain't it? Oh, I'm sorry. You wouldn't know anything about that, would you?"

Dodson and Deronda had a long antagonistic history, and over the years it had only grown worse. They sniped at and diminished each other at every opportunity, and they were very competitive. His up was her down and vice versa. Their last spat had been over their brief but fractious partnership in a food truck, D&D's Downhome Buttermilk Fried Chicken. They'd come together by necessity. Dodson had the financial know-how and it was Deronda's grandmother's recipe.

Unfortunately, working together in close confines hadn't been thoroughly thought out. They both insisted they were the boss and the other was useless. They criticized, complained, argued and yelled at each other every day. The food quality flagged, the reviews got sketchier. They got short with the customers. Dodson remembered one notable encounter. Deronda was at the service window and not in a good mood. A young couple arrived and the woman said, "We don't eat meat, eggs, gluten or soy. What should we get?"

And Deronda said, "The fuck out."

Dodson hadn't been able to stand it anymore and sold his half of the business at an after-Christmas price. He thought he'd gotten off the *Titanic* early but Deronda proved to be a sharp businesswoman, a surprise to them both. All she needed was her independence. She'd made the truck a success, eventually acquiring six trucks that roamed all over the city. They were listed among the top twenty-five in LA, and she'd done interviews for KCAL and KTLA and the *Long Beach Press-Telegram*. She was making good money and had put her son, Janeel, in private school. Dodson tried to convince himself she'd cooked the books, but that was bullshit since no books had been kept.

"How are you, Dodson?" she said. "How's everything in your unemployed world?"

"Everything's aight," Dodson said, looking down and stirring his decaf with his finger.

"And how's Micah? Is he doing all right? Getting fed and everything?"

"The baby's doing fine."

She got out her phone and called someone. While the other end was ringing, she said to Dodson, "Could you get me a caramel macchiato, please? Skim milk. I'm trying to keep my figure." Dodson got the drink and came back but Deronda kept talking for another five minutes. After she ended the call, she checked herself in a compact, patted her hair and said magnanimously, "Now what was it you wanted to talk to me about? Refresh my memory."

"I need a job," Dodson mumbled.

Deronda leaned forward and cupped her ear. "I'm sorry, you're talking very softly, Dodson. That's not like you. Could you say that again?"

Dodson cleared his throat. He took a deep breath so he wouldn't reach over the table and choke her to death. "I said, I need a job."

"My, my, my," Deronda said. "Life is full of surprises, ain't it? Is this the same Dodson that's always disrespected, called me names and questioned my judgment and intelligence? Was that you?"

"I don't think so. You must be talking about somebody else."

"Oh, it was you, all right. You even made fun of my boyfriends."

Dodson shrugged. "Melvin couldn't even read. What'd you expect me to do?"

"You're lucky I have a forgiving nature," Deronda said, "or I'd kick you to the curb like the mangy scoundrel you are. Now if we can get back to business. What kind of position were you looking for? Management? Finance? Human resources?"

"I just need a job."

"Uh-*huh*," she said, nodding. "Well, I believe I can help you with that. I happen to have a position on truck number four—that's four out of six, in case you haven't heard."

"What kind of position is it?" Dodson said.

"The lowest one I can possibly think of," she said. "It pays minimum wage with no benefits of any kind. When can you start?"

"Now."

"Excellent," she said. "Nothing like an eager beaver. If you work hard and keep your ass to the grindstone, I think you'll go far. I'm always looking for people like yourself—you know, desperate with no prospects. My assistant will call you. Have a wonderful day now." She was laughing as she went out the door.

Dodson had always prided himself on being cool, but somewhere during the conversation it had flaked away like dandruff. He almost brushed off his shoulders. He would take a nap before he went to work. Maybe he'd dream about dignity and see what it felt like. Sometimes you get an image of yourself as you are. Not what you used to be, would like to be, hope to be, deserve to be or anything else. Just you as you are. Dodson saw himself as if he were looking in a window; a twenty-nine-year-old ex-convict wearing big rubber gloves, galoshes and a do-rag soaked through with sweat and smelling like burned fried chicken and Tabasco sauce. He saw himself wiping down every surface, sweeping and mopping the floor, emptying the garbage, disposing of the cooking oil, sanitizing the ice machine, cleaning the coolers, appliances, cutting boards, fryers and steam table. He saw himself looking at his phone and reading Deronda's texts. *Be respectful to your superiors. Zero tolerance policy on weed. Hard work is the only way for advancement.*

He couldn't believe he'd reached yet another low point in his life. A graph of his ups and downs would start in the upper left-hand corner and step jaggedly but steadily down to the lower right corner and drop right off the page. The problem was—and always had been—direction, an outlet for his uniqueness, a vehicle for his energy. A place for his abilities. Since he was a kid, he'd been on the lookout for his destiny but nothing had ever seemed right. Maybe he didn't have one. Maybe he'd be one more humdrum, half-ass homeboy who dreamed big and ended up in a small life.

He tried to make a mental list of his accomplishments; a blank page except for a few things, mostly when he was running with Isaiah. He'd done some good, the work a useful outlet for his street acumen and quick wits. They'd partnered briefly, but Dodson's need for independence had overshadowed his judgment and he'd left. Another mistake. Another turning point where he should have gone left instead of right. He had to get back with Isaiah. The hard part would be convincing him.

Isaiah was prideful, prickly, too smart to be a homo sapien and he didn't like people second-guessing him. And he couldn't be hustled. There was no way to do this except go straight at him. Dodson would have to remind him what a great team they were and that everything couldn't be solved with a freakishly large brain. Yeah, they argued a lot but the competitiveness sharpened their wits, hyped up their motivation. Maybe Isaiah didn't see it the same way but that was the truth of it.

The immediate problem was a way in. Dodson had always been too cool to reach out but this was an emergency. His sex life had already been reduced to a kiss on the cheek and a long flannel nightgown. If he touched Cherise's body in a way that wasn't in passing, she gave him a look so threatening his balls took cover in his intestines.

Then he heard Beaumont was shot. It was a sad excuse, shameful in fact, but a bad pretext was better than none and a reason to make contact with Isaiah. The thing at the Hyatt had gone well. Hustling Marlene was easy, but Isaiah didn't seem grateful; he looked resentful. Well, he would be, wouldn't he? He was the same hardheaded ego-centric motherfucker he'd always been but it was time the boy faced facts. He needed a partner whether he wanted one or not. Reaching out would cost Dodson a little more stature with himself but he was barely off the ground as it was.

Dodson finished for the night, locked up the food truck, and headed for his car. He had that urge again. To visit Beaumont and Merrill. It was strong. He didn't so much resist as he did let it happen. He drove to the hospital. It was late and he was tired. What the fuck was he doing? He entered Intensive Care and walked down the hall toward Beaumont's room. A couple of patients slogged past with a mobile IV, others were on gurneys in curtained cubicles, a nurse in green scrubs was staring intently at a clipboard; a voice from the intercom: "Code blue, code blue, level A, twelve eleven, code blue code blue."

Dodson slowed his pace. *What are you going to say, Dodson? Whassup, Merrill? How's it going?* He stopped. He saw Merrill huddled with a doctor and a nurse just outside Beaumont's room, talking seriously, Merrill listening and nodding. Dodson's embarrassment thermometer spiked up to bird flu levels. It was rare for him, not knowing why he was doing something. "This is crazy," he said to himself. He turned quickly and went back the way he came.

Dodson showed up at the house unannounced again.

"Okay," Isaiah said. "What's going on?"

Dodson immediately got chesty. "Ain't nothin' *goin on*. I'm here to help your ass."

"I don't need any help."

"Yeah, I noticed how good things were going with Marlene," Dodson retorted. "You charmed that girl's thong off."

The phone rang. Isaiah had called Jasper four times and the little shit had finally called back. The little shit said, "I can't make it." He was eating something sticky. "I'm doing something."

"Where are you?" Isaiah said.

"Friend's place."

"Then get home *now*."

"I can't right now, okay? I'm doing something."

"Listen to me, Jasper. I'm doing this for your sake so—"

"It'll take me too long," Jasper whined. "I'll have to catch the bus."

"I'll come to you," Isaiah said. "Give me the address."

"You can't now. We're rehearsing."

"Listen to me, you idiot," he said. "I'm trying to keep you out of prison. Do you understand? *Prison.* There are people in there who will turn a spoiled little asshole like you inside out with a broom handle. Now give me the damn address."

CHAPTER ELEVEN

SHIT

Isaiah drove. "I'll tell you again," he said. "I don't need your help."

"Yes, you do," Dodson said.

"Don't I get a say in it?"

"Not if you're wrong."

"Wouldn't I know it if I was wrong?" Isaiah said.

"Sometimes you do and sometimes you don't," Dodson replied. "I don't want to re-litigate the matter but shall we count the number of times I saved your ass from certain death? With Walczak and them I got shot for my troubles, and by the way, you never thanked me for that."

"I came over to see you," Isaiah said, defensively.

"I know you came over to see me," Dodson said, "but you should have said something like, 'You know what, Dodson? The only reason I'm here today is because you're a bad-ass muthafucka and sometimes I think I'm invincible but the fact of the matter is, I'm not. The fact of the matter is, I get in over my head but I won't admit it because I'm prideful to the point of stupidity and I think my freakishly large brain will get me out of anything, which I continue to believe in spite of all evidence to the contrary. My other shortcoming is people, especially women. When it comes to the fairer sex, I am deaf, dumb, blind and lucky beyond measure to have a girlfriend of any kind, let alone Grace.'"

Isaiah looked at him. "You think I should have said all that?"

"Or something like it," Dodson said. Isaiah's phone buzzed.

Dwight was sitting up in bed, his phone on speaker, one hand twirling the stiletto like a cheerleader's baton. He couldn't wait to get out of this cramped, one-bedroom shitbox. There was no room for all his clothes. Suits and dozens of shirts were neatly hung on the curtain rods. They looked like racks at the dry cleaner. The tiny closet and all the drawers were full, piles of neatly folded clothes in and on anywhere there was space; plastic boxes overflowing with underwear, socks and T-shirts.

"Where are you?" Dwight said.

"On my way to Jasper's rehearsal," Isaiah said.

"You're in for a fucking treat, believe me. What's happening?"

"I don't know what that means," Isaiah said.

"It means, have you made any fucking progress," Dwight said, raising his voice. "I've got to tell Angus."

"Making any progress doing what?" Isaiah snapped back. "Chasing the alters around? Talking to them when they have nothing to say? Trying to find evidence that doesn't exist? Tell Angus, yeah, I've made all kinds of progress." He hung up.

Dwight bellowed and threw the stiletto. It tumbled through the air end over end and stuck in the drywall with a *thunk*. The knife was custom made, carbon steel, five-and-a-half inches long, its tip, sharp as a hypodermic. Stilettos were illegal to carry in most of the US. Dwight kept it under his jacket in a tube-like scabbard on his hip. He practiced whipping it out. It took him less than a second.

A true stiletto had no cutting edge, it was strictly for stabbing. The method taught by the *scherma di stiletto siciliano* or the school of Sicilian fighting in the sixteenth century was to plunge the blade into your opponent and twist it around to cause maximum damage. It was Dwight's preferred method too, the one he'd used against seven of Angus's enemies and the one he'd like to use on that prick Isaiah. Stick it through his eardrum and puncture the one on the other side.

His temper was a problem though, coming in bursts like a cannon with a fuse a half inch long. Angus was always restraining him and saying something shitty at the same time. "For fuck's sake," he'd say, "you can't kill *everybody.* Use your fucking head—like Tyler. I wish I had two of him and one less of you." *Tyler,* Dwight thought. *So long, asshole.* He wished he could have been there to watch that know-it-all prick bleed out on the floor.

Dwight grew up in Stoddard, Arizona, off Highway 85, about 150 miles southwest of Phoenix. Take your eyes off the road to read a text and you'd pass right by it. There were no good parts of the Sonoran Desert but Stoddard was an infected toenail or an unwashed ball sack. He couldn't figure out what the town was *doing* out there. Were people farming? Farming what? Cactus? Gila monsters? Rocks? There was no manufacturing or tourists or lakes where you could water-ski. All the trees were plastic and only grew at Christmastime. Everybody lived in crap houses and crap trailers and there was nothing to do but drink, do drugs and try to get a blow job from anybody with lips.

Dwight's family lived on a scrawny ranch and raised a scrawny herd of cattle. They were a lot of fucking work. You needed two acres of pasture to feed an animal for a year. There was a vast tract of federal land around the ranch but it was mostly desert so you didn't need two acres, you needed a whole bunch of fucking acres and somebody had to herd them there on a broken-down ATV that stalled out and left you stranded in the middle of an unwashed ball sack.

Dwight tried really hard, but he could never quite clean the cow turds off of his whole person. There was always a streak on his sleeve, a clod on his boot, a smear on his pants. Delighted, the kids at school nicknamed him "Shit." Not "Dwight's a Shit" or "That Shitty Dwight," just Shit. That's all. SHIT. Even his friends called him that.

"Hey, Shit, howya doing?"

"You going to the game, Shit?"

"You know where I can score, Shit?"

Maybe that was one of the reasons Dwight was always angry. He was the kind of guy who looked for a fight, *wished* for a fight; who hoped some asshole would underestimate him and get the beating of his life.

Dwight wasn't big, but he *seemed* big and nobody who knew him messed with him. In a playground brawl he'd try and kill you. Literally, *kill you*. Even if you could win the fight, who'd want to get into it with somebody who wanted—not to break your nose or give you a black eye—but sincerely wanted you dead? The county sheriff called him the Tasmanian Devil, which Dwight thought was a lot better than SHIT.

Dwight always carried a weapon. A knife, screwdriver, box cutter, rock, brass knuckles, anything really. When he was fourteen years old, he broke his older sister's jaw with a roll of pennies in his hand. His father started to whip him with a piece of garden hose he kept around just for that purpose. Dwight ran into the shed and as his father came after him he clocked the fucker right between his eyes with a shovel. There was a trench in the yard where a sewer line had been dug up. Dwight rolled his father into it and would have buried him if his mother hadn't stopped him. Dwight took his dad's money and car keys and got the fuck out of Stoddard.

He went to Phoenix. He hung out around 19th and Thunderbird, staying away from the Circle K even in the daytime, no point going there unless you're looking to score meth. He robbed street people, broke into apartments and smashed and grabbed. He stole old cars and sold them for scrap. He worked menial jobs like sweeping up and taking out the trash but only if he could rob the place. He slept under a bridge with the bums and the winos. They were noisy and had stupid fights but at least they didn't bother him.

He liked gun shows. Walking up and down the aisles, past table after table and display after display, gawking at the neat rows of weaponry. The handguns, rifles, shotguns, assault rifles, machine guns, antiques and exotics, each with a convenient price tag he couldn't afford. The guns had locks on them so you could pick one up without waiting for a store owner to open a display case. You could aim it, admire it, work the ejector, slide back the bolt, pull the trigger, ask questions— anything you wanted except take the gun home. He imagined shooting people and how cool that would be. No discussion, no argument, no negotiating, just give me the fuck what I want or catch a hollow point in your solar plexus. He thought about all the people he would blast, starting with his father. He'd put that hose in that fucker's mouth and shoot him through the nozzle.

Angus must have been watching him, this kid with a dirty face and raggedy clothes, drooling over the guns but never buying anything. Angus made him an offer. Buy a gun with Angus's money and get paid a commission. Dwight's first reaction was disbelief. Somebody was actually going to *pay* him for that? It was perfect and easy and fun, and after a few purchases, he made enough money to *buy his own fucking gun!* He chose a pre-owned Smith and Wesson Model 29 .44 Magnum revolver, the Dirty Harry gun. It was heavy and only held six rounds but it never jammed and all you needed was one shot to kill anything in America. He shot the shit out of that gun. Half of everything in the desert had a fucking hole in it and there were enough dead rabbits and ground squirrels to feed every carnivore in Africa.

He got along with Angus—sort of. He was demanding, always yelling, and the ugliest fucker Dwight had ever seen. But he paid well enough. Pretty soon, Dwight was making trips from Arizona to California by himself and doing other things for the old man as well. Dwight was the guy on the ground, the middleman, the one who made the sale, picked up the money and took all the risks. Back then, he liked it. He was young, full of testosterone, and was hooked on violence.

Angus had a rival. A middle-aged woman who called herself La Balla. She wore mariachi clothes, including the wide-brimmed white hat and a cluster of fake red carnations behind her ear. Her third husband, a three-time loser, drove her around the neighborhood in a neon green 1972 Lincoln Continental convertible. She was dismissive of Angus and was taking a lot of his gang sales.

Angus sent Dwight to *teach her a lesson.* Underneath her outfit, La Balla wore a corset. She had to. Nobody who was five-two and chunky could have a waist like a ballerina. That worried Dwight. He didn't want to use a gun for his first kill. He wanted to *feel* it, make it personal. He thought about a knife but it might be blocked by a metal stay or an eyelet or a heavy layer of spandex. That's when he came up with the idea to use a stiletto. That's why the weapon was created in the first place. To pierce chain mail and leather armor. Not having an edge allowed it to penetrate deep.

Dwight caught La Balla walking from her car to her house. It was dark and he hid behind a cypress tree that shaded her porch in the daylight. As she opened her bag to get her keys, he stepped up behind her, cupped his hand over her mouth and said, "Buenos noches, bitch." The stupid fucking hat was in his face. He reached around, stabbed her in the chest, twisting the blade for maximum damage. She flopped around like a tied-up alligator before she slumped to the ground. It seemed to take a long time.

Angus was furious. "I told you to teach her a lesson, not kill her!" he bellowed.

"I taught her a lesson," Dwight said. "I taught her how to die."

Everything was more or less okay until Tyler entered the picture. Angus took to him right away; a decorated ex-marine, smart, easy to like, and he knew ordnance. He was good-looking too. The son Angus never had. Angus treated him respectfully, never once calling him a nitwit or dimwit or numbskull, hardly ever raising his voice and asking him his opinion when he was making a decision. And get this: Tyler got a percentage of the profits. Angus made him a fucking partner! All the years Dwight had put in and he was still on a fucking paycheck. Dwight decided that one way or another, that old fuck would get his.

Dwight wasn't looking forward to telling Angus that Isaiah hadn't gotten anywhere. He'd go into one of his rants and blame whoever was in the room. It didn't matter, Dwight thought. Isaiah wasn't going to figure out what happened that night. Nobody could. Not unless they were there.

The address was a two-story commercial building on the funky side of 7th Street. It might have been respectable thirty years before, but now it was dilapidated and listing, bricks missing from the façade, paint peeling. The first floor was an abandoned plumbing-supplies distributor; the second floor had mattresses over the windows. The stairs were narrow and steep. The door on the landing was covered with stickers for various bands. No doorknob, just pliers sticking out of it. Weed smell instead of air. As they reached the top of the stairs they were assaulted by a brain-splattering cacophony that bore no resemblance to music; more like cats in a garbage can getting kicked across a parking lot.

"The fuck is that?" Dodson said. "I bet you any money there ain't no bruthas in there."

The lead singer was dressed in black leather pants, black tank top with an AC/DC logo, shag cut, black-black hair, requisite tats and bare dirty feet. She was strangling the mike and screaming something unintelligible. A chica was on bass—fifties pompadour, wraparounds, black tights, gangsta flannel.

On guitar, a man in his fifties—chinos, a pink polo shirt and a Rolex. He rocked back and forth, eyes closed, as if playing the same three notes over and over again took his full concentration. He was probably financing the band. Jasper was on drums, headbanging while he banged on the drum kit seemingly at random. He was like a hyperactive kid with no talent and a double dose of Ritalin. All he was making was noise.

"The fuck is he doing?" Dodson said, cringing. "I know dogs with a better sense of rhythm."

"Cut, cut, cut," the singer said. "Fuck, Jasper, stay on the goddamn beat. You're the fucking drummer, for Christ's sake. You *are* the beat."

"I'm on the beat," Jasper mumbled dolefully. He picked a bottle of beer off the floor and guzzled it.

"She's right," said the chica. "You're all over the fucking place."

A girl was watching from the shadows. "Leave him alone," she said.

"Eat ass, Lydia," Chica said, sneering. "And you're a lousy lay too."

"You're really bad, Jasper," the older guy said. "I mean *really* bad."

Jasper threw a drumstick at him. "Fuck you, gramps. Go somewhere and have a heart attack."

"Take ten," the singer said. "Maybe when we get back Jasper will play better, fat fucking chance."

Jasper stayed and hung his head, the others dispersing into the warren of rooms. The shadow girl, Lydia, went over to him, put her hands on his face and kissed him. "You were playing great, babe," she said. "Don't pay any attention to that bitch." Jasper saw Isaiah and groaned.

"I'll see you later," Lydia said. She kissed him again and left.

Jasper led Isaiah and Dodson into an anything room. Broken furniture, card table, old amps, a three-legged keyboard, cardboard boxes, clothes, DJ equipment—anything. "Who's this guy?" Jasper said, sneering at Dodson.

"You mean me?" Dodson said. "You better get respectful, son, or I'll beat you to death with them drumsticks."

Jasper smelled like beer and cigarettes. He picked up his jacket and searched around in the pockets. Suddenly, he was alarmed. He turned the pockets inside out. "Shit, man! My ring, man. My fucking ring! It's gone."

"I'll buy you another one," Isaiah said, meaning it.

"No, man. It's the ring Lydia bought me! It was like this cool skull!"

"Later, Jasper."

"No! I've got to find that fucking ring!" Jasper shouted. "Lydia saved up to buy it. She'll be *pissed.*" He started throwing things around and looking in stupid places. "Where is it? Where is it?"

"Jasper, we don't have time for this," Isaiah said, nearing violence. "The ring could be anywhere."

"No, no! I have to find it!"

"I know who's got the ring," Dodson said casually. Isaiah looked at him.

"You do?"

"Remember I was tellin' you about women?"

They found the chica out on the fire escape, smoking a joint. "Who the fuck are you guys?" she said.

"Give the boy his ring back," Dodson said.

She huffed. "I don't have any ring. What are you, a cop?"

"It wasn't the so-called singer," Dodson said. "Jasper plays bad so she steals his ring? That makes no sense. And it wasn't gramps either. What's he gonna do with a cheap-ass skull ring? No, it was you, bitch."

The girl puffed up and stepped forward. "Did you just call me a bitch?"

"You act like a bitch and that's what I'll call you," Dodson said. Fearing a fight, Isaiah stepped between them.

"Okay, that's enough."

"Get out the way, Isaiah," Dodson said, moving him aside. "You said Lydia was a lousy lay," he went on. "You used to be together, didn't you? Jasper took her away from you. You was jealous and stole the ring because Lydia gave it to him. Now quit messing around and hand the damn thing over."

Chica's face flushed. "I'm telling you, I don't have it." Isaiah realized Dodson was right.

"Could be in her bag," he said.

Dodson shook his head. "Have you ever known a woman who would leave her bag somewhere in a house full of people? She doesn't have one. The ring's in her shirt pocket."

"Oh, really?" she said. "How do you know?"

"You're wearing tights. Will you give him back the ring now?"

Jasper was ecstatic to get the ring back, but didn't say thank you and insisted on going back to the condo before he would talk. Isaiah said no, they'd talk outside. They came out of the building. Weirdly, Jasper focused on the scraggly azalea bushes planted around the perimeter of the building. They were flowering despite their condition. Jasper shivered and hugged himself.

"Christ," he said. "Why do they grow those fucking things?"

"What's wrong with azaleas?" Dodson said. "I kind of like 'em myself."

"Let's talk now, Jasper," Isaiah said. Jasper was on the phone.

"Hey, Ma," he said. "Did you do my laundry? Well, I couldn't find my Slayer T-shirt and I need it…no, that's Black Sabbath, stupid. I said *Slayer.* Christ, don't you know anything?"

"Jasper, get off the phone," Isaiah said.

"Just have it ready when I get home, okay?"

"Jasper, *get off the phone.*"

"What do you mean, you're not home?" Jasper said. "Where the fuck are you?" Isaiah grabbed him, got him in an arm lock, and pushed him face-first into the building, the phone clattering to the pavement.

"OWWWW SHIT!" he yelled. "That fucking hurts, dude!"

"What did you see that night?" Isaiah said. His teeth were clenched.

"OWWWW SHIT!"

"Talk to me or I'll snap it off and you'll never play the drums again, which wouldn't be a bad thing. Now answer my questions."

"Okay, okay! Let go of my arm!" Jasper shouted, but Isaiah kept his cheek mashed against the bricks.

"What do you know about Tyler?"

"Him? He was an asshole," Jasper said.

"Because?"

"Because he was messing around with Christiana. He wanted to break us up."

"You wanted him dead, didn't you?" Isaiah said.

Jasper didn't hesitate. "Sure," he replied. "We all wanted him—well, maybe not dead, but fucked up, that's for sure." Isaiah cranked his arm higher. Jasper howled. "OOWWWWWW SHIT!"

"Did you have anything to do with hiring the killers?" Isaiah said.

"Me? Fuck no!" Jasper said. "Are you crazy? I party, man, ask anybody! They'll tell you the same thing!"

"Did you hear anything from the others?"

"No! No! I didn't!" Jasper said. Isaiah looked at Dodson.

"He's lying," Dodson said.

"OOWWWWW SHIT!"

"What happened that night?" Isaiah said.

"I wasn't there!" Jasper said.

"What do you mean?"

"I mean I wasn't there, dude—OOWWWW SHIT! There was all this shit going on and everybody was freaking out! Not my problem. I stayed away." Isaiah held him there, looked at Dodson again. He shrugged.

"Let me fucking go!" Jasper screamed. "You're breaking my goddamn arm! *Pleeease!*" Isaiah let him go, the kid grimacing and rubbing his arm. "Fuck you, asshole!" he said. Then, to Dodson, "You too, you fucking shrimp!" He picked up his phone and made a call while he hurriedly walked away.

"Did you believe him?" Isaiah said. "That he wasn't in on the murder?"

"I tend not to believe anybody," Dodson said, "especially when there's four or five of the same muthafucka. One thing I know, he couldn't have done it by himself."

They drove in silence. Isaiah was dreading the next conversation. Dodson didn't say anything but you could feel his smug satisfaction like cool air blowing in from the dash vents.

"You were right about the ring, okay?" Isaiah said.

"Yes, I know," Dodson said. "This is not a new experience. I'm frequently right but I suppose you would know that better than anyone."

"The case is over," Isaiah said. "Jasper was my last hope." He glanced in the rearview mirror. "I think we've got a tail."

Four or five cars back, a ten-year-old Camaro was changing lanes when Isaiah did, keeping the same number of cars between them and following when he made a turn. "I think those are the killers," Isaiah said.

"I should have took the bus home," Dodson said.

Isaiah wanted a better look at them. He moved into the empty right lane and clicked on the turn signal. The Camaro moved over too. There were no cars between them so it had to pull up right behind him. He saw them clearly.

"Two women."

"We in trouble now," Dodson said.

"They're having some kind of argument," Isaiah said.

"Prob'ly about how to kill us."

Isaiah made the turn and then another into a maze of deserted streets; he didn't want to run over anybody. He accelerated hard, the Kia's engine straining. Then he made a tire-screeching right, then a left, then another right, driving too fast to look back, then a snap turn into an alley, where he rolled to a stop and turned off the lights.

"You left them in the dust." Dodson chuckled. "Don't nobody keep up with my boy." The Camaro turned into the alley, the women were laughing.

"Who the fuck are they?" Dodson said. "Wonder Woman and her sister?"

Isaiah was embarrassed but had to shake them. His advantage: he knew the neighborhood and they didn't. He drove on into traffic, changed lanes a couple of times, putting some cars between himself and his pursuers. He came to a red light at Long Beach Boulevard, didn't stop, and made a sharp right.

"Get ready to jump," he said. Before the Camaro could follow, he pulled over, got out of the car. He and Dodson ran into Nifty Dry Cleaners.

Mrs. Chin, an ex-client, was behind the counter. She was selecting a mystery chocolate from a box of See's while she slowly chewed something caramel. "Youf inf twable, yef?" she said, which Isaiah took to mean, "You in trouble, yes?"

"I need to use your car." She got her bag, threw him a ring of keys.

"Flay fenta," she said.

Isaiah drove the gray Sentra out of the lot and down an alley.

"How'd they get onto you?" Dodson said. "Who told them you was at Jasper's place?" Isaiah was wondering about that himself.

"Gia knew we were going there," he said. "Dwight knew and he probably told Angus. Jasper knew and maybe the other alters picked up on it. In other words, everybody." Isaiah thought a bit, looked at Dodson. "Why didn't Jasper ask for a ride home?" he said.

"Yeah," Dodson said. "Jasper don't drive, his girlfriend left, and nobody else in the band was gonna give him a lift."

"He was on the phone when we left," Isaiah said. "Maybe he called them."

*　　*　　*

Twenty minutes ago, Annie was laughing about catching up to Isaiah, but by the time they got back to the motel room she was her carping self again. "That was so stupid!" Annie said. "I told you not to chase him. Now he knows we're onto him! We'll never get him now."

"We might have caught him," Sal said with a shrug. She found a warm beer and screwed off the cap.

"Caught him?" Annie said. "You mean out there on a public street? And then what? We shoot him in front of a hundred pedestrians? That makes a lot of sense."

Sal shrugged and drank the beer. "I chased him and now it's over so get off my case."

"No, I won't get off your case," Annie said. "You never listen to me and look what happened. You've blown the whole deal, and why? Because you always want to prove you're a swinging dick."

Sal was getting angry. She set the beer down. "You better shut up now, Annie." They went quiet. There's a particular kind of stillness before a fight starts, a moment where you either reconsider or the shit is on. Annie backed up three steps, giving herself room. Sal tensed, bent her knees a little and spread her feet. *The shit was on.*

Annie lowered her voice and spoke steadily without pause. *"Don't tell me to shut up Sal don't you ever tell me to shut up you stupid bitch I'm not afraid of you who do you think you are you stupid fucking bitch you want to get into it let's go—"* Annie didn't raise her voice but the words were getting louder. Sal was breathing hard, her head expanding, her pulse like a war drum, her anger coiling into fury. Annie didn't stop. *I'll fuck you up do you hear me Sal I'll kick your ass so go ahead and make a move I'm fucking ready for you I've always been ready for you don't mean shit to me you never did you stupid fucking bitch—"*

"Shut up, Annie."

"Fuck you shut up you fucking cunt why don't you bring your fat ass over here and make me but you won't because you're a fucking cunt—"

Something broke inside of Sal, a pressure gauge, a release valve. Blindly, wildly, she charged, screaming, "I'll kill you, you fucking bitch!" She grabbed Annie by the shirt, took a punch in the face, and threw her into the credenza, a lamp crashing to the floor. Annie was up in an instant, a fucking *instant*. She hunched low and took a fighting stance as she backed up between the two beds. Sal saw what Annie was going for—her folding knife was lying on the coverlet. She'd used it to cut the pizza. They lunged for the knife at the same time. Annie was quicker, got the knife and rolled off the other side of the bed. In another fucking instant, she was up on her feet, the knife blade open and ready.

Annie was fierce and unafraid, a killer who had killed many times before, but so had Sal. They faced each other, every slight, insult and contemptuous look, every dismissive remark, scowl of disapproval and derisive laugh boiling up inside of them; a surging ruthless energy as unstoppable as an axe descending on a prisoner's neck. Violence between lovers, Sal thought, was never about the present. Each of them was proof of their fucked-up lives. Each was to blame for their barren futures.

Sal had to arm herself. She tried to pick up the chair but it was heavy and awkward and a leg banged into the wall. Annie screamed, lunged forward and slashed Sal's arm. Sal stumbled and fell on her back. Annie was on top of her, the knife raised, Sal holding Annie's wrist, a foot between the knifepoint and her death. Sal punched her with the other hand. Annie cried out and fell to the side. Sal ripped the knife away, wrapped an arm around Annie's neck and held the blade to her throat. "Don't move, Annie, or I'll cut your fucking head off."

"FUCK YOU!" Annie screamed. She grabbed Sal's arm and tried to pull it off while she kicked and writhed. Sal grimaced, growled and pressed the blade in. "I told you not to move!"

Somebody hammered on the door. "Hey! What the fuck are you doing in there?" The guy from the front desk. "You cut that shit out or I'll call the fucking cops!" He banged on the door again. "You hear me in there? And if you fucked up the room you'll pay for it!"

Sal let Annie go. She got up, coughing; she leaned over and vomited. There was a cut on her neck. She touched it and looked at the blood on her fingers. Sal's slashed arm was bleeding heavily, the blood pouring out of the wound. She was going into shock. "Help me," she said.

Annie wiped her hand on her pants and looked at Sal for the longest moment of their lives.

Sal lay on the gurney as the doc and a nurse stanched the wound. "What happened to you?" the doctor said.

"I cut myself shaving," Sal said. They stitched her up, bound her arm and set it in a sling. She got pain medication, a tetanus shot and antibiotics. Annie was let in to see her. She stood alongside the gurney, not speaking, not making eye contact, not saying she was sorry but neither did Sal.

"Go back to the motel," Sal said. Annie left. Sal closed her eyes against the harsh fluorescents and felt the pain meds' slow creep. Amazing, to be so far away from love. Sal didn't know when she'd crossed the line into hatred or maybe there'd never been one. But when this was over, she'd kill Annie. If Annie didn't kill her first.

CHAPTER TWELVE
Some List

Grace walked through McClarin Park. It was a nice day and she was on her way to meet TK for the church picnic. She was looking forward to it, curious about his mysterious love interest and eager to meet his friends. A couple of years ago, she would have been intimidated, worried she'd be rejected and afraid of doing or being the wrong thing.

At the time, her psyche was already fragile. Then the Walczak thing happened and smashed it to pieces. The evil son of a bitch had killed her father and avenging his death had brought her no satisfaction or relief. The pain still visited her every day.

It was agonizing to leave Isaiah but going to New Mexico was good for her. She reconnected with her mom. They hadn't seen each other in ten years and catching up was equal parts heartbreaking and joyful. It was good to get away from Isaiah too. Their time together had been so intense, so fraught with danger and chaos that the artsy town of Santa Fe, with the gentle desert hills rolling into the horizon, was a sanctuary. Peace. She had longed for Isaiah; she daydreamed about him and held his imaginary hand even when she was with Noah.

She meant it when she told Isaiah she still had problems. There was her baggage, of course, but therapy had also uncovered a deep well of self-hatred. Thankfully, Isaiah hadn't seen it and hopefully never would.

Frustration with herself would bring it out. Minor things. She'd get stuck on a painting, she couldn't remember where she parked her car, she burned the eggs, she missed an appointment, someone beat her to the parking space, the shirt she ordered from Amazon was the wrong size. Instead of returning the shirt, she'd throw it in the trash. Instead of finishing the painting she'd slash it with a box cutter. Instead of methodically looking for her car, she'd walk or take the bus, muttering, "Fuck the goddamn car," and with every incident came a torrent of self-abuse, cursing and berating and yelling at herself for being so stupid, clumsy and inept. It went on and on until she was spent and sobbing.

"It's called displacement," her therapist said. Her name was Rebecca. She was somewhere in her fifties; warm, wise and safe. "You're angry about one thing and it comes out in ways that don't have anything to do with the real source."

"What's the real source?" Grace said.

"That's what we're going to talk about."

Grace was angry about a lot of things. Some rational, some not. She was angry about her mother abandoning her and that she was failing as an artist. She was angry because she'd spent so much of her life in self-imposed isolation. She was angry because she had to kill a man and that Walczak had murdered her father. She was angry because she had to leave Isaiah, the love of her life, and go to New Mexico because she was so fucked up. Because she couldn't handle her shit, because her goddamn *problems* dictated what she could and couldn't do. Angry because she was always *always* in her own fucking way. She wondered if there were other people like her; walking around, seemingly normal and workaday, while underneath, a blazing pool of magma waited to erupt, incinerate and lay waste to reason.

Rebecca said the anger was dangerous. She warned Grace that one day it would be about something more than burned eggs or a parking space; it would be about something important. A crisis where the stakes were injury, death or worse.

"Or worse?" Grace said, almost laughing. "That's kind of heavy, isn't it?"

Rebecca stared at her. She was serious. "You see it all the time," she said. "Road rage, a cop beating a bag lady, a parent killing a child, a wife murdering her husband. Something small sets them off and by the time they come out of it, they've done something irreparable. That could happen to you, Grace."

She shifted in her chair. "So what do I do about it?"

"You're not sick and you're not a slave to your emotions," Rebecca said. "When you go off like that it's a decision. A bad habit. Exert control or I'm telling you, in all sincerity, you will live to regret it." Grace came away from the session talking to herself. *That's not gonna happen ever again, do you hear me, asshole? You will be aware. You will handle your shit.*

As the weeks went by, the tantrums lessened but didn't go away. They were less the first-string quarterback and more the substitute, on the bench but warmed up and ready to go. Put me in, Coach. Grace's fear of the present gradually receded, her fear of the future saw possibilities instead of disaster. She spent fewer nights wrestling with her nightmares, fewer nights painting and drinking coffee to keep the demons away. Sometimes she would wake in the morning, feeling—at first, she couldn't identify it until she realized she felt *good*, like the actors in the Sleep-Eze commercials, smiling and yawning as they stretched, ready for another day. It was both strange and exhilarating. How had this happened, she wondered? She marveled at the power of human contact and understanding.

She could remember the exact moment when she decided to go home. It was daybreak. She was standing on her balcony in her boxer shorts and T-shirt, drinking her second cup of coffee, when she heard someone calling her name. At first, it was hollow and distant, as if it was coming from a canyon somewhere in the foothills. Bit by bit, it increased in volume. And then a tiny figure appeared on her heart's horizon, waving wildly and breaking into a run. She could see the familiar outline—tall, straight and sure, and then the contours of his face and the color of his eyes and it was Isaiah and she was crying and there was nothing better in the world than his arms around her, his breath in her ear, his voice, as beautiful as the dawn. The next day, she packed, said goodbye to Noah, and made the long drive to California, wondering all the while, *Am I too late? Is Isaiah with someone else? Has he forgotten me?* In a way, it didn't matter. She would love him whether he liked it or not.

About sixty people had gathered around a cluster of picnic tables, covered with an array of colored bowls, casserole dishes, Dutch ovens and Tupperware. There was macaroni and cheese, macaroni salad, Jell-O salad with shreds of carrot, oxtails, hot wings, green beans with almonds, pig's feet, corn bread, collard greens cooked with ham hocks, red beans and rice, corn on the cob. A feast too good for a mere king.

"Who is this, TK?" Reverend Arnall said with a smile as warm as the day.

"This here's my friend, Grace Monarova," TK said. "Grace, this is Reverend Arnall."

"A pleasure to meet you, Reverend," Grace said. The man had stature; a presence both solid and embracing. In his eyes, you were a child of God.

"No, I'm only the reverend in church," he protested. "At picnics, my name is Daniel."

"Okay, Daniel," she said, with a smile as warm as his.

"We're glad to have you, Grace. Please partake of God's bounty and enjoy yourself."

The women were equally as welcoming; not shy at all about introducing themselves and telling her they were glad she'd come and asking why she was hanging around with an old man like TK. They filled her paper plate with so much food it nearly folded in the middle. She'd never had a meal this good or satisfying. Her limited social life had been spent with artists, everybody with an agenda; wanting something, needing something. There was always intrigue wherever you went but it wasn't evident here. Just ordinary people, talking, laughing, gossiping, scolding their kids, appreciating the food, the weather and the grace of God. Grace had always been iffy about God, but here in the shade of the maple trees, their branches sieving sunlight into gilded beams and backlit by a sky blue as a cornflower, she thought these folks might be onto something.

TK sat down next to her with no plate and a cup of red punch. "There she is over there," he said nervously. "That's Gloria." Grace saw a stout woman in a dark print dress, wearing glasses with rhinestones in them and black shoes with thick crepe soles. She was at the dessert table, seemingly in charge as people brought their offerings. To some, she afforded a charitable smile, to others she reacted as if they'd brought their laundry or a dirty football. She seemed severe to the point of hostility. TK said she had been the vice principal at Carver Middle School for twenty-five years and she definitely looked the part.

Grace swallowed and cleared her throat. "She's very, um, attractive, TK."

"Ain't she though?" TK said, looking at something in a parallel universe. "Now here's where I get stuck, see. How'm I supposed to talk to her when she's all busy like that, and she's *always* busy. I just go on up there out of the blue and say, 'Hi, my name is TK, and I own a wrecking yard'?"

"Yeah, I see your point," Grace said. She understood why TK was so anxious. She didn't know how old he was but there weren't many years left to find love. She was much younger and had felt the same way. She got up from the table.

"Where're you goin'?" TK said.

"To get some help."

"Gloria?" Reverend Arnall intoned, like there was pleasure in saying her name. "I'd like you to meet Thomas Marion Kahill. TK is a respected businessman. We've known each other since we were children. Thomas, this is Gloria Simmons, a stalwart of our church and our community." Grace sat down close enough to hear the conversation.

"Pleased to meet you," TK said, taking off the STP cap he wasn't wearing. Gloria looked at him for what seemed like a long time, as if she were trying to recognize his species or whether he had some kind of mental condition.

Sensing unpleasantness, the reverend said, "Excuse me, I should be mingling," and he moved off like Christ had called him to prayer. TK didn't know what to do with his hands, taking them in and out of his pockets and wiping the invisible oil off on his pants.

"I'm pleased to meet you too, Thomas," Gloria said, with an expression that said she wasn't pleased at all. "I've seen you in church, haven't I?"

"Oh, yes, ma'am," he said. Grace cringed. *She's not your aunt, TK.* He corrected himself but not before Gloria's glare put a knot on his head. "I mean, yes Gloria, you have...seen me in church that is...more than once I'd say." He stood there with a strained smile on his face, a drop of sweat trickling down his neck. Grace couldn't stand it. *Say something, TK!*

"Did you bring a dessert?" Gloria asked sharply.

"No, I'm afraid not," TK said.

"Did you bring anything at all?"

"I was going to but—"

She harrumphed. "Just like a man, showing up empty-handed and expecting to be fed. Well, run along now. I'm busy."

Grace and TK returned to their table. TK looked miserable, dabbing his face with a napkin. "This is hopeless," he said. "I feel like a damn fool. I've only known her a minute and a half and she don't like me already." Grace didn't say anything. Advice to the lovelorn was way outside her wheelhouse.

"I don't know if I would say that," she said. She was a terrible liar.

"I'm goin' back to the yard," TK said. "You comin'?"

"No, I think I'll stay awhile."

She was helping the ladies clean up when a woman about her age approached. She was striking without trying to be. Beautiful, yes, but more than that, she was sure of herself. She knew herself. She was a truth teller. It was obvious.

"Grace? I'm Cherise, Dodson's wife."

"Oh, my God." Grace laughed. "I'm so glad to meet you." They hugged and held on. You can tell a lot from a hug. They were going to be friends for a long time.

"I'm glad to meet you too," Cherise said. "My, oh, my," she said with a wry smile. "We know how to pick 'em, don't we?" They talked about Isaiah and Dodson, their stubbornness, idiosyncrasies and blind spots. They laughed a lot.

"I heard how you met TK," Cherise said. "He's a sweetheart, isn't he?"

"Yeah, he is," Grace said. "Did you know he has a thing about your mom?"

Cherise reared her head back. "*My* mom? Lord have mercy. He'd have a better chance at romancing a gladiator or the Great Wall of China."

"No offense," Grace said. "But I'm a little puzzled myself."

"Mama has a low opinion of men generally," Cherise said. "My father, Josiah, was a womanizer and scoundrel. I told her, *everybody* told her, but she ignored us. When he ran off to North Carolina with a barmaid she finally had to accept it." Cherise looked at her mother, scolding someone about something. "It left a mark," she added. "What's TK going to do?"

"I don't know," Grace said. "There's no place for their paths to cross except church." Cherise thought a moment.

"What?" Grace said.

"Mama belongs to a book club."

Isaiah was wrung out from the car chase but brightened the moment he saw Grace. She was in his living room, waiting for him—*him,* and it was thrilling. She told him about TK and Gloria as they shopped at Vons.

"*Gloria?*" he said.

"I know."

They went to McClarin Park and she watched him play basketball. They stopped by the Coffee Cup and Isaiah introduced Grace to Verna, who always greeted Isaiah with a warm "There's my hero!" He also introduced Grace to Verna's croissants. "She told me her recipe," Isaiah said. "Snowflakes and a tub of butter."

They made brief but fire-breathing love, napped awhile, and took Ruffin for a walk. They went to the movies but neither really watched, content to sit in the dark, eating popcorn and holding hands with buttery fingers. They sat side by side on the back stoop, drinking Heineken, Ruffin lying under the lemon tree snapping at flies, the most aggressive thing he did.

Isaiah told Grace what had happened when he left Jasper's.

"Two *killers* chased you?" she said.

He shrugged. "They didn't catch me."

"That's not the point. You were in serious danger."

"No, I wasn't," he said. He felt like a kid being called a bad name. "They would *not* have caught me."

"*This* time," Grace said, truly alarmed. "My God, Isaiah. How can you treat this like it's routine?"

"Because it is," he said sharply. "I was in danger when I helped you with Walczak and you didn't complain then." He instantly regretted his words and realized with alarm that he knew how to hurt her. "That was a terrible thing to say," he said. "You're worried about me, that's all. I'm sorry. Really. I apologize."

Her chest rose, she thought a moment and exhaled. "No, you were right. It's what you do. I know that and I shouldn't have said what I said." She leaned her head against his shoulder and they stayed like that awhile.

She squeezed his arm. "Let's go for a drive."

Grace and her dad loved Steve McQueen movies, especially *Bullitt*. The chase through the streets of San Francisco in the '68 Mustang GT was their favorite scene of all time. Three versions of the car were used in the movie; one was wrecked and sold for parts. Her dad had found it in a junkyard but was killed before he could work on it. After his death, she'd restored it in his memory. When she'd gone to New Mexico to be with her mother, she left the car with Isaiah. He'd prepped it for long-term storage—changing the oil, filling it with premium gas, installing a battery maintainer, removing the spark plugs, overinflating the tires, and using cedar balls to keep out the mice. The car was Day One fresh.

They drove through Orange County, past Lake Elsinore to Temecula and along a windy, isolated road that braided its way up Palomar Mountain and to the observatory. Grace drove like a normal person instead of her usual Richard Petty with a death wish. The sun was saying good night to the world and the view from the observatory was spectacular. They sat on the parapet, chatting, a new phenomenon to Isaiah. Did Grace know how to make instant coffee yet? Did Isaiah still wear the blue shirt every time he wanted to look nice? They talked about Isaiah getting health insurance because he was a moron if he didn't. Her birthday was June sixth, a Gemini. His was November 3rd, a Sagittarius.

"Geminis gravitate to Sagittarians because we're sexually very compatible," she said.

"I don't need the Zodiac to tell me that," Isaiah said. "Do you really believe in that stuff?"

"No, but Mom's into it. I think it comforts her, thinking she can understand her life by tracking the stars. In a way, I envy her."

"Me too."

Lately, Grace had been looking for a place to live with enough space and light to paint. So far, she'd struck out. "Everything's expensive," she said, "and the dog doesn't help."

"Live with me," Isaiah said, adding quickly, "I mean, if you want." They were smiling at each other, playful but not, his heart drum-rolling in his chest.

"Big step," she said. "Aren't you worried? If you add up all the time we've spent together, what's it come to? A week?"

"More like ten days. Plenty of time."

"What's the rush?"

"I'm not getting any younger," he replied. "Are you?" Now they were grinning.

"Can I think about it?" she said.

"Sure," he said, his eyes never leaving hers. "Take your time."

Isaiah was happy, a circumstance as exhilarating as it was unusual. How could someone reappearing in your life make you do dance steps when you took out the trash and sing "My Girl" while you were folding your laundry and make you feel so corny you wanted to bang your head on the refrigerator? He had invited Grace to live with him. Just like that. No hesitation. No thinking about it. He just did it. He'd never done anything that emotionally declarative in his entire life. She'd said she still had lots of problems. He understood that. Changes on the inside take a while to catch up with changing your ways. He was like that too. Maybe they could help each other and speed things along. Team up. Collaborate. Or maybe they'd be like eagles mating in the sky and get their claws tangled up and plummet screaming into the earth because neither of them was a therapist.

A jolt of guilt rocked him when he thought about Stella. She wasn't overflowing with problems. She was well adjusted, stable, optimistic. No visible wounds on her psyche. Nevertheless, Isaiah wanted Grace. With her hard shell and her wary outlook and a past that would always be there. Oh, she could loosen its bite but it would never let her go. But this wasn't a reasoned choice, he thought. It was like preferring jazz over classical or skiing over rollerblading or playing wide receiver instead of inside linebacker. There was probably a complicated psychological explanation but so what? Did having an explanation for why you felt something change the way you feel? He wanted Grace and that was all there was to it. But why did she want him? he wondered. Was it just that she recognized another flawed soul or were there things about him that were truly lovable? He was good at his job. He wasn't ugly.

"Some list," he said. Then he got on Amazon and ordered a king-size bed.

CHAPTER THIRTEEN

1488

Angus paced around the house, restless and anxious. Too much was happening. Too much to worry about. Christiana, Isaiah, Dwight, Lok, Sidero and the nimrod Starks. And then there was his swan song. The Last Big Deal. Farewell, motherfuckers. I'm riding off into the sunset still in the saddle with a shitload of money on the mule train behind me. He'd made it through his seventy-six years without getting shot, crippled or locked up in Corcoran with the people he'd sold guns to. It was a goddamn miracle. He wouldn't have believed it if he hadn't lived through it.

After Angus left Welch and the coal mines, he rode the rails. He'd heard the life was adventurous; a form of freedom but that turned out to be bullshit. The constant racket from the rails was stupefying and how much fucking scenery could a person appreciate? There was no call of the road, only the need to move. If your life wasn't going anywhere at least you could. Only other hobos could give you a hobo name and Angus was dubbed "Troll," which he didn't appreciate. He decided to go to California. He didn't need a reason.

Angus arrived at the 8th Street train yard in LA. The closest accommodation was on Skid Row; south of 3rd, west of Alameda and north of 7th. There was no south side; poverty, crime and shitty housing extending into South Central, Compton and beyond.

He took up residence on Main Street, the neighborhood's unofficial 5th Avenue. Piles of trash and garbage were heaped on the sidewalks nearly black with grime, the smell an odious mix of alcohol, shit, piss, rotting food and decades of accumulated BO. The homeless camped randomly. Angus's abode was in an alley; a tent-like affair made from orange crates and garbage bags only recently emptied of their garbage. His neighbors were emaciated, obscenely dirty, covered with open sores, their flea-infested dogs as starved as their masters.

For a time, Angus worked as a fry cook at Johnny's Shrimp Boat, a takeout place slightly larger than a kiosk and set in a parking lot full of drunks. The owner, Shig, would scream out orders to him from three feet away. "SIX AND RICE, CHILI ON!" One night, Angus saw Shig's Ruger .357 Magnum on a shelf beneath the register. He stole it and never went back.

Angus sold the gun to the bartender at King Eddy's, bought four Saturday night specials, sold three of them and kept one for himself. He made a good profit, enough to live on for a while. He wanted to sell more guns. He found a Yellow Pages that wasn't ripped to shit and made a list of local gun stores and noted their locations. He didn't want anything close to the Row. He chose Wyatt's Guns and Gunsmith in Burbank, the city nothing like it is now. There was a growing residential area but a lot of it was dreary and lethargic with weedy vacant lots between the low-rise commercial buildings. Angus rode the bus with his gun tucked into the back of his pants. He was so scared he almost turned back, but the thought of returning to the stink and his wretched neighbors made him eager and determined.

Wyatt's store had a folding security gate on the front and back, heavy doors, spotlights that came on at night and a burglar alarm. Surveillance cameras were nonexistent at the time. The most intimidating security feature was a large black German shepherd that stayed in the store overnight. Angus went home, rented a storage locker and wondered if he had the nuts to carry out his plan. Another night in the Villa de Garbage Bags convinced him. If he didn't do something soon, he'd die there.

Eleven thirty in the morning. People were already at work and it was too early for lunch. The street was nearly deserted. Angus walked into Wyatt's. The dog was lying near a rack of shotguns and barely looked up.

"Morning," Wyatt said. "How can I help you?" Angus froze a moment, the buzz of adrenaline in his ears, his eyes wide, forehead dotted with sweat. Wyatt must have recognized the look because he reached under the counter. Angus shot him and then the dog.

He stood there for maybe a minute, breathing in the gun smoke and tamping down his panic, the quiet as bad as any sound he'd ever heard. He listened, waiting for yelling and pounding footsteps and sirens. Nothing. He looked at Wyatt and the dog. They were dead—*fucking dead*, their blood mingling on the linoleum floor, indistinguishable from each other.

With shaking hands and a pounding pulse, he loaded Wyatt's van with rifles and handguns until the suspension sagged. He drove back to LA, numb and glad of it. He put the guns in the storage locker and parked the van where it was sure to be stolen. He dismantled his own gun, wiped down the parts and scattered them in different storm drains. The only thing he felt bad about was the dog. The next day he found a newspaper someone had left on a bus bench. A big article on page 4.

GUN STORE OWNER MURDERED
Police Say Large Cache of Weapons Stolen.

King Eddy's bar, on the corner of 5th and Los Angeles Street, had been there since Prohibition. It was the quintessential dive: dim and gloomy, regulars hovering over their drinks at the long oak bar, glistening bottles of booze on inviting, ascending shelves, a place you looked into your drink so you wouldn't see yourself in the mirror. Eddy's had seen more drunken brawls, stabbings, shootings, vomiting, whispered deal making and ramblings of the insane than all the other bars in the area combined.

Angus sold the guns to carjackers, drug addicts, pimps, hired thugs and especially gangbangers. It was 1987, the crack epidemic had swept through the hood like polio, infecting the poor, the voiceless and people of color. The Crips and Bloods were at war and the demand for guns was high.

When the supply of guns from Wyatt's ran out, Angus hired straw buyers to buy guns in Arizona and Texas. That was how he met Dwight. A scruffy little mutt with an explosive temper, a predilection for violence and a conscience that was MIA. He'd be your best friend while he stole your money and fucked your sister just before he gave you up to the cops. He was mean too. Once he turned off the road to hit a deer and kicked a bag lady because she asked him for a quarter. Dwight favored a stiletto over a gun. "More close-up and personal," he explained. He was a good man to have around. Nobody wanted to fuck with a guy whose street name was Stab You in a Heartbeat.

Angus was making money but even with Dwight's help it was exhausting. The problem was selling guns one at a time. A hundred guns was a hundred transactions and a hundred chances to get busted. He couldn't keep it up and he knew it. His solution came in the form of Tyler Barnes, a former Marine officer back from Iraq with an M16 to sell. Unlike Dwight, Tyler was a nice guy. Even-tempered, unassuming and polite. Angus liked him right off.

The Vietnam War had ended decades ago, leaving thousands and thousands of weapons stored in so many places the military couldn't keep track. And not just assault rifles and pistols, but grenades, land mines, plastic explosives, machine guns and rocket launchers. The wars in Iraq and Afghanistan added more sophisticated weapons to an already massive arsenal. Hundreds of millions of dollars' worth were stolen but it hadn't made a dent. There was a group of navy employees who lifted parts for Phoenix missiles and F-14 fighter jets from the aircraft carrier *Kitty Hawk* and tried to sell them to Iran.

Surplus weapons was a huge problem for the military. You can't sell them off, you couldn't dump them, you could only destroy them. In response, the military developed the "Defense Demilitarization

Procedural Guidance" manual. The manual explained how to destroy a weapon's most vital components with the fewest number of cuts, drill holes and disassembly. One observer called it "haiku with a blowtorch." But that kind of precision takes time and the backlog of weapons was enormous. The arsenals and military bases were a gunrunner's candy store.

Military ordnance was a little high-end for the locals but not for the cartels. Sinaloa, Golfo, Juarez, Tijuana, Los Beltrán-Levya—they were always at war and they'd pay outrageous prices for anything that killed, killed faster, pierced armor, set shit on fire or blew shit up. Angus hired Tyler to get the supply chain organized. The weapons came from vetted military bases. Fort Bragg was especially forthcoming. Angus and Tyler thrived, accumulating wealth and property and toys until there was nothing left to buy. Dwight wasn't happy about Tyler but Angus didn't give a shit. They had moved into a new era. Dwight had to keep up or hit the fucking road.

Angus stopped pacing, went into the kitchen and fed the dog a concoction he made himself. Organic chicken, carrots and broccoli, boiled and chopped up in the food processor. The doctor told him that if he ate as well as his dog he'd live to be a hundred. Angus missed Tyler. Tyler was a man's man, intelligent, brave and honest. Angus considered him his true family. Losing him had weakened Angus's will and made his mortality palpable and more imminent. He realized he'd seen himself and Tyler as one and the same; their energy, loyalty and love— yes, love—made him feel invincible. Without Tyler, Angus was a tired, limbless old man who was in a business he could do without and that could do without him.

Angus never believed he would retire. He thought he'd remain Top Gun until his heart exploded from all the Reuben sandwiches or someone blew his head off and took the title. Until Tyler's death, the Last Big Deal was just another deal, in the making for months. With him gone, it was a last hurrah for a pointless life, a gold watch for a retiring pencil pusher, a souvenir from a bankrupt county fair. Tyler's death had sucked the meaning out of everything. Angus knew that. It was only vanity and the fear of humiliation that kept him going.

When the Deal was over, Angus could devote his time to Christiana, make her life easier and take some of the load off Gia. It all depended on Isaiah. If he got Christiana off, Angus would have a life with purpose. Take that away and there would be nothing left of him but savagery and revenge.

Hugo was hanging at Sidero's place, sprawled on the couch, smoking some tree. Sidero and Jenn were in the bedroom, arguing about something. They were *always* arguing. Hugo wondered why they stayed together. Jenn was hot but fucking her didn't make up for all the shit she heaped on Sidero. Hugo's own marriage worked in its own way. His wife did the wifely shit and the boy did his bit but lately he'd been trouble. Rebellious. Talking back. Sneaking out. Not towing the party line. You could expect that from a teenager, Hugo thought. He'd been the same way at that age. Still, you had to set limits, hard and fast ones and enforce them with your fists if you have to. There was nothing worse than a teenager with his own ideas.

Hugo took another hit off the joint, held it in, and breathed out the smoke. It was potent stuff but not enough to drown out Jenn. When she was pissed, her voice was like shifting gears with a burned-out clutch. It vibrated the air and rattled your eardrums. *Jesus,* he wished she'd shut up. He didn't know how Sidero could stand it. Hugo didn't hit women unless they deserved it and he would have punched Jenn's lights out a long time ago. Do it once and do it good and you never have to do it again. The world was all about respect.

Hugo got much respect from the gang. He'd served a tour in Afghanistan and if you were ex-military you were special. You had skills. You'd been trained by the US Army, the most powerful fighting force in the world. At demonstrations, he was a brawler, another point of pride. Nothing he liked better than thumping some nigger with a sign that said WHITE POWER IS UNAMERICAN or some other stupid shit. Hugo had gone to a white power demonstration in Berkeley. Some Jew girl started screaming at him about being racist scum and he hit her in the face. It was still on YouTube. Everybody had seen it fifty times and laughed like hell fifty times. The first time his son saw it, he laughed but it sounded forced. Hugo let it pass.

He and Sidero were on Angus's payroll. Angus gave the others a cut to split and a discount on guns. It was a bonus. Especially for the guys who joined the gang for reasons that had nothing to do with white nationalism. They were lonely or lost or oddballs or pissed off at life in general or they wanted to belong. If racism was what it took to have drinking buddies and a place to hang, then they were racists all the way.

Hugo was the real thing. He'd been taught by the real thing. His father, Hugo Senior, had a Confederate flag hung over what he'd called "the marriage bed." There were pamphlets all over the house. "The South will Rise Again." "Securing the Future for Our White Children." "Why We're Becoming a Mongrel Race." Logos were tacked on the front door, Senior patiently explaining them. Kekistan is a fictional country and its flag mimics the Nazi war flag. The Kekistan logo replaces the swastika and the green background replaces the red. The Deus Vult was like a cross made with two capital *I*s. It meant "God's Will," supposedly said by Pope Urban in 1095 when he made a speech urging the First Crusaders to free the Holy Land from the Muslim infidels. There were wrought-iron numbers on the front door, 1488, even though that wasn't their address. Fourteen referred to the fourteen-word neo-Nazi slogan: *We must secure the existence of our people and a future for White Children.* And *H* was the eighth letter of the alphabet—88 was another way of saying Heil Hitler. There was other stuff Hugo thought was stupid but he never said it out loud. The Red Wings logo was altered and repurposed by a group of white nationalists who called themselves the Detroit Right Wings.

Every morning, Junior and Senior would give each other a heel-clicking, spine-straightening Nazi salute. Senior said the Jews ran the educational system and that's why Hugo was homeschooled. His mother took care of the three *R*s. Senior taught him the ways of the world. They both enjoyed it. They'd sit on the couch together, Senior's arm around him, calling him *sport* and *buddy* and *pal* while he talked about the coming race war or the extinction of the white race. He made Hugo memorize a passage from Revelation 14. *"If anyone worships the beast and its image and receives a mark on his forehead or on his hand, he also will drink the wine of God's wrath, poured full strength into the cup of his anger, and he will be tormented with fire and sulfur in the presence of the holy angels."*

Jews, Senior explained, not only worshipped the Beast, they had killed Our Lord Jesus too. Those were among Hugo's best memories, safe and cozy on the couch with his father who loved him so very much. They'd thumb through issues of *Guns & Ammo* or *Tactical Life*. They watched action movies, sci-fi and more relevant stuff too. *Romper Stomper, Into the Homeland, Skinheads, American History X, The Infiltrator.* Senior and Junior always rooted for the bad guys. They also watched documentaries about the rise of the Third Reich, Hitler and the Nazis and the so-called Holocaust, Senior pointing out all the things the Jew writers got wrong and all the things that were faked.

But if Hugo didn't pay attention or got sleepy or wanted to watch TV, Senior would get pissed and start screaming and then he'd take his belt off and swing away with that big silver belt buckle, always careful to keep the bruises and welts where the teachers wouldn't see them. Drinking made it worse. It wasn't so much the pain that hurt Hugo, it was Senior's disappointment, his love vanishing like a gunshot, loud and fiery, resounding in your ears, the gun smoke hazing your eyes, and then a breeze, hardly one at all—and it was gone.

There was a lull in the argument. Hugo couldn't hear Jenn's voice anymore. Maybe they'd called a truce or they were fucking or maybe Jenn went to the bathroom—probably the likeliest explanation. Only a bodily function would shut that bitch up. Didn't matter. Maybe it was the weed, but Hugo was in a good mood. He was optimistic about the future. That was the one thing you could thank Obama for. He was a rallying cry for white nationalists all across the country. Hugo was a registered user on Stormfront, a white nationalist website. When

Obama became president there were *thirty thousand* new users, and that was one website. *One.* You project that out to the rest of the country and there were millions of other white nationalists out there; Charlottesville was a call to action. It was time to get serious, quit hiding in the fucking toolies. They were mainstream now. I mean if the goddamn president of the United States is on your side and calls you a very fine person and if governors and state legislators and high-ranking officials were keeping the niggers and Mexicans out of the voting booth, well, hell, what the fuck were you waiting for?

The argument had shifted to the kitchen. Hugo could see Sidero, leaning back against the counter, talking on the phone, Jenn across from him, standing there with her arms folded across her big tits and scowling, her favorite expression.

"Yeah, I know the plan, okay?" Sidero said, exasperated. "Yeah, I already talked to Angus—"

"Tell Dwight to go fuck himself, Sid," Jenn said in a loud whisper.

Sidero sighed into the phone. "Didn't I just say I know the plan?" he said.

Jenn stuck her head out at him, her eyes widening. "Tell him to *fuck off, Sid!*"

Sidero put his hand over his ear. "Angus said what?"

Jenn shouted at him, "Tell him to tell Angus you've got this covered and they should shut the fuck up and mind their business!" Sidero hung up.

"You're such a fucking wimp," Jenn said.

"Yeah, you told me that a hundred times already."

"Why do you take it?" she said, getting earnest. "Come on, tell me once and for all why you put up with this shit?"

Hugo wondered about that himself. If Angus treated him that way he'd put that old fuck in a body bag.

"You wouldn't understand," Sidero said, walking into the hallway.

"Why do you keep saying that? I'm not stupid, you know."

No, she's not stupid, Hugo thought, but she was a badgering ball-buster. He wondered what Isaiah was doing. Angus had fucked him over good. The case, if you could call it that, was a bunch of bullshit. From what Hugo had heard so far, it was Mission: Impossible without the Mission.

Isaiah had nothing on the killers and nothing on who employed them. He had no leads, no suspects, no direction and no possibilities. He was no closer to resolving the case than he was at the beginning. Christiana's arrest hung over him. There would be no warning. One minute, Stella would be safe, and the next, she'd be in serious peril, all her struggle and hard work at risk for something she had no part in. He thought about her, rehearsing Vivaldi, happy in her focus, joy in her intensity, like Grace when she was painting. He thought about Angus's men, grabbing her in a parking lot and smashing her fingers with a hammer against the hood of a car. He thought about her screaming.

It was time to get desperate, he decided. To do something hopeless. To embrace futility. Ordinarily, he would do the job alone but he called Dodson. Maybe because the case was so intractable and his efforts were so pointless, but the truth was, Isaiah was lonely—no, that wasn't it. More like stranded, alone on an uncharted island in the middle of the Pacific, building bonfires that no one would ever see. He wanted company. But there was a hidden agenda too: proving Dodson wrong. Isaiah didn't need help and he didn't need a partner. He was still IQ and a neighborhood icon. Dodson would be reminded of that when he watched Isaiah break the case without his help and come out of it unscathed.

Tyler lived in an older, very exclusive neighborhood in San Joaquin Hills. The houses were large and venerable, the styles traditional. Some of them, Isaiah guessed, might have been built as far back as the thirties. They had shake roofs, wide porch beams and dormer windows. Their lawns were expansive and lush, flanked by flowerbeds and over-hung with mature trees, the kinds of houses that stayed in a family for generations. An odd choice for an ex-marine. Maybe Tyler grew up in a similar house or found serenity here after the ravages of modern warfare. It made sense when you thought about it. Isaiah would've chosen a place like this over a modern house any day.

The layout of the neighborhood made escape difficult. The narrow winding roads were exclusive to the neighborhood. Some ended in cul-de-sacs. The rest led to two public entrances. Easy to cut off for security patrols and law enforcement. Isaiah decided to park below Tyler's house on a street outside the neighborhood, then approach with Dodson from the brushy hill at the back of the property. If they went in daylight, they were too easily seen. At night, they'd have to use flashlights. Isaiah chose evening, when they'd be less visible but there was still enough light to see.

They wore their caps pulled down, latex gloves and dark clothes. They climbed the hill, dust rising in the breeze, the brush thick and thorny, Dodson muttering about fucking up his new Pumas the entire way. Isaiah couldn't stop the loop in his head. *This is stupid. This is really stupid.* It was warm and they were sweating through their clothes by the time they reached Tyler's perimeter fence. It was made of cement and eight feet tall.

"At least there ain't no razor wire," Dodson whispered. "How we gonna get over this bitch?" They walked the fence and found a heavy wooden gate. It was the same height as the fence, an escape hatch for the occupants in case there was a fire, a home invasion or other emergency. Like two burglars breaking into the house. The gate was locked from the inside, probably with a latch and padlock. They looked around and found a loose cinder block. Isaiah stood on it, jumped up, got a hand-hold on the top of the gate and scrambled over. Dodson followed, still complaining about his sneakers.

They crossed the vast backyard. It was dark now. Houses with their lights on flanked them. All it took was a glance from a kid and they were done. *This is stupid. This is really stupid.* They circled the pool, scurried around the patio staying close to the fence, then cut under the portico. No light from inside. The ground-level transoms were dark. They stood there, letting the sweat dry and catching their breath. "This crazy, Isaiah," Dodson said. "Getting in there without the alarm going off ain't even possible."

"Go back if you want," Isaiah said, knowing Dodson wouldn't.

Isaiah had a lot of experience with burglar alarms. He'd handled dozens of burglary cases and personally had bypassed, sabotaged and disconnected more than a few alarms himself.

The green and white signs said ASSURED RESPONSE SECURITY. Isaiah was familiar with their alarms. If a door or a window were opened, the occupant had thirty seconds to enter the passcode on a keypad. Go over the time limit and you tripped the noisemaker. Simultaneously, an alert was sent to the alarm company through the phone line. The system also had a backup. If the phone line were tampered with, a cell signal went out. Either way, a patrol officer would respond and show up on the doorstep with a flashlight and a gun. To get inside Tyler's house, both systems had to be defeated.

Earlier in the day, they'd gone over the plan.

"The first thing we have to do is find the control box, the CPU," Isaiah said. "It controls both the primary and backup alarms. If we disconnect it, the system is cut off from the alarm company completely."

"How big is it?" Dodson asked.

"About the size of a hardback book."

"A hardback book?" Dodson said. "Houses up there in the hills are six, seven thousand square feet. Some of them are bigger than that. How we gonna find something that small in a crib that big, plus all the rooms and furniture and shit. That's like looking for a needle in TK's wrecking yard. They could hide something like that anywhere."

"That's just it," Isaiah said, "they don't have to hide it. It's not like a wall safe. The box only needs to be out of sight, like a fuse box. There's a difference. Say you're the homeowner and there's a false alarm and the keypad won't shut it off. Do you want to run up to the second floor or go out to the garage or move the dresser while a hundred-decibel siren is blasting your ears off? No. You want the box accessible, someplace you can get to in a hurry but a burglar would have to look for it."

"In thirty seconds," Dodson said, with a deep sigh.

"I've seen alarms in all kinds of houses," Isaiah said. "The most common places to put the box are on the first floor—the foyer closet, the hallway closet, the pantry, the laundry room and the utility room. Accessible but out of sight."

"Be serious, Isaiah," Dodson said. "You can't take a piss in that much time."

"Once we're in, we split up," Isaiah replied. "You take some of the places, I take the rest. I know, we'll have to move fast."

Dodson huffed. "That's not cutting it close, that's cutting it off. There's still the backup too. The cell signal."

"I've got it covered."

"Yeah? You better hope you do."

There was activity in the houses next door. Lights going on and off. Doors opening and closing. TV chatter. Voices. Tyler's back door was solid oak and the dead bolt was high quality. The newer locks were immune to picking and bumping. Isaiah drilled out the lock with a high-speed drill and a cobalt bit. He brought out a small electrical device with three stubby antennae.

"Signal blocker," he said. "Disrupts wireless signals, covers eight frequencies. It'll shut down the backup." He put his hand on the doorknob. "You ready?"

"Not especially," Dodson said.

"Soon as I open the door—"

"I know what I'm supposed to do," Dodson said, belligerent. "The question is, should I do it at all?"

Isaiah opened the door and they rushed in. They were in a hallway. *30...29...28.* Dodson made a sharp turn into the laundry room. If the control box wasn't there, his next stop was the kitchen pantry and any other likely places along the way.

Isaiah sprinted down the hall, nearly tripping over a matched set of Louis Vuitton luggage. He raced across the great room, hurdling over the sectional and into the foyer. There was a small closet for coats and rain boots. He slammed open the sliding door. No control box. *23...22...21.* There were stairs leading up to the second floor and another hallway. He took his own advice and chose the hallway, skittering to a stop at a larger closet. He swung the door open. No box.

If Dodson had found the thing he would have shouted. *17...16...15.* Isaiah was either completely wrong or he'd missed something. *He'd missed something.* He knew it. He'd seen something but didn't see it. *12...11...10.*

"Oh *shit*," he said. There were ground-level transoms. The house had a goddamn basement. A rarity in LA. *8...7...6.* How do you get down there? He didn't see the entrance in either of the hallways. Somewhere off the kitchen? No, Dodson would have found it. *5...4...3. Where's the basement door, Isaiah? Where the fuck is it?*

The alarm went off. It was FUCKING LOUD; the piercing WHOOP WHOOP WHOOP! specifically engineered to fuck up your brain cells and scare the living shit out of you. If Isaiah could shut the alarm off in the *next* thirty seconds, the company might think it was a false alarm. *28...27...26.* Dodson came running up to him, shouting, "The fuck are you doing? Wasn't we supposed to abort?" WHOOP WHOOP WHOOP! *Think, Isaiah. It's right in front of you.* "I knew this plan was stupid," Dodson yelled. "I knew it right from the jump. Why in the fuck don't I listen to myself?" *19...18...17.* "Hello?" he continued. "Don't go zombie on me now." Dodson's voice faded in the deafening whoops. Isaiah had to block them out; retreat into the whirrs and clicks of his reasoning mind. *12...11...10.* WHOOP WHOOP WHOOP! The alarm was getting to him; he could smell his own sweat. He cupped his hands over his ears and closed his eyes. *7...6...5.* Dodson was screaming something in his face. WHOOP WHOOP WHOOP!

"It's an old house," Isaiah said. He opened his eyes. *The entrance is underneath the stairs!* He raced over there and yanked open the door. *3...2...1.* The control box was screwed into a two-by-four right inside the basement door. He pried off the cover with a screwdriver and disconnected a couple of wires. The alarm went quiet, its absence like a thing unto itself. They listened. Empty houses have a certain feel, a hollow silence, dense, unbreathed air. The neighbors seemed unperturbed. No one shouting or banging on the door. False alarms happened all the time. The stupid thing goes off for a minute and shuts itself off. Yeah, okay, Isaiah thought. But did the alarm company buy it?

There were odors trapped here since Tyler's last day on earth. Coffee, fabric softener, window cleaner, wine, sauteed fish.

"What are we looking for?" Dodson asked.

"I don't know," Isaiah said.

Dodson looked at him. "I don't know? Is that what you said, *I don't know?*"

"Yes, that's what I said."

"The first time you said that to me was in Vegas," Dodson said. "I didn't like it then and I like it less now. How can we find something when we don't know what it is?"

"I'll know it when I see it," Isaiah said irritably. "Be on the lookout, okay?"

They went down the hallway and looked into Tyler's office. Isaiah had a penlight. He shined it around knowing there would be no open laptops, iPads, cell phones, diaries, answering machines, calendars or balled-up letters in the wastebasket like TV cops always found. Dodson stayed near the windows where he could see the street.

"Find anything?" Dodson said, wryly.

"Be quiet, will you?" Isaiah said.

"Spoiling your concentration?"

"Be quiet, goddammit!"

They went upstairs to the master bedroom. There were numerous suits in the closet, many of them made by Christiana. One of them looked familiar but Isaiah didn't know why. He stopped a moment. It was the same charcoal gray pin-striped material as the vest he found in Marlene's room. Were Tyler and Marlene having an affair?

The dresser drawers held lots of zany socks and Tommy John underwear. "I had a pair of those," Dodson said. At thirty-two dollars each they should come with a pair of pants and a hoodie.

A ring box from Tiffany revealed an engagement ring, the rock the size of cat's-eye marble. Marlene and Tyler were getting *married*? That made no sense at all. There was a small silver box on the bed table containing bindles of cocaine. There were two shopping bags from Saks Fifth Avenue on the bed. Swim trunks, plush beach towel, white linen shirt, and, according to the receipt, two-hundred-dollar flip-flops.

Dodson said, "Did you find anything you can't recognize because you don't know what you're looking for?"

"Will you *please* shut up," Isaiah said. He was embarrassed. He'd come here to do something fruitless and brought along an audience to watch. There was a framed photo of a woman on the dresser. She was at the beach, looking out at the ocean. It was sunset, a glow of heaven's light on her beautiful face; a breeze fanned her hair, pins of green shining from her earrings. Her smile was optimistic, a hint of mischief too. A different look for Marlene.

"Security patrol," Dodson said, peeking through the blinds. "False alarm my ass." A security guard had arrived in a new Ford Escort, green and white with the Assured Response logo on the doors. It looked like it was delivering a pizza. Three seconds later a police car pulled up. Dodson said, "Neighborhoods like this, they don't fuck around, do they?"

The security guard stayed outside and talked importantly on his radio, probably wishing he'd lost twenty pounds and gotten into the academy. The cop went around the side of the house, hand on his gun, looking for the entry point. Isaiah and Dodson took off, racing down the stairs, through the hallway toward the back door, but they heard the cop come in. They turned around, retraced their route, went through the foyer, and darted back up the stairs to the landing. Moments later, the cop entered the foyer, muttering unintelligibly on his radio the way cops do.

"He's calling for backup," Isaiah whispered. The jammer doesn't block radio signals.

"Will he come up here?" Dodson said.

"Not yet."

A police officer never clears a house by himself. The cop left to block the back door and secure the scene, the security guard still out front. Isaiah and Dodson jogged from room to room, but there were no secondary roofs or convenient drainpipes or ceiling hatches or loose tiles so they could hide in the air-conditioning vents. How the hell did Tom Cruise find those things? That left bashing the cop or the security guard over the head with a blunt instrument. That wasn't going to happen. And even if they somehow got past them, they'd have to run across the yard, get over the fence and climb down the hill in what was now complete darkness. Dodson was looking at him. "Well, what do we do now, *IQ*?" he said. No more funny business. He was serious.

Isaiah was panicked and hoped it didn't show. *Fuck, we're fucking trapped! We're fucking trapped! Okay, okay, calm down.* Three more cops arrived. They huddled in the foyer, talking in that deliberate way cops do. Isaiah hoped they'd follow procedure and clear the first floor first.

"I'm getting a little upset here," Dodson said. "I have a criminal record and if I get busted I'll be back in Vacaville eating baloney sandwiches with no mustard and explaining to my serial killer cellmate why I can't give him some head."

The cops were making a lot of noise, radios crackling, doors opening, calling to each other. "Clear! Clear!"

"Well?" Dodson said, his voice rising. "I ain't playing. Isaiah. What's the goddamn plan?" Isaiah smiled. "What the fuck you smiling for?" Dodson said.

He followed Isaiah into the bedroom. Isaiah picked up the silver box and dumped out the bindles of cocaine.

"This ain't *Antiques Roadshow*," Dodson said. "The hell you gonna do with that?"

"Stay behind me," Isaiah said.

The security guard was leaning against his car, poking at his phone. Isaiah came out of the house, double time, holding the silver box straight out in front of him. "Detective Martin, major crimes," he said like he was pissed. "Have you called HQ?" The guard was startled, and before he realized the silver box wasn't a badge, Isaiah punched him in the stomach. The guard wheezed and fell to the ground. Isaiah took his keys just as Dodson came running out. They got in the Escort and drove away, a cop in the rearview mirror yelling at them.

They were not home free. The entrances to the neighborhood might already be blocked and there was only one road leading up to the neighborhood itself. Were those sirens Isaiah was hearing or the adrenaline screaming through his veins? *I told you this was stupid! Didn't I tell you this was stupid?* Isaiah had consulted Google Earth before they'd left and had memorized the layout of the roads. He made a turn, then another, heading back in the direction of Tyler's house.

"Where the fuck are you going?" Dodson said. They reached Tyler's street but on the opposite end from where they'd departed. Isaiah saw a house with its lights off and pulled into the driveway. Tyler's place was maybe fifty yards away, two cops on the sidewalk, talking on their radios, the rest of them had left to pick up the chase.

"Didn't you hear me?" Dodson said. "The fuck are we doing?"

"Let's go," Isaiah said.

"Let's go where?" Dodson said. "Don't think two niggas dressed up like bank robbers might be a little suspicious?"

They got out of the car. The neighbors were coming out onto their lawn to gawk. They saw the security company's car and didn't panic. Isaiah flashed the silver box again. "Undercover!" he said gruffly. "Go back inside." They obeyed. Isaiah and Dodson raced around the side of the dark house. The gate was two feet shorter than Tyler's and they clambered over it. They ran across the yard, climbed over a chain-link fence. They scrambled and stumbled down the hill, the thorns shredding their clothes. They reached the Kia and drove off just as a helicopter arrived and hovered over the development.

They left the windows open so the sweat would dry. They didn't speak until their heart rates had dropped to something near normal. Isaiah could feel Dodson getting ready to unload. Isaiah said, "I got us out of it, didn't I?"

"That's your defense for doing something stupid?" Dodson retorted. "*You got us out of it?* You the one who got us *into* it in the first damn place. I can't believe you dragged us in there when you didn't know what you was looking for. That's like trying to see the North Star but you don't know what a star is. And by the way, did you find anything that's gonna break the case?"

"No."

"No? You mean nothing? No clues? No ideas."

"No."

"And you say you don't need a partner," Dodson huffed. "Son, you need *two* partners. One to help you out and the other to keep you out of jail." Isaiah didn't have an answer. Dodson said, "What am I gonna tell Cherise about all these rips in my clothes?"

"Tell her you found a stray cat and tried to bring it home," Isaiah said.

Dodson glared. "Was that your idea of a joke? Please don't do that anymore. You are the unfunniest motherfucker in the hood and if you don't believe me, ask anybody who knows you." They arrived at Dodson's apartment. He got out of the car, stooped to look back inside and said, "You owe me a new pair of Pumas."

Isaiah drove home and thought about Christiana, the long colorful dresses in her closet and the travel brochures to Fiji and the picture of the house at the edge of the sea. He thought about the pin-striped vest he found in Marlene's room. He thought about the Saks Fifth Avenue bag and the Tiffany engagement ring he found in Tyler's bedroom and the photo of Marlene on the bed table. He thought about her earrings like pinpoints of green. He thought about her saying, *Oh I knew him, all right. He was like every other man I've ever met.* Like every other man who wanted sex. He thought about the suit Christiana was making for Tyler the night he was killed. He thought about Gia saying Christiana didn't like to be touched. He thought about the alters and how every one of them disdained Tyler.

The next day he found Christiana at the shop, hand-sewing contentedly.

"You and Tyler were going to get married," Isaiah said. She stopped what she was doing but didn't look at him and didn't put the needle down.

"That's not true."

"That's why Tyler grabbed Pearl in the shop and kissed her neck," he said. "He thought it was you. You didn't want Pearl to talk to me because she's weak and might have said something she shouldn't have. You don't like to be touched. That's why Marlene was having sex with Tyler instead of you and that's why she hates you both. The picture on his bed table was of you. I could tell because of the jade earrings. Those long dresses in your closet? They're for warm weather, someplace like Fiji, for instance, and so was the linen suit you were making for Tyler. That's why you got emotional, isn't it?" Christiana didn't look up.

Isaiah went on. "Tyler had bought some things from Saks. Beach clothes, and there was luggage under your bed that should have been in storage, and Tyler's luggage was in his hallway. He had a diamond ring from Tiffany, your engagement ring. You were eloping."

She shook her head adamantly but he continued. "That photo in your room, the one of the house on the beach with the forest behind it. That's your dream house, isn't it? On the Oregon coast? That's where Tyler was from." Christiana's hands were over her face. She was crying. Isaiah didn't let up. "You kept it a secret because if Angus found out there'd be no telling what he'd do. Tyler, the trusted one, was taking his little girl away."

"It doesn't matter," she sobbed. "Tyler is dead."

"It *does* matter," Isaiah said. "Because you're thinking what I'm thinking. That one of the alters, or maybe all of them together, hired the killers."

"It wasn't them, I know it wasn't!" she sobbed.

"They all despised Tyler, even Pearl. Why should that be? He was a nice guy, nice enough for you to marry him. They didn't like him because if you married Tyler, they'd *all* be marrying Tyler." Isaiah considered what he'd say next. The guilty might go unpunished but a moral compass at this point wouldn't save Stella.

He lowered his voice. "Now here's what you have to do, Christiana," he said. "I need more information. You have to convince the others to tell me everything they know about that night. Maybe they were involved, maybe not, but if I know for certain, I'll know what I'm working with. I can figure out what the police have and if I know that, maybe I can come up with a way to divert them. Do you understand?" She was trembling. She nodded. "Will you try?" he asked. He was as desperate as she was.

"Yes," she said. "I will try."

Grace was at Cherokee's place, wearing rubber gloves and cleaning the stove. Once again, she was imposing on her friend so it was the least she could do. Grace thought about Isaiah's invitation. Was she really going to move in with him? She wanted to. *Home* was not a word she used or had thought about much but the urge to create one was tempting and powerful. She'd talked it over with Cherokee before she left and almost regretted it. Nothing like a spoilsport and the voice of reason to mess up your day. She told Grace she was nuts.

"Maybe wait another week," Cherokee said, "until you really get to know him."

The doorbell rang. Grace peered through the peephole. Her first reaction was alarm. *What the hell is he doing here?* Then she remembered the goddamn stupid fucking duffel bag. She took a deep breath and gathered herself. She paused. For some reason she wanted him to wait. He rang the bell again. She put on her calm face and opened the door.

"Hi," Noah said. He smiled warmly. "I'm really glad to see you."

"Hi," Grace said. "I'm glad to see you too."

Noah DeMarco moved easily, smoothly, like his joints were oiled, surprising for a tall man. He was blue-eyed, legitimately rugged, sun-streaked hair touching his shoulders. He had a deep tan but it was different from the bronzed surfers in Malibu; less like a uniform, more like he'd earned it riding a horse, rounding up cattle all day. He reminded her of a young Sam Shepard.

"This is your friend's place?" he said.

"Cherokee. She's great."

"I'd like to meet her," he said. She didn't answer. She got him a bottle of water and they sat on the green velvet couch. Conflicting emotions swirled around her like fireflies. She was surprisingly glad to see him. *Tamp it down, girl. Get him out of here.*

"How are you?" he said.

"I'm good. You?" she said.

"I'm fine. I had a good trip." He talked about driving here from New Mexico on his bike. The vistas he'd seen, the people he'd met. It was a pleasant travelogue, nothing showy, no death-defying adventures. His voice was calm and self-deprecating, so different from before. She was suddenly afraid Isaiah would walk in.

Grace had been in New Mexico almost a year, lonely and pining for Isaiah. One of her friends hosted a dinner party. The guests were a mix of local artists, normal people, dedicated narcissists and your garden-variety flakes.

Everybody brought wine. Noah brought a big bouquet of desert flowers in an old ceramic vase. Beaming, the host set them down as a centerpiece and pronounced Noah a sweetheart. Grace was on the other side of the table, the flowers between them. When Noah stood up to greet someone she took a good look at him. *Wow. He's good looking.* She felt guilty just for thinking it.

Between the desert marigolds and red chuparosa and the feathery apache plumes, she caught brief glimpses of him—an amused blue eye, a forelock brushed away, a smile brilliant against his tan. Somehow, the puzzle pieces made him more intriguing.

She heard snippets of what he said. Hardly anything about himself, freakish in this crowd. He sounded hyper but charming. He made the people beside him laugh and she wished she could laugh too. It had been a while and she'd almost forgotten how. She looked at him through the leaves and stems. He was looking back at her. She smiled, embarrassed, and he was too. They both stood up, reached over the foliage, and shook hands.

"Noah," he said. "Nice to meet you."

"Grace. Nice to meet you too." It was the kind of connection people noticed.

Later they talked, mostly about their work. He was intense,

knowledgeable and a little full of himself but tolerably so. She asked to see pictures of his work. He was talented. Really talented. She showed him what she'd been doing and he was impressed too, but his work was clearly better. It was nice talking to another artist. He understood what she was getting at and the references to other artists. He listened too, not waiting to top her anecdote with a better one. Rare in a man. Rare in anybody. It reminded her of Isaiah but she shut that out.

A mild evening in New Mexico was romantic all by itself. But with the moon close enough to kiss and the stars gathering to greet one another and the breeze smelling of damp earth and sage, you either fell in love or wished that you could. Segovia played under Chinese lanterns and she danced with him, feeling guilty the whole time. She imagined Isaiah longing for her while she flirted with a handsome artist who thankfully, wore no beads, didn't have a man bun or talk about his trips to Paris. The wine made it okay to be dancing with him. At one point, her face touched his chest and she quickly withdrew it. She did that with Isaiah. She said an abrupt goodbye and left, Noah not saying anything stupid like *When will I see you again?*

She regretted leaving. She wasn't doing anything wrong. Noah was a nice guy and she was attracted to him. So what was the problem? She repeated her mantra. *I have issues to resolve. A relationship is not a good idea.* That was one of the reasons she'd left Isaiah, wasn't it? To get her head straight? Resolve her terrible past? Why move eight hundred miles away only to be entangled with someone you didn't love?

Two days later Noah called and asked her to coffee. Nothing wrong with that; she had coffee with friends all the time. She almost put on something prettier than her usual chambray shirt over a T-shirt but caught herself and wore what she wore. Don't be an idiot, she thought. It's fucking coffee.

They met at Lucinda's in the afternoon. They both worked mornings to catch the early light and they both smelled of turpentine and had paint on their hands. It was like a membership card. As artists, they had the same central issue: how to capture and illuminate human nature; the nuance in a glance, the feeling between the feelings, the words being said when nobody was saying anything. Joy and pain and isolation without being maudlin.

"It's so frustrating," he said. "I feel like I paint around it, behind it, or I overpaint because I'm trying too hard."

"And when you're done," Grace added, "you feel like you quit the race five yards from the finish line."

"Exactly," he said, and they smiled.

He invited her to go for a ride in the desert on his motorcycle but she declined. Too much like a Julia Roberts movie. They'd need a soundtrack. He was cool about it, didn't ask for a reason or a consolation prize like dinner. He was either a gifted romantic or a genuinely nice guy. She casually asked around about him. Girlfriend? No. Bad habits? Nothing anybody knew about it. Drugs? Recreational like everybody else. She was surprised when he didn't call.

She didn't see him again until two weeks later at a friend's exhibition in Albuquerque. She was surprisingly glad to see him and he obviously felt the same. They hugged and held on a moment longer than necessary. Afterward they went for a walk, had dinner and talked for a long time. He walked her to her car and kissed her. A sweet kiss. A just-right kiss. Grace was wary by nature, sometimes bordering on paranoia. Rebecca told her, "Trust requires practice, and in those terms you're a lazy bum."

She wondered if Noah would be another in a long line of losers. A man who talked a good game, seemed to be good-hearted but turned out to be a grown-up adolescent, a mama's boy or an egocentric asshole who talked constantly while the world revolved around his head. How could you know? It was a fantasy to think that you could. You made the jump and whatever happened happened. Anyway, she was independent, comfortable with her sexuality and in need of male companionship. It had nothing to do with Isaiah. Waiting until she was more trusting was like waiting for retirement. She went over to Noah's place. He opened the door. She looked at him a lingering moment, he smiled, and she went inside.

She spent a lot of time at the old adobe house Noah had rented. It was bigger and cooler than her cramped apartment. He was neat, thank God, considerate and good in bed. He worked hard. She liked him a lot. They became a couple. People invited them places together. She assumed he would call every day. Her mother liked him. Sometimes she thought there might be a future with him, something she hadn't thought about until she'd met Isaiah. But he was there and she was here. Sometimes she couldn't conjure up his face and at others she could feel him inside her and remember every word he'd said.

Noah became part of her routine, part of her life. Sure, he had his moments. A jealous rant about another artist. A bout of feeling sorry for himself. A dismissal of something she said. But they were brief, he apologized and they went on.

Noah was preparing for an exhibition, a one-man show at a prestigious gallery. He painted in a frenzy, staying up until three a.m., losing weight and brooding, rife with self-doubt. Every now and then he'd snort a few lines of coke. She was okay with it; she did it herself. The exhibition was a huge success, nearly all his paintings sold. His notoriety spread. He had money. He got an agent.

He bought clothes that were new but looked vintage. He grew a beard. He didn't listen anymore. He waited until she was done talking, like a plane had flown past, and then launched into something about himself. He got another show and bragged about it. He snorted more coke and stayed out late with his friends. He was critical of her work and gave her a lot of advice. She put up with it for a while. Sometimes you do that because you don't want to admit you've wasted so much time and emotion. One night, he was high and yelled at her for not cleaning up his part of the studio. He had commitments, he had deadlines—didn't she understand that? She told him to fuck off forever, gathered her things and went back to her apartment.

She chided herself for missing the signs and not leaving sooner. Once again, she'd seen a man not for himself but what she hoped he would be. She forgave herself. It takes time to find that out. Rebecca said this wasn't an indictment of trust, but Grace wasn't so sure. Noah called, came around and sent a lot of emails but she didn't answer her door or respond.

She thought about Isaiah and wondered why she'd wasted her time with anybody else. "You love him, you stupid bitch," she said to the bathroom mirror. On the day she left New Mexico, Noah came over. He said he was sorry for the way things had ended and that he'd been an asshole. He asked her to take a duffel bag with her. He was going on a trip to get his head straight and there was no room on his bike. He would stop in LA to pick it up. She knew it was a ruse to see her again but said yes so he'd leave.

Noah took a sip of coffee, put the mug down and didn't pick it up again. "Are you painting?" he asked.

"Only a little," she said. "I have to find a space." She waited for him to talk about his amazing new work or upcoming show in Miami or New York but he didn't. He seemed mellower, more relaxed and not high. "What?" he said.

"Nothing. Are you moving here?"

"I'm not sure," he said with a sigh. "I'm staying with a buddy for a few days. I've been at loose ends, sort of. That self-doubt thing."

"*You* have self-doubts?" she said with a little laugh.

"Yeah," he said with a little laugh himself. "My massive ego started cracking right after you left and then it fell apart completely. I was a mess." He looked at his brown hands. "I'm sorry for what happened. It was my fault completely."

"Forget about it."

"No, let me say this. I should have said it to you a long time ago. I was pigheaded and arrogant and you were far more patient than you needed to be. Thanks for that. And I'm clean, by the way."

"I'm glad," she said. "I've always wished you well."

He got up. "I'll get out of your hair." He gave her a brief hug. "I hope we see each other again."

She didn't answer and he left.

*   *   *

She was in Isaiah's backyard, painting. She needed new ideas. She needed to make progress. Seeing Noah sparked it. He was so good it made her jealous. Usually she started with a shape or a color or some vague emotional impulse, going wherever her instincts led her. But she'd decided it was kind of a cop-out. How do you know you're growing if you have no intention to? It was like kids with finger paints. They painted whatever and whatever was fine. She had never started a painting thinking about an objective or an idea. Whenever she managed to capture something truthful it was happenstance, like closing your eyes and hitting an RBI. Today, she had restrained her ambition to depict the whole of human nature and decided to paint Ruffin, or rather, the feeling of Ruffin—his innocence, his purity, his pleasure at a scratch behind the ear, his complete contentment doing nothing more complicated than lying under the lemon tree.

It took some experimenting but she was onto something. She'd found the colors and visualized the composition. After some experimenting, it started to flow, becoming less cerebral and more a direct connection from the paintbrush to her feelings for the dog.

Isaiah came out the back door. He was brooding and troubled. Again. She put down her brush and waited. He'd speak when he was ready.

"I've got nothing," he said. "Really nothing."

"I'm sorry."

Grace was deflated. She felt silly, painting a dog—the *feeling* of a dog—while he was working on a complex problem with someone's future at risk. She looked at him. He'd gone still, in the zone. She waited. He stood up straighter and made a face like he'd stepped out of a warm room into a cool breeze.

He smiled and said, "The guns."

CHAPTER FOURTEEN
Deagle

Angus watched Hugo, Lowell and Johnny mount his new baby on the jeep. The fucking thing was beautiful. Looking at it scared the shit out of you. Whoever designed this thing was a goddamn maniac. Yes, this would be fitting for the Last Big Deal. A high note to go out on; the Top Gun still on top.

"This motherfucker is badass," Hugo said, grinning.

"It sure is," Angus said, grinning back.

Angus used to rationalize about his business. If the narcos didn't kill people with guns they bought from him, they'd kill people with guns they bought from somebody else. Besides, you couldn't control what a customer did once the gun was sold. If he went out and killed somebody that wasn't your fault. Look at it this way. Suppose that same guy drove his Camry into a crowd at the bus stop. Would you blame Toyota? No, of course not. Guns don't kill people, people do, and they kill them with all kinds of things. Knives, hammers, tire irons, baseball bats and bolt-action deer rifles. The blame lies with the bearer. True enough, Angus thought, as far as it went. But what you can't do with any of those things is go into a classroom at an elementary school and slaughter all the children at the same time.

And what was that other chestnut? Oh, yeah. That you needed an AR-15, a thirty-round clip and a thousand rounds of ammo to defend your family against—what exactly? The neighbors? Rioting minorities? An invading army from Canada?

No. The real reason gun advocates believed they needed an arsenal was to defend themselves against the US government, when, in clear violation of the Second Amendment, its agents came to confiscate your guns. Angus shook his head whenever he heard some numbskull say that. Make no mistake, there were lots of people who *wanted* to see the guns confiscated, but nobody thought it was possible. Not Hillary, Michael Moore, Al Gore, Peter Pan or that lesbian on TV, Rachel something.

There were three hundred million guns in the country. The government couldn't confiscate three hundred million car keys—but okay, just for the sake of argument, how would the government implement that policy in say, oh, I don't know—Compton or Dade County or Flatbush or Mack Avenue in Detroit? Give the gangbangers a Del Taco coupon in exchange for their Glocks and Mac 10s? And what would the government do about the countless guns that people would hide in their backyards, give to friends or bury in the desert? And did anybody really think the NRA's thousands of members were going to voluntarily give up their weapons?

Or how about this? How would the government get the guns out of *Texas*? Yeah, that sounds plausible. What would be the plan? Go from house to house, apartment to apartment, ranch to ranch? Get a couple of cops to ring the bell and say, "We need you to turn in your guns, sir," and what if the guy says, "No, I don't think I will." Then what? Wake up a judge and get a search warrant? Get dozens of officers to set up a perimeter, evacuate the schools, call in the SWAT team and the helicopters and the armored vehicles every time someone resists? The only way to get the guns out of Texas is to nuke the place.

Angus always wanted to tell the "cold dead hands" people they could let go of that fantasy. The government has no interest in confiscating your guns, and that means the small fortune you spent on the private arsenal in your basement should have gone toward a sun porch or your retirement account. But let's say you're a hard-ass and you're going to stockpile weapons anyway. That's fine, just be honest about it. You're doing it because you want to, not because you need to.

Not that Angus gave a shit. People would always want guns and people would always sell them no matter what the government did or didn't do. There was no stopping the arms trade or even slowing it down and if you're a ball bearing somewhere in that wheel, don't be a pussy. Accept your part in it. It disgusted Angus when he heard gun people try and weasel out of their responsibilities. If you profited from a product manufactured specifically to kill people you were, to one degree or another, culpable, and if you can't handle it, take an immunity pill from human suffering and get on with your fucking business.

Isaiah drove. Angus owned property out near Barstow, a vast tract of desert, nothing on it but scrub brush and brown foothills. He used the place to demonstrate his wares to prospective customers. Isaiah was usually watchful no matter where he was. There was always something to learn or at least observe but a black fog of guilt had clouded the landscape. *Guilt.* There was always something to feel guilty about. He didn't think he was unique in that way but he wondered if other people suffered from so much of it. Supposedly, guilt was useful, a deterrent to harming others, but most of the time it arrived too late, after the harm was done. *Stella*, he thought. He had to warn her about Angus but how could he do that without distracting her from the music? How could she focus on the Vivaldi with the threat of crushed fingers and the end of her career? He called her. He'd think of something. He was good on his feet.

"Isaiah! How are you?" Stella said. She sounded happy. Joyful even.

"I'm okay," he said, trying to put a smile in his voice. "How are things going?"

"Wonderfully!" she said. *Of course they are,* he thought. She went on. "The conductor is very happy and so am I. I'm finding things in the piece I didn't know were there. It's exhilarating!" The temperature in the car hadn't changed but he was sweating. *You're so fucked, Isaiah.*

"That's great, really great," he said. *Tell her, Isaiah. Tell her!* His entire vocabulary had vanished. In an awful moment, he realized he was quick on his feet but not with words. Could he really destroy her innocence? Her vibrancy. Her life?

"Hello? Are you still there?" she said. *Tell her, Isaiah. Tell her!*

"Yeah, yeah," he said, "I, uh, was just calling to say hi and to, um, wish you luck." *You're a coward, you truly are.*

"Are you okay?" she asked. "You sound funny."

"No, I'm good, I'm fine. I'm really happy for you."

"Can't wait to see you!"

"Yeah, me too!" he yodeled.

The call ended. He wanted to get out of the car and run over himself.

Angus had replaced his Maybach with an identical one. It was parked in a clot of other cars and pickup trucks that belonged to the Starks. A white stallion amid a herd of nags. Isaiah parked and got out of the Kia. The looks he got from the gang members weren't dirty; they were blackened with fecal matter and studded with dagger points.

There wasn't much here. A metal roof over a row of shooters' tables. About two dozen people firing rifles and handguns. There were heavy sheets of fiberboard painted with people of various ethnicities and sexual preferences. Most of those were blown to shit. There were paper targets on wooden posts, metal ones shaped like a feral hog or turkey, long-range targets hanging like dinner plates. With everybody shooting, the sound was one long barrage. That was another thing the movies got wrong. Guns are *loud*, louder than a thunderclap, scare-the-shit-out-of-you loud, each round packing enough decibels to put a long-term hurt on your eardrums. The shooters had ear protection. Isaiah had to stand away just to make it bearable. Fumes from the smokeless powder were heavy. They smelled and tasted a little like fireworks; the mercury fulminate in the primer gave it a metallic edge. People thought it was Cordite but Cordite was a brand name for a gunpowder that hadn't been used in sixty years.

Isaiah leaned against Sidero's truck. Since the last time he'd seen it,

Sidero had put on new tires. It had a big cab. The space behind the front seats was crammed with random piles of stuff. Clothes still on their hangers, a juicer, DVDs in a box, fishing poles, a laundry basket full of shoes, a TV, a couple of rifles, a basketball, a space heater, stereo speakers and a jumble of other things.

Isaiah had been curious about Sidero's name. It sounded ethnic and Sidero's skin was a little dark for a white guy. Isaiah had looked the name up. Kevin Boyd was right. The name was Latin. It meant "evil nymph." Appropriate, Isaiah had thought.

Since he'd confronted Christiana in the shop, Isaiah had become skeptical about the alters as killers. They were so at odds with each other and Gia said they argued about everything. Collusion seemed unlikely. And really, Christiana had minimal influence on the others. Isaiah was in a better position to get info than she was. In his desperation, he'd grabbed at straws and tried to make a bale of hay. He'd been thoroughly discouraged until the pieces of another idea snapped into place. He wished his thinking process was more linear; that he could coalesce the clues more quickly, but relevancy came to him as it pleased, without regard for urgency or timing. His new conclusion wouldn't resolve the problem of exonerating Christiana, but he was in the hunt, and despite all his protestations about the case, he was excited. He was IQ and he was doing his job.

He felt sorry for Christiana and the alters, victimized by their father and facing the possibility of prison time for something they possibly didn't do. Even if the threat to Stella was removed, Isaiah would have still carried on. He wanted very much to prove the alters innocent. He felt for victims. He felt their suffering and bewilderment and fear. Grace told him he felt too much. It was one thing to recognize the pain of others, it was another thing to try it on for size.

The red-haired woman Isaiah had seen at the Den was apparently a gun enthusiast. She was wearing full camo and yellow shooting glasses, firing a mint, pre-ban, Polytech AK assault rifle with an extended clip and a huge sniper scope, the ventilated barrel resting on a small tripod. A weird combination. An assault rifle was a short- to medium-range weapon. If shooting at a distance, why not use a sniper rifle like a Barrett .300 or an M24? Just something to do, Isaiah thought. If you weren't actually killing niggers and Mexicans, what else could you do with a gun like that except *pretend* to shoot niggers and Mexicans from far away?

Set next to the tripod was a spotting scope to check the cluster. A ballistic chronograph was in front of the barrel. It consisted of two triangular antennae that extended from a small electronic device. Fire through the triangles and the device measured bullet velocity so you would know how fast the round was going when it passed through the burglar's lung. The red-haired woman loaded her own cartridges. She was serious. This was another thing Isaiah had never gotten into: gear. All that spandex and Gore-Tex and carbon fiber and breathability and sport-specific shoes and COOLMAX socks and gizmos to measure your vitals while you ran around the block. These days, it cost you a couple grand to just get on a bicycle.

Isaiah didn't see Angus around. Sidero and some others were trying out a "Deagle," the Desert Eagle .50-caliber handgun. Isaiah eschewed guns but he knew a lot about them. The Deagle was so powerful you could shoot through a chimney, kill Santa, Rudolph and the guy in the next house. The .50-caliber round was the largest you were legally allowed to load into a handgun. Put the shell next to a .45 and it looked like Mr. Bullet taking his young son to kindergarten. Gangstas were into them as showpieces.

Sidero fired off a couple of shots. BOOOMMMM! BOOOMMMM! More like explosions than gunshots, the gun bucking so hard he couldn't control it. The first chipped a big chunk off a random boulder. The second killed an angel lounging in the clouds.

The raw power delighted the onlookers. *Oh, shit! That fucking thing's a cannon! Gimme a turn, I want to shoot it. You could knock down a synagogue with that bad boy.* Dwight stood well apart from the others. It seemed deliberate. Him in his fancy suit and shiny shoes, everybody else in T-shirts and jeans. He looked like Sonny Corleone at a skateboard park. He was firing a .44 mag with one hand, the heavy recoil hardly affecting him. He shot rapidly, the clanks from the metal targets telling you he didn't miss. He held another gun at his side.

Hugo drove up in an open jeep and skittered to a halt, kicking up a shower of dirt. Angus was manning a machine gun mounted on the roll bar, a gun Isaiah had never seen before. It was shorter and more compact than the conventional machine gun and the barrel was stubbier. It looked like a lesser cousin or last year's model except for the ammo belts feeding into both sides of the breech. The way the Starks whooped and cheered you'd have thought it was an Abrams battle tank. Isaiah wondered why until the realization swept over him and his mouth fell open. No, it couldn't be.

Angus stood up. "Gather round, boys and girls. This is what I've been telling you about." He wheeled the weapon back and forth, grinning with pride. "This is the M134 Minigun. Six rotating barrels, forty-four-hundred-round magazine, three thousand rounds per minute. That's fifty rounds a fucking second!" More cheers and woo-hoos.

There was nothing mini about Angus's new toy. It was the modern version of the Gatling gun. Most military machine guns were gas operated, recoiled with every shot and maxed out around five hundred rounds per minute and nine or ten shots per second. The guns were air- or water-cooled but could still overheat, getting hot enough for the gun to fire without pulling the trigger. To keep the weapon at operating temperature, the gunner had to control the number of rounds in a given amount of time.

Inside the Mini's stubby barrel were six smaller rotating barrels that didn't overheat, had virtually no recoil, and with a 4,400-round magazine firing at fifty rounds per second, the 7.6mm supersonic armor-piercing rounds came at you in a continuous stream. Because the gun was more stable, it was far more accurate than a conventional machine gun and at a longer range. The Mini was something you'd see mounted on a Black Hawk or an armored vehicle. This was no street weapon, it was *ordnance*. It wasn't designed to kill people; it was meant to decimate them wholesale, to bust down walls, slash through sandbags, annihilate bunkers and kill your whole fucking battalion.

Angus swung the gun toward the target area, laughed like a ghoul and opened up. Isaiah had never in his life seen a weapon perform like this. At first, it didn't seem that impressive because it was quieter than a conventional machine gun but the rate of gunfire was cartoon fast, the spent shells like brass popcorn, ejected into the air and spilling onto the ground. Not one target escaped, all of them were hit multiple times in a cataclysmic salvo of lead. Anything wooden was blown apart, explosions of dirt on the hill behind them, the metal targets swinging wildly, clanging like church bells on meth, echoing through the hills, apeshit and celebratory. The shooting stopped, a cloud of smoke drifting over the range, Angus was sweating and grinning. The Starks burst into cheers, high-fiving and throwing their fists in the air.

"This baby is for the Sinaloa cartel," he shouted. "They were the highest bidder, and are you ready for it? A *millllion* bucks! On one sale for one fucking gun! Fuck you, Lok! Do you hear me? And bonuses for everybody!" There were cheers and shouts, beer bottles raised to the sky, more high fives and fist bumps and excited laughter all around. Angus saw Isaiah and took a deep breath.

Angus, Dwight, and Isaiah gathered under the metal roof. The others were packing away their guns and picking up the shell casings. Sidero was nearby, messing with the Deagle, something wrong with it, sliding the ejector back and forth.

Angus said, "Are you still fucking around with that piece of junk? A useless gun if there ever was one."

"It's a great gun," Sidero puzzled. "What are you talking about?"

Angus snatched the Deagle away and hefted it in his hand. "Look at this piece of shit. It weighs five goddamn pounds. What are you gonna do with it? Put it in a holster and you'll tilt to one side. You need a fucking golf cart to carry it around." Angus tossed the gun away.

"I like it," Sidero said, like he was surprised anyone would think otherwise. He must have known it was the wrong thing to say because he took a step backward.

"You like it?" Angus said. "You *like* it? You *like* a gun that isn't good for anything but killing redwoods? What the fuck is *wrong* with you?

You're dumber than I ever thought possible." Angus stepped closer, Sidero retreating, still with his palms out. He glanced at the redhead; arms folded across her chest, lips pursed, glaring as if to say, *stand up to him, don't take that shit.* Momentarily, that steeled him. He stopped, straightened up and looked Angus in the eye. "I like the gun, okay?"

"What's this?" Angus said, sneering. "You think you're a man now, you sniveling little shit?" He gave Sidero a two-handed shove that sent him stumbling back.

"Leave him alone, Angus," the redhead said.

"Shut up, you cunt," Angus replied. "Why don't you go home and bake a pie?"

Sidero tried to stand tall but he was clearly afraid. Angus shoved him again. He staggered backward and fell to the ground. Everybody was staring agog at Angus's cruelty and Sidero's cowardice. The redhead was storming away with her fists clenched by her side.

Angus stood over him. "I asked you a goddamn question, you useless fuck. *Do you think you're a man now? Answer me!*" Sidero was resting back on his elbows, looking at his boots. He was breathing heavily, eyes like flaming cauldrons, boiling over with hate. "That's what I thought," Angus said. "Get out of here." Sidero got up and walked away. He got to his truck, the redhead inside, angry and disappointed, the red of her face matching her hair. They drove away shouting at each other.

The others dispersed, probably wondering what Isaiah was wondering. What could Sidero have possibly done to deserve such venom? This obviously wasn't about the Deagle or manhood. Something else was at work.

"Well?" Angus said. "What's going on?" Isaiah had remembered a conversation with Dodson about the East Side Longos and how they were all packing new Berettas.

"The guns that went missing?" Isaiah said. "Dwight stole them."

Dwight's head went back in surprise. He scoffed and said, "Me? You're full of shit. I never got them and Sidero never did either. Like I said, Tyler must have fucked something up with the sellers."

"Tyler didn't fuck up," Angus said. "He never fucked up."

"Tyler wasn't perfect, okay?" Dwight said. "And maybe the shipment never got here or maybe they're in Tyler's house."

"They're not in his house or anywhere on the property," Isaiah said, keeping a straight face while he lied. "I was there. I searched everything." That drew a look from Angus. "And Tyler didn't handle the inventory," Isaiah said. "You did, Dwight."

"Bullshit," he said. "It was probably the sellers. Those assholes are always trying to screw us."

"No, Dwight," Isaiah said evenly. If he raised his voice, they'd start yelling over each other like the pundits on CNN. "You stole the guns and then you sold them."

Dwight huffed. "You're making shit up. And even if I did steal them how would you know?"

Isaiah remembered what Dodson had told him. "The East Side Longos," Isaiah said. "That's what they're packing now. Brand-new Beretta, PX4 Compacts. All twenty or so gang members with the same gun. How did that happen, Dwight? A coincidence?" Dwight was caught. He had his hands on his hips and was looking at the ground.

"You *stole* from me?" Angus hissed. His face was inflated and flush, the red-veined big eyes even bigger. "You fucking weasel! I found you in the goddamn trash heap! You were nothing, a fucking bum, and this is what you do to me?"

"There's more," Isaiah said. "You hired the killers, Dwight. You had Tyler murdered."

Dwight reacted with what seemed like real outrage. "*What?* What a load of bullshit! I didn't like the guy and I'm glad he's gone but that doesn't mean I had him killed."

Isaiah said, "The night he was killed he told Christiana he was upset about something. He said someone had disappointed him and he'd have to tell Angus and things would be bad. He was talking about you. He caught you stealing the guns."

Angus had reached some other level of anger. The veins in his neck were like whipcords in bas-relief. He wasn't so much trembling as he was vibrating at a frequency so high you could almost hear it. He stepped toward Dwight, flexing his liver-spotted hands, readying to strangle him.

"I stole the guns, okay?" Dwight confessed. "And Tyler busted me, but he said he wouldn't tell you if I paid for them. He gave me six months to come up with the money. I have half of it already. I can show it to you if you want."

"Show me money in a bank account?" Angus huffed. "What the fuck does that prove, you piece of shit? Who knows what else you've stolen from me!"

Isaiah went on. "There was another reason why you had Tyler killed."

"I didn't have him killed!" Dwight shouted.

"You didn't just dislike him. You *hated* him. You hated him more than anything."

It was Dwight's turn to be furious. His smug face sharpened into chisels, his eyes, glowing meteors burning through the stratosphere. He glared bitterly at Angus, who was glaring back the same way.

"Fuck yeah, I hated Tyler," Dwight said. "I worked my ass off for all those years and what happens? Tyler is a goddamn partner and I'm still getting a paycheck! He was wonder boy and I was nothing, a goddamn flunky. Yeah, I get to be the idiot who takes all the risks, driving around in the middle of the fucking night with a pile of guns in the truck, scared I'll get pulled over and hoping Sidero doesn't do something stupid." Dwight stepped forward and poked a finger into Angus's ossified chest.

"Want to hear another perk?" Dwight said. "I get to meet the customers. The Latino gangs, the black gangs, the Asian gangs—the cartels too. One of their sales reps showed me his chain saw. A Black & Decker about ten feet long. He said they had a barbecue and he sawed a cow in half while it was still alive." Dwight nodded furiously, poking harder. "Yeah, that's the kind of shit I have to deal—wait, I'm forgetting something. Oh, yeah, the Russians. Do you know those guys? They dress like Stallone in the first Rocky movie and call themselves Odessa. *Really* nice people. They'll kill you for parting your hair on the wrong side." Dwight smiled sardonically. "But they're good businessmen, I gotta give 'em that."

He went on. "Let's say you're a hooker in Vegas and you fuck a high roller and make yourself ten grand. You keep five hundred, the pimp gets seven-fifty, Odessa gets fifty-five hundred, and the thirty-two fifty left over gets sent to Moscow. And who's it addressed to? *Vladimir Putin!* Yeah, that crazy asshole who throws you in jail for mispronouncing his name and then kills you with a poison dart. *That's* who I have to deal with, Angus! And did I tell you I get threats all the time? These motherfuckers know where I live, what car I drive, what bars I drink at. One day there was an envelope on my windshield. I thought it was a parking ticket. You know what it was? A picture of Jenn with her eyes blacked out. How's that for a fucking message? And where is Tyler all this time? Sitting in his mansion getting his dick sucked by a movie star and drinking champagne with you." Dwight was so close to Angus they were breathing on each other. Angus didn't move, fierce and implacable. "Did I hate Tyler?" Dwight growled. "You're goddamn fucking right I did, but I didn't have him killed."

"You cheated me and you lied," Angus said. "Why should I believe you now?"

"Because if I had anybody killed, it wouldn't be Tyler." Dwight's face was gnarled with a rabid, unquenchable hatred. "It would be *you.*" One moment, Dwight was standing there bare-handed and in the next, the stiletto's needle-sharp tip was pressed just under Angus's right eye. Isaiah didn't move. Angus had lost his bluster and was standing absolutely still, trembling, eyes cast down at the stiletto and breathing harshly through his nose. This wasn't a bluff. Dwight was homicidal.

"What else, Angus?" Dwight said. "Any more insults? Huh? Any more criticism? Any other *names* you wanna call me? Me, the guy who makes the money for you? What's the matter? Am I making you nervous? Maybe dock my paycheck, Angus. Yeah, teach me a lesson. Cut me down to nothing like you do all the fucking time." Dwight pressed the tip in harder, blood running down Angus's cheek, mixing with the rivulets of sweat. Angus drew in a breath and pulled his head back, but Dwight grabbed him by the jaw and put the stiletto in his mouth. Angus said something but he might have been gagging, his tongue was bloody. There was nothing Isaiah or anyone could do. Stabbing Angus would take a millisecond. "Too bad Tyler's not here," Dwight said. "Wonder Boy to the rescue. But he's not here, Angus. *There's only fucking me!*" Dwight raised his elbow, about to ram the stiletto down Angus's throat. Angus let out a gargled scream—

"Don't," Hugo said. He was aiming the Deagle at Dwight. He was calm, in his element, a confrontation with a gun was what he lived for. "Drop the knife. Just drop it. You know I'll shoot you and won't think a thing of it."

Dwight hesitated. His eyes flared with defiance. He put the stiletto back in its scabbard. Hugo abruptly handed the Deagle to Isaiah. "You know how to use it? I've got things to do." Angus gave Hugo an awkward nod of thanks and Hugo walked away.

As the adrenaline dissipated and everyone caught their breath, Isaiah set the gun down on a shooter's table and wiped the sweat off his face with his forearm. He was stupefied by Angus and people like him. If only Angus had treated Dwight with the slightest *hint* of care and consideration this would not have happened. *This would not have happened.* He would not have had a stiletto stuck in his mouth by his own employee and he would not have been scared shitless and spitting up blood and vomiting like he was now. How could he not see that? Angus thought the only way to control people was power, because the opposite of power was weakness. He thought only about threats and sanctions. *If you don't do what I say bad shit will happen to you.* The problem was that as soon as you couldn't carry out those threats and enforce those sanctions, even for a short time, the people you were controlling turned on you just like Dwight had done. What Angus didn't understand was that you didn't have to *exert* your power, even if you had it, and that didn't make you weak. It made you a leader.

People aren't afraid of leaders, they *follow* their leaders because they know they are fair and knowledgeable and respectful and the leader has shown them that he acts in everyone's interests and takes care with their dignity. Angus was a tyrant who'd created a nest of vipers and now he was outraged because one he'd been stepping on for years and years wanted to sink its fangs into his neck and surprise, surprise.

The encounter had drained Dwight of emotion, Angus too. They looked like two dead palm trees. Isaiah was exhausted. Nobody spoke. Angus took a deep breath and said blankly, "Go back to work." Dwight stood there a moment, then turned and walked away.

"Big risk," Isaiah said.

Angus's voice was crusty. There was blood around his mouth like he'd been eating fresh roadkill. "Nah," he said. "What's he going to do without me? He'd be on the streets or locked up on death row and he knows it."

Don't ever lose your leverage, Isaiah thought, not even for a moment, unless you want another stiletto stuck in your mouth. Angus was stupid and would always be so.

The old man glowered at Isaiah, pale, his sweat pink with blood. "Well, that was a fucking bust," he said. "You're supposed to be smart and the best you can do is this crap? I'm starting to think you're as dumb as Sidero."

Isaiah's frustration boiled over. "I have nothing to go on! Not a goddamn thing and you know it! You want to fire me, Angus? Because I'm dumb? Because I'm a nimrod? Do it! Put Dwight on the case or one of your half-ass Nazis! See if they can do better. Come on, Angus, hand me my fucking pink slip!"

"My daughter's got a record, did you know that?" Angus said. "Marlene stabbed a cocktail waitress. Bertrand hit some guy with a golf club and fractured his jaw. It cost me a shitload of money to get them out of that. Can you imagine how a jury would see it? A spoiled rich kid who thinks the law doesn't apply to her, and even if she gets off with involuntary manslaughter she'll be in prison until she's a goddamn senior citizen."

Angus was skinny and old but terrifying nonetheless because he didn't bluff. He'd tortured his own daughter and smashing Stella's future would be nothing at all. The old man's eyes had gone colorless and runny. He hated and feared Isaiah. If Isaiah failed he'd deprive him of atonement.

"Now you listen, you useless fuck," Angus snarled. "Time is running out. You get my kid out of this, do you hear me? Do you? Because if you don't, I'll turn the Starks loose on your girlfriend and they'll do more than break her hands. *And you'll be next.*"

Isaiah was apoplectic with rage, this evil bastard moving him around like a human pawn, keeping him away from Grace, making him do things and face dangers that could get him killed. Angus had no right. *He had no fucking right.*

"Are you trying to intimidate me?" Isaiah said. "Because I've dealt with assholes that make you look like Winnie-the-Fucking-Pooh. You say you're gonna break Stella's hands? Then get ready to have your own stomped into kindling. You won't be able to pull a trigger, pick up a butter knife or wipe your bony ass. You say I'm next? That time is running out? My time is your time, old man." Isaiah moved close so Angus could feel his ferocity, smell the fever on his breath.

"If you hurt Stella," he said, "I'll break your back and put you in a ventilator for the rest of your fucked-up life. Are you hearing me, Angus? You say you don't bluff? Well neither do I, motherfucker. *Neither do I.*"

Angus moved back a bit. Apparently, he wasn't used to being threatened. In business, maybe, but not like this. Not with someone so smart and capable and determined. He said quickly, "Go about your business." He brushed past Isaiah and walked away.

Isaiah tried never to threaten people with bodily harm. You were only daring yourself to do it and he avoided violence whenever possible. As his fury receded, he knew he couldn't break Angus's back or anything like it. Revenge. Retaliation. It came up again and again. Was it human nature? It was definitely universal. From powerful politicians to kids on a schoolyard to primitive tribes in the wilds of the rain forest—you hurt me, I hurt you back. But revenge is emotional, like Isaiah was now. You might feel justified but that's not justice. Justice is for everybody. Revenge is all about you. It's not justice to act the same way as your victimizer. The same way as Angus. Justice isn't personal—it's about principles. Do we obey the law? Do we adhere to a moral code? High minded, Isaiah thought. A hard thing to be in this world. Nearly impossible.

He drove home, wrung out and wasted. Angus was right about Christiana. If by reason of insanity was a tough defense, multiple personalities would be even more perilous. There were plenty of doctors and researchers who thought the condition didn't exist and saw it as an excuse for criminal behavior. Juries were rarely persuaded. *Let's see if I get this straight. You're saying that Mr. Smith isn't guilty of killing Grandma because he was Mr. Jones when he swung the hatchet? Oh, please. That's like punching a guy in the face and blaming your fist.*

The great IQ, the neighborhood icon, wanted to pull over to the side of the road and cry. He knew that one or all of the alters had hired the killers. There were no more suspects, no more motives. The ending was predictable. Christiana would get arrested. Then Angus would send the Starks to break Stella's hands and she'd have to leave town and the Long Beach Symphony Orchestra behind. Then Isaiah would hunt down Angus, clash with the Starks, more people would be killed or wounded and Grace would no doubt leave him for good. All he wanted to do was be with her and the pale green eyes and the beguiling face and sit on the back stoop, drink a beer and watch Ruffin sleeping under the lemon tree.

Beaumont lay unconscious under his hospital covers. He was still and ghostly. Most of the lights were off, the beeps muted, the lines barely moving, distant voices in the hall. Merrill was asleep in a hard plastic chair, his head skewed to one side, arms folded in an X across his chest.

"Merrill?" Dodson said.

Merrill opened his eyes, took a deep breath and blinked a few times. Surprised, he said, "Dodson?"

"Thought you'd be here." Dodson put a paper bag down on the

food tray. He took out some plastic containers, a plastic fork and some napkins. "Cherise's mother, Gloria. She sent some food over. She's a scary old bitch but she can cook."

"Thanks," Merrill said, "I appreciate that. There's only so much nutrition you can get from a vending machine." Dodson took the other chair. Merrill opened the containers. There was a deep, rich chili and warm corn bread.

"Oh, my," Merrill said. He ate with gusto, making *mmm* sounds and shaking his head.

Dodson was self-conscious and imagined Merrill was too; two people sitting in a room with a dying man, one of them eating chili and corn bread, the other one watching him. It was quiet for a time. Dodson said, "I'm sorry, for all the things I did back then. To you. To Beaumont."

Again, Merrill was surprised. He stopped eating. "It was a long time ago," he said. "It's all forgotten."

Dodson shook his head. "Not by me." He had no idea why he was saying these things and he didn't know if he really meant them. "I did a lot of stupid shit," he continued. "Stupid and wrong. I can apologize to you but not your father. Not anymore."

"Everybody does things they wish they could take back," Merrill said. "The bad thing is to let yourself be defined by them. You're not the person who did those wrong and stupid things anymore. You can lay that burden down, Dodson."

Suddenly, Beaumont inhaled sharply and then he went still again. It happened too fast for Dodson to be startled by it. He wondered if the old man was dreaming about the bullets that tore holes through his chest. Dodson felt worse than when he arrived. He was supposed to be consoling Merrill and was being consoled himself.

"Did you know my dad at all?" Merrill asked. "I mean, outside of the store?"

"No, I didn't."

"Except for the family, he kept to himself. He was a very kind man despite what people thought. Everybody complained that his prices were high. They were, but he couldn't buy in quantity like the supermarkets and his margins were piddling." Merrill smiled and tapped his plastic spoon in the air. He seemed to relax some. "Dad gave away a lot of stuff," he said. "More than he should have, if you ask me. Food, water, toilet paper, aspirin, all kinds of things, mostly to shut-ins and people who couldn't feed their kids. Delivered it to their doors and nobody ever knew. I didn't know until Mom told me."

Dodson had no idea either. The grouchy old man had a soft side? A nice thing but for some reason it didn't make him feel nice.

"Remember Dancy Walgreen?" Merrill said. "The wino who used to hang around with Mo? A few months ago, he got sick, liver cancer. He didn't tell anybody, not even his wino friends. He said they'd fuss over him and try and cure him, especially Mo. Mo had a remedy for every-thing and most of them involved chicken parts, hot water and chewing tobacco." Merrill laughed. "Dancy said he wouldn't go to the hospital, they couldn't do anything for him anyway. He wanted to go home to Texas to see his kin before he died but he had no way to get there."

"What did he do?" Dodson asked.

"Dad drove him."

"Beaumont drove Dancy all the way to Texas?"

"Yeah. He did." Merrill was beaming. "That's the way he was." Dodson was feeling worse and worse. He had to get out of there but Merrill still had the spoon in the air and had only eaten half the chili.

"Dad was in Vietnam," Merrill went on. "Drang Valley, Khe Sanh. Saw a lot of bloodshed. A lot." Dodson knew what was coming. Beaumont was a hero. Right on cue, Merrill said, "He was awarded a Bronze Star and a Purple Heart. He never said anything about it. I only found out when I was cleaning the garage and found the medals in a toolbox." Merrill huffed in admiration. "Everybody in the family asked him what happened. He said it was too terrible to talk about and that whatever he'd done it wasn't enough."

Dodson was starting to resent Beaumont. The old geezer who wore the same green apron every day and called Dodson a hooligan and kept a .45 Colt Commander under the register was a hero who fed poor people and reunited winos with their families. Who the fuck knew?

With growing irritation, Dodson listened as Merrill kept talking about Beaumont's love of history, especially the Civil War and how he'd taken the family on a road trip to Gettysburg, Antietam and Shiloh and that their house was too small to have a dog but Beaumont loved animals and helped Harry Haldeman at the animal shelter early in the mornings and how Beaumont and TK were the only old-timers left who'd built successful businesses from scratch and how proud Merrill was of both of them. Dodson felt like his lungs had shrunk and he couldn't get enough air.

"I've gotta go," he said.

"Thank Gloria for me," Merrill said. "The food was really delicious." Dodson got up and went to the door. "And Dodson?" Merrill said. "Thanks for letting me talk. I guess I needed to do that."

Dodson left the hospital as fast as he could without running and went next door to the parking garage. He walked down the deserted aisle to his car. He felt strange. Off. His irritation had turned into something else but he didn't know what. It had started earlier in the evening. He'd come home from work, taken a shower and put on clean clothes. Then he sat on the sofa with Micah and read him a story about a pig named Andy Bacon. Dodson felt good reading to his kid. He felt fatherly, he felt like a man. Cherise walked past and gave him a big smile. He was getting to the part where Andy comes home from the supermarket crying when he noticed Micah was asleep.

Dodson put the boy to bed. Then he asked Gloria if she'd make something for Merrill. He was probably at the hospital. She was happy to do it, she'd known Beaumont for years and years. She was going to take the food to Merrill herself but Dodson said it was late and he'd get it over there. He didn't know why he'd done any of that.

Dodson always wondered how people in the movies ended up in a deserted parking garage in the middle of the night but here he was, in a deserted parking garage in the middle of the night. Something was creeping up on him but there were no footsteps and no need to look back. It was sadness, heavy and dark with outstretched hands and curled fingers. He could sense it getting closer and almost started to run when it overtook him and wrapped him in its smothering arms. He didn't know why Merrill had affected him so. He wasn't a personal friend and neither was Beaumont. There was no reason to feel this way.

Dodson got in his car and drove but he couldn't shake it. He drove faster but it wouldn't go away.

CHAPTER FIFTEEN
Who's Cliff?

The Ladies of Color Turning Pages book club met in the church library once a month. Twelve women sat around the table; most of them TK had seen at the picnic. He was the only man. The women were surprised when he came in, expressing some suspicion about his motives but nothing outright negative.

Louella Barnes said her husband didn't read because it took time away from the TV. Marcie said her fiancé wouldn't read anything but the instructions on a power drill. After much discussion, they decided to *see what Gloria thinks*. TK was already sweating. The windows didn't open and his suit was made of heavy wool.

Gloria entered and the chatting ceased.

"Good evening, ladies. I'm glad you could all make it tonight." She looked around, her eyes skipping over TK like he was a shadow or oxygen before quickly coming back to him. "I see we have a guest. What brings you here tonight, Thomas?"

"My friends call me TK," he said with a feeble smile.

"I'm aware of that, Thomas. Are you waiting for someone? Is someone picking you up?"

"No, I'm just here like everybody else."

"I see." Gloria gave him the same querying, dissatisfied look she'd given him at the picnic. "Let me ask you, Thomas, when you were deciding to attend tonight, did the name of the club suggest anything to you?"

"Yes. It suggested the club was just women."

"But you decided to show up anyway?"

He'd rehearsed the answer with Grace. "I wouldn't have done it but there's no book club for men, or none I know about anyway." The other women muttered and nodded their agreement.

"Although we've never made it a rule," Gloria said with forced patience, "I believe the intention of this club was to allow women to express their opinions without the distraction of men."

"Oh, let him stay, Gloria," Cecile said. "If the man wants to talk about books, that's a good thing. I've never seen it before, have you?"

"Besides," Delores added, "he's cute."

"You think everybody's cute, Delores," Gloria said. She sighed. "Here's how it works, Thomas. You can say anything you want as long as you're civil."

"You don't need to keep bringing that up," Simone grumbled. She glared at Cecile. "I didn't actually run over you, did I?"

"Moving on," Gloria said. "This week's selection is Toni Morrison's *God Help the Child*. Are you acquainted with her work, Thomas?"

"No, I'm not."

"I see," Gloria said, like he was wearing a Speedo and a top hat. The women discussed the book in terms TK wasn't familiar with: character development, plots and subplots, themes, pacing, whether something was a symbol or metaphor for this or that. It wasn't like men talking, he thought. They weren't trying to top each other or argue their points. It was like they were trying to add something, fill in the picture, point out something the others might have missed. Helping one another to understand. TK was as impressed as he was surprised. He'd known these women only in passing. Cecile was a bus driver, Delores was a checkout clerk at Vons, Simone a crossing guard for the school district, but here they were, talking about all these complicated things. He shook his head with wonder. The consensus was that it was an impressive book, not Morrison's best but certainly worth the read.

When the discussion was over, Gloria said, "Our book selections are done by committee, Thomas. Three members take a book home and read it. If they all agree the book is worthwhile, then everybody reads it and we talk about it like we did tonight."

"I gotcha," TK said, putting his hand up like he was way ahead of her.

"The book under consideration is Colson Whitehead's new one, *Underground Railroad*. It's Louella's and Simone's turn to be on the selection committee but Consuelo is home sick. Would you like to take her place, Thomas?"

"Me?" he said looking over his shoulder.

"Is there some other Thomas sitting behind you?" Gloria said. "I'm asking if you would read the book and tell us your opinion." This was going too fast for TK. He didn't know what to say. "Of course," she added, "if you think that's too much for you—"

"No, no, I'll read it," he blurted out cheerfully. "I love to read. I read all the time."

"Good for you. Now, several members are going on vacation and would like to take some books along so we're meeting again on Thursday." She gave him a look that was part challenge, part low expectations. "Do you think you'll be ready by then?"

He tried to look confident. "Oh, I'll be ready. No doubt about it."

He left the library before everyone else, ripping off the tie before he choked, his shirt sticking to his back. He knew what Gloria was up to. She didn't want him in the club so she was setting him up to fail. Evidently she didn't know who she was messing with. He'd never backed down from anything in his life. His body was frail but what was left was all gristle. He hadn't read a novel in decades but he'd read this railroad book and show Gloria and the whole damn club he was as smart and sophisticated as any of them.

They were sitting at the back of the Coffee Cup where there was less noise. "Have you read it?" Grace said.

"I tried. I just can't settle my mind to it," TK said. "I'm not used to reading so much at one time."

"What do you know so far?" Grace asked.

"Not much. Book happens in slavery times. A girl named Ajarry gets kidnapped and brought to America. Poor thing. Makes your blood boil just reading about it. Then she dies and Cora takes over. It was hard to follow; too many people start showing up. The Randalls, Blake—a real SOB, that one. Then there's Mabel, Jockey, Caesar, a boy named Chester and some others—I can't remember 'em all. Then it gets too far-fetched for me. In the book, the underground railroad is a real goddamn train and it runs *underground*! Now I know that ain't true. The underground railroad was just some folks who helped slaves escape to the north. Gave 'em shelter and such.

"And then the damn book jumps around in time. All of a sudden, Cora is living on a farm somewhere in Indiana! I didn't get close to finishing. You know that book goes on for *three hundred pages*? The installation manual for a dual clutch six-speed transmission ain't half that long. Who in the hell's got that much to say? This Colson fella needs to get himself a hobby." He sighed and sat back in his chair. "I'm not going on Thursday. No sense making a fool out of myself."

Grace nearly agreed, but the book club was her stupid idea in the first place. She couldn't let him down. "You know what?" she said excitedly. "I'm gonna get you some Cliff Notes!"

"Who's Cliff?" TK said. "Did he read the book too?"

After leaving TK, Grace went back to Cherokee's place and downloaded the CliffsNotes online. She went through them but couldn't concentrate, preoccupied with Isaiah. Since her return, they'd chatted and bantered and made innuendos about living together but beyond that, everything had been about his case. She felt neglected. Was she being petty? Yes. The case was about life, death and broken hands. When she was painting in Isaiah's backyard, he assumed it was okay to interrupt her. He didn't ask for her permission or say he was sorry. He just started talking. Is that the way it would be? Because the case would always be about life, death and broken hands, and it would always be more important than a painting about a dog. She wondered if her life would be subsumed in his.

The doorbell rang. It was Noah, holding his helmet under his arm and looking sheepish. "I forgot the duffel bag. Sorry." This time Grace wasn't alarmed. She didn't know how she felt. She wondered if he'd forgotten the bag on purpose. But she'd forgotten it too.

"Want some coffee?" she said.

"That would be great." She made him instant. She only drank brewed coffee if Isaiah made it or they were outside somewhere.

Noah sipped his mug and grimaced. "I didn't want to say anything before but this is the same crap you drank in New Mexico."

"I happen to like it," she said, amused.

"I remember you making it. You were like a mad scientist, measuring the stuff like that would make it taste better." She laughed. "I went to MOCA yesterday," he said. He talked about Rosenquist, Rauschenberg, Joe Goode and Arshile Gorky. Noah was animated, wondrous, inquisitive, his love of art gleaming in his blue eyes, in his entire self. His devotion was one of the things she'd admired about him. He said he was staying in LA for a few days but that was a lie. He smelled like paint and turpentine. He'd set up shop somewhere. And Noah didn't like the city. He'd come for her. She was suddenly curious. She wanted to see his paintings, see if he'd progressed and made use of his tremendous talent.

"Let me see the new stuff," she said.

He got out his phone. He'd painted a series of horizons. They were gorgeous, ingenious, different things going on above and below the line of sky and water. She felt embarrassed about painting *the feeling of a dog*.

"Amazing," she said. "Really, Noah. These are great."

His face wallowed in the praise, his ears turning red. "I better go," he said, rising. "By the way, there's a Martin Basher exhibition opening at Anat Ebgi. Want to go? I could meet you there."

Basher wasn't among Grace's favorites but his work was interesting; installations about consumerism and retail architecture. It was a weird situation. She couldn't tell Noah to back off because he hadn't made an advance. Thankfully, she'd already made plans to go with Isaiah.

"I'm already going," she said.

"Great. See you there," he said.

"Don't forget the duffel bag."

This was turning out better than she'd thought. She'd be at the show with Isaiah, Noah would get the message, and that would be that.

When Sal returned to the motel, Annie was in bed watching TV with the covers pulled up to her chin. "How are you?" she said.

"Okay," Sal replied, and that had been the extent of their conversation for the last two hours.

"What are we going to do?" Annie said finally. "We've still got our loose end."

"Why are you asking me?" Sal said. "I'm the stupid cunt who fucked up everything, remember?"

"Could we forget that for now?" Annie said. "What are we going to do?"

I'll never forget, you wait and see, bitch, Sal thought. He had come up with a plan in the hospital. "Angus hired IQ, right?" Sal said. "Angus is his employer."

"Yeah. What about it?" Annie said, changing the channel.

"What if Angus was dead?"

"What do you mean?"

"I mean, if my employer was dead, I wouldn't keep working for him, would you?"

Angus sat at his desk with Weiner in his lap. He got up with the dog in his arms and wandered aimlessly around the house. Everything was riding on Isaiah coming through. Christiana wouldn't last long in jail, caged up like a fucking zoo animal and the dykes would eat her alive. He went back to his desk, sat down and tried to calm himself. Looking at the photo helped. It was old, the colors fading, the silver frame tarnished nearly black. He wouldn't let the cleaning lady touch it. It showed Angus sitting in a wheelchair, a woman standing behind him. She was small and dark, wearing a blue sweater and a smile so warm it spiked his heart with longing and regret.

He'd split with Gia and was living in a gargantuan house on Balboa Island when he fell down the stairs and broke his hip. He had the hip replaced and was laid up for a while. He went through an agency and hired a nurse to take care of him. Her name was Virginia. She was forty or thereabouts. She'd recently arrived from the Philippines and had come to the US on a work visa. She told him she was pregnant but in her first trimester. Angus's recovery time would be about six weeks. By the time she was too pregnant to work, he'd be on his feet again.

His ugliness didn't seem to matter to her. She looked him in the eye when they talked, smiled a lot, picked crumbs off his face, and read to him when he said his eyes were tired. She helped him with his physical therapy. She cooked for him and cleaned the house. She was quiet, undemanding and cheerful. But never submissive. Ask her to do something and she'd think a moment before she decided. She was in charge of herself, not him.

Virginia was the kindest, most patient person Angus had ever met. He didn't know people like that existed. It was like discovering a new kind of rose or that there was such a thing as sunsets. He paid her overtime so she would stay longer, and all the while he was waiting for her to laugh at him or steal from him or catch her on the phone telling her girlfriend that she worked for a circus freak.

She talked about her family back in the Philippines. She missed them. She had a grandmother here but it wasn't the same. The father of the baby had left when he found out she was pregnant. "Filipino men are bad," she said.

"All men are bad," Angus replied, and she laughed. He told her about his legit businesses: car washes, parking lots, taco stands, beauty salons, but nothing else. He told her about Gia, but not Christiana. He told her about growing up in Welch and being a coal miner and living on Skid Row.

If she wasn't interested, she *seemed* interested, and after a while he got the feeling it wasn't the story that involved her, it was him—the guy whose job interviews were three minutes long. Don't be an idiot, he said to himself. That can't be right. But when he thought about it, he'd been nice to her. He hadn't asked her for a lap dance so she probably saw him as a gentleman. He paid her well so he wasn't a tightwad. He didn't swear in her presence, go on tirades or belittle his employees. He was different around her and he liked it. It took energy to be angry and suspicious and domineering. He could relax.

She was plain but it didn't matter. He wanted her, and as flamboyant and aggressive as he was in business, he was equally insecure and unnerved by her. She wasn't in awe of his affluence. That made him anxious too, that his money didn't count. It wasn't part of the equation like it was with Gia, and Angus minus money equaled an ugly guy who was broke. He looked for signs of affection, of something beyond nurse and patient, but she was the same all the time. Maddening. He could read his customers like an issue of *Guns & Ammo*. Virginia was like the phone book in Braille.

Unfortunately, she'd been right about his recovery. In six weeks, his hip had pretty much healed. He pretended it wasn't; hobbling and wincing, using crutches and complaining. She was surprised since she'd helped him with his physical therapy. "Don't go," he said. "I still need help."

She was nearing the end of her second term but agreed to stay on. One morning, she came in early and caught him tossing a tennis ball at the garage and catching it again. "You look good," she said. "Very healthy." She took the tennis ball out of his hand. "You like me, don't you?"

"Well, sure, of course I like you," he said sheepishly. "You take good care of me."

"Don't be stupid, Angus. I mean *like* me." He looked at his shoes.

"Well, yeah, I mean, you know. Sure. Yes. I like you." She touched his face.

"You're a good man. I know it in my heart."

Not long after, she moved in and the man who thought he'd be alone forever was loved. They got married in Vegas and Angus, to his stunned amazement, was happy. Happy had always been a word and that was all, said in sarcasm or to describe someone crazy or stupid or naïve. Okay, maybe happy was a little over the top. It was more about feeling—what would you call it?—*normal,* he supposed. He never knew what normal people did without the rush of danger, the fear of getting killed and the exhilaration of getting away with murder, corruption or somebody else's money. He didn't know what they did without *real* stakes. I mean suppose you're an ordinary schmo and your quarterly sales numbers were down. What happens? You lose your Christmas bonus and your two weeks playing shuffleboard on a cruise ship to Mazatlán. Why is that a reason to get up in the morning?

But Virginia had redefined normal. What that word really meant was taking pleasure in small things. Like getting up and having an actual breakfast with an actual human being, instead of gulping down a McShit burger with Dwight on your way to getting shot at, or watching TV with your wife cozied in your arms and taking walks to places you had heretofore studiously avoided, like parks and beaches and anyplace there were trees. It meant reading a book without feeling you were missing something and putting birdseed in the bird feeder and making a sandwich for someone besides yourself.

Predictably, there were problems. Stay indoors your whole life with the lights off and never let anyone know you existed and there would *still* be fucking problems. Apparently, *normal* didn't quench the need to be a ruthless motherfucker and the undisputed champion of the illegal gun trade who took on all challengers and blasted them into oblivion. On that, *normal* had no effect. Angus had been that way long before he met Virginia and changing it would be like trading in his DNA for a bus pass or a used car. He decided he would do both. Strike a balance. Yin and yang. Good and bad. It went that way for a while. A perfect world. And then Virginia died in childbirth.

Her grandmother took the baby. Angus was catatonic with grief. He hired a team of house cleaners to remove her smell. None of them could identify what he was talking about. They worked for a week scrubbing and washing and steam cleaning.

"I still smell it," Angus said.

"I don't smell anything," the supervisor said.

"Come back tomorrow and I'll pay you double." The team worked for another week but Angus claimed the smell was still there. In the end, he couldn't stand it anymore. He sold the house at a loss and moved out of the neighborhood.

Angus stopped looking at Virginia's photo. Not because he wanted to but because his eyes were tired. He thought about taking a nap, but knew he wouldn't sleep. He picked up Weiner and took her outside to pee. The grounds were beautiful. A black-bottom pool, lush garden, a white lattice gazebo nestled among the willows, aspens and sycamore trees. It could have been a garbage-strewn alley full of crackheads for all he cared.

He couldn't remember exactly when the guilt he'd suppressed for decades had come crashing into his conscience, or when he realized he might as well have chopped off his daughter's legs or blinded her. In some ways, that would have been better. Those were disabilities that could be coped with, handicaps to be minimized. But this. This uncontrollable, unpredictable, invisible butcher knife that severed and cleaved, that separated you from yourself, that let you glimpse your wants, needs and aspirations just long enough for you to recognize them, and then they—and you—were gone again. And again. And again.

He took a hot bath for the first time in years. He thought it was a waste of time but Virginia told him it was soothing and of course, she'd been right. He lay in the warm, soapy water looking at his bony feet and wondering how his life had become this fucked up, how he'd become so lonely. Only recently, he had realized that the need for love doesn't go away. It doesn't matter how callused and inhumane you are or what hideous things you've done in your life. The need might be dormant or cast aside or long forgotten, but if the meagerest possibility of love arose, however unexpected or unlikely, it exploded; tumultuous, unstoppable and rapacious. He had Weiner and no one else.

He was thinking his life couldn't get any worse when his phone buzzed. It was resting on the edge of the tub. He fumbled with it, dropped it in the water, cursed and retrieved it. Maybe it was good news for a change. It wasn't. It was Gia. Between sobs she said, "Christiana's been arrested."

The officers came to the condo and told her she was under arrest. Gia was hysterical but they ordered her to stand aside or she'd be arrested too. Christiana had to restrain herself from screaming when they cuffed her. The alters went berserk, everyone gathered in her head howling and sobbing at the same time. Christiana supposed she was switching out because she was in the elevator with the cops and when she returned she was in the back of the police car and when she switched out again they were on the freeway and the cop was saying, "Could you hold it down back there?" And the next thing she knew a frightening thing was happening. They'd just gotten out of the car and the officer was standing very close, bending over so their faces were even. He had an enormous bald head and small round eyes that seemed to see right into her brain. His voice was low and his breath smelled like cooked meat. He said, "You threaten me one more time, Miss Byrne, and you're in for a very hard time." *Damn Marlene,* Christiana thought, that temper of hers. She probably tried to seduce him first.

Christiana was processed and fingerprinted. The switching out was going so fast she only got glimpses of things. A female officer telling her to stay against the wall. A big woman with a copper-colored wig saying, "You're gonna get your ass kicked, bitch." In a line with other women, the one in front of her turning and saying, "You one of them transvestites, ain't you?"

She was in a holding cell with three Latino women who had tattoos and looked at her like she was an angel food cake. Then she was on the floor, being beaten by one of them, who said, "You wanna fuck with *me*?" every time she hit her. And now she was sitting on a cot in a cell by herself. She was bruised all over, a clump of her hair was torn out. Other prisoners were yelling, the officers yelling back, the alters screaming and crying and cursing. She clamped her hands over her ears and tried to block out the sound but there was no way to block something if it was inside your brain and she prayed she'd switch out before she got up, took a running start and rammed her head into the cement wall.

Isaiah was in the bedroom getting dressed for the Basher exhibition. Grace was excited. They were going to a gallery, her world. They'd drink wine and look at art and meet some people who weren't cutthroats. She could show off a little too. Noah would be there and she'd be glad to be rid of him. He was in her head far too much.

Isaiah came in, hurriedly, upset. Again. "What's the matter?" she said.

"Gia called," he said. "Christiana's been arrested. I have to go—"

"—warn Stella," she said.

He didn't apologize and her disappointment curdled into anger as he went out the door. She fumed a few moments. She was being small but couldn't help it. She fed Ruffin, put fresh water in his water bowl and left for the exhibit.

Stella's concert was at the Terrace Theater. He'd forgotten all about it. She'd left a ticket for him at Will Call. By the time he got there, the concert was over. They had agreed to meet in the lobby afterward, and he stood around waiting as the audience streamed out of the double doors, talking and laughing. The space emptied and there was nothing but the shimmering chandeliers and a vast expanse of carpet, Vivaldi lingering like a scent. He rehearsed what he would say and each word sounded like bullshit before he said it. He couldn't stand the idea that she might be crippled, that there would be no more performances, no more music, no more Stella.

Stella and three other musicians came out carrying instrument cases. She hugged them in turn. "Thank you, thank you, I'll meet you there." They moved off and she turned to Isaiah. There was hurt in her eyes, a quiver in her voice. "Your seat was empty," she said. "Where were you?" He opened his mouth but nothing came out. "It was my first solo performance," she said. "It was important to me. My family was here, my friends were here, but not you. Not my boyfriend." Tears ran down her lovely face. "How could you do that to me?"

He explained about the case, about Angus and the threat. She was furious. "I don't believe this!" she said. "This man is going to break my hands? That's insane!"

"I know and I'm sorry—"

"Did you call the police?"

"I don't have anything to tell them," Isaiah said. "He hasn't done anything yet."

"*Done anything?* You mean I have to have my hands broken before he can be arrested?"

"Stella, I—"

"Well, what am I supposed to do, Isaiah? Go into hiding?"

"Yes," he said, adding quickly, "temporarily. I'll have it cleared up in—" He didn't want to lie. "Soon."

"You're telling me that if I walk out that door, I'm in danger?"

"Probably not, but I...I wouldn't go home. For now."

She put her hands out, beseeching the heavens, as if to call back a future that was already destroyed. "How could you do this to me, Isaiah? I haven't done anything! I'm not part of your world!"

He was desperate to comfort her, but *I'm sorry* seemed inadequate to the point of insulting. He said it anyway. "I'm sorry. I had no idea he would—"

"I don't want to hear it!" Her words were like teeth, tearing the last bits of flesh off his conscience. "I'll stay at my parents' place. Call me when this is over." She backed away, aiming a finger at him. "You and I are done, do you hear me? Completely done!" She whirled around and was gone. This woman who had come up the hard way and always knew she'd be a musician and worked at a laundromat when she was nine years old and could only afford three lessons and took two jobs in the summertime and earned a scholarship to a good school and played in Michael Bublé's orchestra at the Mirage and worked for seven years to become first chair in the Long Beach Symphony Orchestra—was terrified and had every right to be. Her entire life was under threat and it was all because of him.

*   *   *

The Basher show was stunning. His trademark paintings in gradated, shimmering stripes, his industrial installations intriguing and architectural. Grace liked his work more than she'd thought. Cherokee showed up. It was almost a surprise to see her outside the apartment, where they always wore sweatpants, no makeup or shoes.

"Where's Isaiah?" Cherokee said. "I really want to meet him."

"He couldn't come," Grace said. "Work." She felt worse saying it out loud. Noah came in. She turned away so it wouldn't seem like she was waiting for him. Had she been waiting for him?

"Who's that?" Cherokee said.

"My old boyfriend from New Mexico."

"The one you told me about? Is he sniffing around you again?"

"Yeah, I think so. Don't look at me like that. He doesn't mean anything."

Cherokee was uncomfortable and left to talk to her friends. Grace and Noah looked at Basher's work together and went for a drink. Grey Goose for her, beer for him. He really had changed. He talked about relationships, that he wasn't prepared for one, not understanding what it was about, what it meant. "Nobody teaches you about those things," he said. "It's trial and error and a lot of stupidity."

"Agreed," she said, smiling. "You were a real bastard."

He smiled back. She knew he liked that about her. Never trying to soften things or gloss over them. "Are you seeing someone?" he ventured.

"Yes, I am. He's a wonderful guy."

"I guess he'd have to be." He sighed. "Ah, well. All the good ones are taken." He kissed her on the cheek when they said goodbye. She drove home, feeling an odd sense of loss, more so than when they'd broken up. Maybe it was the finality of it; all the feelings they'd had for each other turned to nothing. They would never see each other again. It's surprisingly hard to give up a fantasy, even when you know it was a placeholder, even when you know for certain it was the best thing to do.

She thought about Isaiah. She wanted to kiss him and go to bed with him and whisper in his ear and tell him everything would be okay.

Stella was fair game now. Isaiah couldn't protect her. Dwight, Sidero, Hugo, and the rest of those barbarians would be hunting for her and there was no way of knowing when and where they'd strike. Sometimes, when evil was imminent, you reached a point where there was no more room for maneuvering, quick wits, trickery or sleight of hand. Extremes were necessary. What Isaiah contemplated was beyond anything he'd done or even imagined.

They were on PCH, heading into Cambodia Town.

"Whatever you're up to," Dodson said, "it's a giant can of worms, and you know what's gonna happen? What *always* happens."

"Which is?" Isaiah said.

"Which is—there won't be no worms," Dodson replied. "They'll be some life-threatening shit you never saw coming but you won't care cuz you think you know everything even when you don't and I'll end up dead or at the very least seriously wounded."

"That's not true," Isaiah said, unconvincingly.

"Then spill it. Why do you want to see him?"

"It's hard to explain."

"Hard to explain?" Dodson said. "I understand English, I even read and write some too." He thought a moment and looked sharply at Isaiah. "Oh, shit. You got one of them special plans of yours, don't you? One of your high-risk, death-defying, all-or-nothin' muthafuckas with a million moving parts." He started to lift his T-shirt. "Have you seen the bullet hole I got from the last time you had a special plan? You remember, don't you? Them Abu Ghraib sons of bitches had guns and we had a slingshot and flamethrower made out of a caulking gun?"

"Let's just see how this goes, all right?" Isaiah said.

"You called Lok so that means you're offering him something," Dodson mused. "Probably your skills. What else have you got? My question is, what do you want from a killa thug like that muthafucka?" Dodson's eyes widened with alarm. "*Oh, shit.* You're meeting him because he *is* a killa muthafucka."

"I said we'll see how it goes."

"Ohhh, shit!"

"Will you stop saying that?"

They drove into Cambodia Town. The hood is the hood, Isaiah thought. If the Starship *Enterprise* beamed you up from South Central and beamed you down in Cambodia Town, the only things you wouldn't recognize would be the names of the gangs. The Mother of All Ghetto Housing had birthed a million identical offspring; Lok's place was an elder child. A pink L-shaped stucco building, two stories, casement windows that didn't open, iron railings, graffiti scarred, all the doors facing the V-shaped parking lot. Old men played dominoes at a card table, smoking cigars and drinking 40s. Women sat outside their doors in housecoats, fanning themselves and gossiping with their neighbors.

Isaiah was an almanac of gang lore. In the eighties, hundreds of thousands of Cambodians fled Pol Pot's genocide and the Khmer Rouge. A million and a half people were murdered in the killing fields. Isaiah couldn't get over it, any more than he could get over the Holocaust. The numbers were horrifying, but equally so were the people who could kill with such wanton savagery. History hadn't washed them away. They were still here. Rwanda, Bosnia, Darfur and a bunch more would-be tyrants with Nazism in their hearts, mulling over which races, religions and sexual preferences they would eradicate if only they had the chance.

A large number of Cambodian refugees settled in East Long Beach. Adapting was hard. They were poor, rootless, uneducated, spoke Khmer, and there was no network to help them adjust. Many were traumatized by their experiences and suffered from PTSD. Here, they were less than strangers, they were interlopers in a space already crowded with the needy and the powerless. They were strangers to themselves as well. If you're defined by your world, who are you when your world kicks you out and leaves you to die?

Good parenting was hard to come by. The kids were neglected, adrift, stunted by poverty, alcohol and drugs. At the time, Cambodians had the highest dropout rate in the city and were brutalized by the black and Latino gangs. A simple trip to the store was dangerous.

The Tiny Rascals Gang, or TRG, was formed in the eighties for protection. The name referred to a favorite TV show, *The Little Rascals,* an OG going so far as to name himself Alfalfa. Other members took names from the show, too: Spanky, Stymie and Butch. But as the gang grew and got more ruthless, the reference became embarrassing and the story changed. The name came about because they were all just tiny rascals. Blue and red were taken as gang colors so TRG settled on gray, which looked drab to Isaiah.

As conditions in the area worsened, the gang evolved into one more Army of the Damned, descending in concentric circles into a burning pit of extortion, robbery, drugs and murder. TRG formed alliances with the Chinese Triads, the Ghost Shadows, On Leong Tong, 14K and Wo Hop To.

It said something about the country that TRG grew so rapidly. Other Southeast Asians, even Latinos and blacks, joined up. The gang spread to other cities and now they were ten thousand strong, the largest Asian gang in the country. There were sets all over LA. The Tiny Insane Criminals, the Lynwood Varrio Tiny Locos, Alley Tiny Criminals, Paramount Varrio Tiny Sureños and Lok's gang—the Tiny Enforcerz Crew. TEC. Their formal name was Tiny Enforcerz Crew L59, the L59 referring to the gang's fiefdom, Lindenhurst Ave, 5900 block.

Though its turf was larger than that, the block was TEC's home base, its fortress; trespass and you were likely to catch a bullet. Its gang sign was so complicated, you needed two people and four hands to assemble it.

"When we get in there let me do the talking," Dodson said.

"Why? It's my proposal," Isaiah replied.

"Why? I'll tell you why. Because in addition to your ignorance about women, your sense of decorum in a business situation lacks finesse, acumen and sensitivity, and if Lok shoots you, he'll shoot me too."

Isaiah and Lok had gotten into a serious beef a while back. Back in the day, Dodson sold weed to Lok and dated one of his cousins. Dodson hadn't gotten her pregnant—a rarity—and Lok was appreciative. Isaiah would never say it out loud but it was reassuring having Dodson along, knowing how cool he was in a crunch, how fearless and loyal.

Lok's apartment was a three bedroom he shared with his homies. You didn't have to see it to know what it was like. There'd be a TV the size of a ping-pong table, a fucked-up sofa, a couple of PlayStation controllers, white plastic chairs, a mattress on the floor, a coffee table for rolling joints and resting your Glock, and a beat-to-shit, mustard-colored carpet stained to death and only vacuumed when somebody's mom came over. There was no point talking about the smell. The only thing Isaiah was wrong about was the carpet. It was brown.

Lok was seated on the edge of the sofa, clutching the controller, thumbs working the buttons, his eyes superglued to the screen. Isaiah couldn't stomach video games. There was enough violence in real life. Making a game of it was like the Muppets singing a song about starvation.

"What's up, Lok?" Dodson said as they sat down. "How you been?"

"Aight," he said without looking up. "I'm cool." There was nothing to suggest he was the leader of a notorious gang. Pudgy, shaved head, a frown like he was pondering world peace. Studious wire-rimmed glasses.

"Isaiah's got something for you," Dodson said. "A business opportunity."

"I hear you got two females on a string, Q," Lok said, steadily working the controller. "A white girl and a sista. Not bad, dude. I never would have guessed."

Isaiah wondered how Lok knew about Stella and Grace. It was one of the worst things about his job, people all up in your business. He started to snap back but Dodson silenced him with a look.

"You want some advice?" Lok offered. "Stick to your own kind. White bitches ain't nothing but trouble. All they want to talk about is *relationships*. Shit. Only relationships I got are with my money and my car."

"There's some wisdom right there," Dodson said, hiding his ring finger. "Trust a woman and you put your shit on the line. Last time I had faith in one, I woke up naked with no wallet, no watch and my weed was gone too. Only thing the bitch left behind was my socks."

Lok chuckled and scratched his nose with his shoulder. "You nearly got me busted, Q. You remember that? Me and Gentry Green was doing that deal and you brought the pigs down on us. I barely got away. Gentry's still in Corcoran, did you know that?"

"No," Isaiah said. "Gentry and I aren't in touch."

"Could have been me, locked up for ten to twenty."

"Could have been," Isaiah said, adding, "You were lucky."

Dodson winced. Lok turned hostile. "I'm always lucky, nigga, but you got some muthafuckin' nerve coming down here. I should be cuttin' your throat 'stead of sitting here bullshitting."

"Ease up," Dodson said. "We come in peace. My boy's got something good on tap."

"Were you like, poor?" Lok said for no apparent reason. "I mean, like really poor, like no lunch, and soup for dinner? That's how I grew up. Shit makes you hard, you know what I'm saying? When school started, Mom would buy me a new pair of pants and my brother a new shirt. We switched every day."

Isaiah was on the fence about growing up hard, whether it was a reason or pretext for being a criminal. The difference between Stella and Ponlok wasn't their financial struggles, gang temptations, bad schools or fewer opportunities. It was their families. A kid deprived of love, that kernel of what makes us human, will grow up stunted and mean and might well become the leader of a Cambodian street gang. Grow up loved and nourished and you might well become first chair in the Long Beach Symphony Orchestra. It reminded Isaiah of Angus, his favorite son, Tyler, thriving and esteemed, and the neglected ones, Sidero and Dwight, eating themselves alive with hatred and self-loathing.

Lok's gaze never left the screen, his avatar mowing down the bad guys while it ran full out, dodging enemy fire, leaping over chasms and downed bridges, rolling away from explosions and firing everything from handguns to RPGs and flamethrowers. Lok had remarkable hand-eye coordination. Isaiah thought he should quit this gangsta bullshit and fly an F-15, protect his country, do something useful.

"Oh, shit," Lok said. He'd hit a tricky part of the game. He worked the controller furiously, ducking his head as tracer rounds zipped past, his shoulders shifting back and forth. Dodson glanced at Isaiah. *Be patient.*

There were footsteps and voices from the hallway. Smells preceded them. Garlic, lemongrass, ginger, curry. Three homies came in carrying Styrofoam boxes, Guda one of them. The group had that look seen in every gang photo ever taken: scruffy and disorganized, like everybody tried to dress the same without having the same clothes. They glanced at Lok and ignored Isaiah and Dodson. Guda looked at the floor as if he'd never seen it before. They all stood there a moment. If you had food, it was your prerogative to watch TV.

"Come on," Lok said. "Let's go outside."

"Your mom's pork and rice is crazy good," one of the homies said. "Is there any beer left?"

"Hey, man," said another, "I don't think this is my box."

Lok, Dodson and Isaiah went outside on the balcony and stood at the railing. There was nothing to look at but the parking lot, two dumpsters and some kids running around, having fun even in a shithole like this.

"So?" Lok said, lighting up a J. "What's this about?"

"Angus is selling a Gatling gun," Isaiah said. "It's new. Forty-four-hundred-round magazine, fires three thousand rounds a minute. Never saw anything like it. You could kill everybody on the block and still have ammo left over."

"No shit?" the gang leader said. "Fuckin' Angus's gonna make some stacks behind that bad boy. Why you telling me this?"

"Because I can help you steal it."

Lok thought a moment. He tipped his head back as if he needed more distance to focus. "How do you know this shit? I need more chapter."

"I know because I know," Isaiah said. "The same way I knew you and Gentry were making that deal. This isn't a sales pitch. If you're interested, fine. If you're not, I know people who will be."

Lok sneered. "Oh, yeah? Like who?"

"The Locos, the Boulevard Mafia, the East Side Longos, Sons of Samoa, Armand Duprée on the west side, JJ Hardaway in Cerritos—"

Lok chuckled. "Okay, okay, you got your shit down, I should have known." He looked hard at Isaiah, searching for a crack in his confidence. "You sure about this?"

"You know I don't bullshit," Isaiah said.

Lok nodded. "I'm in, aight?" They pounded fists. "Who are the buyers?"

"I don't know yet."

"I'll put the fam on it, see if they can come with something." Lok smiled. "What do you want, Q? I know you ain't doing this for free."

Isaiah could hardly believe he was saying the words. "I want you to kill Angus."

They drove away from Lok's place, Dodson incredulous. He'd expected a deal but nothing like this. He hadn't realized Isaiah was under so much stress. This was contracting a hit. This was muthafuckin' murder.

"Don't you think you're being a little extreme?" Dodson said.

"I don't know any other way to get Stella out from under this, okay?" Isaiah said heatedly. "Have you got any better ideas?"

"Yes, and here it is. Calm your ass down. I don't know if you're aware of it yet but I'm on your goddamn side. I can worry about you if I want to and you got shit-all to say about it." Isaiah's teeth were clenched, his eyes narrowed. He hadn't swallowed since they started the conversation. "Take a breath," Dodson said. "I'm serious. Take a breath." Amazingly, Isaiah complied, filling up his chest and letting it go. He did it a second time. His shoulders relaxed. "And I'd be remiss," Dodson went on, "if I didn't remind you that the laws regarding killing people are not debatable. There is no wiggle room, there are no do-overs."

Isaiah ignored that. "Something else just occurred to me," he said. "Angus may have hired the killers himself."

"What? What for?" Dodson asked.

"It's the same thing I told Christiana," Isaiah said. "If Tyler took her away, Angus would be losing his little girl, the one he owes and can never pay back. What he couldn't anticipate was that the killers would shoot Tyler in Christiana's shop. It was bad luck. The killers had no reason to know he had a daughter."

"Then why did Angus hire you?" Dodson said.

"Desperation," Isaiah said. "The only way he could get the heat off of Christiana was to point the police in another direction. If they were convinced there were more plausible suspects than Christiana, they might leave her alone."

"What if the cops found the killers?" Dodson said. "Wouldn't they rat Angus out?"

"Angus took a chance," Isaiah said. "What else could he do?" They rode in silence awhile. Isaiah knew Dodson wanted to say *Are you sure about this?* But wisely, he didn't.

"Ain't the worst thing I can think of," Dodson said, "having Angus gone the fuck outta here. That's more like my code of honor than yours. Personally I got no problem with it. I'm thinking about you. You the one that's gonna suffer behind this. The question is, will you suffer more for Stella or Angus?" Isaiah didn't say anything. "Okay," Dodson said as if he'd heard an answer. "Tell me what the plan is—don't look at me like that. I'm not trying to take over your life."

"Oh yeah?" Isaiah said, still defensive. "Then what *are* you doing?"

"I'm trying to keep you from ending up with a bullet hole in your head and buried in Angus's backyard. Now quit being so hardheaded and tell me the goddamn plan."

CHAPTER SIXTEEN

The Junior from Anywhere High

Isaiah and Dodson drove out to the Den. They parked on the road, went by the empty kiosk, and crossed the city parking lot. It was the weekend and the forklifts and earth movers were lined up in rows, the office trailers and warehouses were closed. Isaiah and Dodson went through the grove of scraggly trees and stopped at the tree line.

The Den was set in a large, weedy area with a barbed-wire fence around the perimeter, an open gate in front, fourteen Starks milling around in the yard, most holding a beer. A couple of kettle barbecues were smoldering, filling the breeze with the summer smells of charcoal and barbecued chicken.

"Damn, that smells good," Dodson said. "And it tastes good no matter who cooks it." Hate rap was thundering out of the windows, assaulting the sky, the clouds wincing and moving away. "Ain't this a bitch?" Dodson said. "Muthafuckas using nigga music to put down niggas." A few of them were dancing halfheartedly, shuffling around and bobbing their heads more than anything else. "Will you look at this," Dodson said. "Tryin' to move to the beat and they off by the whole fuckin' song."

"Be quiet, will you?" Isaiah said.

There were four women. Isaiah thought their lack of numbers was another sign of women's superior intelligence. Three of them were

218

wearing mom jeans and oversize sweatshirts. The fourth was the red-head from the firing range; cutoffs, a tank top and cowboy boots. If you can't get attention in the real world, why not be this year's Miss California Bigotry?

A dog was meandering around, a bullmastiff. Majestic and hulking with its big square head and floppy black muzzle; a brindle, tawny striping over black, a hundred thirty pounds of get the fuck out of my way.

"Oh, shit," Dodson said.

Isaiah noticed a kid off by himself, leaning on a car, smoking a cigarette. He was fifteen or sixteen, reclusive face, an absorbent gaze and a seedling soul patch. A junior at Anywhere High School in his white T-shirt and jeans. He was trying to be casual but it came off as self-conscious and awkward, that age when you're scouting around for an identity but not quite ready to hop on a bandwagon. Isaiah wondered if the kid's parents were here and whether they'd taught their son to hate the conniving Jews and the fucking blacks and the lazy illegal Mexicans and if they'd instilled in him the belief that the mainstream media were out to destroy the white race. He wondered if the kid had stood respectfully at the Robert E. Lee monument or read about the made-up Holocaust or was handed an AR-15 for the coming race war or whether he had an option to see the world any other way. It was a crime and tragedy but that was freedom for you. A good idea that was never on sale.

The dog worried Isaiah as much as it did Dodson. Bullmastiffs originated in Britain two hundred years ago. The privileged class bred them to attack poachers nabbing a rabbit and trying to feed their families. The dogs' masters preferred brindles because of their excellent camouflage.

Isaiah and Dodson watched the house for an hour. It was getting dark. Somebody turned on the porch lights. Sidero came out. He shouted something and everyone went inside. Fortunately, the dog did too. The music was turned off. Sidero could be heard ranting, and then the Starks began singing the most off-key, caterwauling, embarrassingly bad version of "Dixie" in the history of the Deep South. "They can't sing neither," Dodson said.

Isaiah knew Dodson had a phobia about dogs, and for good reason too. When he was a kid, a pit bull had mauled him, leaving scars all over his back and arms. During the Black the Knife case, Dodson was nearly eaten by a giant pit bull named Goliath.

"It's a one-man job," Isaiah said. "Stay here."

Dodson watched Isaiah dart across the road, through the gate and into a cluster of cars parked haphazardly around the house. The destination was Sidero's truck, which, of course, was parked right next to the porch. Between the truck and Isaiah was an empty stretch of ground with no cover.

Dodson whispered, "Pick your moment, Isaiah." The Starks started chanting, "Blood and soil! Blood and soil!" Whatever the fuck that meant. "Go now, Isaiah!"

As if Isaiah had heard him, he dashed across the space and slipped under the truck. Fucking Isaiah was fearless. Dodson couldn't see him, but he knew Isaiah was attaching a magnetized GPS unit to the frame. He stuck his head out to see if the coast was clear. He started to scramble out but three guys came out of the house.

"Go back, Isaiah! Go back!" Dodson said, trying to keep his voice down. Two of the guys were holding a drunken colleague by the armpits. Without a word, they dropped him on the ground and went back inside. The drunk's face was turned sideways, his cheek in the dirt. All he had to do was open his eyes and he'd be looking directly at Isaiah.

"Oh, shit," Dodson said. He swallowed hard and blinked the sweat out of his eyes. He wanted to run over there but didn't know what he'd do. The drunk got to his hands and knees, silvery drool hanging from his open mouth. A gun fell out of his belt. "Oh, *shit*," Dodson said again. He knew what Isaiah was thinking. The shortest way out was the way he'd come in, but he'd have to run right past the drunk, sprint across the yard, over the road and into the trees. Would the drunk see him and have time to shoot?

Isaiah's other option was longer; get out on the other side of the truck, run across a stretch of weedy field and over the barbed-wire fence. Dodson couldn't stand it. *Make up your mind, Q. Go one way or the other!* The chanting had stopped and the meeting was breaking up, chairs moving, talking, loud laughter. *Make up your mind, Isaiah. Make your fucking move!*

Too late. The group came out, footsteps thumping down the wooden stoop. "Damn, Isaiah," Dodson said. "Why didn't you make a fucking move?"

Isaiah was berating himself. *Why didn't you make a fucking move?* He was surrounded by a forest of legs and loud babble. He was overwhelmed with fear for the thousandth time in his life. The people were all so close. He could hear their stupid conversations. The drunk was lying flat now, eyes closed. *Stay asleep. Stay asleep.* The drunk opened his eyes. He stared, wrinkling his brow and squinting as if he wasn't sure what he was seeing. "Sidero?" he said. "I slee a nigger."

Sidero snorted. "I'll bet you do, you drunk son of a bitch."

"No, no, man, I thwear to God, I slee a nigger."

"Oh, yeah? Where?"

The drunk vomited, causing an outpouring of disgust. Moving legs blocked Isaiah's view. The reprieve was momentary. The dog was twenty feet away, sniffing the ground intently. In the miasma of smells, it had no reason to home in on Isaiah but it was coming this way. *Sniff sniff sniff sniff sniff sniff.* Isaiah had rarely experienced full-on panic, fear so intense it paralyzed your limbs and stomped on your logical mind. He fought the urge to run. The dog was getting closer. *Sniff sniff sniff sniff sniff sniff.* The fucking thing was relentless. What was it looking for? Isaiah remembered: the barbecue. The dog was looking for scraps! There was a greasy chicken bone a foot and a half away from Isaiah. He'd have to reach out from under the car. Would somebody see his hand? *Do it, just do it. One...two...THREE.*

He snatched the bone and flung it sideways. The dog sensed it and moved off. Isaiah's head sunk with relief, his forehead touching the ground. He looked up again. The dog had been blocking the drunk's view. The guy was slightly more sober now, sitting up, bending at the waist to peer under the car.

"Hey, Sidero. I'm not kibbing. There's a nigger under your car."

"You're hallucinating."

"No, I'm not. Here, takes a look for yourself."

Isaiah watched Sidero's feet move toward the drunk. *It's over. I'm done.* Sidero grabbed the drunk by his collar and hauled him to his feet.

"Come on, asshole. We're gonna hose you off."

"No, wait, I thwear—"

The drunk was hauled away. Another reprieve. Engines were starting, people were leaving. Sidero would too. The moment he backed out his car, Isaiah would be exposed and these drunk, angry clods would beat him, cripple him or worse. He hoped Dodson wouldn't do anything foolish.

One by one the cars departed, tires spraying gravel as they sped off, the drivers yodeling rebel yells, Heil Hitlers and fuck the fill-in-the-blanks. Isaiah's brain was churning but he had nothing. Five cars were left...four...three, the roaring engines fading into quiet. Two left. Sidero's truck and somebody's Charger. Were they in the house? *Go now, Isaiah!* Too late. Sidero and Hugo approached. They stopped next to a bicycle leaning against the porch.

"You ready, bro?" Hugo said.

"Ready as I'm gonna be," Sidero said, not sounding especially confident. "All I want to do is get this over with and collect our money. Fucking Angus. God, what a prick."

"I hear you, man, I'll see you later."

The two men went to their cars. Sidero wore heavy boots, the thick soles scraping against the ground, dust rising with every footfall. He opened the door, got in and slammed it shut. The engine started, the vibration loosening grit that fell on Isaiah's head. He stifled the urge to sneeze. Hugo started his Charger but neither of the vehicles moved. They're on their phones, Isaiah thought. The first thing you do. Hugo had to leave first or he'd be left in the open. *Come on, asshole, go.*

Isaiah waited. Another death watch. Another instance where his fate would be decided by someone else's random behavior. Hugo left first. *Hallefuckinglujah!* Only Sidero remained. Wouldn't he just love to shoot a nigger? Tell the guys about it? Get a skull tattoo to commemorate the accomplishment? Put a notch on his gun next to the one for Beaumont?

A quick calculation. The truck was parked head-in. Sidero would back out, arc to the right, and come to a stop before turning left toward the gate. Until he made that turn, Isaiah would be completely in the open and the fucking porch lights were still on. The option. When Sidero backed out, he'd be looking over his right shoulder. That would give Isaiah three, maybe four seconds to get up and scramble over the porch railing. The support posts were thick so he'd be out of view.

He waited. The truck's huffing idle was like a lion panting, the exhaust fumes nauseating. Sidero put the car in reverse and backed out. Isaiah waited until he was exposed, leaped up, grabbed the porch railing and flung himself over. He landed hard, rolled and slammed into the wall. He waited, listened. Sidero's car was moving—and then stopped. Was he making a call or had he seen Isaiah?

Sidero drove away.

Isaiah sat up, leaned back against the wall and tried to compose himself. This shit was getting old. He'd been thinking about it a lot these days, how routinely risking his life wasn't a sustainable career path. Grace made his life worth more. When people heard he'd been in a scary situation, they imagined it was exciting and on some level, fun. It wasn't. It really wasn't. Experiences like this were nightmare-inducing and put black holes in your health. They were also a prognosis. Keep this shit up and you will not live a long time.

Isaiah sucked in a deep breath and started to get up. He wondered why the porch lights were still on. Had someone forgotten to turn them off? And that bicycle was still leaning against the stoop. Had someone forgotten that too? Isaiah sucked in a breath. "Oh no," he breathed. *Someone was still in the house.*

The Junior from Anywhere High came out on the porch, a mop

in one hand, a gun in the other. He looked at Isaiah. He didn't seem angry or triumphant, more curious and confused. A few minutes ago, he'd been demonizing niggers just like everybody else, and here he was face-to-face with an actual nigger in the flesh. Isaiah's ethnicity was a crime in itself, and he'd been spying on them. If the kid shot the black bastard, the gang would throw him a party.

Through the railing, Isaiah saw Dodson emerge from the tree line. He was coming to the rescue. *Don't do it, Dodson! Go back!* The kid bent his knees and put the mop down on the floor, carefully, as if it might break. He stood, sighed and looked across the field at the barbed-wire fence, seemingly ambivalent, like his mom was calling him home. Dodson was hunched low. He reached the front gate, hid behind a post and peeked around it. He kept coming. *Go back, Dodson! For fuck's sake, pleeease go back!* Isaiah didn't think his heart could stand any more pounding or that his lungs could take another heaving breath. His sweat glands were drowning. He wondered how it was possible for a kid—*a fifteen-year-old kid*—to even consider shooting another person, as if he were deciding whether to drop out of school or have sex without a condom.

The kid gripped the gun tighter and looked at Isaiah again. Dodson was crouched and moving slowly, halfway across the yard now. He had a rock in his hand the size of a softball. *You're gonna get killed, you idiot. These people train their kids with guns.*

The kid was sullen now, like this was a problem he didn't want, a question he couldn't answer. He was anxious too, breathing in sighs, his finger moving on and off the trigger; hate versus humanity flickering through his fledgling eyes. He took another deep breath as if preparing himself. Dodson was ten feet away, tiptoeing up behind him, hefting the rock. Isaiah tensed, ready to jump the kid if he aimed at Dodson. The kid looked off again.

"You better go," he said. Then he turned and went back inside.

Chip looked through the window. The second black guy had joined the first one and they were running into the trees. Chip had seen the second guy in his peripheral vision. Another reason to come inside.

Shooting one of them would have been hard. Shooting them both was unthinkable.

Chip still had the gun in his hand. His dad had given it to him on his thirteenth birthday. A Walther PPK because they liked to watch James Bond movies together. The gun was used but it fired just fine and he was a good shot. His dad thought he should join the military. College was for the hoity-toity rich kids, he said, and it filled your head with socialist propaganda. Chip knew what socialists were. He'd studied it in history class. He was pretty sure he knew more than his dad. He seemed to think it was some kind of group dictatorship.

Chip imagined what would have happened if he'd shot the black guy. The gang would have been happy. Overjoyed, in fact. They'd slap him on the back and ruffle his hair and offer him a beer. His dad would have held him up on his shoulders and ran down the middle of the street yelling his head off. His dad seemed to think he had no ideas of his own, that he swallowed the party line whole and that he didn't consider other opinions or beliefs, that he didn't read the paper or watch the news.

His dad was always talking about a race war; that it was bound to happen and they should be prepared. Race war, Chip thought. *Race war?* So the black kids at school would go out and get guns and mow down all the white kids because—because what? They had to protect their privileged position in society and nip this white resurgence thing in the bud? How stupid did his dad think he was?

Chip went back to mopping but his hands were shaking. It was a scary situation, out there holding a gun on somebody while another guy snuck up behind you with a rock. It was okay though, he thought. He could forget about it. He was sure something like that would never happen again.

Isaiah and Dodson hiked back through the trees. Isaiah was exhausted and shaken, stumbling several times and falling down. They crossed the parking lot, went past the kiosk and got in the car. They sat there awhile, Dodson with his head back, Isaiah resting his forehead on the steering wheel. The world was too much for him. If he could have walked off into the dark never to be seen again he would have, if it wasn't for Grace.

Hugo had said *I'll see you later,* which could mean he'd see Sidero whenever or they were meeting again that night. The blue GPS dot settled on an address nearby. It was a small, untidy house, Sidero's truck under the carport. Isaiah parked and settled in.

"Nothing to do but wait," he said.

This was a big night in Sidero's shitty life. Another fantastic opportunity to fuck shit up and piss off Angus again. Him and his *millllion*-dollar deal, the mean old fuck lording it over you, calling you nimrod and dummy and knocking you down right in front of the crew, always explaining things a thousand times because he thought you were stupid. That asshole scores big and you get the fucking crumbs. Angus was a legend and you're what you always were. A nobody in a shit pile of nothing.

Jenn, his girlfriend, was a hard-core white nationalist, which was cool, but she was goddamn strict about it. She wouldn't let him watch basketball games because seventy-five percent of NBA players were black. "Doesn't that tell you something?" she said. Uh-huh, he thought. It tells me niggers can run fast and jump out of their socks. She could be a bitch too, always saying he should stand up to Angus and tell him to fuck off and that he was a wimp for taking it. She didn't understand, although he'd tried to explain himself a hundred times.

Sidero had wanted to dump her a long time ago but he had a thing for redheads. That, and she had something on him. They were at Rafters on a Saturday night, standing room only, fuck the fire marshal. Everybody was dancing, drinking, sweating, waving a bottle of booze in the air. It was Sidero's birthday and he was drunk out of his mind. He didn't dance but Jenn did, with a bulked-up jarhead, wagging her booty while the guy air-fucked her, his boner nudging her cutoffs. Goddamn slut. If the guy hadn't been so big, Sidero would have broken a beer bottle over his head.

Sidero was standing at the back, leaning against a wall so he wouldn't fall over. The club was dark to begin with but he was under the loft, people partying up there. You couldn't see anything except when the disco ball angled the right way and the gleam made you blink. It was coming around again and Sidero turned his head aside.

A black guy was standing at his shoulder, looking at him. Not angry or scared or anything else. Just looking. Though he'd tried many times since, Sidero couldn't remember the man's face, only that his eyes were soft and in the instant before the gleam left them and the darkness returned, Sidero leaned over and kissed the man. He didn't know why. He just did it. And then Jenn was there.

"Let's go," she said. Her voice was as flat as sheetrock and she was close enough to touch him—hit him—but there was nothing in her expression. Not shock, surprise, disgust or anything else. She turned around and pushed her way through the crowd. He hurried to catch up and didn't look back.

They never talked about it, but it was always there. Like a shiv or an ace up her sleeve; something she could hurt you with whenever she wanted. Sometimes when they were arguing, she'd look at him as if to say, *I saw you kiss a black man, you nigger-loving homo.* He wasn't either of those things. He was sure of it.

Although he'd never admit it, there was nothing Sidero wanted more than to please Angus. His need pissed him off and made him feel shittier about himself than he already did. What if he messed up again? He wouldn't. He couldn't. He'd promised himself. He'd do exactly what Angus said and he'd have Hugo and Dwight to back him up.

Sidero had been planning to leave town for a while now but he'd always chickened out. He'd load his stuff into the truck, be all ready to go and think, maybe *this time* he could make Angus happy. The need drove him to try over and over again, even with the abuse, even with the humiliation.

The realization had been coming for some time now. There was no way to please Angus. It was impossible. Sidero's sins were biblical and he'd be in hell forever. He decided after the shooting range that he'd had enough. When the Gatling gun deal was done he'd get the fuck out of Dodge. And Jenn? So long you miserable cunt. You just got dumped by a wimp.

Sidero had just dozed off when Jenn woke him up. "Time to go," she said. She gave him that *I don't know who you are* look, and just to be a bitch, she added, "We don't want to be late."

Isaiah and Dodson followed Sidero and the redhead back to the dirt road that led to the Den. Isaiah parked and waited.

"You think it's coming down tonight?" Dodson asked.

Isaiah nodded. He was glad he hadn't told Grace. This was going to be bad and he didn't want to lie, keep secrets and try to smile. Fifteen minutes later, Hugo and Dwight showed up in a green delivery van. They were grim and tense. The Gatling gun was in there.

Isaiah called Lok. "Be ready. It's happening."

"Fuck yeah," Lok said.

Isaiah's unease was turning into horror. He had set this up and people might—would certainly—be killed. He rationalized. Nobody told the gangsters to do this, they were volunteers. They'd chosen this life. They knew they could be killed at any time and many of them were killers themselves. The world wouldn't miss them any more than it missed the countless numbers of other gangsters who had died violent deaths they probably deserved. How was this any different? Isaiah sighed, shook his head and wondered why he kept bullshitting himself. Whatever happened, he owned it. He had to think of Stella before he fell apart.

CHAPTER SEVENTEEN
The Deal of the Century

A little after midnight, Sidero's truck and the green van emerged from the dirt road. Isaiah followed. Willow to the 710 and then north on the 405, Isaiah keeping Lok informed. When they exited at El Segundo Boulevard, Isaiah knew where they were going. "The industrial zone," he told Lok. "Don't get any closer than Sepulveda."

The zone was a large expanse of acreage, bleak in the daytime when people were around. At night, it was a forgotten outpost, survivors from the apocalypse awaiting death. A massive oil refinery loomed out of the dark, a tangle of pipes and tall fire stacks emitting clouds of steam, escaping gases burning into water vapor, random lights illuming flurries of insects. There were immense storage tanks, rusted-out railcars, sludge pools, stretches of weedy ground, old tractor tires, piles of rebar, clustered labyrinths of pipes with no end or beginning and low buildings dingy with pollution, the whole area thick with the smell of oil and cancer.

Isaiah positioned the car on a rise from where he could see most of the area. Sidero's truck and the green van were waiting on the south end of the zone, their engines running, the lights off. Isaiah waited, fear and anxiety rioting inside of him. He heard distant engines approaching; the buyers were coming. He still didn't know who they were. Dodson didn't seem especially anxious, more excited, something

Isaiah admired. Dodson liked action, craved adrenaline. Isaiah texted Lok. *Be ready.*

On the north end, the sellers showed up, only the shapes of their vehicles visible. At exactly twelve thirty, Sidero flashed his lights three times and then once. The reverse code came back from the buyers. All the vehicles turned on their lights and started down the long, roughly paved road that ran from border to border. Isaiah imagined how Sidero must be feeling, his heart in his throat, Angus yelling in his ear, a gun on the console, sweaty hands clamped down on the steering wheel, every instinct telling him to get the fuck out of there and that well of fear when he realized there was nowhere to go but straight ahead.

The two sides stopped thirty feet apart. They were in different lanes so the headlights didn't blind them.

"I'm going to text Lok," Isaiah said.

"I'd wait a minute," Dodson said. "Wait till they get out of the cars and they're on foot. You wanna make sure the Gatling's in that van. Nobody can trust nobody."

Dodson was right, of course. If Isaiah hadn't been so nervous, he'd have thought of it himself.

Sidero got out of his truck, no gun visible but for sure he had one. Hugo and Dwight stayed in the van, an arsenal in there with them. Over the idling engines, there was the swish of traffic and crickets trilling in the darkness. The buyer emerged from his vehicle by himself. As he came into the light, Isaiah saw his face. "Oh, shit," he whispered.

"Oh, shit," Dodson said.

It was Manzo.

The Locos were acting as middlemen for the Sinaloa cartel, charged with making a smooth transaction. Manzo had a full-size suitcase. He set it on the hood of the pickup and opened it, revealing bundles of cash. Sidero began counting the money. Manzo turned and gestured. A Loco got out of a car. He went around to the back of the van, Hugo opening the door for him. The Loco went in, turned on a flashlight and scuffled around with something. It was going smoothly enough. Willing businessmen making a deal.

Dodson nodded and Isaiah texted Lok. *Now.* He waited, his chest clenched, his breathing short, the full impact of what he'd done landing on him like a grenade, his conscience exploding into shrapnel. This would result in carnage. Young men would die tonight. *Die.* And their families would too but slower, like arsenic dripping through an IV, sickening them with loss for the rest of their lives. The Loco got out of the van and nodded. Everything was cool. Sidero said something that might have been, *It's all good.*

"Where the fuck is Lok?" Dodson said. "This shit is gonna be over in a minute."

A dozen cars appeared on the south end, behind Sidero's crew. They bounced over the bumpy road, engines roaring, blasting DMX's "X Gon' Give It to Ya" out multiple stereos, the TECs yelling and pointing guns out the windows. They weren't in range but started shooting anyway, Isaiah chanting in his head, *For Stella for Stella for Stella.*

Manzo crouched low and ran back toward the Locos, bullets zipping past him and kicking up dirt. Sidero's crew was trapped between the TECs and the Locos. Hugo and Dwight ran into the darkness and began shooting back in both directions. Sidero was underneath the truck with his hands over his head. He wanted no part of the fight. At first it seemed stupid but the kid had made a smart calculation. He couldn't be seen under there and no one had an angle on him. Out there in the dark, anything could happen. He'd left the briefcase on the hood of the truck. Isaiah wondered if he'd done it on purpose.

Because the TECs had come up behind Sidero, the Locos thought the two forces were on the same side. A huge salvo erupted. Gunshots popping, flaring, hundreds of them, the bright flashes lighting the shooter and going out again.

"Damn, man," Dodson said. "Vietnam just came to Long Beach."

Somebody shot at the truck, cracking the windshield and punching holes in the fenders. Sidero rolled out from underneath and crawled into the brush.

A Loco shouted, "Cover him!" A volley of gunfire from the Locos. Manzo ran out of the dark, hunched low. He jumped into the green van, the engine still running. Vehicles were blocking the way but Manzo drove around them into the scrabble.

"Oh, no," Isaiah said. The van made it to the perimeter road and sped toward the north-side exit. *The Gatling gun was getting away!* Isaiah put the Kia in gear, stomped on the gas and took off in pursuit. The four-cylinder engine was hard-pressed to follow but eventually caught up when Manzo slowed for traffic. The gang leader drove at the speed limit, going south on Anaheim. As soon as he made the turn onto Long Beach Boulevard, Isaiah knew where he was going.

"The storage place?" Dodson said. Isaiah nodded. He'd had a locker there for years.

Isaiah knew Manzo would use a key card to get in and the gate would close behind him. He also knew the place was surrounded by a twelve-foot chain-link fence with razor wire coiled along the top. Isaiah parked nearby and went into the trunk of the Kia. He had transferred his gear from the Audi. Make it simple this time. The collapsible baton and a Taser.

"You still got that pepperball gun?" Dodson said. "I like that thing."

"You're not coming. If something happened to you, Cherise would kill me twice." Dodson didn't argue.

Isaiah cut through the fence with a bolt cutter. Nothing but rows and rows of identical lockers with roll-up doors, the aisles wide and empty. In the sulfurous light, it looked like a set for a horror movie. He found Manzo in Aisle 3. The back of the van was inside the locker. Manzo was out of view.

Isaiah stayed close to the locker doors and reached the van. He cursed himself for not wearing a mask. He turned into the locker and with aching slowness, slipped alongside the van, sweat stinging his eyes, trying to breathe without making a sound. He could hear Manzo inside the cargo bay, sliding the Gatling gun to the rear of the van. He jumped out and went toward a dolly leaning against the wall, his back turned. Isaiah made his move the moment Manzo turned around.

"Isaiah?" he said. Isaiah plunged the Taser into his chest.

"Motherfucker!" Manzo screamed.

While he grunted in agony and writhed on the ground, Isaiah shut the cargo bay and drove the van away.

Dodson called. "You okay?"

"Yeah, I've got the Gatling," Isaiah said. "Take the Kia and go home."

"You sound like something's wrong."

"Manzo saw me."

"Lord have mercy," Dodson said. "Can't you do anything without somebody else wantin' to kill you?"

"No, I guess not," Isaiah said.

Next day, Dodson went with Isaiah to deliver the Gatling gun to Lok. They met in an alley somewhere in Cambodia Town. It only took a minute for Lok's boys to heft the PVC crate into a pickup truck, cover it with stained drop cloths, paint buckets and some gardening tools to pin it down.

"You true to your word, Q," Lok said, grinning. "I saw you going after Manzo. That was some bad shit right there." Lok took a fat envelope out of his pocket. "A little sumpin'-sumpin' for you. Call it a gratuity." To Dodson's surprise, Isaiah took the envelope and put it in his pocket.

"I need Angus to be gone," Isaiah said.

"I know," Lok said, "it'll take me some time."

"I don't have time," Isaiah said. He was angry, looking directly into Lok's eyes, a challenge anywhere there are gangstas. Lok was nodding, lips pursed, reassessing. Dodson tensed, ready to get into it. The fellas in the truck were watching, one of them with his hand behind him, a gun in the back of his pants. Lok was still considering. He knew nobody fucked around with the homeboy they called IQ. Cheat him, shoot at him, mess with his friends, even fuck with his dog or in any way try to undermine him and you could find yourself in jail, hiding from your own people or deep in poverty without a place to live and a bus pass as your primary means of transportation.

"I'm not fuckin' with you, Q," Lok said. "Angus is as good as dead." Isaiah kept his voice low. *"We had a deal."*

"And I'm keepin' the deal," Lok said, belligerent now. "Don't disrespect me, Q. I don't take this shit from nobody, even you. This shit takes time to organize. I already tried once so what am I supposed to do—go to his crib, knock on the door, get past all them skinheads he keeps around and say, 'Let me in, Angus, I need to kill your ass immediately'? If you're in such a big fuckin' hurry, go on and do it yourself." All the air went out of Isaiah at the same time. "I always keep my promises," Lok said. "Ask anybody."

Isaiah drove, staring and silent. Lok was right. In his panic about Stella, he'd made a huge mistake. Why hadn't he thought of it? Killing Angus would, in fact, take time. *You're so stupid. You're so fucking stupid!*

Lok was right about the other thing too. If Isaiah wanted Angus gone in a hurry, he'd have to take him out himself. He thought about it, deliberately killing another human being with malice aforethought. Could he do it with his own hands? How? Gun, knife, baseball bat, garrote, ice pick, bow and arrow? He groaned aloud, bullshitting himself yet again. He'd seen people get killed and the reactions of the ones who'd killed them.

He remembered Novelle standing in his driveway with a pistol in his hand, the shot still resounding, staring at his girlfriend, Leslie Garza, crumpled on the ground. In one cathartic moment, Clarence had turned her into *a thing*, an object you could shoot with impunity. You could see it in his eyes, the realization that she wasn't a thing. She was a person, lying there as a pool of blood expanded around her. Clarence dropped the gun, went to her and fell to his knees, whispering *oh no oh no oh no oh no oh no.* He grabbed her and shook her, screaming, "COME BACK COME BACK!" But Leslie was gone and not ever coming back. Weeping, Clarence held her in his arms and rocked her back and forth, as if she were a sleeping baby who would wake soon and be whole again.

Even if you shot somebody climbing in your window with a butcher knife and a roll of duct tape, something dies inside you right along with the life you've taken. Isaiah wasn't a spiritual kind of guy, but he believed there was a bond between human beings, not of brotherhood but of evolution—a species that survived by keeping each other safe, and when you broke that bond, you broke the tether that held you to humanity.

He thought of that night in the industrial zone, and the screams of the dying and wounded. He might as well have shot them himself. The overwhelming awfulness reminded him of Flaco, the ten-year-old boy who'd been shot in the head during a gang war. The boy was a young man now, cheerful and industrious. He lived in the condo Isaiah and Dodson had bought for him. He married his girlfriend, Debbie, who had Down Syndrome and he'd been promoted to cashier at the pet boutique. But his brain injuries had stunted his abilities, his aspirations, the fullness of his life. He never complained, maybe because he'd forgotten who he could have been.

In a world where mass shootings, murderous antiheroes, glamorized bad guys, terrorist bombings, and ethnic cleansing were routine, people forgot, or maybe they never knew, how devastating the consequences of violence could be. Isaiah had suffered no brain damage in the gang war, but he'd been partially responsible for it happening and the guilt had injured him somewhere deep inside; an inoperable wound that pulsed and hemorrhaged every time he saw Flaco.

He wondered if saving Stella would have been worth the lives that were lost and the grief of their families. No, he thought, but saving Stella would have been some small consolation, an over-the-counter analgesic for a massive stroke. But he couldn't save Stella. He'd failed. He'd failed in every way possible.

Headlines blared:

GANGLAND SHOOTOUT IN LONG BEACH; POLICE CHIEF SAYS IT WAS
OK CORRAL
GANG WAR EXPLODES IN LONG BEACH
GANGS OUT OF CONTROL, RESIDENTS SAY
BIGGEST GUNFIGHT IN SOCAL HISTORY LEAVES THREE DEAD,
MANY WOUNDED.

Grace knew Isaiah was involved. The TECs, the Locos, Angus, Lok, the Starks, the Gatling gun. None were mentioned in the news but it all fit together. She watched the coverage and read the reports. She went into the kitchen. Isaiah was standing at the counter, looking into a bowl of oatmeal as he slowly took bites.

"The gunfight," she said. "Did you have anything to do with it?" She sounded severe and shrewish but she couldn't help it. He sighed and put down his spoon but didn't answer. "Isaiah," she said, "I asked you if you had anything to do with this."

"Yes, I did," he said quietly, his eyes still on his oatmeal. "It was my idea. I set it up." He told her why and how and left out nothing.

Grace felt a rising fever, an illness spreading through her system. Isaiah had delivered a weapon of inestimable power to some unbounded maniacs, and people had been killed in the process. Something even more terrible occurred to her.

"What did you want from Lok in return?" she asked. She couldn't look at him, the man she loved. Revered. He was stripped of his skin, his naked self in such pain she couldn't bear it.

His voice was broken and doomed. He said, "If I got him the Gatling gun, he would kill Angus." A smothering silence descended on them.

She was hesitant about judging him. She had killed a man herself and she could see what a terrible bind he was in and that what he did had come from compassion. But some things were wrong no matter what the reason. Isaiah had orchestrated a situation where *he knew in advance* people would be killed. Her love for him, her sense of right and wrong and her humanity, argued and fought, leaving her with only bewilderment and a dizzying sense of loss.

"I, um, I'm gonna go to Cherokee's," she said. "I need to think about things."

She left as confused and heartsick as she'd ever been. THREE DEAD AND MANY WOUNDED. She couldn't get over it. She needed to talk, but Cherokee had gone camping with her girlfriend. She met Noah at McClarin Park. He knew her. She could unload on him and it would be all right.

"I'm glad you called," he said. They sat across from each other at a picnic table. She told him about Isaiah and how he'd orchestrated the gunfight. "He knew people would be killed," she said. "He did it because he had to. I know that but some things can't be parsed. Some things are wrong no matter what the reason."

"He went too far," Noah said.

"Yes! He went too far! It's unforgivable." She said it knowing she hadn't forgiven herself for killing the man she thought murdered her father.

"Do you love him?" Noah said. She nodded. "Then I guess the question is," he said, "can you forgive him the unforgivable?"

"I don't know." She was crying now. He went around to her side of the table and held her hand in both of his. "*Damn* him," she said. "He went *too fucking far!*"

"Yes," Noah said gently, "but is it too far for you?"

She cried a long time and he held her and stroked her hair. He walked her back to Cherokee's place, his arm around her shoulders.

When they got to the apartment, he said, "I'm going on a little trip, up the coast, to Big Sur maybe. You can come along if you want." He put up his palms. "No, no romance. Just some time to clear your head, get some perspective. I'm your friend, you know."

"Thanks, Noah. I'll let you know."

Isaiah stood on the stoop staring at the place under the lemon tree where Ruffin liked to sleep. There was a barren spot among twigs and fallen leaves where the dog walked in circles before lying down. Isaiah noticed the tree was dying and somehow it seemed right. Didn't Grace know he had no other choice? Didn't she know he would have done the same for her? He wanted to explain again. Maybe he hadn't said it right. Maybe he hadn't been clear. Maybe she hadn't understood the pressure he was under. No, he thought, she understood. She understood everything. And then she drove away.

He went inside and paced. He was all self-revulsion and guilt-driven energy. He couldn't just stew about it; he had to act. He had to *do* something. He needed some small degree of redemption, however small, and the more he thought about it, the more he needed it *right fucking now.* The Gatling gun, he decided, would never reach its customer.

CHAPTER EIGHTEEN

LTEC

Isaiah had transferred the weapon to Lok in an alley in Cambodia Town. He didn't know what had happened to it after that. Would the gangster have taken it to a storage locker? No. There were cameras and people going in and out. Manzo had done it because he'd been under threat and had no immediate alternative. The safest place to hide the gun was in Lok's hood.

"Thanks for coming," Isaiah said. "I could do it myself but—"

"Nobody said you couldn't," Dodson replied. "My question is, why do it at all? You could leave that goddamn gun right where it is and it don't mean nothing 'cept some useless muthafuckas who deserve to be dead get what they deserve. You think there's a shortage of gangstas out there? Nigga, please. It ain't no different than throwing out the garbage. The only thing you'd notice was that the stink was less."

"I have to do it," Isaiah said.

"No, you don't," Dodson replied. "That's just what you say when you gonna do something that makes no sense. Are you really gonna risk your life behind this bullshit? You could die, Isaiah. Don't that ever occur to you? That your freakishly large brain don't make you immortal?"

"Yes, it occurs to me," Isaiah said.

"What about Grace?" Dodson said. "I don't know the girl but I'm pretty sure she wants your ass around for a while."

"I'm not so sure."

"Yeah, but I know you want to be around for her."

That was Dodson, Isaiah thought. Combative, contrary, sanctimonious and unyielding unless he was forced at gunpoint.

"Do you want to be partners again?" Isaiah said.

"I do if you do," Dodson said. "But you know how I am."

Isaiah said, with no small amount of trepidation, "Yeah, I do."

Lindenhurst Ave, the 5900 block, was no different than the blocks that came before or after it. Run-down houses and apartment buildings, chipped stucco, gang graffiti, littered streets, chain-link fences and worn-out banana palms, their edges brown and dry. Five gangstas were hanging out on a porch. Other than the Asian faces, they were indistinguishable from any other squad across the nation. They called each other *nigga,* wore the tats and chains and waved guns in their videos. A statement, Isaiah thought: *We are outlaws.* Funny, though, being apart by being the same.

Who would Lok trust to hold the Gatling gun? There was no room in his apartment and it was risky. A raid could put the crew away for decades. Other homies? Possibly. But Lok would worry they'd open the crate and show the gun to their girlfriends. Family, then. Brothers or sisters? No. Same problem, and they might be upright citizens like the great majority of people in the neighborhood.

Dodson was quiet and thoughtful. Isaiah didn't like it. "You're trying to get ahead of me, aren't you?" he said. "Figure out the move before I do."

"Yes, I am," his partner replied. "That's my job. To push you into doin' shit you wouldn't do if I wasn't here so go back to your cogitatin' and leave my ass alone."

Because of their fluctuating incomes, many gangsters lived with their parents, which made it hard to be completely independent. It wasn't uncommon for mom and dad to look the other way when it came to their kids' criminal activities. If they helped support the family, why ask questions? Times were hard and Pol Pot's genocide made selling a Gatling gun not such a big deal. Survival was survival.

"His parents," Isaiah said.

"That's what I was thinking too," Dodson said.

Lok's family name was Heng, but it turned out to be a very popular name in Cambodia Town and Cambodia as well.

Okay, Isaiah, what do you know? All he had to work with was what he'd gleaned from his visit to Lok's place. He remembered talking with Lok while he played the video game. There was nothing in the décor that referenced the gangster's parents. Isaiah remembered smelling the food as the homies came in, everybody with a Styrofoam box. They ignored him and then he, Lok, and Dodson went out on the balcony. *Go back, Isaiah, you missed something.*

"Remember when we were in Lok's apartment?" he said. "We were talking to Lok and then his homeboys came in with the food?"

"Yeah, I remember," Dodson said.

"They wanted to watch TV so we went outside and as we were leaving, one of them said something. What was it?" They thought a moment, their faces screwed up.

"He said he had the wrong box," Dodson said, pleased with himself.

"No, it was before that, something about the food."

"Yeah, yeah," Dodson said, nodding. A moment passed, both of them staring out of the window at the contest they were having.

"Pork and rice," Isaiah said. "The homie said your old lady's pork and rice is crazy good and he was talking to Lok."

"Damn, your memory is tight," said Dodson appreciatively. "But what about it? Lok's mom is a good cook. That don't mean nothin'."

"The food was in Styrofoam boxes," Isaiah said, his smile victorious. "Lok's parents have a restaurant."

"Fuck you, Isaiah," Dodson said.

There were six Cambodian restaurants in the area. Conveniently, one was called Heng Cambodian Food. It wasn't far away. They took a quick look inside. Thirty seats, twelve customers, prints of Cambodian dancers on the walls and bottles of fish sauce on the tables. Mrs. Heng was at the cashier's desk doing something on a calculator. She was thick, white-haired and grim.

"Can I help you?" she said.

"Can I get some kung pao chicken to go?" Dodson said.

"Kung pao chicken Chinese," she said, insulted. "This Cambodian food. Don't you read sign?"

They walked through the parking lot. Three spaces were designated STAFF ONLY. Two cars were aging, dull paint and Bondo patches. The third was a new Camry, XLE, the up model, retail around thirty thousand dollars.

"That's a lotta car for somebody who owns a little restaurant," Dodson said. "I think Lok's helping her. The least she could do is keep the Gatling gun for him and open herself up to prosecution."

"Do you want to do it?" Isaiah said. "You're good at this."

Dodson called the restaurant and in an impressively officious voice, said, "Is this Mrs. Heng?"

"Yes, I Mrs. Heng. What you want?"

"My name is Walt Jacobson from FedEx security."

"FedEx? We get FedEx?"

"That's the problem, ma'am. We tried to deliver a package but it was the wrong address. Do you live at fifty-nine eighty-two Lindenhurst Avenue?"

"No, you wrong," she said sharply. "Two blocks down. Sixty one twelve. You get that? *Sixty one twelve.*"

"Thank you, ma'am. Someone has to sign for it. Will anybody be home?"

"My niece there. I have to go now."

Isaiah parked in the alley behind the house at 6112. The partners stood on their tiptoes and peered over the cinder-block wall. Hopefully there'd be a garage suitable for storing a big PVC crate, but there was only a square of fractured cement, a carport and a driveway off to one side. Why can't something be easy? Isaiah thought. If the crate was here, it was inside the house.

He got his binoculars from the car and checked out the dead bolt on the back door. There was a tiny hole adjacent to the keyway. It was a so-called smart lock and connected with a phone app. You opened it by simply touching the lock. People thought they were more secure because the locks couldn't be picked and you could rekey them yourself. Not true. Because of the extra components, manufacturers saved money on the lock itself. It was weak, poorly designed and more vulnerable to duress.

In his quest to keep up with modern advances, Isaiah had acquired a force tool specifically designed to defeat popular brands of smart locks. It was a #3 key blank adapted to fit a ratchet wrench. He went over the wall and hurried across the cement square to the back door. He could hear a TV, an action movie judging from the slam-bang music. He inserted the blank into the lock's keyway and ratcheted the wrench. Because there were no cuts in the key and the lock was weak, the whole cylinder turned and the dead bolt slid back into the strike plate.

The door was open. God help me if there's a dog, he thought. He slipped inside the kitchen. He waited, listened. No dog. Good. The movie was still playing. He crept through the kitchen and the small dining room to a doorway. It opened onto the living room. He peered around the corner.

A girl was sitting on the sofa, facing away from him, talking on the phone and watching *Batman v Superman*. Judging from her voice, T-shirt and the sheen of her hair, she was in her late teens. There was a mishmash of tats on her arm, the only legible things being four letters in fancy script: LTEC. Lady Tiny Enforcerz Crew, the female wing of the gang.

"*Shit,*" Isaiah hissed. On the end table nearest her was a handgun. This girl wasn't just hanging out at her aunt's house. She was the goddamn security guard.

There wasn't a big crate within viewing distance so it had to be in a bedroom, assuming it was here at all. The hallway was on the other side of the room. Isaiah would have to creep past the girl and hope she didn't turn around. Even without looking, she might detect him by the movement of the air.

He got down on his hands and knees and crawled. The fucking hallway looked ten miles away.

The girl got off the phone and stretched. Was she going to the bathroom? Getting an extra clip for that gun? Gratefully, she stayed seated.

Isaiah was halfway across the room when he heard a man's voice.

"Get me a soda, Jorani."

Her boyfriend! The voice was raspy with sleep. The guy was probably lying down with his head in her lap. Given the macho nature of gangs, he was the real security guard. The girl was there to keep him company.

"You get it," she said. "I'm not your fucking slave."

The room was hot, Isaiah's heart pulsing in his throat, sweat dripping like he was under a heat lamp at Robert Earl's BBQ. Why was it always ninety degrees when he was in dire jeopardy?

The boyfriend sat up, yawned and ran a hand over his shaved head. *Guda.*

Isaiah resumed crawling, fighting the urge to speed up.

Guda groaned. "Fuck, man, it's fucking boring. When's Jessie gonna be here?"

"I don't know."

Isaiah was fifteen feet away from the hall. Guda stood up and stretched his massive bulk, his arms like grain silos.

Isaiah kept crawling. *Almost there, keep going!*

"Is he gonna be here soon?" Guda asked.

"I told you," the girl groaned. "I don't know. Quit bugging me, okay?"

Ten feet away.

"Fuck, man. What a bitch."

"You don't say that when I'm giving you head."

Five feet away.

"I'm going to call him," Guda said.

"Good. Call him."

Two feet away.

Guda turned around, poking at his phone.

Safe! Isaiah was in the hallway, out of view. He sat up, rubbed his aching wrists, and sucked in a deep breath. He got to his feet and tiptoed to the first door. It was a bedroom, no crate. Next was the bathroom, and then a second bedroom, still no crate. There was one more door at the end of the hall. He started toward it.

"I'm going home," the girl said.

"No, don't," Guda whined. "Don't leave me here by myself."

"I've got things to do."

Isaiah heard her get up. He stepped into the second bedroom and saw the girl's handbag was on the bed. *Shit!* She was coming in here. There was no place to hide except the tiny closet. He got in and squeezed himself into the narrow space beside the door. It smelled like old shoes. He heard the girl enter and rustle around in her bag.

"Where's my car keys? Guda? Do you have my keys?"

Guda came in. "Come here, baby," he said playfully. "Come on and gimme some."

"'Come on and gimme some'?" she said. "Now? Fuck no." Isaiah visualized their movements from the sounds. A rustle of clothing, shuffling of feet, a deep sigh. Guda had come up from behind and wrapped her in his arms.

"Don't, Guda," she said. More rustling and shuffling. "I said, don't!" She was trying to wriggle away and he wouldn't let go.

"Come on, don't be like that."

"I have to go, okay?"

"Ten minutes, that's all," he said, like he was selling pressure cookers or car wax.

"Ten minutes? Gee, that sounds like fun. *Let me go!*"

They were struggling now. She was twisting around, grunting angrily, but he held on easily, chuckling. "Fuck, Guda!" she shouted. "I swear to God, I'll break up with you!"

"Do it. I don't care," he said. His flimsy idea of manhood was at risk. He needed control. The struggle was escalating. They were moving around the room, banging into things. Isaiah was stuck. Put a stop to it? He'd expose himself to Guda and what if he'd brought the gun in with him?

"Don't fight me, bitch!" Guda said, getting pissed. He threw her on the bed and got on top of her. The bed springs bottomed out, she grunted from his weight. They grappled, but he had her pinned.

"Get off me!" she screamed. *"Get off me!"*

He hit her. She yelped. The struggling stopped and there was only heavy breathing. What a coward, Isaiah thought. What was it about a girlfriend that gave you permission to assault her? Guda gave the age-old line men used to justify violence. "I told you not to fight me, didn't I?" he said.

She was crying. "Okay, okay, fuck. Let me take my pants off."

"Yeah, let me see that ass." He chuckled. They got off the bed. Isaiah heard an ugly wallop, fist against face. "Oh *fuck!*" Guda shouted. He staggered but didn't fall down. She ran out of the room. "I'm gonna fucking kill you!" he screamed and went after her.

Isaiah came out of the closet and went into the hall. The happy couple was in the living room, screaming at each other and throwing things. Mrs. Heng was coming home to a disaster. Isaiah hustled to the door at the end of the hall, opened it and smiled. The crate was leaning against the wall like a sarcophagus in a museum basement.

He went back down the hall and peeked into the living room. The fighting had reached another level. Guda's shirt was torn, scratches on his neck and face. The girl's hair was a fright wig, her nose bleeding, a bruise on her cheekbone. They were standing on opposite sides of the sofa, glaring murderously and breathing like racehorses.

"Get away from me!" she said. "I'm going to tell my brother, you know!"

"Fuck your brother," Guda said. "I'm gonna kick your ass."

The doorbell rang. *BRRRINNG.* Isaiah had been here too long, Dodson had gotten worried and circled around to the front of the house. It's good to have a partner.

Guda lunged over the sofa. He almost grabbed her but she dodged away, knocking over the end table on her way to the floor. Guda snarled and came after her again. Isaiah was about to make his move when the girl got to her feet. She was holding the gun.

"The fuck are you doing?!" Guda shouted.

BRRRINNG.

Isaiah thought of Cherise and Micah. *Stay away, Dodson. Stay away!*

BRRRINNG. BRRRINNG, BRRRING, BRRRING.

The gun infuriated Guda all the more, this bitch trying to back him down with his own goddamn strap. He was a gangsta and that shit was never going to happen. Guda went toward her with his chest out, pounding it like a pissed-off silverback. "Come on, bitch, shoot me!"

She backed away, holding the gun in two hands. She was sobbing, garbling her words. "Stay away from me, Guda. I'm not bullshitting."

"Have you lost your fucking mind?"

"You hit me, you fucking prick. You said you'd never do that!"

"Put down the fucking gun!" he bellowed and kept coming.

She backed into the wall and fired. *BLAM BLAM!* The gun bucked harder than she'd expected, the shots going wide, blowing up a plastic crucifix and fracturing the TV screen. Guda stumbled back, arms over his head. "ARE YOU FUCKING CRAZY?"

Isaiah hid his face with his hands and took off, racing across the living room.

BRRRINNG. BRRRINNG.

"Hey!" the girl said, and aimed at Isaiah. *BLAM BLAM!* But he was already gone.

"That was Isaiah!" Guda shouted. "Gimme the fucking gun!"

"No! Fuck you!"

Isaiah burst out the back door, leaped off the stoop, ran across the cement square and tripped on a crack. He fell, scrambled to his feet, but it was too late. Guda tackled him from behind and they went sprawling, Isaiah flat on his stomach. He tried to turn over but got only halfway. Guda was on top of him, rearing back to punch. Isaiah had no leverage so he reached up and clawed Guda's eyes. He howled and his hands went to his face. Isaiah shoved him off and stood up, but Guda grabbed him and tried to drag him down. Isaiah tried to wriggle free while he hammer-fisted Guda on the head.

"You motherfucker," Guda yelled. "You're fucking dead!"

The hammer fists were having no effect. Isaiah was pulled to his knees. BLAM! A bullet zinged past them and whanged into a garbage can. The girl was on the stoop, aiming the gun. It wasn't clear if she was shooting at Isaiah or her boyfriend.

"The fuck are you doing?" Guda yodeled.

"Get out of the way!" she screamed. She'd gangsta'd up, holding the gun sideways. It looked cool but you can't aim for shit. *BLAM! BLAM!* The shots hit three feet from the fighters, ricocheting, powdering the cement. Dodson came around the corner of the house.

"Could I ask you to tone it down? I sleep in the daytime." The girl shot at him but Dodson had already stepped back.

Isaiah took off. *BLAM BLAM BLAM!* Bullets flying as he swung over the cinder-block wall, Guda screaming, "STOP SHOOTING, YOU'RE HITTING THE HOUSE NEXT DOOR!"

"How many times do I have to save your life?" Dodson said as they drove out of the alley. "This shit is getting tiresome. If Cherise finds out I was anywhere near a gunshot, she'll shoot me herself."

"Guda saw me," Isaiah said.

Dodson shook his head. "I didn't think things could get no worse but that's seriously fucked up, Isaiah. You don't have a death wish, you have a stupid wish. I told you this would happen, didn't I?"

"Yes, you did."

"But that had no effect on you, did it?"

"No, it didn't," Isaiah said, "and what pisses me off? I can't get to the Gatling gun now."

"You already did," Dodson said.

"How do you figure that?"

"Wait for it," Dodson said. Five or six seconds went by before they heard the wailing sirens of every police car in the area.

Fist pound.

*   *   *

It was evening. Dodson stood with a bag of warm food in his arms and watched from the doorway. The beeping had stopped, the oscillating lines were still. Merrill, his wife, and some others were gathered around Beaumont. The doctor was shining a light into Beaumont's eyes. The doctor squeezed his fingernail for a moment or two and listened with his stethoscope; everyone tense as if Beaumont might still be alive. The doctor said, "I'm sorry."

Merrill bent low and kissed his father on the forehead. "I love you, Pop," he whispered. "I'll miss you." Merrill's wife put her hand on his back. There were murmurs: *He was a good man, Merrill. He was a rock. Everybody loved him, Merrill. Your father was the best. Stronger than iron. He was a hero and nobody knew.*

Dodson turned and left. He went outside, wandered over to McClarin Park and sat down on a bench. He wished he had a joint. He wished he was with Isaiah. He wished he was running from the cops and getting shot at by gangsters. He'd never been so lost, so confused, not having any answers because nobody had asked him any questions. This was like a white people problem. A crisis that was all in your head. This wasn't real. This was bullshit. "Get your shit together," he said to himself, "before the shit gets you."

His phone buzzed. It was Cherise, wondering if he was still at the hospital. He told her that Beaumont had died and he'd be home in a few minutes. He gave the food to a homeless couple and heard them arguing as he walked away.

Christiana was in an isolation cell. Cement cubicle, windowless except for the meal slot in the door. It was close and dark and cold. She was sitting on the bed, wedged into a corner, holding her knees. She'd been beaten up again. Her face was swollen. An arm had nearly been torn out of its socket. She didn't mind the pain.

The noise from the other inmates was less here, but not from the alters. There was a continuous roar of fear and anger and bewilderment.

It didn't stop, it went on and on. She could pick out Angie's voice now, a braying, blistering screech of invective. Christiana pleaded with them to stop but they wouldn't. She couldn't take it, she couldn't stand it. She put her hands over her ears and screamed, "STOP! PLEASE STOP!" And miraculously they did. The quiet was startling and felt incredibly tenuous, a mouse with one foot on the trap, another step and the spring would snap and the voices would begin and she would go mad. She waited. No one spoke. She waited.

CHAPTER NINETEEN

Just Tea?

Nothing was happening at the church on Thursday night, TK's footsteps sounding hollow as he went down the long hallway. No one was around. If the hall wasn't lined with children's drawings, he might have been in the joint, on his way to a parole hearing. He had abandoned the suit and bought a polo shirt. Grace had steered him from orange and bright yellow to dark blue.

"You mean I gotta dress like her too?" he said.

He was early. Delores was the only one there, a couple of gold teeth glinting in her wide smile. She was not a small woman. Her dress was very tight and showed a lot of cleavage, her titties so close together you couldn't slip a putty knife in there. Her perfume smelled like a truck full of strawberry jam had tipped over on the freeway.

"Hello, TK," she cooed.

"Hello, Delores," he said, wondering if he'd come on the wrong night.

"Come sit over here." She patted the chair next to her.

"Uh, well—" He didn't see how he could refuse. "All right."

He sat down. Delores scooched closer. "Don't be so far away," she said. She was still smiling. It seemed like her gold teeth had gotten brighter and they'd grown in number. It was a struggle not to look at her chest. It was like trying to ignore a mountain range as your plane passed between the peaks. "How've you been, TK?"

"Old and slow," he said, his usual answer to that question.

"You might be old but I don't know about slow," she said. She winked, her false eyelash flapping like a bat wing.

"How's Terry?" he said.

"My husband? He's been dead for a year."

"Well, I'm sorry to hear that."

"I'm not," Delores said. "I waited a long time for him to die." She put her hand on TK's knee. "Are you busy later?" she said. "Maybe we can go somewhere and have a drink." She looked like she was going to kiss him, pulling back suddenly when Gloria came in. Gloria stood there in her dark print dress and her dark expression, looking at them like the vice principal of Carver Middle School. A boy and girl sitting next to each other in a room full of empty chairs. She grimaced.

"Who likes strawberries?"

Gloria brought everyone to order and the meeting began. "The book under consideration is *The Underground Railroad* by Colson Whitehead. Can we hear from the selection committee?" Simone and Louella spoke first. They summarized the story, gave thumbnail sketches of the characters, talked about what they liked and disliked and how they felt about the characters' sadness, terror and cruelty. Simone was nearly in tears.

"Thomas," Gloria said, "do you have anything to say? There has to be a consensus before we select the book."

He cleared his throat. He felt pretty good about this. Cliff was a smart guy and he was really well organized, everything in neat little sections. "Well, the story is about a woman named Cora—" he began.

"We've already heard about the story and the character, Thomas," Gloria said. "Tell us something else. What would you say are the book's themes?" She was deliberately torturing him, he thought. He wasn't a prospect, he was a target.

He stalled for time. "Well, now, that's a big question," he said with a serious nod. "Very big. Really big." The stuff in CliffsNotes about themes was the hardest to understand. He couldn't remember what it said exactly except something about unifying ideas, which didn't clear up anything.

"Big picture," Grace had said. "Life and death, right and wrong, love and hate. That's simplistic but that's what a good novel does. It illuminates our humanity." Which didn't clear up anything either.

"Thomas?" Gloria said. Everyone had leaned over the table to get a better look at him. Delores leaned back as if her titties might impede their curiosity.

"Uh, well," TK said. "I'd say in this case, it's life and death." That got no response of any kind. "Or right and wrong." Still nothing. "Or love and, uh..." He couldn't for the life of him remember what came next so he said, "Not love." There was no spit in his mouth but he went on anyway. "The big picture in other words. Who humanity is and what he's up to. Unifyin' this thing or that, illuminatin' and whatnot." The silence was excruciating. The women were still looking at him as if they hadn't heard him correctly or he'd said something in Farsi. TK had let women down before but only one at a time. It was a new experience disappointing twelve of them simultaneously. To his great relief, they looked away, somebody coughing, somebody else clearing her throat.

"Thank you for that, Thomas," Gloria said. "*The Underground Railroad* has been accepted."

Grace was waiting outside the church. "How'd it go?"

"It didn't," TK said, throwing the book into someone's yard. "But the next time I see Cliff I'm gonna kick his ass."

She offered to take him out for dinner but he refused, saying he had to get home. She felt awful. She felt terrible. This sweet old man swept aside because she was as clueless as she was incompetent. She didn't know what to do but she was hungry. She went to In-N-Out and had a cheeseburger and a shake. The food didn't quell the guilt but at least she was full.

*   *   *

Gloria had come over to babysit so Cherise could go to the movies with her friend. "How was the book club?" Cherise said, as she gathered her things.

"A complete disaster," Gloria replied.

"A disaster? Why is that?"

"Thomas Kahill showed up."

"You mean TK? What's wrong with that?"

"Well, he's only semiliterate for one thing," Gloria said. "Can you imagine? Someone like that coming to a women's book club? I don't know what he was thinking. He might have been drunk or high on drugs, I wouldn't be surprised."

"He wasn't high and he wasn't drunk, mama," Cherise said. "TK is not like that."

"Well, obviously you don't know him as well as you think you do," Gloria replied. "What self-respecting man brings his hussy to a church picnic. Did you see her? A white girl, no less. She was young enough to be his granddaughter."

"Are you talking about Grace?" Cherise said.

"And I'll tell you something else," Gloria went on. "Last night, Mr. Kahill and Delores Mason were about to do something nasty. If I hadn't come in they would have rutted like animals right there in the church library."

"Mama," Cherise said. "Grace is Isaiah's girlfriend. TK is just a friend and you know as well as I do, Delores was putting a move on him. She puts a move on anything with body heat."

"Well why did he do something as silly as come to our book club?" Gloria said.

"He *likes* you, mama," Cherise said, "and he didn't know any other way to hook up."

"Nonsense," she huffed. "Why would he be interested in me?"

"Yeah, it's got me wondering too," Cherise said. "Being nicer wouldn't hurt you, mama, no matter how you feel about him."

"I don't feel anything at all," Gloria said.

"Give him a chance," Cherise said, moving for the door. "TK is a good man with a good heart."

For the last three hours, TK had been dismantling a Fiat with its front stove in. Didn't matter much, he thought, the car looked like a garden snail when it was new. He stood in the shade of the warehouse and drank a beer. People said water was better for you but they were young and didn't know any better. His old bones ached. He'd have to hire some help soon. The goddamn arthritis had caught up with him years ago but he'd refused to surrender. He looked around at the stacks of eyeless wrecks, the rusty, looming crane, the piles of fenders, bumpers, mufflers and engine blocks, chips of broken glass sparkling in the dirt. It wasn't pretty, but he was proud of it nonetheless. Running a business by yourself for forty years was an accomplishment. Big companies with big bank accounts had come and gone, but he was still standing, doing something necessary and paying his taxes. Some people would say it was sappy, but it made him feel like a productive citizen, like an American, like he could hold his head up anywhere in the world.

It was good of Grace to help him but nothing was going to happen with Gloria now or ever. That was as obvious as the egg on his face. He'd never felt this foolish or embarrassed. It was time to look reality in its cloudy eyes. He was old and falling apart. There was no more romance in his future. The love he'd received so far was all the love he was going to get. He shouldn't have waited so long. After Etta left him, he'd dated a few women but they weren't to his taste. He supposed he could have picked someone easier than Gloria, someone who didn't dislike him for being alive and breathing.

He knew she wasn't an obvious choice, but there were some people you had a sense about and he had a sense about Gloria. Underneath her hard shell and harsh words there was a loving heart. He knew it like he knew the wrecking yard. He knew it when he met Grace and he knew it when he met Isaiah, two people so detached they could have been spirits, floating around among us, unseen and unheard. He knew it when he met Harry Haldeman, the belligerent, ill-tempered old man who ran the animal shelter and never had a kind word for anybody. Maybe so, but watch Harry around dogs. Watch him calm a pit bull, abused and snarling, ready to chew your arm off, Harry approaching so slowly he seemed to be stationary, talking soft, telling it his human secrets, sitting down nearby, still talking, his voice kind and soothing, and then watch the dog sense safety and an end to its loneliness, edging over, sniffing and sniffing, licking Harry's face, eventually lying down with its head in Harry's lap. Nobody knew it, but Harry was a loving man.

TK made up his mind about Gloria one night when he saw her on the pier at Shoreline Village. He'd gone for a walk to breathe in something besides gasoline and motor oil. Nothing like a clear night and the smell of the ocean, he thought. He was lucky. He saw Gloria with Cherise and the new baby. They had stopped to take a picture, Cherise smiling happily, holding the baby's little hand up to wave. Cherise continued walking but Gloria stayed a moment, watching her daughter nuzzle the baby's face while she sang a lullaby that lilted on the breeze. If you were going to build a monument to love, it would look like Gloria in that moment, so pure and certain and all-encompassing. It warmed him just to be near her.

A Prius pulled into the yard. He'd seen it before but forgot whose it was. He thought he was hallucinating when Gloria got out and walked toward him. What was she doing here? Did she want him to dismantle her car? Did she want to grill him some more about themes?

"Hello, Thomas," she said, stiffly.

"Hello, Gloria," he said. She hesitated, holding something back.

"Is there something I can do for you?" he asked.

"Not that I can think of," she replied brusquely. She stood there, fanning herself with a folded flyer and looking around with distaste.

"You didn't have to drive all the way out here," he said. "A phone call would have done it."

"I wanted to see your circumstances," she said. "Is this your property, Thomas?"

"Yes, it's mine," he said, and for some reason he felt embarrassed.

"I see," she said. She took a deep breath. "I understand you'd like to go out with me."

"Beg your pardon?" He turned his head sideways so he could hear her better.

She sighed impatiently. "I *said*, it's my understanding that you'd like to go out with me."

He didn't know whether to fess up. Maybe this was a trap. "Uh, well, now that you ask me, I'd have to say yes. Yes, I do."

She turned and moved back toward her car. "All right, fine. Tomorrow. Three o'clock. We'll have tea."

That didn't seem right. "*Just* tea?" he said. She said something else about Lisa or Elsie or Evelyn's room but he couldn't make out the rest because she'd started her car. Why did they need another woman around to have tea? he wondered. He could make it himself with a tea bag.

"That's great, TK," Grace said. "It's like a real date, and the best part is, she asked *you!*" TK did not share her elation. He looked confused.

"That's all we do?" he said. "Drink tea?"

Grace was at the far edge of her knowledge base. "There's food involved, but mostly it's a nice way to have a conversation."

"I don't like tea."

"Drink it anyway. It's simpler."

"What do we talk about?" he asked. Grace wasn't great at chitchatting and TK was asking for specifics.

"Oh, anything, really," she said cavalierly. "You're just getting to know each other." Grace had spent most of her life walling off scrutiny of any kind. She thought about how she and Isaiah got to know each other, a torturous process between two unwilling people that only happened because of several near-death experiences.

"What should I wear?" he said. "The suit or the polo shirt?" Another challenging question. She was surprised how easy it came to her.

"Wear the polo shirt *under* the jacket. You'll look casual but not too casual."

"Thanks, Grace, I really appreciate your help."

"Glad to do it, TK." She couldn't wait for this to be over. This was the ignorant leading the innocent.

"Any advice?" he asked. She thought about it. Did she have anything useful to say to an old man going on a first date in fifteen years? No, she didn't. TK was looking at her expectantly.

"Uh, well, be yourself," she said. She had never dispensed a homily before and it felt awful.

"Why would I do that?" TK said. "We already know she doesn't like me."

Good point, she thought. She winged it. "She only dislikes you because she doesn't know you yet."

"I appreciate this, Grace," TK said. "I truly do."

"What are friends for?" Jesus, she thought, another homily.

He nodded thoughtfully. "Be myself, huh?"

Isaiah got the word from Gia: Christiana had been released on bail. A reprieve for Stella but it was temporary. He was brooding, trying to keep his mind off his troubles by reading the paper. An article described how the police found a dangerous weapon in a house on Lindenhurst Avenue in Cambodia Town. Gunfire was heard by the neighbors and two people were arrested. Witnesses saw officers in hazmat suits removing a large PVC crate out of the house and loading it into a police van. The spokesperson for the department wouldn't identify the contents of the crate, saying only that it was a threat to the entire community. There was some speculation it was a military weapon but that hadn't been confirmed.

Isaiah felt a moment's satisfaction. At least he'd done something. He wondered if Grace had seen the report and if she knew it was him. He wondered if that was enough. But Grace hadn't called and he didn't have the nerve to call her. He sat in the armchair, drinking cold espresso. *Three dead and many more wounded.* Stella still at risk. Nothing had changed. He was right back where he'd started. No, it was worse than that. He'd created new problems along the way.

He got up, kicked the wastebasket and screamed in the shower, accomplishing nothing before gathering himself and getting back to work. He reviewed the case microfiche-style, frame by frame projected onto the backs of his eyelids. He waited for a discrepancy, something that didn't fit or was supposed to be there but wasn't or was the other way around, or where the words were at odds with the facts at hand. He'd been doing this for a long time now and his unconscious often put things together before he did.

He thought about Jasper's room and the Fender Stratocaster leaning in the corner. It shouldn't have been there. Neither should the empty bottles of Everclear or the toolbox under the bed or the boots with the monk straps, the left sole worn down to nothing. He thought about his first conversation with Pearl and what she'd said at the end. He thought about how the alters smelled of cigarettes and the posters of bands on the walls. He thought about the fist dents in the wall. None of it fit.

Jasper didn't play a Fender Stratocaster; he played the drums. The boots were motorcycle boots, the left one worn down because the left foot scraped the ground at stops and starts. Jasper didn't drive and why would he need a toolbox?

Everclear was grain alcohol, 190-proof. Jasper drank beer. The alters smelled like cigarettes but none of them smoked. The posters didn't match. The Ramones and the Dead Kennedys were punk. The New York Dolls, Kiss, and Twisted Sister were glam rock. Jasper was rock and roll. Who liked punk? Punching walls wasn't in Bertrand's character. When Isaiah talked to Pearl she said she had to leave or she'd get in trouble. In trouble with who?

Isaiah thought about what he'd read. How each alter played a role that helped them survive the abuse. Christiana was day to day, Pearl was submissive, Marlene was salacious, and Bertrand was protective. But where was the anger? Where was the hatred for what Angus had done? The night of the murder, Bertrand said he watched the woman in black climb up a rope. Then he came inside but the alters were switching out too fast and he didn't remember anything beyond that. Then there was another time gap between then and Marlene standing in the front door, feeling the temperature change and sweating. Presumably, either Christiana, Pearl or Jasper had switched out with Bertrand, and whoever that was ran through the cutting room, hopped over Tyler's dead body, continued through the showroom, out the front door, down the block and then returned, switching out with Marlene who felt the temperature change and was sweating as she reentered the shop. That made no sense. Isaiah couldn't imagine any of them doing something like that.

There was another alter.

Isaiah sent a text to Christiana's phone. *To the sixth alter. I know you're there. You are in serious jeopardy. Desperate to talk.* Fifteen minutes later, he got a return text. *Hollywood Palladium.* He was hesitant to call Grace. Would she hang up on him?

"I need your help," he said.

"Okay. Come pick me up."

The east end of Sunset Boulevard was another anonymous stretch of urban sprawl with that cluttered, you-could-be-anywhere-in-LA look. Billboards, strip malls, fast-food restaurants, gas stations, nail salons, palm trees spaced too far apart to be glamorous, and more dry cleaners per square foot than anywhere in America. There were a few tattered reminders of the past. The Seventh Veil Strip Club, a former hot spot, now shabby and neglected, thick layers of pollution darkening the lavender paint. There were photos of strippers gone by in the dusty window boxes and a life-size Venus de Milo wishing you hot lap dances as you went through the door.

TK had told Isaiah about the Hollywood Palladium; TK had been there many times in his youth. It was built in the forties, styled in sleek art deco, aqua and white. Everybody from Tommy Dorsey to Frank Sinatra, Tito Puente and Stevie Wonder had played there. *The Lawrence Welk Show* made its home at the Palladium. TK's grandmother had watched the show regularly. The Champagne Lady, the Lennon Sisters, Al Hirt and Arthur Duncan—a tap dancer and the only person of color to ever make it on the show, which ran for twenty-seven years. TK said, "They couldn't find another black man who could sing or dance?"

The Palladium might have gone the way of the Seventh Veil but some investors had come to the rescue and gave the place a complete makeover. Jay Z performed at the grand reopening. Isaiah and Grace didn't talk on the drive over. She was distant but held his hand. Did this mean she'd seen the news video with the police carrying the big crate out of Mrs. Heng's house? Did she understand what it was and that he'd made it happen?

The marquee said OXY. "Is that a band?" Isaiah said.

Grace nodded at the people in line. "Yeah, they're punk," she said. "Was into it for a while. This is after my Motown phase." She told him about the Sex Pistols, Ramones, the Slits and Green Day. "Punk was about rebellion and resisting the establishment," she said. "If you were a good musician, you were suspect. The bands did outrageous things but it got to be self-conscious. Vomiting onstage, rolling in broken glass. Donita Sparks threw a bloody tampon at the crowd. Eventually I lost interest. I don't trust anything with its own fashion. Have you ever seen a mosh pit?"

"Not in person," Isaiah said.

"It's a trip."

"What does mosh mean?"

"Move over, shithead."

The Palladium was much bigger than he anticipated. Huge dance floor, people packed in like too many sheep herded into a holding pen. A flying saucer of klieg lights and strobes hung overhead, flashing and beaming and sweeping across a thousand sweaty faces. A banner hung from the balcony that said MAKE AMERICA RAGE AGAIN.

The music was so loud it was like a wall closing in, something you had to push back on for fear of being smashed. It sounded to Isaiah like one continuous car crash. The band was onstage, backed by a massive video screen flashing a jangle of images: Mona Lisa with a green mohawk, gargoyles with glowing eyes, Andy Warhol's checkerboard of Marilyns, a baby wearing a diaper and a medieval helmet, a vulture carrying a peace sign in its claws, Beelzebub in various forms and a lot of different skulls.

Four shirtless white dudes made up the band, headbanging to their waists, jumping up and down like hysterical chimps, the drummer hammering more than playing, the lead singer choking the mike to death, braying in anger, self-indulgence and lunacy. What was he in the daytime? Isaiah wondered. A dog walker? A mechanic at Jiffy Lube?

The crowd was into it, headbanging, shouting and screaming, their pumping fists silhouetted against the stage lights. It was as sweltering and muggy as the Amazon, somehow appropriate for a jungle jammed with primitives on the edge of control. There was a mosh pit in the middle of the dance floor, a maelstrom of young men shoving and shouldering and bullying one another aside while they staggered and careened around drunkenly. No women. They weren't stupid. Maybe it was his vantage point but Isaiah couldn't see anyone of color. Only white people would do this, he thought.

Grace was delighted, like she was remembering fun times. "Oh, yeah!" she exclaimed. They kept moving but it was pointless. The crowd was too thick to locate anyone in particular.

"What are we going to do?" she shouted.

"Try to get lucky," Isaiah shouted back.

The music stopped. It was like a terrible pain had suddenly vanished. The houselights went on. The crowd was revealed. A scroungy, heavy-breathing bunch of kids, their eyes glinting with hormones, adrenaline and ecstasy. The bandleader shouted into a mike. "All right, ladies, are you ready for a death wall?" There were raised fists and screams of excitement. Grace screamed too, hands cupped around her mouth.

"Yeah, let's do it!"

"Death wall?" Isaiah said.

"Everybody get back," the band leader shouted. "This is ladies only!" The middle of the dance floor cleared. Women emerged from the crowd, dozens of them, grinning with anticipation. They formed two lines, facing each other, about thirty feet apart. Isaiah saw her—*the sixth alt!* Christiana was wearing an oversize T-shirt and a fierce attitude and she was stripped of makeup. She gave the illusion of bulk.

Isaiah pointed. "Grace, do you see her?"

He turned but Grace was gone. He turned back to the dance floor. *Grace was in line,* grinning and eager like the others. Directly across from her was the sixth alt. The band began to play a tick-tock rhythm, getting louder and louder, the women leaning forward like runners on the starting line, the crowd cheering and hooting, berserk with excitement. As the music reached a crescendo, the band leader shouted, "One…two…THREE!"

The lines charged. Like no shit, they really charged, smashing together like the armies in *Braveheart.* They moshed with abandon. The sixth alter got lost in the chaos, but there was Grace, fierce little Grace, in the middle of it, giving as good as she got. The lights went out, the strobes came on, and it was too dark to see. Isaiah was afraid for her, even though he knew it was everybody else who should be afraid.

He texted her. *I'm in the lobby.* He waited, the same song playing endlessly. The song changed to another but he could hardly tell the difference. Grace and the sixth alter came out into the lobby, sweaty and disheveled. Grace's shirt was torn. The alter looked angry and resentful.

"I'm Isaiah."

"I know," the alter said.

"Let's talk." They started for the exit but the alter stopped and glared at Grace.

"Could you go get lost somewhere?" she said.

"Um, sure," Grace said. She looked at Isaiah. "I'll meet you at the car."

They sat outside on a bus bench.

"I don't know your name," Isaiah said.

"Angie," she said.

"What's your problem with Grace?"

"I don't like chicks, that's all. So what?" Isaiah noted a bruise on her face and a bald spot just above her forehead.

"What happened to you?" he asked.

She touched the bald spot. "I got into a fight when I was in jail. It was nothing."

"Do any of the others know about you?" Isaiah said.

She shrugged. "Just Pearl. I think the others kinda know I'm around, but really? They don't want to know." She smiled grimly. "If they knew how much shit I do for them..." She found a pack of Camels, lit one and blew the smoke out of her nose.

"I want to know what you saw that night," Isaiah said.

Angie searched her mouth with her tongue, found a shred of tobacco, and spit it out. "I saw everything. I can see through everybody's eyes." Isaiah remembered Gia saying that was possible. Angie went on. "I saw that fucking bitch come in the back and shoot Tyler and I saw her climb the rope. I switched out with that doofus Bertrand and went after her. I knew where she was going. The building next door. On the other side, there's an old-fashioned fire escape. So I ran outside—"

"Through the front door?"

"Yeah. I ran down to the corner and I was right. The fire escape was all the way down, but that bitch was gone. Then I came back to the showroom and Marlene took over. There was some random switching around. Christiana was last, kneeling down next to Tyler." Angie shuddered with anger.

"He wouldn't give me a chance!" she said. She blurted it out in a sob. "He was too busy fucking Marlene and gushing over Christiana. He *loved* her! He fucking *loved* her!" Her voice quavered and went lower. "He couldn't *stand* me. I'd come out for three fucking seconds and he'd look at me like I was shit!" She wept. Isaiah felt sorry for her. This fraction of a person with her fraction of a life, her past too horrifying to contemplate, her present a fugue state understood only in remnants. Unrestrained rage swept through her, the hatred so intense he thought she might catch fire.

"Now I'm all messed up!" she screamed. "Fucking Tyler. *Fucking* Tyler! I wish he was alive so I could kill him again!" Was that a figure of speech or an admission? She sneered at him. "Angus brought you into this, didn't he? Yeah, nobody as straight as you would work for him. He's got something on you." She huffed, admiringly. "Yeah, that's Pop for you. He doesn't fuck around. He was always like that. He never asked; he took what he wanted and if you fucked with him, he'd fucking destroy you. I worked for him for a couple of months. He thought I was Jasper. It was cool, you know? Seeing how the old man operated." She brightened into what looked like nostalgia. She laughed. "Fuck, he was ruthless! *Fuck!*"

"Angie," Isaiah said. "If I'm going to help you I have to know. Did you have Tyler killed?"

She looked at him, her gaze dripping with disgust, malice and glee. "I've gotta go," she said. Then she got up and went back inside.

CHAPTER TWENTY
This Is Our Life

Angus was roaming aimlessly around his house. He wished he liked to watch TV, have something mind-numbing to do. The theft of the Gatling gun was infuriating. It was the goddamn trifecta: a blow to his pocketbook, ego and reputation. And that bonehead Sidero had lost the fucking briefcase to the goddamn Cambodians. A milllllion fucking dollars in there. He left it on purpose, Angus thought. Oh how that little shit would suffer. He would no longer remember what manhood meant. If only Tyler had been around. He'd have kept his cool, just like he had in Afghanistan when he ran across open ground, grabbed an RPG and blew the shit out of the enemy and saved the rest of his platoon. Where the fuck do you find guys like that? They're all cops or FBI agents or straight-shooting assholes like Isaiah.

The last time anybody saw the Gatling was when the leader of the Locos was driving away with it. It was probably in Culiacán already, mowing down campesinos digging in the fields and minding their own business. Rage made the house seem small and close. He wanted to kick something, destroy something, but he bellowed his fury instead, his head back, arms out like a crucifix, repeating the outcry over and over again, until his breathing was a hacking cough and he felt his ugliness like a tumor on his heart. Somebody—*everybody*, would pay. Including that goddamn Isaiah and his goddamn girlfriend.

The thing that really snagged in his throat? How did Lok know about the delivery? How did he know to be there in the industrial zone? Someone told him. Someone was a rat. It was so precise it felt personal. Someone wanted him to ride off into the sunset a worn-out old man. Someone wanted the Top Gun to be humiliated. He pondered that awhile. *Sidero.* It had to be him. Isaiah had called, saying he wanted to come over. As soon as he left, that little prick would be dealt with. Angus's outrage had frightened Weiner. He found the dog under his desk. He sat down with the dog trembling in his lap.

"It's okay, boy," he said, stroking its ears. "Everything's all right."

Aside from Christiana being released on bail, everything was fucked. All the years he'd spent struggling and killing and creating mayhem, and for what? To preside over a snake pit of traitors, liars and incompetents? To sit on a useless shit pile of money? There was nothing left to do, no more to be gained, no limelight to bask in, no love to be discovered, no comfort or joy left in the world. He longed for Virginia and normal life and pleasure in small things, but their possibility was as finished as he was. At first he didn't recognize them, but there were so many tears falling rapidly, one after the other, beading like jewels on the dog's soft brown fur.

They were driving over to Angus's place. "Angie admired her father?" Grace said. "That makes no sense at all."

"I've been wondering about that," said Isaiah. "Maybe a family connection is better than no connection at all. Love from your parents is a powerful thing." He was thinking about Marcus and how his death had left him with a massive emptiness. He was still in high school at the time and was so desperate to fill the void he'd let Dodson, a drug dealer and a gangster, move into his apartment. He went on. "Maybe it helps Angie feel less, I don't know—more normal."

"Maybe," Grace said. "But I still don't understand it."

Harsh spotlights lit up Angus's massive concrete house. Add some gun slits and it could have been a bunker above Normandy beach. Isaiah parked in the driveway. Some of the Starks were milling around,

Hugo and Sidero among them. Isaiah didn't ask Grace if she'd be all right because he knew she would be.

"Good luck," she said as he got out of the car.

"Howya doin', asshole?" Sidero said. He eyed Grace. "A white chick, huh? Why don't you stay with your own kind?"

"Why don't you stay with yours?" Isaiah said, as he walked past him. "You know, stupid people."

Grace got out of the car to stretch, the Starks looking her over.

"What is it about white girls and niggers?" Hugo said. "Can't get enough of that black meat?"

"You're right," Grace said. "I should have settled for a pea-brain Nazi asshole like you."

"Fuck you," he replied.

"'Fuck you'?" she said. "That's the best you can do? Say, haven't I seen you before? Sure, it was in a movie. You were retarded and playing the banjo for Burt Reynolds."

"Shut up, bitch."

"I'll never shut up, dickhead, and unless you've got the balls to kill me right now, go home and fuck your cousin."

Grace wondered why she was here, trading zingers with a bunch of bottom-feeders. She wasn't exactly swimming with them, but she was down in the muck. She didn't need this. If she'd never seen, heard or spoken with them she wouldn't have been the lesser for it.

She got back in the car and wished Isaiah would hurry up. A woman came out of the house, a redhead in shorts and cowboy boots. She put her arm around Sidero and whispered something in his ear. Grace couldn't believe it. That moron actually had a girlfriend? The redhead could do better picking somebody out of a drunk tank or a soup kitchen.

"Another alt?" Angus said. "That's ridiculous." His eyes were red and puffy.

"No, it's not," Isaiah said. "I met her. Her name is Angie. I think she had Tyler killed."

"Bullshit."

"There are no other suspects, Angus."

"That's insane!" the old man shouted. "You're off your goddamn rocker. That's not fucking possible!"

"She worked for you," Isaiah said.

"No, she didn't. It was Jasper. I gave him the job because I thought it would be good for him."

"Would Jasper kick your dog?" Isaiah said. "He knows you'd be pissed. Marlene is a bitch but would she *stab* somebody? Bertrand calls himself the protector but would he hit somebody with a golf club and fracture their jaw? If Christiana was attacked, Bertrand's more likely to give the guy a stern talking-to."

Angus looked stumped and then stern and then angry and then exasperated. Voices in his head, arguing. "But how would she make contact with hired killers?" he said. "Those people aren't just anybody. They're hard to get to."

"Ever leave your computer on?" Isaiah said. "A file drawer open? Ever been on the phone with someone who might know a contractor? Has an alter ever been around when your associates came over? Did she meet any of them? Talk to them? Angie had access. She knew who you knew. It wouldn't be hard. She makes a call to someone with connections, says it's on your behalf and who wouldn't want to get in good with the Top Gun's daughter?"

"Why are you telling me this?" Angus said. "Christiana is still in danger and it's your fucking fault!"

"No, it isn't," Isaiah said. "It's her father's fault. The one who tortured her, the one who—"

"I DIDN'T DO ANYTHING!" Angus screamed. "DO YOU HEAR ME? I—DIDN'T—DO—ANYTHING!" An unseen hand clawed the old man's eyes, distorting them beyond insanity. He was muttering and shaking his head, his gaze moving wildly as if he was trying to see in a blacked-out room. His liver spots were darker, his sweaty scalp shining through his meager hair, his stoop more curved. He was in agony, his mouth open, bestial and crazed, a grimace like a branding iron searing his heart, in as much emotional pain as Isaiah had ever witnessed. How terrible a conscience can be. Angus quieted down, his breathing ragged as he morphed into a crone, cruel and unyielding, his voice so low and ghostly it might have been coming from an air vent or a darkening sky. "Get her out of it, Isaiah," he said. "Get her out of it or I'll kill you and everyone you love."

Angus sent the Starks away. He took a Valium, sat on the sofa with Weiner in his lap. Since Isaiah left, he'd settled down some. He was too exhausted to deal with Sidero but he would. In a way it was a good thing. The betrayal freed him from his promise and that little fuck was going to get it. Maybe not killed. But close.

The doorbell rang. He was overjoyed to see Christiana but it wasn't her. It was the new one, Angie. Slovenly, scornful, a poisonous look that could have killed Angus all by itself. She looked twenty pounds heavier than Christiana.

"Hello," he said with a weak smile. "I don't believe we've met."

"Oh, we've met, motherfucker. We met a long time ago."

She meandered around the study, eyeing things disdainfully. She picked up an antique vase from Italy and dropped it on the floor. Weiner yipped and scrabbled under the desk. She kicked over a side table, toppling the porcelain lamp, the bronze stag a customer had given him and an ivory bust of Napoleon he'd bought at an auction. She pulled books off the shelves, upturned the ottoman, tipped over chairs and with one violent sweep of her arm, cleared the photos off the mantel. She stood there in the mess, looking at him, waiting for him to challenge her.

"I, um, I've always wanted to apologize," Angus said. Her presence made him feel more fragile than his age.

"*Shut up,*" she said. "Just shut the fuck up, you fucking coward. You goddamn fucking pig."

"I'm sorry," he whispered.

The words seemed to enrage her even more. She picked up the bust of Napoleon and hurled it, hitting him on his forehead. He cried out, staggered back, his hand over his face, blood running through his fingers.

She strode over to him and hit him with a backhand, hard. "Pig, you fucking pig!" She snarled like a beast, her eyes strobing. She slapped him again and again and on and on, her invective in one long unintelligible stream.

He didn't try to protect himself. He stood there and took it. He would always take it. He welcomed it. Now she was hitting him with her fists, blow upon blow, a boxer pounding the heavy bag. It was almost a relief to feel his guilt as physical pain. Finally, she stopped. She was keening with her mouth open, drool hanging from her lips, the blood from his nose and torn lip splattered on her face. And those eyes. Bludgeoning, slashing, demolishing.

"I should kill you right fucking now!" she said. He hoped she'd do it. He'd give her the gun in the desk drawer and wait impatiently for the bullet to end his torment.

He heard someone running down the front stairs, no attempt at stealth. "Who the hell is that?" It was two people, not one. They reached the foyer. How the fuck did they get in? Swing from a tree? Angus knew instantly it was danger. He went to his desk and found the gun.

"What's the matter?" Angie said.

Angus heard them coming up the hallway toward the study. He fired into the wall. *BLAM BLAM BLAM BLAM BLAM!*

"Get back, Annie!" one of them shouted. Women? Not that it mattered. They fired back, the silenced rounds punching through the wall, chipping fragments off the fireplace and tearing holes in the furniture. Who are they? Angus thought. Why are they here? Why are they shooting at him? He grabbed Angie's hand, pulled her into the den and shut the door. She was terrified.

"What's going on?" she said.

"Shit!" he spat. He turned, opened the door again, fired off a few more rounds, then hurried to his desk. He reached underneath and picked up his shivering dog. "It's okay, Weiner," he said. More rounds blew through the wall. He went back into the den and led

Angie into the billiard room. He slid the heavy door closed and stopped.

He was wheezing, sticky with his own blood, his heart thumping—but he wasn't panicked. His body was old but his ferocity and fearlessness were still present and accounted for. Angie was looking at him, a scared little kid. It warmed him for a moment.

"Who are they?" she said. "What do they want?"

Angus said nothing, enjoying his brief omniscience. He knew what the shooters would do. One would stay on the chase. The other would circle around to the back and cut them off. The house was huge. It would take her a while to get there.

He led Angie down a hallway, through the dining room to the kitchen and up a narrow back stairway. Where was his private security? he wondered. What the fuck was he paying them for? The dog was getting heavier. Angus was shaky, his chest heaving. Angie helped him up the rest of the way, an arm around his waist, a hand on his elbow. Even under the circumstances it felt wonderful. They reached the second floor. Angus had to stop again, catch his breath.

If he'd calculated correctly, the front door was unguarded. He and Angie hurried down the main hallway and started down the long curving staircase that ended in the foyer. They were halfway to the bottom when gunfire erupted, the ejected shells clinking on the marble steps. One of the women was at the top of the stairs, shooting down at them. They made it around the curve out of view but were stuck there. By the time they reached the foyer, they'd be shot in the back. They had to hurry, the other shooter no doubt on her way.

"Angie, go on," Angus said. "The front door. Go!" He gave her a shove.

She bounded down the rest of the stairs and out the front door. Angus had to make a break for it, but the shooter was right around the corner and he was old and creaky. Clutching Weiner with one arm, he circled the other around the curve, shot three quick rounds, then stumbled down the rest of the stairs. The front door was open but he didn't want them to go after Angie. He closed it and heard sirens. *It's about fucking time!* If he could hold off the killers for another two minutes, he'd be okay. He hurried into the hall and cut through his office and the den, panting, bleeding, his head ringing from Angie's blows. He opened the door to the billiard room and met a tiny woman dressed in black and aiming a gun that was too big for her hand. Someone else came up behind him and pressed a barrel into his back. "Drop the gun," she said. He obeyed. "Now move, Angus."

They tried to make him leave the dog but he wouldn't. Now he was in the backseat of a car, the tiny one sitting next to him jamming her gun into his ribs. The bigger one was driving one-handed, the other arm in a sling. They weren't ugly but weren't pretty, either. The tiny one was okay if you liked titless dwarves.

"What the hell is this?" he said. "What do you want?"

"First of all, we want you to shut up," the driver said.

"You're them, aren't you?" Angus said. "The contractors that work as a team." They didn't answer. "Why would you want to kill me, for fuck's sake? What did I do?"

"Like you don't know," Tiny said.

"I don't, goddammit. Tell me."

"You hired us to kill Tyler and then you sent IQ to track us down," she said. "You double-crossed us."

"That's bullshit!" Angus said. "I didn't hire you! Why would I want to off Tyler? That makes no sense. He was the only guy I trusted. He practically ran the business. I didn't want to kill him. I wanted to clone him!" That gave the women pause. "Who did you talk to?" Angus continued. "Who gave you the job? Because it wasn't me."

"Your daughter," the driver said. Angus's insides froze. *Angie.* Isaiah was right. The driver said, "She told us Tyler was stealing and you wanted to take him out. We wanted to talk to you directly but she said you don't do that anymore."

"She said it was an emergency," Tiny said. "She said you'd pay double and you'd send the money up front."

"More bullshit," Angus retorted, "and you know what else? The police think Christiana did it. You guys left no evidence, unless you spit on the floor or took a piss and forgot to flush. I don't know how you did it, but the cameras didn't catch you and the only witness was my daughter and she couldn't recognize you because you wore masks and gloves, didn't you? The police don't know you exist." That put the women back on their heels.

"What do we do about IQ?" Tiny said.

Angus was loving it, browbeating these two assholes. The excitement was bringing him back to life. He felt like he did forty years ago. A slippery, conniving, ferocious motherfucker from the coal mines of West Virginia who mowed down his rivals and robbed them blind while he did it.

"What am I, your manager?" he said. "Leave town for a while. Isaiah's not the police. He's one guy from the fucking ghetto. If you don't knock on his door and confess, you'll never see him again."

Tiny was looking at the dog, a slight smile on her face.

Angus thought a moment. If they thought he'd hired Isaiah, why hadn't they killed him back at the house? Taking him along only slowed them down. When the answer came to him, he suppressed a smile of his own. Amateurs. They didn't know who they were fooling with.

"Could we stop a minute?" he said. "Weiner's gotta pee."

"Who the hell is—you mean the dog?" the driver said. "Forget it."

"It'll only take a minute," he said. "And if the car smells like dog piss, I might not feel like talking."

"Talking about what?"

"Paying you off."

They pulled over behind a gas station. Angus let the dog go and it wandered around, sniffing and sniffing and sniffing.

"Hurry up, Weiner," Angus said. "What are you looking for, a urinal?"

Tiny's eyes were riveted on the dog, like she was hoping it would find a suitable place.

"We want five hundred thousand," the driver said.

"Don't be stupid," Angus scoffed. "I can't get five hundred thousand dollars. Who has that kind of cash lying around?"

"Stop bullshitting," Tiny said. "We know who you are. Don't tell us you're not loaded."

"You're damn right, I am loaded," Angus said. "Loaded to the goddamn gills. Now let's go find an ATM that'll cough up five hundred grand. Look, you dummies, I don't have a goddamn savings account at Wells Fargo. My money's offshore. It's in Panama and Cyprus, and it's not in cash. It's invested in equities and bonds and real estate. I'm not a goddamn drug dealer." The women looked at each other. Angus sighed. "What are you, fucking hayseeds? Do I seem like the kind of guy who's gonna keep his money under a floorboard? I'm a businessman. Use your goddamn brains, will you?"

"How much can you get now?" Tiny said. The driver sighed and shook her head. Inwardly, Angus sneered. *Look at them. Tiny wants a deal but the driver doesn't want to back down. Divide and conquer.*

"Right now?" Angus said, scratching his head. "I've got what, a hundred grand or so in an ETF." *Like they know what that means.* "Are you guys set up to receive a wire transfer? No? Well, that's stupid. Some pros you are."

Tiny was bent down, holding her hand out to the dog and making kissing noises. The dog ignored her and walked through a puddle.

"For fuck's sake, Weiner," Angus said.

"When can you get it?" the driver said.

A mistake. Now they're committed to a hundred grand. Keep them on defense. "What is it, Saturday?" he said. "I can have it for you in cash by the end of next week."

"No, Monday," the driver said.

"Don't be a moron," he said. "Do you know how an ETF works? It's a mutual fund. If you want cash, you have to sell shares, which means I have to talk to my broker and he doesn't work weekends. Monday I'll tell him what I need, he'll make the order, but the transaction has to be confirmed. That'll take two or three days, and when the shares are sold, the money has to be transferred into my account and there's another day before it posts. Once it's there, I still have to go down to the bank and wait for them to gather up a hundred K in cash while the manager gives me the stink eye. It's the best I can do—are you done, Weiner? Jesus, it took you long enough."

The dog waddled over to him and he picked it up. Tiny looked disappointed, like she'd wanted Weiner to come to her.

"How do we know you'll pay?" the driver said.

Angus smiled. The clincher. "Because if I don't, you'll come back and kill me."

The driver huffed. "No. That gives you time to kill *us*."

She's not completely stupid, Angus thought. "Oh, for fuck's sake!" he said, getting loud. "Will you clowns get it together? Don't you want to go home? We have a deal, okay? A hundred thousand dollars in cash! Are we agreed?"

"No," the driver said stubbornly. "That requires trust and we don't have any."

Tiny reached out tentatively and patted the dog. Angus turned it away from her. "What the fuck do you want me to do?" he said. "Get the lawyers involved? Draw up a goddamn contract? You want to follow me around all week with a gun to my head?" The driver was stumped.

Tiny looked wistfully at Weiner. "He'll give us the money," she said.

"How do you know?" the driver said.

"Because if he doesn't, we'll kill the dog."

Sal drove away, Angus in the rearview mirror, yelling something about taking care of the dog. Sal thought, this is it. This is our life. Leaving a vicious old man at a gas station, a man they'd tried to kill and extort for money. This is our life. Annie in the backseat, snuggling with a kidnapped dachshund named Weiner as they drove back to their fucked-up house three blocks from Long Beach Gas and Oil, smelling of sweat, gun smoke and wet dog. This is our life. They were hired killers on the brink of sanity who'd murdered a long list of people and there was no way they could be anything else and there was no chance anyone else would have them.

This is our fucking life.

*   *   *

There was police tape strung around the house, the front door battered down. The cops had come and gone. Angus hobbled inside, aching, limping, his face bruised and crusted with blood. He wished he had a crutch or a wheelchair. He wished he had Virginia.

Angie was leaning against his desk, drinking eighteen-year-old scotch out of a coffee mug. "Surprised you made it back," she said. He hoped she would ask him if he was all right but she didn't. She looked at him, hostile and challenging, like whatever he said would be wrong and stupid and useless.

"What did you tell the cops?" he asked.

"That it was a home invasion," she said.

"What did you say about me?"

"That you were traveling, on an airplane somewhere."

Angus hesitated. Had she realized he'd risked his life for her? That he'd saved her? Would this be the beginning of forgiveness? "Why did you stay?" he asked hopefully. He could see the fury rising in her again, her eyes surging with hatred so pure and limitless he thought he would faint.

She came in close. "I'm going to let you live, Angus. Because that way I can punish you forever." There was a long, still moment. She looked at him as if he were a tick swollen with blood or a smear of shit on her hand. She spit in his face. And then she left.

Angus let the drops dry. They felt like abrasions, like scabs. He wished they were tattoos, like the ones the Nazis forced on the Jews, a dehumanizing string of numbers that marked them for suffering. Marked them for doom. He closed his eyes and saw Christiana, eight years old, hanging from a closet bar, a wire coat hanger twisted around her wrists so tightly her hands were purple. Her hair was filthy and ropy and stuck to her face with sweat, grime and tears. Strands covered her eyes but she saw him. She saw her father looking at his daughter in a torn lavender dress, piss and shit running down her legs. She saw him recoil at the smell. She saw him almost say something but change his mind. She saw the darkness coming and felt the air compress as he closed the door.

Angus sat down at his desk and thought he might stay there until he perished from hunger or thirst or was, in some other way, dead on arrival.

Deronda had left ten minutes ago. Dodson's soul still stinging from her taunts. He was cleaning truck number three. It was parked in a lot with Deronda's five other trucks. He couldn't bear to look at them. He couldn't stand thinking that they might have been his and how there'd be twenty or thirty of them if he had been in charge. He kept his head down and went through the routine. Sweeping, mopping, emptying the garbage, disposing of the cooking oil, sanitizing the ice machine, cleaning the coolers. Usually, he listened to old-school beats. Tupac, Biggie, Nas and the like, but lately, he'd been leaving his headphones in the car. The music reminded him of who he thought he'd be. He took a break. There was a lot left to do.

Headlights turned into the lot. He could tell from the driver's profile it was Cherise. Something about the way she carried her head. He didn't want to see her. He didn't want her to see him. There was no way to escape so he took a deep breath and waited. He imagined what she saw. Her broke-down husband, standing there in a sweaty do-rag and a filthy apron, holding a mop stuck in a bucket of soapy water. Shame was new to him and he almost turned and ran. She pulled up alongside.

"Hi, baby," she said. "Just wondering if you were okay."

"I am as you see me," he said. She didn't flinch.

"It had to be this way." She wasn't smug or condemning. Just a fact.

"I know," he said. "I'm not complaining. Where's Micah?" She turned her head. The boy was asleep in the backseat. No teddy bear and Dodson was glad. The idea that his son would need a stuffed animal for comfort was somehow pussyish. He wished Cherise would hurry this up and drive the fuck away.

"I love you, Juanell," she said. "I want you to know that." He wished she'd keep her voice down. He didn't want the boy to wake up.

In nearly a whisper, he said, "I know."

"Do you?" she said.

"Yes, I do," he answered.

He didn't look at her, his eyes cast downward at the dirty mop water.

"I'll see you at home," she said. "I'll have dinner waiting."

She drove away and Dodson watched the taillights grow dim and disappear. He wondered what people would say about him when he was lying in a mess of tubes and white tape and catheters; what they'd say when the beeping stopped and the lines had leveled. He remembered what they'd said about Beaumont. *He was a good man, Merrill. He was a rock. Everybody loved him, Merrill. Your father was the best. Stronger than iron. He was a hero and nobody knew.* Would anybody say things like that about him? No, they wouldn't. They couldn't.

He wondered what Micah would say to someone who brought him chili and warm corn bread at his father's deathbed. Someone he hardly knew. Would he say his father was brave and kind and loved history and gave free food to strangers and built a business from scratch that had lasted for decades? Would Micah say that he was proud of his father? No, he wouldn't. He couldn't. Because if Micah was honest, he'd say his father was a small-time criminal who wasted his life on schemes and dreams and playing private detective. If he said anything at all.

A pang went through him, the kind he hadn't felt since he was a boy. It was the pang that broke through your defenses and rose in your throat and forced tears out of your eyes. Dodson let go of the mop handle, bowed his head and cried like a fucking baby.

CHAPTER TWENTY-ONE
You Stupid Fucking Cow

TK stood in the entrance of Elise's Tea Room. He nearly turned around and left. Most people would think the room was lovely and inviting, but to TK it was like a fancy china shop where you weren't allowed to touch anything and were in constant danger of breaking something priceless. The room was painted a frosty pink with fancy drapes, glass chandeliers, old paintings and plates with pictures on them on the wall. Classical music was playing, which made everything seem all the more breakable.

The server led him to a small round table, so crowded he could hardly see the tablecloth. There were wine-colored napkins folded into pyramids, a lot of shiny utensils, so many he wondered if more people were coming. There was a centerpiece of flowers and fancy teacups with fancy saucers, the kind that would shatter if you breathed too hard.

He sat down. He felt huge, like he'd been assigned to the kiddie table. He unfolded the napkin and laid it across his lap. He wondered if he'd done it too soon. Maybe it was more polite to wait for his date. He hastily tried folding it back into a pyramid but didn't come close. He put it back on the table and drank a full glass of water.

Gloria arrived. She looked at the napkin lying there like a broken kite. "Hello, Thomas," she said. "You're early."

Realizing he should be standing, he got up quickly, his thighs hitting the edge of the table, everything on it jumping up and crashing back down again. He'd made less noise shooting skeet with his shotgun. The room went silent.

Gloria sat down. She had on a gray suit, black pumps and a necklace made of blue stones. On her, it looked frilly.

"Great to see you, Gloria," he said. "It's nice in here."

"I like it," she said, as if expecting an argument. The server brought the menus. "Not necessary," she said. "We'll have the full tea."

The server left and a pause fell over them. Gloria seemed to be waiting for something—him, probably, to start a conversation so they could get to know each other. This was a dumb way to do it, he thought. You don't get to know people sitting at a table with all this stuff around you. You got to know them fishing from the same boat or playing poker or watching a game and yelling at the TV.

Gloria sighed and looked around like there might be something more interesting to do. TK was desperate. He remembered what Grace had said. *Be yourself.* "Have you heard this one?" he said. "There's this fella, you see, and one Sunday he goes to church and when the sermon was over, the fella goes up to the preacher and says, 'That was one helluva sermon. I never heard a better one,' and the preacher said, 'Well, thank you, sir, but the Lord would appreciate it if you didn't swear in his house.' And the fella says, 'Sorry about that, but it was a *damn* good sermon.' Well, the preacher shakes his head and says, 'I'm sorry, sir, but I'm afraid you have to leave. I simply won't allow that kind of language in my church,' and the fella says, 'All right, I'll go now, and by the way, I left a thousand dollars in the collection plate,' and the preacher says, 'No shit?'"

TK had told lots of jokes that had fallen flat, but this one hit bottom like it had been thrown out of an airplane. To her credit, Gloria tried to smile. Either that or she had a stomachache.

"That's very funny, Thomas."

The food came. Tiny little sandwiches cut into triangles with the crusts removed. They were hardly worth bothering with. He ate the egg-salad one in two bites. Then he ate the salmon one in two bites.

Gloria was looking at him. She hadn't touched hers; she was still sipping her tea.

"Hungry," he said. "I missed breakfast."

There were also some things called scones, which turned out to be the driest biscuits he'd ever had, and there was nothing to wash them down with except the bitter-ass tea. Time slowed. TK could hear the seconds trudging past. Conversation was like someone swept away in white-water rapids, bobbing up every now and then only to sputter and disappear under waves.

"How long have you owned that junkyard?" she said.

"It's not a junkyard. It's a wrecking yard."

"Is there a difference?" He didn't like her tone. "I don't know how you can stand it, really," she continued. "All those old cars. Everything rusty and dirty. What do you do there, anyway? Repair them? It seems to me it's a waste of space."

A vein began pulsing in his neck. "There must be a better use for it," she went on. "A playground, a park, even a parking lot. Anything would be better than that mess." His hand was trembling, the teacup rattling as he set it down.

"Gloria," he said. "I want you to be quiet now."

She stiffened. " 'Be quiet now'? How dare you tell me to—"

"Gloria, *shut your mouth*," he snapped. She froze, her lips parted. He leaned forward, speaking softly, his anger held back by a thread. "My people are from Louisiana. They cut sugarcane all day and lived in shacks and didn't go to school. They came here with nothing and my parents had nothing. I'm the only one in the family to make something of hisself. Now I know I'm not much to look at or talk to, but you don't get to insult my place of business, not to my face, not in my company. And something else you should know. You are the rudest person I've ever met. You're disrespectful every time you open your mouth, and for somebody who's supposed to be a lady, you got no manners at all. You judge people before you even know them, before you even give 'em a chance."

"Thomas—"

"I'm not done yet," he hissed. "See, I knew your husband. I knew him well. He was a bum, a liar and a cheater. He didn't deserve that half-wit girl he ran off with, let alone a beautiful woman like you, and one more thing before we part company forever? *I am not him.* I am Thomas Marion Kahill, and passing me by is the worst mistake you've ever made in your life." He got up, threw some bills on the table and walked out.

He was so angry, he could hardly drive. He wished he'd yelled at her and pushed those scones into her face. What had he seen in that spiteful old witch in the first damn place? Loving heart, my loving ass. How could somebody his age make a mistake like that? He was getting senile, losing his marbles.

When he drove through the gate, he saw what she saw. A junkyard full of junk. Everything rusty and dirty. A space better used for a parking lot. He went into the warehouse and got a beer out of the fridge. He took a long gulp and hurled the bottle at the wall. He couldn't stop his hands from shaking. When a tear rolled down his cheek he knew— it was time to sell the business. Time to pack up and leave.

His phone buzzed. Probably Grace, wanting to know what happened. He rejected the call. The phone buzzed again. He'd have to talk to her sooner or later.

"It didn't work out, Grace," he said. "I thank you for your help but—"

"Thomas? It's Gloria." She was crying. "I'm sorry." She paused to sniffle. "You were right about everything. I was horrible and I'm thoroughly ashamed of myself."

"No argument here," he said.

"When I get nervous or anxious I lash out like that," she said. "It's ridiculous. I hope you'll accept my apology."

He didn't but said, "Fine. I accept. I gotta go now. A new shipment of junk just came in."

"Thomas, wait. I can't tell you how humiliated I feel. I realize there's no way to make it up to you—"

"No, there ain't," TK said.

"Could we give it another try?" she said. *"Please?"* He took a breath to calm himself. He heard her sweating through the phone and liked it. "Please, Thomas?"

He took a few moments before answering. "All right. Wear comfortable clothes. No dresses, nothing fancy."

"May I ask where we're going?"

He thought a moment and said, "Have you ever seen an elephant dance?"

Christiana was curled on the black leather sofa between the giant stuffed panda and the HOME IS LOVE pillow. She was alone and in the dark, the chaos and mess a shadowed moonscape. Everyone had gathered in the house inside her head. Lockup had chastened them. Before, their prison was the walls within Christiana's mind. But there were other kinds of prisons they'd learned, other terrors, and there were people who didn't care about Angus or Gia or that they were rich. There were people outside the bubble of their insulated world who misunderstood and ridiculed alters and switching out and different voices and different everything. Even hating them. Such things made them targets. Such things made them bull's-eyes. Those people were everywhere.

There was silence but she didn't trust it. She stood and walked carefully through the mess and down the hall to her room. She left the light off. She went to her desk, opened a drawer and brought out a pen and a sheet of paper. She signed the paper and left it there. Faint light slipped through the blinds, casting lines of shadow across the photo on her nightstand. The house at the edge of the sea, the dark forest behind it. She could barely see it but she saw everything. She took the photo out of the frame and looked at it for a long time.

Isaiah slept restlessly and, no, things didn't look better in the morning. They hardly ever did. He'd identified Angie as the conspirator but Angus wouldn't let Stella off the hook. Isaiah went to the Coffee Cup. He drank a double espresso but it did nothing for his energy level or his sense of desolation. He left the croissants on the plate.

He thought about Grace. He loved her without question. There was the emotional part, the overwhelming need to be with her, care for her and be cared for in return. But he also admired her. She impressed him. Even if they weren't together, he was glad to know someone so brave and smart, so self-reliant and resourceful. There was no one like her and never would be.

Three dead and many wounded. He wondered if he was irredeemable, to her and to himself. Yes, there were reasons for what he'd done, but reasons were intangible, invisible, electrons sparking through a synapse with no more materiality than a song. But a dead body was real. It had structure. Weight. You could see it. You could roll it over and find the bullet hole. You could watch the family grieve. He had to talk to Grace. See her face. See where things were and ask for forgiveness. He texted her. *Can I see you?* She replied immediately. *I'm at the house.* She was waiting for him and that made him happy.

He went out to the street and automatically looked for the Audi. Man, he missed that car. He thought he heard its roaring engine. He turned and saw a tricked-out Impala speeding right toward him. A Loco named Estevan was holding an Uzi out the window, cranked up, screaming and out of his fucking mind. Isaiah hesitated. There was no cover. He could race in front of the Impala, get to the other side of the street—no time, he'd get run over. Run away, get shot in the back. The car was *coming* and coming *fucking fast!* He had to take away Estevan's angle. He ran *toward* the car. Estevan was grinning, gibbering insanely. He started shooting, *BLAM BLAM BLAM BLAM,* the thirty-round mag spitting brass casings, the trajectory of the salvo and Isaiah's path about to meet head-on—Isaiah hit the ground and rolled toward the street. Estevan couldn't angle the gun down low enough, emptying the magazine over Isaiah's head. The Impala sped on, turned a corner and was gone. Isaiah got up on his hands and knees. Mouth open, spittle dripping out, breathing hard, wrists scraped to shit, bleeding from breaking his fall. People were peeking out of the shops and stores, tentative, not sure the shooting was over. Isaiah stood up, trudged toward his car. He had to get out of here before the cops showed up.

His phone buzzed. "Still alive, motherfucker?" Manzo said. "Enjoy

JOE IDE

it while you can. It's not just us that's coming for you. Our allies too. Varrio Longos, Barrio Pobre, Poker Town Flats and every fucking Sureños gang in LA. Dig a hole, you fucking puta, because that's where you're gonna be." Manzo hung up.

Isaiah plodded back to the Kia. He sat there awhile with his forehead on the steering wheel. He'd fucked up in every way imaginable. Lok wanted to kill him for the betrayal and Angus did too. Sidero and Hugo were lurking out there somewhere and Manzo had called in the troops. Every killer in SoCal would be after him. He needed time to get himself together and figure out what was next. He couldn't go back to the house; they might be waiting for him. He'd stay with TK and lay low for a while. A jolt of alarm made him lift his head. The house.

The house where Grace was waiting for him.

Frantically, he called her. No answer. He raced home, cursing the car and its puny engine. He called her twice more, letting it ring until he got her voice mail. He drove into his driveway and jumped out. The house was impenetrable: steel-core doors, unbreakable locks and burglar bars. Grace was safe unless they caught her outside, but why hadn't she answered her phone? He looked down the driveway and saw her GTI in front of the garage. The driver's door was open, a Starbucks cup on the ground.

"No!" he shouted. He ran down the driveway. As he approached the car, Sidero, Hugo and two other Starks came out of hiding. They encircled him, aiming guns.

"What's up, Sambo?" Sidero said gleefully. "Told you I'd get you, didn't I?"

She decided not to go with Noah to Big Sur. What was she going to do? Compare him side by side with Isaiah and see which one had more checkmarks on her what-I'm-looking-for-in-a-man list? Noah lied when he said no romance. *Of course* there'd be romance. If she went with him she wouldn't come back and the idea of never seeing Isaiah again made her love startling and intense, a beacon piercing through the fog, everything around it murky and ill-defined.

She realized her dithering wasn't about Noah, it was about her insecurities, her self-doubt, her fear of being less than Isaiah's expectations. She didn't know what those were or how exactly she would disappoint him, but Isaiah would love her anyway, and that in itself was a miracle. They would always have hard times. They would always struggle. There would always be doubt and pain and grueling decisions. No one escaped. Karma is karma. No matter how much you fretted and worried about the future, you changed nothing. A trillion elements converged to create a single human event. Your angst was a rain cloud in the solar system.

She was exhausted and wondered if she'd locked the car. She fell asleep in Isaiah's bed. Her phone was on vibrate. A commotion outside the window woke her up. She peeked through the blinds and saw Sidero and three other men carrying/dragging Isaiah up the driveway. He was bleeding from a gash on his head. "Motherfuckers!" she shouted.

She ran into the living room, snatched the collapsible baton off the coffee table and opened the front door. A van bumped over the sidewalk onto the lawn just as Isaiah and his attackers came out of the driveway. The door slid open.

"Let him go!" she yelled. She charged them.

One of the men came forward to meet her, his hands ready to grab. The baton was unimpressive. It looked like the handgrip on a wheelchair. Isaiah had taught her to use it. She curled her wrist inward and snapped the baton downward to its full length. Raising it high and wide gave the attacker more time to block the blow. She kept the baton close to her body, held it back over her shoulder and swung, putting her hips and shoulders into it, the metal rod slicing through the air. *THWACK!*

The blow hit the guy in the rib cage. He screamed and whirled away. The second guy was huge and came in low like a linebacker. She hit him on the shoulder. He cried out but kept coming, grabbing her around the middle and flinging her to the ground. She landed hard, the wind knocked out of her. By the time she recovered, the van and Isaiah were gone.

"GODDAMMIT!" she screamed.

Mrs. Marquez was across the street, hysterical and waving her cell phone. "I called the police."

"No! No police!" Grace shouted.

"Why?"

"I can't tell you now. Please trust me. Tell the police you made a mistake."

Grace got in her car and drove in the direction of the van. It was too far ahead. Chasing it was futile. She pulled over in the Vons parking lot. She questioned her decision about not calling the police but decided she'd done the right thing. Angus had his men kidnap Isaiah and why do that unless they were going to kill him? Or worse. They'd probably have their fun first. She didn't want to think about that. But if those assholes got a hint the cops were involved they'd kill Isaiah immediately.

She'd have to rescue him. At least she'd have to try. Before falling asleep she'd decided to move in with him—repaint the place, add some color, hang some paintings, get some furniture. Make it look like a home instead of a monastery. She'd always thought the nesting thing was corny but she'd never had a reason to consider it before. Marriage? Kids? The idea of spending the rest of her life with one of her asshole boyfriends had been laughable. Until Isaiah came along.

She turned off the engine and collected herself. How could she possibly find him? She had no leads, no clues, and she was no Isaiah. She was dumb to even consider it. "No, Grace," she said aloud. "You have to do this! It's Isaiah, you moron!"

It was warm in the car. She got out and breathed deeply, trying to calm herself. *Okay, Grace. Channel Isaiah. Start with what you know.* She stood there a minute, her head empty, nothing occurring to her. "I don't know anything," she said. She started pacing. "What am I supposed to do?" she asked the sky. "I don't know *anything!*" She thought about Isaiah, bleeding and helpless as those motherfuckers dragged him into the van. She thought about what they were doing to him, how they were hurting him. She couldn't stand herself. "YOU STUPID FUCK-ING COW!" she shouted. She stopped, put her palms on her temples and pressed hard. She heard Rebecca's voice. *When you go off like that it's a decision. A bad habit. Exert control or I'm telling you, in all sincerity, you will live to regret it.* "Okay, okay," she said. She started walking. *Okay, where would they take him?* she thought. *There was this fucked-up place where they had their meetings—what did Isaiah call it? The Den, that's right. He said it was an old house. Where was it? Think, Grace. What did he say?* She couldn't think of anything and walked faster, running her hands through her hair. Still, nothing came to her. "Come on, Grace," she said aloud. "What did he say? What did he say?" She lost it. "GODDAMN YOU, GRACE! GODDAMN YOUR FUCKING—" She stopped. *Calm down, calm down, it's for Isaiah. Don't you dare break down.* She remembered. "When I asked him where it was he said *it's on the way to the airport!*"

She was pleased with herself for exactly two seconds, and then she slapped herself on the forehead. *So what? There's a million ways to get to the fucking air—no, no, Grace, don't go there, just think. What the fuck else did he say?* She kept walking around, running her hands through her hair so often it was turning greasy. She tried to keep herself from seeing fists smashing Isaiah's face, boots stomping his bones. She put her hands out in supplication. "STOP IT, GRACE!" She wanted to choke herself until she passed out. *He said something else, Grace...something else...what was it? What the fuck was it?* It felt like she was birthing a car or a picnic bench. "He said...he said...*he stopped at the cemetery!*" she shouted.

She fumbled with her phone, her fingers suddenly fat. She brought up a map. The Sunshine Cemetery was on California Street and Willow. Willow was a straight shot to the airport. *Okay, good, Grace.* Isaiah had driven on Willow past California and the cemetery, heading toward the airport, the farthest east he would have gone. The Den was somewhere between those two points. She smiled and then frowned. "Big help," she said. He could have turned off on any of the dozens of side streets.

She walked in circles but nothing was coming to her. She took off her jacket and dropped it on the ground. *Come on Grace come on Grace come on Grace come on you stupid fucking moron bitch!* "Please, Grace!" she shouted. She was crying now, tears and mucus streaming down her face. *Come on Grace come on Grace come on Grace come on you goddamn fucking idiot!* She grabbed a shopping cart and shoved it as hard as she could. It rolled, hit a parking block and fell over. A store manager approached her.

"Excuse me, miss," he said, "but you're scaring the customers and—"

"GET THE FUCK AWAY FROM ME, ASSHOLE!" she screamed. He scurried off, his hands over his head in case she threw a rock.

She stopped, panting, her hand over her mouth. She shut her eyes and heard Isaiah say—what? *What did he say, Grace?* "He said his blood sugar was low," she said. "He said he stopped at the park and had an energy bar!" She went back to the map. She scrolled too far and then not far enough. "Where's the goddamn park?" she said. The only park between the cemetery and the airport was Willow Springs Park on Orange Street. He had turned off Willow onto Orange heading east. The house had to be around there someplace. Otherwise, he would have turned off Willow before or after Orange. But how far did he go? she thought. Orange went on forever.

He said something else. *One more thing, Grace.* She was sweating and her throat was raw. Her head was booming like a kettle drum, her anger and self-hatred brawling with her intelligence. She had to relax, breathe like she didn't have asthma and let her brain cells reorganize. *Okay, Grace. Empty your head for fifteen seconds, you can do that, can't you?* She counted aloud. "One." *They have Isaiah; they're hurting him.* "Two." *Sidero hates him. He won't stop until Isaiah is dead.* "Three." *Isaiah is in pain. Terrible pain.* "Four." *He's calling out to me. He's calling my name.* "WHAT DID HE SAY TO YOU, YOU FUCKING ASSHOLE? REMEMBER OR I'LL FUCKING KILL YOU!" she screamed. She stood there, shoulders slumped, staring at the asphalt. The tears and mucus had dried, a second skin of futility. She blinked twice. *"The freeway,"* she breathed. "He said he should have taken the freeway!" Back to the map. Orange intersected with the freeway. She had four sides of a box. California Street on the north, Willow on the west, Orange on the south and the freeway on the east. Isaiah was somewhere within that perimeter. She got in the car, started the engine and put on her safety belt. She filled her lungs, exhaled slowly and settled herself. She put the car in gear, popped the clutch and slammed her foot to the floor.

CHAPTER TWENTY-TWO

How Many Daughters
Does Angus Have?

Isaiah thought he'd seen her drive fast but that was nothing. That was bumper cars. Willow Street was her own personal Grand Prix. She weaved and darted and cut people off. She ran red lights, swerved up onto the sidewalk and drove into oncoming cars to get around traffic. Her eyes widened, she grinned. "There's the cemetery!" she shouted. "There's the goddamn ceme—SHIT!" Orange had come up quicker than she'd thought and she'd gone past it. She did a quick, tire-smoking, death-defying U-turn and turned onto Orange. She slowed. Willow Springs Park was next. That's where Isaiah had stopped to eat an energy bar.

It was an ugly, desolate area. Dead trees, bobbing oil wells, storage yards for heavy equipment, a gravel pit and swaths of arid nothing. "Where are you where are you where are you?" she muttered. And then, "YESSS!" There was the goddamn park. Not much of one, more like an extension of what was around it.

The house was around here someplace. *Isaiah* was around here someplace. She could feel it. A moment's elation—a dirt road! No. It led to the stupid gravel pit. Then was more arid nothing and a power station that seemed to bristle with voltage and danger. In front of her was the freeway, the eastern border of the box. Had Isaiah been talking about here? Was this the place he could have gotten to faster if he'd have taken the freeway? She consulted the map again. It was an industrial area.

Apparently zoned that way because there were no houses. If she continued east on Orange and went past the freeway, she'd enter a vast and densely populated residential area. Lakewood, Bellflower, Paramount, on and on across the breadth of LA. She could see no place isolated enough that the neighbors wouldn't complain about a bunch of drunk skinheads playing hate rock. She went over the map again. The house had to be on or near Orange, and on this side of the freeway; nothing else fit. *But there were no fucking houses.*

She was desperately thirsty and hadn't brought water. "You're a moron, Grace," she said. Okay, maybe it wasn't a residential house. Maybe Isaiah meant a frat house or clubhouse. She drove around the box at walking speed, looking for anything that could serve as the house or something that might be hiding a house from view. She was back on Orange again and the place where she'd started. She stopped, muttered expletives, her hands clenched on the steering wheel. Her thinking was faulty. Suppose Orange wasn't the southern border? Suppose it was the northern border and the box was to the south?

She drove around the new, bigger box. Still nothing. She was back on Orange *again.* She covered her head with her arms and wept. "GODDAMN YOU, GRACE! GODDAMN YOU, YOU STUPID FUCKING—" She made herself stop. Was she really going to give up now? Leave Isaiah to the wolves? *Think it through again, just like Isaiah would.*

She remembered something. One of her professors had told her that when you've run out of ways to solve a problem, *break set.* In other words, break your mind-set, throw out your assumptions and redefine the problem. Okay, what were her assumptions? There were two. That the house was somewhere in the expanded perimeter and that Isaiah had driven down Orange and stopped at the freeway. But what if the house wasn't in the box and Isaiah had kept going on Orange past the freeway? She brought up Google Maps, the street view.

Just on the other side of the overpass was a no-man's-land. One of those spaces immediately adjacent to freeways where the homeless lived and people dumped their old appliances. There was no obvious way to get to it. Grace drove across the overpass and there it was, off to her left. A road too insignificant for Google Maps to show. It ran alongside the huge abutments, unpaved and wide enough for only one car. *This is it, Grace. This has got to be it!* Somewhere down that road was the love of her life.

Grace drove slowly, bumping through potholes, the gravel clattering against the catalytic converter. She was coming around a curve when she saw a car blocking the road, two Starks leaning against it. Thankfully they weren't ones she'd seen before. She stopped and one of them came up to her window. She could see a lump under his shirt. A gun tucked away.

"This is private property," he said.

"I'm sorry. I'm lost," she said.

"Well, you can't come in here. Go back. Now."

She had to drive on the shoulder to turn around. As she made the turn, she glimpsed a rooftop. Was that the Den? She had to take a look. She wondered how Isaiah had done it. There was a grove of trees on the other side of the road. Had Isaiah come through there? She went back to Orange, turned left and drove past the grove. It was hemmed in on this side by a tall, chain-link fence and NO TRESPASSING signs. She drove a little farther. The fencing continued past a vast, empty parking lot. On the other side, forklifts and earth movers were parked in rows. There were some warehouses in the distance. No one was in the kiosk. She parked on the road, jogged across the parking lot and walked quickly into the trees.

The trees were misshapen and sapless, litter and broken glass on the ground. It was dusk. There were gullies to get over, thickets to get around. She stumbled and ran into things. She reached the tree line and stayed behind some brush. The Den was on the other side of the road, as broken down as the gang's ideas. Spotlights lit a group of men standing around in the yard. There were what, fifteen of them? Talking, smoking, drinking, joking, playing tug-of-war with a dog. Grace looked for signs of Isaiah but saw nothing.

An hour went by. The drinking got heavier, the laughter rowdier, the fucked-up music louder. Three women arrived and dispersed themselves among the men. In the harsh white light and deep black shadows, the gathering reminded Grace of news clips from the sixties: Selma, Montgomery, Birmingham, the crowds of white faces seething with hatred for people they'd never met. People who held their innermost fears. Who were too much like them to be tolerated.

They were waiting for something, Grace thought. A pep rally? A cross burning? For their white robes to come back from the cleaners? Or maybe they'd come to watch a nigger get beaten and tortured and hung from a tree. It seemed shockingly possible. The idea made her heart pound and her hands sweat. *Don't wimp out now, you bitch.*

She had to find out if Isaiah was in there. There was no way to get past that bunch of assholes without a box of grenades and an RPG. Call the police? Not yet. Suppose Isaiah was being held someplace else? If the cops showed up and Angus heard about it, Isaiah was dead. *What now what now what now?*

"Okay, Grace," she whispered, *"break set."* The assumption: she had to go through or around the Starks to get to the house. Was that true? Not necessarily. Redefine the problem. What if she didn't have to go through or around them? What if...what if...*what if they left?* What if they were called away? They'd have to have a really good reason. Had Angus watched the news? Had he heard about the police and the house in Cambodia Town? She hoped he hadn't. Isaiah's life depended on it.

Angus was feeling a little better. He'd taken a couple more Valium and rested. His control had returned, the craziness held in check. His phone rang. Unknown caller. Not unusual, the nimrods used burners. He was about to call Sidero anyway and find out about Isaiah.

"Well?" Angus said.

"Angus, this is Grace. Isaiah's girlfriend."

"Grace?" Angus said. "What happened to Stella?"

"She got scared about your threat and went into hiding," Grace said. "It's me now."

Angus hesitated. He'd heard about this girl. A ballbuster, according to Sidero and Hugo. "Well, I can't say I approve of your choice of men, young lady," he said. "What can I do for you?"

"You have Isaiah."

"Do I? I don't know what you mean."

"I want to make a deal."

Angus shook his head. Was she actually trying to hustle him? Women always think they're smarter than men. A load of crap. Except for Virginia. "Go on," he said.

"I know where the Gatling gun is," she said.

Usually, Angus could tell right off if someone was bullshitting, but this girl was straightforward, all business, not fucking around. If Isaiah had a girlfriend, this is exactly what she'd be like.

Angus tried to sound indifferent. "Oh, really? Well, that's interesting, Grace. Was there anything else?"

"The Locos have the gun."

"Christ," he scoffed. "You don't think I know that? You're as dumb as your goddamn boyfriend. I wonder what happened to him, anyway. I hear he's gone missing."

"Could you shut up a minute?" she snapped. "I know *exactly* where the gun is. I'm talking about an address and I'm talking about now."

"And how would you know that?" Angus said.

"During the shootout, Manzo took off with the gun, right?"

"That's what I heard."

"Isaiah was there and he went after him," she said. "Didn't anybody see him?" Hugo had told Angus someone had gone after Manzo, but he thought it was some of the Locos.

"It was Isaiah," Grace said. "And the car was red." Angus took a moment. Hugo had said that too, the girl adding, "How would I even know that unless somebody who was there told me? Think about it, Angus. Who do you think called Lok's people in? Who do you think ratted you out? One of your moron crew had the balls and the smarts to orchestrate something like that? It was Isaiah, no one else could have done it." She was right again, Angus thought.

Angus said, "What was Isaiah going to get out of it?"

"Lok was going to give him a cut," she said, "a hundred grand. Isaiah was going to give it to you in exchange for not hurting Stella." Yeah, Angus thought, Sir Galahad would do something like that. If he inexplicably saved Angus's life in that sewer pipe, he'd do something as idiotic as this. That Isaiah had stabbed him in the back was outrageous, but he'd get his. "What do you want?" Angus said.

"The gun for his life," Grace said. "I know what you're going to say. How do you know I'll play it straight? I'll go first. I'll tell you where the gun is. When you get it, you release Isaiah."

What an idiot, Angus thought. She should take a lesson from the titless dwarf who took Weiner.

"Okay," he said. "It's a deal."

"The guns are at an apartment." She gave him the address.

"This is useless," Angus said, writing it down. "You expect my guys to go in there with guns blazing? It'll be a bloodbath."

"No, it won't," she said. She'd found a building on Google Earth. Run-down, four stories, off by itself. "The front and back doors are always open," she said. "It's a shitty building, nobody cares." She reminded Angus it was Saturday night, and the gang would be out partying. If somebody was in the apartment, it was probably one of the younger guys or maybe even a sister or grandmother. "Shouldn't be a problem for your crew," she said. There were fifteen or so gang members at the Den. She wanted them all to leave. "The real problem is keeping other people out of it," she said.

Angus was Google Earthing the address. Shitty area, no streetlights, neighbors were mostly small houses, fewer people to call the police or come running with a pistol. A good place to hide the Gatling gun. Grace said the Starks should secure the fire stairs, elevator, both ends of the hall, as well as the parking lot, all of which she'd never seen. Lookouts too, in case a Loco happened to drive by.

"I don't know," Angus said. "A lot of things could go wrong."

"Yeah, it's risky," she said. "It depends on how much you want your self-respect back."

When this is over, Angus thought, I'm going to throw this whore in a landfill. "You'd better not be bullshitting or I'll—"

"I know, I know," Grace said wearily. "You'll kill me and you'll kill Isaiah. I get that, okay? But I've got no choice. Isaiah means everything to me. So just do it, okay? I don't want this to fuck up because the gun isn't there."

"Why wouldn't it be there?" Angus said.

"Manzo's already made a deal," she said. "The handover's happening soon, maybe tomorrow for all I know. But the gun is there now. I've seen it. I hang with one of the Loco girls."

"Oh, really?" Angus said, testing her. "What does the gun look like?" Grace had seen it on the news.

"I don't know," she said. "It was in a big plastic crate." She asked him to call when it was over and recited her number. He didn't write it down. "A word of advice?" she said.

"What's that?"

"It's in Manzo's hood. Go big or go home."

Grace ended the call and was immediately kicking herself. Did she say too much? Too little? *Go big or go home?* She couldn't believe she'd said that. How obvious could she be? Angus was probably laughing at her right now and even if he did take the bait, would he act on it now or put it off? She was sitting with her arms around her knees, watching the Starks through a veil of leaves and branches. The gathering itself hadn't changed. If the scene was running on a loop, you wouldn't be able to tell. A fight broke out. Two drunk guys throwing wild punches, grappling and ripping each other's T-shirts, the crowd egging them on, glad to have some entertainment.

Sidero came out of the house, and there was immediate quiet. Everyone gathered around the porch. Sidero stood straight, breathed in deep and waited until every eye was on him. He spoke, his words riling up the crowd, invoking angry shouts and raised fists. Grace was breathless. *It's working!* Sidero gave them instructions, pointing at different members, getting enthusiastic nods in return. How many would leave? Grace wondered. It had to be all of them or she'd be back where she started. *Go big or go home—please.* Sidero shouted something and the whole fucking bunch of them dispersed to their cars. *Oh my God, Grace. You're a genius!*

The engines started almost simultaneously, the thunderous roar filling the night with violence. Sleeping birds took off, the mosquitos disappeared, leaves shook down from the trees. The cars lined up and sped off down the narrow road, great clouds of dust in their wake. The sound faded and an amazing quiet descended, as if noise had been banished from the world.

The three women were left on the porch. A big dog was sitting there too. The women talked for a bit and went into the house. The dog remained, nose up, sniffing the darkness for enemies, sniffing for Grace. She had to take a look. Creep up and peek in a window? No, the dog would be on her. She thought about the women. When the men drove away, they looked bereft, like they'd missed the bus to the big game. Grace had used her sex against Gordo, the creep from her foster home. Women would be a different story.

Grace drove the GTI down the dirt road, going way too fast. She downshifted into second, turned hard through the gate, simultaneously releasing the clutch and yanking the hand brake, the car sliding sideways right up to the house, stopping hard, a wave of dirt and gravel thrown up on the porch. The dog was barking savagely. The women came bursting out the door wielding guns.

"What the fuck are you doing?" the redhead said. "Have you lost your goddamn mind?" Another woman held on to the dog.

Grace got out of the car and slammed the door. "Goddammit, I'm late! Fucking shit! When did they leave?"

"First of all," the redhead said, "who are you?"

"Who am I?" Grace feigned surprise. "I'm Angus's daughter, Grace."

The women glanced at one another. "Angus's daughter?" the redhead said. "I thought she was a dressmaker or something."

"That's my sister, Christiana," Grace said. "Prissy little bitch."

The women looked her up and down. *Stand your ground, Grace. Stay calm. Stay fierce.* The heavyset brunette wasn't having it.

"Let me see your ID," she said. Grace handed over her license. The brunette held it so the others could see it. "Says your name is Grace Mon-a-ro-va," she said.

"Is that Jewish?" the redhead said.

"My ex-husband was from Belgium," Grace said, "and I'm Angus's kid. I'm as white as you are." The women were still eyeing her skeptically. "What's the matter?" Grace said, sounding a little annoyed.

The brunette went back to the license. "Your address is 231 Latimer Street. Where is that, East Long Beach, right? It's full of niggers and Mexicans. If you're Angus's daughter, why are you living there?"

"I told Angus I wasn't a baby anymore and that I'd do whatever I want. He cut me off, the prick. Rent is cheap there. What else can I say?" She put her hands on her hips and stomped her foot. "I can't believe I'm late!"

"What do you care?" the brunette said. "You weren't going anyway."

"That's my point," Grace said. "Why do the men always leave us out of things? Haven't you noticed that? We're their best buddies when they're fucking us and bringing them beer, but when it's crunch time, we're on the sidelines."

"I'm not on the sidelines," the redhead said. "None of us are."

"Oh, really?" Grace replied. "Then why didn't you go with them to kidnap the nigger? I'll tell you why. You're a woman, that's the only reason." Grace chuckled. "I mean, seriously. Are you telling me you're not as good in the field as any of those assholes? Give me a break." She huffed. "Happens every fucking time. Like tonight. They run off like heroes to get the Gatling gun and what are we doing? Nothing."

"Wait," the brunette said. "If you're cut off from Angus, how do you know about that?"

Grace shrugged. "Sidero called me."

The redhead took a step forward. "*Sidero* called you?"

"Yeah. We're hooked up." She'd seen them together outside Angus's house. The redhead inhaled the air out of the world and dropped her chin to her chest. She glared at the ground, trembling.

"What?" Grace said. "What'd I say?"

"She's with Sidero too," the third woman said.

"You're kidding me."

"Mother*fucker!*" the redhead screeched. She walked in a circle, clutching an assault rifle and shaking it. "I swear to God, I'm going to shoot that bastard as soon as he gets back!"

Grace's eyes widened. "That's why he didn't want me to join up! He said he wanted me in reserve!"

"I should have known," the redhead said, "I should have *known!* I'm gonna kill that prick!"

"I'm sorry," Grace said. "I didn't know."

"It's not your fault," the brunette said. "God, what a rat." She put her arm around the redhead. "Come on, Jenn. Let's have a drink." They went into the house.

The third woman remained. She was older, hair streaked with gray. "We told her a million times but what can you do? I'm Samantha, by the way. Come on in. We can plan how to kill Sidero."

The living room was large, plastic chairs in uneven rows. A tattered Confederate flag on one wall, white nationalist signs on another, stuck there in disarray like stickers on a suitcase. A table with a coffeemaker. A cluster of tiki torches leaning in a corner. Samantha put the dog in another room and Grace trailed her down the hall to the kitchen. A fridge, a microwave, dirty dishes in the sink and an overflowing trash can. The brunette was sitting at a folding table, smoking and talking on her phone. A bottle of scotch and plastic cups in front of her. She ended the call.

"I'm Ida," she said.

"Grace. Nice to meet you."

"I thought Chip was supposed to clean up in here," Samantha said.

"Who knows?" Ida said. "It's not like Sidero pays him. You want a drink or a beer?"

"Beer," Grace said.

Samantha got beers out of the fridge and gave Grace one. They sat down at the table. "I still can't believe that asshole," Grace said.

"Take it from me," Ida said, "never date a white nationalist and especially don't marry one."

"Why not?"

"Because they're angry."

They drank their beers. Ida finished her drink and stubbed out her cigarette. "Wonder how the boys are doing?" she said.

Samantha smiled at Grace. "Maybe Sidero will get killed and save you the trouble." Grace smiled back and they clinked beer bottles.

Ida and Samantha started talking about their kids. Grace took stock. Samantha had a gun in a back holster. Ida's was on the table. The redhead's assault rifle was leaning against the sink. Maybe she was in the bathroom. Was Isaiah here? Grace was wary of asking directly. If she knew about the kidnapping and the Gatling gun, she should also know where Isaiah was being kept.

Ida kept glancing at her, as if she knew Grace but didn't quite recognize her. Grace smiled and joined the chatter. She never realized how hard it was to seem casual. *Don't just sit there, Grace. Make a move.*

Angus wondered what the Starks were doing. Would Sidero fuck this up, too? Maybe he'd been too rash, sending them out on something like this, but he wanted that goddamn Gatling gun. He *needed* it. The boys would deal with Isaiah very soon now. Angus told Hugo to go crazy, do whatever they wanted until there was nothing left of Isaiah but his fillings.

He worried about Grace. Had she told him the truth? Was this some kind of elaborate scam? He should have done surveillance, come up with a plan. There was still time to call them back. He picked up his phone.

Dwight came in. "I'm going home."

"No, stick around," Angus said. "I may need you."

"Why? I've got something going."

"For one, because I say so," Angus said. "And for two, I've got something going too." He told Dwight about the girl calling and the Gatling gun.

Dwight's forehead furrowed. He opened his mouth but didn't respond.

"What's wrong with you?" Angus said.

Dwight fumbled in his pocket for his phone. He dabbed at it, nervous because Angus was watching.

"How long is this going to take?" Angus said. Dwight found an article from a local paper. "Read," he said.

The article said the police had confiscated an unidentified weapon from an address in Cambodia Town. Angus read aloud. "Police were seen removing a large crate from the house, leading to speculation that—that fucking bitch lied!" he screeched. "When was this?"

"Two days ago," Dwight said.

"Why didn't you tell me?"

"I thought you knew."

Angus paused, his face swelling and turning red. *"Call Sidero!"*

The Starks were on Willow, heading into East Long Beach. Hugo drove. He hoped this worked out. If it didn't, Angus might fire the bunch of them and he'd be really fucked. He was otherwise un-employed. The old lady worked at a daycare center. Their unplanned second kid was on the way. They borrowed money from their parents and had seventeen grand in credit card debt. Nobody said The Cause would pay, but it was one more reason to be pissed. Here you were, saving the country from the niggers and the Mexicans and what do you get for your trouble? Bill collectors calling you every five fucking minutes.

Hugo looked at Sidero, one lane over. Something was wrong. He was on the phone, yelling, pounding on the steering wheel, so angry the car was weaving. He rolled down his window and Hugo did the same.

"What's up?" Hugo said. Sidero looked deranged.

He screamed, "We've got to go back!" and he peeled off into a U-turn, bumped over the center divider and hurled his truck into the night.

* * *

Sidero drove, his pulse as high as the RPMs. They wouldn't get the Gatling gun but at least it wasn't his fault. It cracked him up, really, Angus getting fucked over by the asshole he'd hired. Who's the moron now? He couldn't wait to get there. That prick Isaiah. Oh, my God, he would fuck that nigger up. The idea made him punch the accelerator and leave the others behind. He didn't have words for what he'd do to him, he didn't have thoughts. There was only the car's roaring engine, the blood thumping against his temples, and his heart screaming *death to the nigger!*

Ida left to see about Jenn. Grace had chanced it and asked Samantha if she could see the nigger. Every time she said the word it felt terrible, like she'd lost her integrity. She followed Samantha down the basement stairs. It was cool, lit by grim fluorescents, a labyrinth of pipes on the ceiling, everything draped in cobwebs. Grace smelled dust, mold and wet cement. She knew Isaiah would be in bad shape. *Don't freak out. You're happy about this, remember?* They made a turn around the water heater and she nearly retched. He'd been beaten and hog-tied. Lying on his stomach, his hands duct-taped behind him, feet bound, a short rope connecting his wrists to his ankles. He was forced to bend backward, his neck sticking out like a masthead. He was in great pain, his eyes wide with panic, sweat was dripping from every pore. There was a strip of duct tape over his mouth, and he was sucking in long breaths through his nose.

Don't lose it, Grace.

"That must hurt," Samantha said.

Grace made eye contact and forced a smile. "Only what he deserves," she said.

Ida hadn't liked Grace right off. Something about her. She wasn't just folks. She didn't wear any jewelry for one thing, and her nails weren't polished. Ida and the other wives painted theirs every color in the Crayon box and had designs on them, ranging from snowflakes and unicorns to AKs and swastikas. Nobody she knew drove a little car like that or kept it that clean, and the tough talk sounded fake. But there was something else about her—what was it? Ida pursed her lips and nodded. Grace looked like a liberal.

"Hello, Dwight? This is Ida. Do you remember me?"

"Yeah, I remember," Dwight replied impatiently. "Is Isaiah secure?"

"Yeah, he's down in the basement, hog-tied. He's not going anywhere."

"I'm busy, Ida. Why are you calling me?"

"Just a question. How many daughters does Angus have?"

CHAPTER TWENTY-THREE

Us Against Me

Samantha had taken the tape off Isaiah's mouth. She was kneeling and giving him water, most of it dribbling down his chin.

Do it, Grace. Now or never.

Grace came up behind her, put one hand on her neck to hold her down, and with the other she yanked the gun from her back holster.

"Hey!" Samantha said. Grace stepped away and aimed the gun.

"Fuck around and I'll kneecap you," she said.

"I knew it. *I knew it*," Samantha said. "I sensed it right from the start."

"Shut up," Grace said. "Sit down by the wall. Face the other way. Lace your fingers over your head." She'd seen somebody do that in a movie.

"You're fucking up big-time," Samantha said, but she did what she was told. Grace put the gun down and used her pocketknife to cut the rope connecting Isaiah's wrists with his ankles. She took the duct tape off his mouth. He grunted with relief, lay flat and breathed deeply.

"Hold on," Grace said. She started cutting the duct tape around his wrists.

"Stay right there," a hard voice said. Grace turned. It was Ida and Jenn, pointing her assault rifle. "Drop the knife and step away from the gun." Grace obeyed. Samantha got to her feet, picked up her gun. She walked over to Grace and stuck the barrel under her chin. "You're going to die tonight, bitch. And so is the nigger."

The women had gone upstairs. Isaiah pretended he was unconscious. He didn't want to be hog-tied again. He was bruised, in pain and exhausted from the rope and the beating. He could hear the women upstairs, screaming at Grace. There were scuffling feet and chairs knocked over. They were beating her up. He tried every way he knew to loosen the duct tape. Nothing worked. The beating went on. He heard Grace crying out, telling them to stop. Isaiah cursed and thrashed, rolling over and over, but all that did was exhaust him all the more. He sobbed, grime and dirt sticking to his face.

The beating stopped. He wondered what was worse—listening to the beating or wondering what they'd done to her. In addition to all his other fuck-ups, he'd brought Grace into this.

The women dragged Grace into the living room and slammed her into the wall. Ida had a gun pressed to the back of her head. "I say we kill her now," Ida said.

"We should wait for Sidero," Samantha said.

Then Jenn huffed and shook her head. "Why? So he can give us orders for something we can do ourselves?"

"We can bury her near the old septic tank," Ida said. "Nobody ever goes back there." A teenage boy was standing in the doorway. He looked terrified.

"Mom? Are you going to kill her?"

"That's nothing for you to worry about," Ida said. "Go on home, Chip."

"But are you? Are you going to kill her?"

"I said, *go on home!*"

The kid left, and for the second time since Grace had known Isaiah, she knew she was going to die.

*   *   *

Chip didn't go home. He stood outside next to the window, listening to the women argue. Samantha was making excuses for why they should wait for Sidero. To make it official, she said, to make sure there was a consensus and what if Angus had other plans? Ida and Jenn were yelling at her, calling her a coward and a fucking phony.

Chip was more afraid than he'd ever been. Was his mom actually going to take part in double fucking homicide? His *mom?* No, she wouldn't, she's not that crazy—but she sure *sounded* crazy. Go home, Chip, he thought. If you don't know about it, it didn't happen. But he knew that was bullshit. If a tree falls in the forest and nobody hears it, the fucking tree is still dead and if the guy who didn't hear it went looking for it, he'd find it full of termites and lying on the ground.

Chip was sweating even in the cool air, things his mom and dad said to him rushing through his head in a torrent. *There's a kike infestation and people don't know it, Chip. It's a scientific fact that blacks are genetically inferior to whites in every way you can think of. The so-called native Americans have never done anything for this country except kill white settlers. Jews are at the root of the sand nigger problem. No Jews, no problem. We're fighting for survival, Chip. The liberal elite are trying to exterminate the white race. Hell yeah, build a wall and throw out the ones that are already here. Fuck the dreamers. Aren't white people dreamers too? Even if there was a Holocaust, which there wasn't, so what? Hitler did us a favor. The president is speaking in code, Chip. He's on our side. It's dog eat dog, Chip. It's kill or be killed. It's us against them.*

Chip didn't understand why his parents kept believing in things that were obviously wrong. It didn't matter where the information came from, if it didn't line up with what they were already thinking, they ignored it. Chip understood now, that facts didn't matter to people like his mom and dad. Facts were raw clay—adaptable, malleable, useful when you're building a wall between the hateful and the hated. What's that you say? We *hate* minorities? Oh, no, not us! We're just honest, God-fearing Americans trying to rescue our country from the niggers, spics, wetbacks, gooks and faggots. *Didn't you hear what the president said? We're very fine people, Chip.*

Really? Chip thought. Were his folks very fine people? Were Samantha and Jenn and Sidero very fine people? Were the Starks? Was the guy who ran over people in Charlottesville? Was Chip? His mother and her friends were about to murder two people and bury them near the old septic tank. No, he wasn't a very fine person. Not if he went home and didn't hear the tree being blown to shit with an assault rifle. It's not us against them, Chip decided. It's us against me.

Isaiah lay on the cement floor in utter despair. He'd been helpless before but nothing like this. There was always an option, always something to try. But this time there was nothing. They would kill him and Grace too.

He heard a noise and looked up. It was the Junior from Anywhere High. He was scared, his breathing short, sweat making his acne gleam. He had a box cutter in his hand. He hesitated, torn between his loyalties and his conscience. He knelt down and cut Isaiah loose.

"Thank you," Isaiah whispered.

"Here," he said, giving Isaiah a gun. "There's no bullets in it. I don't want my mom to get hurt."

Isaiah nodded. "What's your name?"

"Chip."

"You're going to be all right, Chip. You're going to be fine."

Isaiah stood in the darkness of the hallway, getting his strength back. The women were arguing. Two of them had pistols; the redhead's assault rifle was lying on the table. Grace had the side of her face pressed to the wall. She saw him and narrowed her eyes. A signal. He didn't know what she was going to do but he knew he'd have to move fast. The women grabbed Grace and were moving for the door when suddenly Grace groaned, went limp like she'd fainted and collapsed to the floor.

"Oh, for fuck's sake," one of them said.

Isaiah burst out of the hallway with his arm straight out, his gun aimed at her head. "Don't you fucking bitches move!" he shouted like a crazy nigger who hated white people. "Go for your gun, aight? I *want* you to!"

Grace jumped up and disarmed the women, sticking their handguns into her belt and picking up the assault rifle. They had to get out of here, Isaiah thought. There was no time to tie all three of them up. "Get in the bathroom!" he screamed. "RIGHT FUCKING NOW!" The women paraded into the bathroom with their hands up. "Come out of there and see if I don't blow your muthafuckin' heads off!" He slammed the door behind him and gestured for Grace to give him one of the women's guns. He fired two shots through the door, aiming too high to hit them. *BLAM! BLAM!* "I ain't playin', bitches!" he added.

He and Grace slipped quietly out of the house. When they got outside, they popped the magazines out of the handguns and scattered everything in the bushes. They raced across the road to the sound of roaring engines. Headlights hit them. The Starks were back.

Grace and Isaiah limped into the trees. It was dark and they were hurt and they couldn't move fast. They heard car doors slamming and Sidero shouting and the women yelling and then a wild uproar of voices. Isaiah looked back. *Flashlights.* A bunch of them.

"Spread out!" Sidero commanded. The Starks began moving in a line, orbs of light like cyclops eyes, flashing through the naked trees.

Isaiah and Grace stopped to catch a breath.

"We forgot our phones," she said.

"They're too close," Isaiah said. "Slow them down."

Grace aimed the assault rifle high and pulled the trigger, the rounds cutting a swath through the tree branches. The recoil surprised her and the gun nearly jumped out of her hands. In less than five seconds, she'd emptied the magazine. "That's all?" she said. She dropped the rifle and they continued running. The flashlights were farther back. Isaiah heard the mastiff barking but it wasn't a tracking dog. It would stay with the Starks.

"Give it to 'em!" Sidero bellowed.

The Starks opened up. *BLAM BLAM BLAM BLAM BLAM BLAM!* The rounds shredding bark and snapping off branches, killing squirrels and beheading the stunted pines. Two assault rifles went off but the bursts were brief, like Grace's. Grace and Isaiah ran with their backs directly in line with a tree so they couldn't catch one in the back of the head.

They reached a gulley and ran through it until they reached the parking lot. They were cut off from the street by the chain-link fence and the entrance to the parking lot was too far away. They'd get caught before they got there.

"Isaiah?" Grace said.

He didn't say anything. He was in the zone. He thought about what he'd seen the first time he was here: men in orange hard hats driving forklifts, delivering building supplies to a warehouse through the big roll-up door. The voices were getting louder. The mastiff was barking.

"Stay with me," he said.

They raced across the lot to the warehouse. The door was heavy and sheathed in metal but the lock was an ordinary Schlage.

"What are we doing?" Grace said.

Isaiah stared at the door, gathering his energy. He heard Ari's voice. *Kick through the bag. Like you're trying to kill someone on the other side.* He raised his knee and kicked the strike plate, his leg like a cannon shot. Three kicks and the dead bolt was torn right out of the wooden frame.

He pulled Grace inside and shut the door. He looked around, his gaze stopping on a pile of sixty-pound sacks of cement. He picked up one and set it down next to the door. He and Grace worked together, lifting bags, grunting from the effort, piling up five more on top of the first one. Three hundred and eighty pounds' worth. They carried three more bags across the warehouse to the fire door and set them down in the same way. They were exhausted, in pain, bent over, hands on their knees, sucking in air.

"I can't...I can't do this anymore," she said, and Isaiah knew he couldn't either.

"Quick," he said. He grabbed a length of rebar and braced it against the door, the other end buttressed against a stack of cinder blocks. They got three more in place before the Starks arrived. They kicked and pounded on both doors but they held.

"You're in for it now, motherfucker!" Sidero shouted. "All you did was trap yourself."

Grace was realizing too. Isaiah grabbed her hand and pulled her behind a forklift just as the Starks started shooting through the door. It was a tremendous, deafening barrage, a mob of racists unleashing their unfulfilled lives and splintered dreams in sound and fury. It was as if the Confederacy had awakened and an army of zombie rednecks had risen from battlefields to take their revenge and release their long-held inexplicable fury against the blameless. They concentrated on the front door. Dozens of shots were fired into it, the metal sheathing holding the wooden core together. The salvo was surprisingly brief, dwindling to a few scattered shots and then stopping.

"Cease fire," Sidero said unnecessarily.

Isaiah had counted on this. The Starks had given chase quickly and fired off a lot of rounds. They had few, if any, spare clips.

"Johnny, Lowell," Sidero said, "go back to the house and get more ammo. Everything we've got." Sidero pounded on the door, exuberant. "You and that bitch are fucked! We'll run a train on her and then we'll lynch you, motherfucker. We'll string you up by your goddamn neck just like the old days!" The mob laughed and hooted and banged on the walls. Isaiah calculated it would take Lowell and Johnny about fifteen minutes to get to the Den and back. Fifteen minutes before the door was demolished by gunfire and barbarians breached the gap. Isaiah stood there, staring at nothing. He knew what he was going to do. He had visualized the steps. He wondered if it was possible.

Grace couldn't hide her fear. She imagined Lowell and Johnny, skipping and laughing through the trees with their arms full of ammo.

Isaiah came out of his reverie. "Give me one of your shoes."

She knew questioning him would waste time so she handed him

her shoe and didn't say a word. He stuck it into the back of his pants and climbed into the forklift's cab. The engine sputtered to life, chains rattling, spewing black exhaust.

"Hey, what're you doing in there, Sambo?" Sidero shouted. "Digging a tunnel?"

TK had a forklift at the wrecking yard and Isaiah had driven it a hundred times. He deftly picked up a stack of wooden pallets and placed them directly beneath the transoms. He estimated they were twenty-five feet off the floor.

The max height of the forklift was eight feet. The stack of pallets was six feet and that left an eleven-foot gap between the top of the stack and the transoms. Isaiah maneuvered the forklift, picked up a second stack of pallets and placed them on top of the first. Then he carefully picked up the whole arrangement and raised it as far as it would go. The top of the stack was five feet from the transoms.

Isaiah got out of the cab and clambered onto the roof of the forklift and then up the mast to the elevated forks. That was easy, but now he had to ascend a twelve-foot tower of wooden pallets and hope they wouldn't topple over and send him headfirst into the cement floor. He used his fingertips and the toes of his shoes, inserting them into the sides of the pallets, going slowly and methodically like a sloth or a rock climber. He could hear the Starks cheering. The ammo must have arrived. Shit, that was fast. There were laughs and whoops as the Starks loaded fresh clips into their Glocks, Sig Sauers, Berettas, S&Ws, Tech tens and AKs.

Sidero shouted, "Let 'em fucking have it!"

The mob let loose another tremendous salvo. Isaiah tried to stay calm. Sweat was running into his eyes and the barrage was unrelenting. It was like walking a tightrope with a klaxon blasting in your ears and sharks circling beneath you. *Keep going, Isaiah. Focus.*

Grace watched him, wondering what the hell he was doing. Didn't he know the same long drop was on the other side of the transom? He was climbing the second stack of pallets when his foot slipped. "Oh, no!" She hurried closer to catch him. He held on. The tower had moved slightly; it was out of balance. Isaiah climbed more cautiously but that slowed him down.

The Starks had blasted a hole in the door big enough for Jack Nicholson to stick his head through. Sidero looked in but didn't have the angle to see them. He stuck his gun through, curved his wrist around and emptied a clip.

"Here we come, motherfucker!" he roared.

Ida screamed, "You're dead, bitch!"

The shooting commenced again. Soon the door would be one big hole and that would be the end. The women would be turned loose on Grace. They would beat her, torture her and kill her while the men did the same to Isaiah.

Isaiah was still climbing. She watched him, her hands clenched together, her breathing fast and shallow. "Come on, Isaiah," she whispered. "Come on!" When he reached the top, Grace had a moment's relief. She expected him to pull off some genius move she never expected, something right in front of her that she hadn't seen because she wasn't Isaiah. But all he did was break the transom with her shoe.

Two minutes later, most of the door was gone. The Starks bulled through the bags of cement and stampeded into the warehouse. They saw the forklift and the pallets and the broken transom.

"Shit!" Sidero shouted.

The whole group ran out and around to the side of the building. They found a girl's shoe and some broken glass. Sidero looked up at the transoms. "That's a long drop. She must have busted her ankle."

"He'd have to carry her," Hugo said. "They couldn't have gone far."

"Split up!"

A few minutes later, Grace crawled out of the cement mixer and Isaiah slithered from beneath rolls of chicken wire. They looked outside. The Starks were gone. Sirens approached. She took his hand and they ran off.

* * *

Dodson finished up for the night. He dumped the mop water at the curb, wrung out the mop, put everything away and locked up the truck. When he got into his car he saw a lunch bag on the seat that wasn't there before. At first, he was pissed. A prank, he thought. The bag was full of peanut shells or dog shit. But that made no sense. Somebody took the trouble to break into his car, left a bag and didn't bother to rip out the stereo or rifle through the glove box?

Dodson got in the car. Warily, he gently squeezed the bag. He knew instantly what it was. A stack of bills bound in a rubber band. It was the money Ponlok had given Isaiah as a gratuity. "That's my boy," Dodson said, with an affectionate shake of his head. He wondered at the time why Isaiah accepted it. For him, it was blood money. Dodson, however, had no such scruples, and his eagerness to restore the partnership was a tip-off he was broke. Isaiah took the money because he knew he would give it to Dodson.

Dodson would quit his job tonight. A relief but it was only temporary. Cherise would insist the lion's share of the money go to Micah's college fund. Whatever was left wouldn't last long. Gloria would call it welfare and another kind of food stamps and she wouldn't be wrong. He had to make Cherise proud of him. He had to make Micah proud of his father. He sighed. He was right back where he started. Adrift.

He started the engine and sat there a moment, listening to it idle. He stared through the windshield at the food trucks, a herd of shiny moneymakers lined up getting their rest, another long week ahead. That pang went through him again but he stifled it. And then he went still, brow bunched up, a realization sweeping over him. He'd stopped believing in himself. He'd stopped believing that the world didn't happen to him, he happened to the world. Would he fail again, quit trying and go back to the streets like every other punk-ass loser in the hood? End up visiting Micah on Sundays, buying him birthday presents with drug money and beating himself up for losing his family for the rest of his life? Fuck no. He was Juanell Dodson. *The* Juanell Dodson. The quickest, most streetwise, fearless ex-hustler this side of the Long Beach

Freeway. He'd forgotten, that was all. He nodded, resolute. "Do your thing, son," he said to himself, "and y'all gonna be all right." He called Cherise and told her he had a surprise for her. He took off the do-rag and tossed it out of the window. Then he put on some Tupac and drove out of the lot, bobbing his head to the beat.

Deronda had left Dodson to his cleaning duties. She was starting to feel bad about giving him such a hard time, not that he didn't deserve it. Maybe she should let up on him, give him a raise or something. She and Cherise were friends after all. She could afford to be generous. She was where she always thought she should be. At the top. With money. Money made you invincible. If you wanted something, you bought it. If there was a problem, you could pay somebody else to solve it for you. Her son, Janeel, was in private school. She had a new car. She was looking to buy a house. She had a boyfriend, Robert, who was beautiful and had an uptown job.

The *LA Times Magazine* had done a feature on her and the business. Color pictures of the trucks, the long lines of customers and a few of her. In one, she was standing next to a truck, beaming. In another, she and Janeel were mugging for the camera. The caption: *Deronda's son, Janeel. "I do it all for him."* She must have said "That's you and me, baby. Don't we look good?" to Janeel five hundred times. Business had gone up twelve percent since the article came out. She had plans to expand the business. More trucks in Riverside and Orange County. Maybe sell franchises. Put Popeye's out of business. She smiled and patted her hair. There was no other way to bake that cake. Her life was lit up.

A phone call, private number. Everybody had a private number so she answered it.

"Deronda? This is Bobby James."

"Bobby who?" she said.

"You don't remember me? You should."

"Oh yeah?" she said with a huff. "And why is that?"

"As of now, I'm the most important man in your life." He sounded cocky and sure of himself, like he had selfies of you bent over and smiling between your legs. She'd never heard of him. He was probably selling something.

"I don't know who you are," she said, "but you're not the most important anything in my life. I got dead plants that are more important than you. I got toenail clippings that are more important than you. I don't have a dog but even if I did, the hair on his ass would be more important than you. Now was there anything else you wanted to say before I hang the fuck up?"

He snorted. "No, bitch, you don't want to do that," he said. "You really don't."

"Oh, I'm a bitch now?" she said.

"You're *my* bitch now," he said. Deronda shook her head with wonder. Where did these motherfuckers come from? Did somebody have a 3-D printer and a template for a deluded fool? "Goodbye, you poor, sad-ass loser," she said. Her finger was a millimeter from the *end call* button but stopped when he said, "I'm Janeel's father."

Deronda stopped breathing. Was that his name? Bobby James? The guy she'd had sex with in the bathroom at an underground club in Compton back when she was Captain of the All-American Ho Team?

"Nice try," she said. "I know who the father is and he sho' the fuck ain't you."

"Oh, it's me, all right," Bobby said. "You don't remember? It was at that no-name club over on Rosecrans, right near the freeway, was downstairs somewhere, like a basement. I bought you your favorite drink, seven and sevens—remember the bathroom? It was painted orange, the sinks didn't work and there was water on the floor. We hit it in the third stall from the left." He laughed. "*Doggie style.* You were wearing a pink miniskirt, high heels and no panties. You said if I quit before you got yours, you'd turn around and twist my dick off. You don't remember that?"

She didn't remember all of it but it sounded right. The dress, the bathroom painted orange, the water on the floor and especially the thing about twisting his dick off. She'd said that on more than a few occasions.

"Man," he said. "I saw that picture of Janeel in the paper and I couldn't believe it. We look almost exactly alike. I said to myself, damn, brother, that's your son."

For the second or third time in her life, Deronda had nothing to say. Bobby laughed again, but it wasn't a ha-ha kind of laugh. It was more like a your-shit-is-over kind of laugh.

"And you know what else?" Bobby James said. "I want custody."

CHAPTER TWENTY-FOUR
Evil Nymph

Grace went to Cherokee's. Isaiah was beat up, bedraggled and as tired as he'd ever been. He was afraid of going home so he went to the wrecking yard. TK took one look at him and said, "At it again, huh?" During the Walczak case, Isaiah had cleared a space in the loft for Grace. She needed a place to hide. He trudged up the steps, took off his shoes and fell on the futon.

His nerves were sizzling at the ends. *Sleep. Your problems will still be there when you wake up.* He closed his eyes. One minute later, he opened them and sat up. Something was bothering him. Something *always* bothered him when he finished a case, successfully or not. Obsessively, he always went over the events again no matter how sure he was of the resolution. He didn't like missing puzzle pieces. Ridiculous, really. Even if Florida and Ohio were missing from the map you still knew it was the United States. *Okay, Isaiah. What is it? What is it this time?*

It was the infamous sticking point. That moment in the case where a single revelation could turn everything around and predictably, it was an inch from his face, too close to focus on. And then, as frequently happened, another lens brought clarity. Many murders had their origins in the past. Isaiah remembered his conversation with Gia. She told him Angus had married a Filipino woman named Virginia. They were in love and happy but she died in childbirth. Isaiah wondered what had happened to the baby. Gia said it went to the grandmother—but forever? The grandmother would have been elderly already. At some point, the child would have gone back to its father. Back to Angus. That child would be grown up by now. Isaiah didn't know the statistics but in his experience, the number one reason for murdering somebody was revenge. That uncontrollable rage that comes with suffering a loss so great, it was unbearable. Loss of your spouse, a family member, a fortune, a career. Loss of dignity and self-worth.

Angus had tortured Christiana. Wouldn't he also torture the child who killed his beloved Virginia merely by entering the world? And when the child grew up, wouldn't he hate his father? And what better way to take their revenge than to kill the man their father needed and admired? Angus would be cruel and merciless to that child. He'd treat them like scum, like garbage, like shit. He'd treat that child the way he treated Sidero. Sidero's last name was Bernal. A Filipino name. Virginia's last name, and a reminder every time Sidero made his signature that he'd killed his own mother. Gia said Angus had taken a long time to name his son; to find the Latin word for "evil nymph."

How would Sidero pull it off? Isaiah thought. Call the killers himself? Probably not. Too easily traced. If he was smart he'd have let his girlfriend do it. From the looks she gave him at the gun range she hated Angus too. She'd say she was Angus's daughter so if he found out, it wouldn't come back on her or Sidero. A realization smacked him upside the head. "Shit!" he said. Sidero's truck was at the gun range. It had new tires and the backseat was full of clothes still on their hangers, a juicer, DVDs in a box, fishing poles, a laundry basket full of shoes, a space heater and a bunch of other things. Stuff you'd take *when you're leaving town.*

Sidero had almost made a clean getaway but forgot the TV. It was his, he'd bought it before Jenn had moved in. It cost him almost a thousand bucks. He was trying to take it off the wall bracket but Jenn was distracting him. She was fucking pissed, pacing around, crying, taking deep breaths through her nose, her fists balled up.

"You motherfucker!" she screamed. "You mother*fucker!*"

"You said that already," Sidero replied. She'd been yelling and foaming at the mouth ever since he walked in the door. Before he came back for the TV, he'd sent her a text. *I'm leaving you you fucking bitch. Have a nice life and go fuck yourself.* He wished he hadn't done that. It sent her from crazy to fucking insane. Oh my fucking God, he couldn't wait to get out of there.

She came close so she could yell in his ear, "Everything I've done for you! Everything I've fucking done for you!"

"Like what?" Sidero said. "Could you stand back a ways? I'm trying to do this." He was going to take the wall bracket too, but changed his mind. He had to get away from her before he grabbed her assault rifle off the coffee table and shot her.

"All this time I stuck with you!" she screamed. "You fucking wimp! You coward! Who stuck up for you, Sid? Who? *Me*, you bastard! It sure the fuck wasn't you!" Sidero got the TV off the bracket. He held it in front of him and turned for the door. Jenn stood in his way.

"Move, Jenn," he said. She was grinning now. It was a really fucked-up grin. Like a nigger hanging from a tree. "Remember the night at Rafters?" she said. "Remember? Did I say anything? Huh? Did I say anything, you fucking faggot?"

"*Move*, Jenn."

"I'm telling everybody!" she shouted. "Everybody! *I'm telling your dad!*"

He shoved her with the TV. She fell back and toppled over the coffee table, everything crashing to the floor. She was stunned, sitting there in a mess of beer cans, cigarette butts, loose ammo, tabloids and dirty paper plates. Her gun had a moldering slice of pizza on it.

"I told you to move, didn't I?" he shouted. He started for the door again but she crawled over and grabbed him around the knees.

"Don't leave me, Sid!" she sobbed. "I won't let you! You can't leave me!" She was pitiful. He'd never seen her like this. Hair all fucked up, makeup and snot all over her face. She was disgusting. He tried to walk out of her grasp but she held on. "No, no, no, Sid!" she cried. "Please, *pleease* don't go!" He liked it, her begging. "Let go, Jenn," he said. "It's fucking over!" She held on tighter. "Goddammit, Jenn, get off me!" he shouted. He twisted away from her and dropped the TV. "Fuck!" he barked. The screen was cracked. "Goddamn you, Jenn! Goddamn your fucking ass!" She was on her feet now, zombie-walking toward him, muttering *please please please*. Furious and half-pleading, he yelled, "Stay the fuck away from me!"

"Please, Sid," she sobbed. She tried to put her arms around him and he punched her in the face, hard. He could feel her cheekbone break. She fell into the mess again. He pushed open the screen door and charged out. He heard her scream, a wordless howl, so sharp and ugly he put his hands over his ears. He walked quickly toward his truck parked in the driveway. Neighbors had come out to watch. "What the fuck are you looking at?" he yelled at them. He heard the screen slam open behind him. "Leave me alone, Jenn!" he said.

"You're not leaving me," she said. He caught a glimpse of her as he got in the truck, bloody, limp and reeling, aiming the assault rifle from the hip. She screamed, "YOU'RE NOT FUCKING LEAVING ME!" He saw the barrel flash, a round jolted him, and then another. Surprisingly, he felt no pain, only a loosening, a letting go, and then his vision was blurry and there was no sound and he was falling and falling and then there was nothing.

Isaiah stood beside the Kia, openmouthed and staring. The neighbors were screaming and hurrying back inside. The redhead had dropped the gun. She stood there in utter shock, knees unsteady, the look on her face exactly like Clarence Novelle's. For a moment, it was remarkably quiet, remarkably still, nothing moving except the blue smoke drifting over Sidero's body like a ghost.

Isaiah returned to the car and sat there a moment. There was something ineffably sad about Sidero even when he was alive. He longed for the love of his father who was only capable of hate and greed. Sidero wouldn't accept it. He'd fought for that love, hated that love and was humiliated by that love his entire life. One of the hardest things anyone can do is to accept the fact that no matter how much you love your mother and father and no matter how hard you try, they will never love you back. Sidero didn't want to escape and he didn't want to be his own man. He would have stayed in his chains forever but Angus set him free.

Angus didn't know what to do without Weiner. Those two bitches would scream for death if they hurt that dog. Their suffering would be creative and would involve every orifice. It occurred to him that the dog was the only thing in the world that loved him and the only thing in the world that allowed him to love it back.

The attorney called. Christiana's bail had been revoked. She got into a fight and resisted arrest. *It was Angie,* Angus thought. "The judge ordered a psych exam," the attorney went on, "and I'm afraid she could be held until her trial. The date hasn't been set."

Angus hung up. He couldn't breathe and had to sit down. Isaiah called.

"Sidero hired the killers," Isaiah said. "And you know why."

"Where is he?" Angus said.

"He's dead. His girlfriend shot him."

Angus was dumbfounded. He said, "Sidero is dead?"

"Yes, he is," Isaiah said.

Angus dropped the phone. He'd been tough on the boy. He hated him, in fact, but he might have lightened up some. He'd promised Virginia he'd take care of the little shit. He did the best he could with the best he had in him, which wasn't much. His girlfriend shot him; it wasn't Angus's fault.

He was suddenly nauseous. He staggered into his private bathroom and threw up in the sink. He glanced at the mirror and was horrified. He looked a thousand years old. Oddly, his ugliness was less pronounced, everything washed out like a portrait in watercolors. He held on to the sink with both hands and opened his mouth so wide he could see his palate, his molars, his tonsils, so wide he thought his jaw would break. He tried to scream but nothing came out. He thought he might kill himself but decided it was too easy. He had to stay alive so God could punish him.

* * *

Dwight was in the hallway. He'd listened to Angus talk to Isaiah on the phone. When the call ended, he found the old man in the study, flopped down in one of his fancy chairs. His head was back, his arms dangling, unblinking eyes staring at the ceiling. He didn't look dead, he looked slaughtered. Dwight put his hands on the armrests and leaned in, their faces as close as they'd been at the gun range.

"You got everything you deserved, Angus," Dwight said. "Everything except a bullet in the head." Angus's eyes were blank and unfocused. "Now you've got nothing," Dwight went on. "No son, no daughter, no Tyler. Only me. Only stupid, useless, fucked-up me." Dwight stood back, smiled and inhaled a triumphant breath. "Actually, that's not true. Wanna hear something funny? I kept the money from the last six sales, and the cash you had in the safe is mine too. I've known the combination for years. Didn't know that, did you? And by the way? Your jewelry and watches are in my safety-deposit box." Dwight looked off. "There was something else too, what was it?" He snapped his fingers. "Oh I remember! The guns we stored in the warehouse? I sold them. The fucking Russians are loading them into their trucks right about now." Dwight stretched and yawned. "I'm going on a trip, Angus. The Bahamas or Costa Rica, someplace like that. Maybe I'll move there, who knows?" Dwight grinned. "I'll send you a fucking fruit basket, asshole." He left the room and walked down the hall, tossing the keys to the Maybach up and catching them again.

CHAPTER TWENTY-FIVE

Have You Ever Seen
an Elephant Dance?

He was in his room playing *Call of Duty* when Hugo burst in, grabbed him by the neck and threw him into the wall. "My son's a nigger lover?" he screamed. "My son's a fucking traitor?" He came in swinging, but Chip held his ground even as the blows fell and his vision turned to stars and the pain was a sledgehammer pounding him into the floor. He looked straight at the stupid cocksucker and smiled through his bloody teeth.

In the days following the warehouse disaster, Chip was bombarded with threatening emails, voice mails and texts. The Starks and their families hated him and he hated them back. They posted a bunch of shit on his Facebook page until he took it down. He didn't care. You could spend half your life posting idiotic selfies and pictures of the chili cheese fries at Fatburger.

He came home from school and noticed an envelope on the floor. Somebody had slipped it under the window. He imagined all the fucked-up things the message would say and he wondered if there was anthrax on the paper. But there was only a car key tied to a piece of red ribbon. He looked at it, and then he went outside.

A car was parked across the street, a red ribbon tied around the door handle. It was a Kia sedan, red, five, maybe six years old but in really good shape and detailed too. The chrome shined and the interior smelled like pine trees. Chip put the key in the ignition and the engine vroomed to life. It sounded good. From Isaiah, he thought. He nodded to himself. He'd done the right thing and that felt good. Maybe they'd meet somewhere down the road.

Chip lowered the window and drove around the neighborhood. The car ran perfectly. The stereo was new. He came to a traffic light and stopped. He smiled big and patted the dashboard like it was a puppy. The light turned green and he drove off again. This is great, he thought. When he ran away from home, he wouldn't have to take the bus.

Sal and Annie were home now and amazingly, things were better. Annie was still doing her Martha Stewart thing but the nagging had all but disappeared. They had sex and Annie squealed and thrashed and grabbed Sal's hair just like the old days. It was worth giving up Angus's payoff. Sal smelled dinner and it wasn't meat loaf.

Annie came in. "Oh, my sweet baby," she cooed. "You're so beautiful, aren't you? Yes, you are! Yes, you are!" Sal didn't like it. It was unsanitary but Annie held the dog up and kissed it on the lips. Sal thought, this is our life.

This is our fucking life.

After the craziness at the warehouse, Grace went back to Cherokee's apartment to get rid of the shakes, dig that bottle of Grey Goose out of the freezer and get away from Isaiah. They'd seen a little too much of each other in the last forty-eight hours. She'd gone through harrowing times with him but this felt different. This time she was with the man she loved, the man she wanted to be with forever.

It struck her again that what they'd gone through wasn't an anomaly. This was Isaiah's life and she would be part of it. Part of the danger and terror and life-threatening situations. True, she didn't have to participate in his cases but what if things like this came up again—and they *would* come up again—what would she do? Turn him down when he said he needed help? Do nothing if she saw him get kidnapped? What would she do if Isaiah came home and told her there were another three dead and many wounded? How could her artist's life compete with all of that?

She thought about the good things. He was, after all, Isaiah. A man among assholes. The sweetest, smartest, truest person she'd ever met. If she left him, she'd deprive herself of a love that would never, ever happen again. She was certain of that. She wished she was with Ruffin or TK, the only two males she knew who wouldn't upset her. She would talk things over with Cherokee when she got home, or maybe become a lesbian like her and abandon men altogether. It didn't seem like a bad idea. But she loved Isaiah, and it felt good. It felt right. "What are you going to do, Grace?" she said aloud, and she replied, "I don't know, Grace. I really don't."

Isaiah was glad to be alone. Every minute Grace spent with him was like punishing her for being his girlfriend, and the more intimate they became, the more his faults were revealed and the worse he felt about himself. He was stupidly obsessive. Anytime anything triggered his curiosity, he was off and running. He *had* to find out what was really going on, even if arriving at the answer was costly and unnecessary. This flaw in his personality had never been so obvious before. You never know what you're really like until someone is watching you. Sizing you up. Loving you. Grace reflected his weaknesses and that was the scariest part. Seeing who you really were.

Maybe the invitation to live with him had been premature. Maybe he should step back, get some perspective, be the adult in the room. That thought lasted all of three seconds. He didn't want to step back, he didn't want perspective, and the whole adult thing was up in the air. What he wanted was Grace. People said you don't choose who you love. Bullshit. You *do* choose, but you have to fix the problems you cause and understand yourself better so you don't create them in the first place. Sadly, the caveat was that you had to know how. He wished he had a dog. Not Ruffin necessarily. A dog who liked him would be enough.

His joints ached and his bruises hurt. He took a handful of Tylenol but didn't get in bed because he didn't want to look at Grace's painting.

Even in the dark he could see it. He couldn't sit on the back stoop and drink a beer either. It felt wrong without her there. He had his beer lying back in the easy chair. He put on some Thelonious Monk and tried to relax.

But he didn't. Instead, he thought about the alters locked up in a cell, dumbfounded as they appeared, vanished and reappeared, their collective lives an endless retribution for being abused. Monk's number ended and in those seconds before the next song began, he felt it again. *No, not now. Please, Isaiah. Didn't we just talk about this?*

He'd missed something.

"Who cares?" he shouted at the ceiling. Whatever he'd overlooked wouldn't affect anything now. Any more effort was pathetic and futile. Was he really a slave to his obsession? *Take control. How weak are you?* He breathed deeply, felt calmer and more sure of himself. That moment lasted seven seconds. A new record. He sat up. *What is it now, Isaiah?* Frames again. Fast. No spaces in between.

Gia talking to him about her marriage. The faint scar on Angus's head. Jasper reacting vehemently to the azalea bushes. Bertrand agitated about the song "Maybellene." Angie sending Grace away at the Palladium. The alters, trashing the condo. Angus screaming, "I didn't do anything!"

Angus's white scar was on his right temple, close to his eye, the same place Gia said she was hit with an ashtray on Christmas day. Angus didn't throw it, she did. Gia's favorite color was lavender, the color she dressed little Christiana in. The same color as the azaleas that repulsed Jasper. Angie rebuffed Grace because she didn't like women. Women like her mother. In one of Christiana's photos, a framed poster of Chuck Berry was in the background. One of his hits was "Maybellene." The alters weren't just messy, they deliberately destroyed the condo to punish Gia and keep her running ragged. When she told Isaiah about their marriage, she tried to make herself the victim and Angus the guilty one. When Angus screamed he didn't do anything, he wasn't proclaiming innocence. He meant he'd stood by. He'd known but did nothing. Gia committed the horrors. Gia was the torturer.

Isaiah put a narrative together. It was always a precarious thing to do but he had confidence in himself. He'd been doing it a long time. Gia knew about the elopement. How could she not? She hovered over Christiana's every move. She was terrified Tyler was taking her daughter away and she'd have no way to assuage her guilt. No salve, no relief, no redemption, in hell until the day she went to hell. She hired the killers. She was Angus's bookkeeper and had access to his files, phone calls and contacts. She knew his secret codes. When she talked to the killers she said she was Angus's daughter. Maybe she saw an email or overheard a conversation but she knew the elopement would happen soon. She told the killers it was urgent but Tyler was an ex-marine, armed and wary. Getting him alone and vulnerable was tough. Gia was afraid the elopement could happen at any time and grew desperate. She knew about the appointment with Tyler after hours. She told the killers to do it there. Tyler would be relaxed and it's hard to try on a suit when you're wearing a gun. If Christiana was a witness all the better. She'd see for herself that Tyler was gone and the shock would make her more dependent on her mother. Gia left the logistics to the killers. They were professionals, the details were in their hands. She had no way of knowing Christiana would become a suspect. It must have been horrifying, her plan backfiring, causing the opposite of what she wanted. She appeared helpless because she was helpless. She didn't know what to do. She could give up the killers but even if they could be found, they would turn on her and she'd go to prison, locked away from Christiana for the rest of her life, as distant as if Christiana had eloped to Fiji. Isaiah was making a lot of conjecturing, but if he was off, it wasn't by much. He was IQ and of that, he was proud.

Gia didn't answer her phone. Isaiah found her in the shop, tidying things up as if tomorrow would be just another day.

"I've been waiting for you," she said.

"What are you going to do?" he asked.

She seemed to lose awareness of him. She put away a roll of fabric, turned off the sewing machine, inspected an unfinished sport coat and laid it carefully on the cutting table. Then she turned and walked away.

* * *

It was dusk at the LA Zoo. The parking lot was nearly empty, car doors were closing, people walking slowly out of the entrance, lines of children waiting to board their school buses. Gloria hadn't been here for a long time, and other than the smell of alfalfa and manure she had no memories of her previous experience. She and TK hadn't talked on the drive over. He'd been quiet and remote. She'd wanted to say something but felt so terrible she didn't dare. Thomas had been right about Josiah. Her ex was a bum and a liar and a number of other things as well. But when he'd left her for that barmaid, he'd taken more than their marriage. He'd taken a life lived. He'd taken every loving moment and declared it a lie.

Gloria and TK moved toward the entrance and went through the turnstile. TK had some sort of membership and they didn't have to pay. He was carrying a small suitcase, nearly square, something that might hold an old-fashioned typewriter. He didn't say what was in it and she didn't ask. They took a tram up the wide cement road, not much to see, the animal enclosures behind the shrubbery. They got off and walked a short distance to the aviary, circus tents of netting, tall and wide enough for a bird in flight to feel a few seconds of freedom.

"There's somebody here I have to see," he said. A path led through a manicured rain forest and the damp smell of earth and moss and climbing vines, a stream meandering alongside. Birds with riotous colors and unusual profiles flew and glided and stalked in long steps through the foliage.

"Here," TK said.

They sat on a bench. The path had ascended and they could see over an expanse of forest. They heard cheeps, clicks, chitters and calls, an incantation, mystical and rhythmic, a dozen alien languages spoken at once.

"We have to wait till he recognizes me," TK said.

She wondered who he was talking about. Did he know the ornithologist? Why did he have to be recognized? Was someone watching them?

She looked at him and thought she'd never seen a man so content and peaceful as TK sitting there basking in the greening light. She saw something else too. Relief. His eyes, tired of straight lines and right angles, resting now on the curves and patterns of God's fertile earth.

The little red bird appeared so suddenly, it surprised her. "Oh!" she said. It perched on the railing that followed the path.

"Hello, Red," TK said. "It's been a while." He found some birdseed in his pocket and held it out in a cupped palm. She was sure it was against the rules. The vice principal in her almost spoke but didn't.

The bird tipped its head back and forth, its shiny black eyes wary and curious. TK's calloused hand was as steady as the railing. Red flitted over and rested on TK's thumb. The tiny thing was breathtaking. The color was glorious, the feathers so well fitted they formed one sleek surface. The beak was yellow and perfect, the bird's movements so precise they could have been digitized. When Red flew away, it felt like a friend had left on a long trip.

Gloria and TK left the aviary and went into an enclosure area. TK walked fast, taking none of the side paths to the animals. They heard a lion roar, magnificent and plaintive. They arrived at the elephant compound. It was surprisingly large, several acres at least. An elephant was standing under a tumbling waterfall, showering before supper.

"That's Billy," TK said. "Been here for twenty-five, thirty years. Stood around in a dirt corral until they built this place. A damn shame is what it was."

They walked around the perimeter of the compound. There were trails and pools and rock formations, shady places under big trees. "In the wild, an elephant stays where the food is," TK said, "so the zoo people got smart. They put the food everywhere; they even hide some of it. If the elephants want to eat, they gotta go find it, move around, get some exercise."

They stopped at a viewing section. A wooden rail held back the onlookers. A few feet farther on was a fence made of thick strands of wire, set apart so the view was nearly unobstructed. Two elephants were lounging in a pool some distance away.

"Tina and Jewel," TK said. "They've lived together for over thirty years."

They were magnificent, ancient and wise and stoic. They should be wandering the veld, Gloria thought, but now they're here so people can see them before they vanish from the world forever.

She hadn't noticed TK opening the little suitcase. It held a concertina, a Cajun accordion. "TK?" she said.

He didn't answer and slipped the straps over his shoulders. It was a complicated thing made of varnished wood. There was a tiny keyboard and dozens of other knobs and buttons, their functions unfathomable. TK squeezed and separated the bellows, playing a few random chords. There was nothing like the sound of an accordion. Multiple chords at multiple registers, whining and groaning, an infant church organ. TK began to play a zydeco song, one of those meo mio irresistible toe-tappers that made you want to go dancing in the Big Easy and eat a crawfish pie. People turned to watch and listen and smile. It was wonderful, this unabashedly joyful music in such an unexpected place.

Gloria glanced at Tina and Jewel. They were lumbering straight toward them. "Goodness," she said.

The elephants were unmistakably drawn by the music. There was an urgency about them, like they were late for the concert. They arrived at the wire fence and stood shoulder-to-shoulder. And then, miraculously, *they danced*. There was nothing else to call it. Swaying back and forth and back and forth, their trunks swinging and reaching and weaving in the air, the crowd was as delighted as it was mesmerized.

TK was playing with a grin as wide as the sky, and Gloria realized he had introduced himself. His gentleness, his peace, his enjoyment of life. No, she'd never ever seen an elephant dance, and she'd never met a man like Thomas Marion Kahill.

The waiter didn't bother bringing Angus a menu. He hadn't ordered anything but a Reuben sandwich in fifteen years. He'd read the article in the *Telegram*. Lately, he'd been taking more interest in the news. All charges against Christiana Byrne for the murder of Tyler Barnes had been dropped. Gia had turned herself in. He should have been locked up with her, in adjacent cells where they could look at each other and wonder how they could have ever been so evil.

Christiana had been released. She was probably holed up at the condo. He'd called her twenty times but she didn't pick up. He fretted, worried. She was probably zonked out on meds. Yes, she was out of jail, but in truth, she would never be free and neither would he. The little girl in the lavender dress hanging from a closet bar would always be there, staring at him through strands of filthy hair, hating him and haunting them both forever.

After the fiasco at the warehouse, the area was flooded by cops. A few of the extra stupid morons had decided to get drunk and hang out at the Den until they were arrested. Angus had dutifully bailed them out as part of their pact. He got them decent lawyers and promised to give them a big bonus if they kept their mouths shut. They wouldn't, of course. They would find the DA on vacation in the Bahamas to give up their boss. Angus's lawyers told him in that noncommittal, boiler-plate way they have that there was reason to be cautiously optimistic. There were no incriminating documents, bank records, tapes or photos. Angus had used a burner to make his criminal phone calls. He had no bankruptcies, lawsuits or indictments. He'd never been arrested and for all intents and purposes was a legitimate businessman. Bottom line, the lawyers said, it would be his word against a bunch of ex-convict skinhead assholes. Angus liked his odds.

The Reuben arrived and he took his first humongous bite. He moaned. Fuck, it was good. Just the right combination of carbohydrates and grease with that perfect zing of sauerkraut. It was his only pleasure now, the only thing that kept his mind off his guilt and the blazing need for revenge. That son of a bitch Isaiah had not only double-crossed him, but that devious bitch of his had spun him like a top. Angus had plans for them. He'd been hateful before but now that's all there was; all that was keeping him alive. Isaiah and his girl would never be safe. Never. And neither would the violin player. After he was through with her she wouldn't be able to whistle. Last night, he'd dreamed of Isaiah, sprawled on the sidewalk, a pool of red expanding around him as if the sky had rained blood. That day would come. The two fucking killers had never returned with Weiner and never got their payoff. Angus wished they had, he'd have paid them gladly. He missed Weiner desperately. He ached for his little pal. Getting another dog seemed wrong. Sacrilege.

The front door of the restaurant opened and two guys came in. Angus glanced at them and went back to his food. He was chewing another mouthful of corned beef when he realized the men were dark-skinned Asians with flat noses. One of them was Ponlok.

"Hello, Angus," Lok said.

Angus set the sandwich down and wiped his mouth with a napkin. "Look, this war has gone on long enough," he said. "There's enough business for the both of us. Sit down and have something to eat. The Reuben is great."

"You sent Isaiah to steal the Gatling gun," Lok said.

"No, I didn't," Angus scoffed. "I would have if I could, but how would I know where you were keeping it?"

"That's why you sent Isaiah. That motherfucker can find anything."

"I didn't send him," Angus said adamantly. "I wanted to kill him. He brought you guys in to steal the goddamn gun from me."

Lok sat down across from Angus and set his pistol next to the jar of hot mustard. "Then tell me something," Lok said. "Why did Isaiah risk his life and bring the cops down on my mother's house if you didn't send him?"

"Because he thinks he's a hero, that's why," Angus replied. "He didn't want Sinaloa to have the gun and I don't know why you're complaining in the first place. You got my million dollars, didn't you? Are you gonna give it back?"

Lok considered that a moment and nodded. "Yeah, I can see Isaiah doing that. I'll spend your money wisely, Angus. You take care." Lok and his friend left.

Angus wasn't hungry anymore and pushed his plate away. He was in a rental car backing out of the parking space when a car pulled up next to him. Lok was in the passenger seat aiming a gun.

"What the hell is this?" Angus said.

"The end, motherfucker."

Angus saw the flashes but didn't hear the shots. He slumped sideways and hung there by the seat belt. He was numb, his vision dimming, and in his last moments of life, he wished he'd finished the sandwich.

Grace was relieved Angus was dead but nothing was finished. That big guy from the Starks especially. Isaiah had corrupted his son and he would take his revenge sooner or later. The rest of the Starks, Manzo, and a thousand other cutthroats were hunting him as well. Grace heard from Deronda that a bounty was on Isaiah's head and special hit teams were searching for him everywhere. Manzo even put up WANTED posters: A twenty-five-thousand-dollar reward and much respect, for Isaiah dead or alive meant cabdrivers, mail carriers, hookers, dope dealers, busboys, janitors, crackheads, security guards, store clerks, and entire families would be looking for him too.

Isaiah had to leave town; he had no other option. At first, Grace thought there was a way around it. That they could live somewhere else in LA—it's an immense area—but word would get around. IQ, the unlicensed, underground PI who made things right when no one else cared, was living in Culver City or Hollywood or the San Fernando Valley. He could lie low but she knew Isaiah wouldn't do that. He wouldn't hide. He'd go someplace where he could be himself.

Her life was here. She wasn't going to run and wasn't going to live on the road. She thought Isaiah could come back someday and everything would be the same and she'd repaint the house and get some furniture and they'd have a baby and—no. That wasn't going to happen. She'd seen her friends go through it. Living apart from their spouses or lovers, pledging their loyalty, calling and emailing every day until that faded to nothing as they created new lives. So would Isaiah. She couldn't imagine what that life might be but it would happen. He couldn't be rootless forever. He would meet someone else, but she couldn't think about that. There was that saying, *It was better to have loved and lost than never to have loved at all.* Maybe that was true, she thought, but there should be a door prize for the anguish, something besides memories. Memories were gossamer and momentary. Isaiah was flesh and blood and there was no one else like him.

She drove through the neighborhood, tears spilling from the pale green eyes he cherished so. She drove past places they'd taken for granted, where small things happened that now seemed so meaningful. Shopping together at Vons, playing basketball at McClarin Park, ordering takeout from the Mandarin Palace, eating warm croissants at the Coffee Cup and the movie theater where they didn't watch the movie and the nightclub where she'd danced and danced and loved Isaiah. She thought about drinking beers on the back stoop and her painting on the bedroom wall and Ruffin sleeping under the lemon tree and the kitchen where they'd washed dishes side by side and made out with soapy hands and went to bed in the middle of the day. All the things that were no longer theirs.

The evening was appropriately gray and washed out. She drove into the wrecking yard and there he was, waiting for her with his hands in his front pockets and leaning against a battered Jeep with a canvas top. With a single look, she knew he was leaving without her, no matter what she said or did. He was thinking of her. He was Isaiah after all.

She went to him and put her head against his chest and his arms enclosed her for the last time. Their hearts matched beats. Her insides felt carved out as if they knew there was only emptiness to come. He didn't say anything. It was one of the best things about him—not asking questions that didn't have answers. Not saying what didn't need to be said. The moment was the moment, and it didn't need elaboration or even goodbyes. Let the pain breathe of its own accord. Let their love ebb in silence. After a long time that wasn't long enough, he raised her chin. She was trembling and so was he.

"I owe you," she said.

"Owe me? For what?"

"Ruffin. He was your dog. You gave him to me. He kept me safe, just like you said, remember?" She slipped the keys into his hand. He turned, threw a duffel bag into the Mustang and drove away.

She lingered, remembering how she'd driven away from him and how he'd looked bereft and forsaken and she supposed she looked that way now. Ruffin came over and sat down next to her. "Hello, friend," she said. Then she kneeled and hugged him and breathed in his smell and held on to him for dear life.

EPILOGUE

It was late and the traffic was light. The Mustang's engine droned but it helped him not to think. He'd heard Angus was dead and he'd seen on the news that Gia had turned herself in. That was something at least. He'd texted Stella, telling her she wasn't in danger anymore. She didn't answer back.

Isaiah thought about Beaumont. His store closed, the windows boarded up, the last vestige of him a green apron torn through with bullet holes. Earlier, he'd called Merrill. He told him that the man behind his father's murder had been killed by a rival. There was silence. Merrill said without inflection, "Oh. Well, thanks for telling me," and he ended the call.

Isaiah felt deflated. He had expected to hear some sense of relief or satisfaction. Instead it felt more like despair. Well, why wouldn't it? he thought. Pointless killing after pointless killing. It made Beaumont's death seem more meaningless than it already was. But wasn't that a fitting end for Angus? Wasn't that only right? Wasn't that justice? Poetic justice if there was such a thing? Yeah, maybe, Isaiah mused. Or maybe it was nothing at all.

Christiana had hung herself from a closet rod. Not with rope, but with wire from a coat hanger. Carter Samuels, a police officer and former client, told Isaiah there was a note but no one could decipher it. It appeared to have been signed by Christiana and five other people. It was as if they'd made some sort of pact, some group decision, but the five others couldn't be located and none of the neighbors seemed to know who they were. Another odd thing, Carter added. There was a crumpled photo in Christiana's hand that hadn't been dislodged even in the agonies of suicide. The photo was of a small house at the edge of the sea, a dark forest behind it. Who it belonged to and why Christiana wouldn't let it go, the police had no idea.

Isaiah drove on in a strange car with no woman, no past, no future and nothing to go back to. He didn't know where he was going and he didn't know what he would do. There was only the road and the taillights in front of him and the empty darkness beyond.

Acknowledgments

My thanks to Elyse Dinh-McCrillis, a specialist in finding lost stories and bringing them home again, and to Felix Zayde, for his keen, discerning insights into many aspects of the book. My unending gratitude to the good folks at Little, Brown and Mulholland Books. They continue to endure my quirks, misgivings, missteps and shortfalls with unwavering patience and kindness. My debt to them has grown and accumulated interest to an amount so enormous I could never pay back an iota of what I owe. *Hi Five* was another collaborative effort with Josh Kendall, an experience that was no less enjoyable and edifying than with the previous books. I am lobbying to have his name put on the covers. My deepest appreciation to Dr. Steve Marmer. His vast knowledge and understanding of multiple personality disorder were absolutely invaluable to the writing of *Hi Five*. Any mistakes, inaccuracies, flights of fancy or dramatic license are mine and mine alone. And to Diane. The sweetest person in the world.

16/11/26

BETTWS